ALSO BY BETSY WOODMAN

Jana Bibi's Excellent Fortunes

Love Potion Number 10

Love Potion Number 10

A Jana Bibi Adventure

Betsy Woodman

HENRY HOLT AND COMPANY   NEW YORK

Henry Holt and Company, LLC
Publishers since 1866
175 Fifth Avenue
New York, New York 10010
www.henryholt.com

Henry Holt® and ® are registered trademarks of
Henry Holt and Company, LLC.

Library of Congress Cataloging-in-Publication Data
Woodman, Betsy.
    Love potion number 10 : a Jana Bibi adventure / Betsy
Woodman. — 1st ed.
        p.   cm.
    ISBN 978-0-8050-9957-7
    1. Fortune-tellers—Fiction.   2. Single women—Fiction.
    3. Scots—India—Fiction.   4. India—Fiction.   I. Title.
    PS3623.O666L68 2013
    813'.6—dc23   2012027367

Henry Holt books are available for special promotions and
premiums. For details contact: Director, Special Markets.

First Edition 2013

Designed by Kelly S. Too

Printed in the United States of America
1 3 5 7 9 10 8 6 4 2

To Elizabeth Berg

AUTHOR'S NOTE

I have set *Love Potion Number 10* in 1961, and used the names current at the time, for example, Bombay instead of Mumbai.

The currency exchange rate was roughly 4.8 Indian rupees to the U.S. dollar. The rupee was divided into 100 *naye paise* ("new money"), but old coins were also still in use, 16 annas to a rupee.

Hamara Nagar is a fictional town; it would be somewhere in today's Uttarakhand, a state that got carved out of Uttar Pradesh in 2000. Similarly, Terauli is not on any real map.

The Thirty-eighth King's Own Scottish Borderers is a fictional regiment, and the Symphony Lovers' Club of Bombay a made-up organization. Similarly, you will not find the tunes of Jana's family's butler in any Scottish fiddle music collection.

A glossary is provided at the end of the book for terms that may be unfamiliar.

To pronounce Jana Bibi's name, start to say Janet and change your mind. Bibi sounds like BB, as in the pellets.

Love Potion Number 10

Best Foot Forward

◦ß *Drip, Drip, Drip*

Jana awoke abruptly. Downstairs, in the fortune-telling salon, Mr. Ganguly was screeching something like "Water! Cold! Help!" She had not heard him put those words together before. She sat up in bed, still groggy, now hearing footsteps on the staircase and, next, a frantic knocking on the bedroom door.

"Jana mem!" came Mary's voice. "Come now! Come quickly!"

Jana pushed her feet into her bedroom slippers and grabbed her heavy wool dressing gown off the foot of the bed, hurriedly wrapping it around herself as she made her way down the stairs. In the salon, Mr. Ganguly was flapping and jumping, trying to avoid drops of water coming from the ceiling through the elaborate wrought-iron filigree of his enormous cage.

"Bloody hell!" Jana almost never used unladylike language, but this occasion called for it. Water was dripping down one wall, ruining last year's paint job, soaking the painting of Mughal ladies feeding parrots, and turning a deck of tarot cards that Jana had left on the side table into a soggy sponge.

She quickly got Mr. Ganguly out of his cage and onto her shoulder, then turned and ran up to the bathroom off her bedroom. There was no water to be seen there. She held the flowered enamel washbowl under the tap on the wall and twisted open the handle. A very few drops could be coaxed out.

She went downstairs again, and now the whole household was awake. Lal Bahadur Pun came running from his night watchman's post in the courtyard, small Tilku and old Munar from the room they shared in the basement. Mary was moving surprisingly fast for her bulk, hurrying to the kitchen building and calling for Lal Bahadur Pun to follow her. Between the two of them, they finally managed to turn off the main water line from the town water supply to the compound.

Jana went back into the salon. The water had stopped dripping, but it was puddling on the polished cement floor, and heading straight for the rug she had bought at the Kashmiri Palace. She quickly bent down and felt dampness on one corner of it. Not *too* bad, she thought, and began rolling it up. Mary and Lal Bahadur Pun arrived back with rags and started mopping here and there, Mary throwing a rag at Tilku and yelling at him to make himself useful. Munar fetched his broom of long soft sticks and swished it around, which merely served to make dirty swirls on the wet floor.

Finally, all five members of the household stood and stared and tried to assess the damage.

"Pipe froze," said Lal Bahadur Pun.

"Too cold in this place," said Mary.

"We should turn the water off at night," said Lal Bahadur Pun.

"*Now* you are saying that," said Mary.

"Jana mem, I thought the house was falling down, everyone was yelling so much!" Tilku said.

"At least we don't need to wash the floor today," said Munar, though that wasn't exactly true.

"Water! Cold!" Mr. Ganguly observed and flapped his wings as if shaking off the water from a birdbath.

"It had to happen *today*, of course," said Jana.

Of course. It had to happen on the day that the reporter was coming from the *Illustrated Weekly of India* to interview Jana and photograph all of them.

"I suppose we still have to do the photo shoot," said Jana. "We'll just have to keep to the dry side of the salon. And perhaps take some of the pictures outside."

"We will put our best foot forward," said Lal Bahadur Pun. "Only show the good side."

Best foot forward. That should be our motto, thought Jana. All of a sudden, she was desperately in need of a good pot of tea. Some fried eggs and toast with butter and guava jelly wouldn't hurt, either.

The others, too, all seemed to be thinking suddenly of tea.

"But tea requires water," said Lal Bahadur Pun.

"There's still a full jug from yesterday," Mary said. "Already boiled."

"Bit of a waste to boil it again," Jana said, "with fuel so expensive." Seeing the unanimously horrified looks, she added quickly, "But better than going without tea."

Lal Bahadur Pun and Mary and Jana went out the side door and through the courtyard to the kitchen, where, as Mary had said, the big clay jug of water from the day before was still full. Mary put the kettle on the electric hot plate, and Jana filled a small bowl, found some parched grains in the food cupboard, and went to feed Mr. Ganguly.

Meanwhile, Lal Bahadur Pun went back and forth inspecting the pipes, figuring out how to allow the water to flow to the kitchen building without having it reach the broken pipe upstairs in the house. "There must be a valve somewhere," he kept saying. Finally, he found an ancient rusty valve on the kitchen wall, which grudgingly allowed itself to be turned shut.

⚘ *The Show Must Go On*

By eleven A.M, when the reporter was due, there was a semblance of normality in the house, although half the salon was damp and forlorn. Mary and Jana had carried a couple of kerosene tins of water from the kitchen up to Jana's bathroom, allowing Jana to heat a bowlful with the immersion heater and take a makeshift sponge bath.

To think, Jana scolded herself, that she had been growing impatient with her bathing arrangements! She had been longing for a modern bathroom, with a large gleaming white tub like the one she'd had at the nawab's, and hot and cold running water going to a lavabo with a drainpipe, not a bowl you had to empty down the hole in the corner of the floor. At least yesterday the water had come out of the tap on demand—better than today's situation. She should have known when she was lucky! A memory popped into her head of her grandfather boasting about the house having running water. The pipes are probably the original ones he put in, she thought; they should have been replaced long ago.

After washing up, she dressed in her green silk fortune-telling costume, complete with the emerald necklace she had thought was just costume jewelry when Ramachandran had given it to her from the storeroom at the Treasure Emporium. On discovering that it was genuine, she had considered locking it in a bank vault, but today she was glad that she didn't have to go fetch it. Really, why have an expensive necklace if it caused you a lot of bother?

Moreover, she had to admit (although vanity was not her habit) that the green of the gems brought out the green in her hazel eyes. Would the photos for the *Weekly* be taken in color? Surely so, if they wanted to make the best of Mr. Ganguly's brilliant green plumage and bright red beak.

It remained to do something with her mane of hair, which was long and curly to the point of unruliness. "Oh dear," muttered Jana, looking in the mirror. "This mop!" Usually she tucked it into two simple braids, but with her fortune-telling garb, she needed something more formal.

"Mary, can you do anything with this hair?"

"Of course, Jana mem." Mary took up the hairbrush and studied Jana's head.

When Jana's two little daughters were still alive, Mary had always made small feeder braids at their temples, then woven them back into the main braids. Now she did something similar to Jana's hair, but also concocted an elegant swirling chignon.

"Jana mem, you tell that man from the *Weekly* that he is lucky that we are talking to him today," Mary said, brushing, twisting, and plaiting with deft flicks of her fingers, without even looking at what she was doing.

"I think we'll just act as if everything is normal," Jana said.

A skeptical look crossed Mary's round, pockmarked face. "Normal. Well, normal for this household is not normal for anyone else."

"Would you want it to be?" Jana asked.

Mary put the last few hairpins in Jana's hairdo. "This house—and the people in it—are usually better than normal," she said. "But pipes bursting is worse."

Jana sighed, and Mary went on: "Not many other people's

pipes burst last night. On Maharajah's Hill, no one lost water."

"How do you know this, Mary?"

"The potato wallah told me. He also said that here in the Central Bazaar, only two, three other houses had pipes burst. Old houses, like this one."

"Aha. Well, perhaps we'll do a renovation soon. Maybe put in a hot-water boiler."

A smile flashed across Mary's face. "Very good idea. On a cold morning, very nice. Even that boy Tilku might wash."

When Mary had left, the thought occurred to Jana that the emerald necklace would pay for a modern bathroom, with a shower as well as a real bathtub, long enough to lie down in, and a boiler. Something to decide later, she said to herself, as she checked to see if it was securely fastened around her neck.

A Reporter

Young Mr. Gopal at first aroused Jana's protective instinct. He was thin and stoop-shouldered, like an impoverished university student who scrimps on meals to buy textbooks and burns the midnight oil before exams. His smile was perhaps too ingratiating, but Jana chalked that up to nervousness.

She tried to put him at ease. "I'm so sorry you had to brave the cold. It's quite unusual even for this altitude." With Mr. Ganguly on her shoulder, she led the reporter into her sitting-room-dining-room-fortune-telling salon and pointed to the stained wall. "You can see that the frost last night was too much for our old plumbing."

Mr. Gopal gave a long, drawn-out wiggle of his head to express concern.

"Bad bird!" Mr. Ganguly squawked, and Mr. Gopal drew back with a start.

"Don't mind him. He had a rude awakening this morning," Jana explained, transferring the parrot to his perch. "It may put him in a bad mood for the whole day."

"I am very sorry about that," said Mr. Gopal, with a worried frown.

"Come, let's sit here," Jana said, gesturing to the table in front of the bay window, and Mr. Gopal put his shoulder bag down and faced the view.

"Beautiful!" he exclaimed. "Lovely!"

"It is, isn't it?" Jana always liked it when someone complimented her on the majestic mountain panorama, as if she'd had some part in creating it. "Tea, Mr. Gopal?"

First he refused, and then she insisted, and finally he agreed. Mary brought the tea tray and they each had a cup. Then Mr. Gopal began his interview, or, as Jana soon felt, his interrogation. I suppose he's just being conscientious and wants to do a thorough job, she thought.

"*Achcha*, Mrs. Laird, please give me your full name."

"I was born Janet Louisa Caroline Elizabeth MacPherson. I married Mr. William Laird, so Laird is my name now."

"I see. Thank you. Your date and time of birth?"

He wrote it carefully in his notebook: January 26, 1902.

"So, you are now fifty-nine years of age," he said. "You are quite well preserved."

Well! The cheek of the fellow!

"Your time of birth?" he continued.

Six A.M. Jana remembered her mother telling her.

"Are you going to cast my horoscope, Mr. Gopal?" she asked.

He looked puzzled for a moment, then said, "Oh, no, no, that's not *my* line of work. I just want to be on solid ground when gathering information. And you have lived in India all your life?"

"Almost all," said Jana. "I was back in Scotland from . . . let's see . . . 1919 to 1925. Otherwise I've been here. Well, not *here*. First at a mission station—my late husband was a missionary—then in Bombay, then at Terauli, just south of Delhi, where I was violin tutor to the nawab's children."

"And here, in Hamara Nagar—how did you happen to become a fortune-teller?"

Jana, after some thought, replied: "It was—community service, I suppose you might say. Some leading merchants of the town thought we needed an extra tourist attraction in the Central Bazaar, to help put the town on the map. They wanted to persuade people in the government not to place a large dam here."

"I see. Congratulations on the town still being here," Mr. Gopal said. "Now, you're living alone here—that is, without family?"

"My household staff *is* family to me," Jana said. "We take care of one another."

"I see. Including that rather fierce-looking man at the gate? A Gurkha, is it not? What's that costume he is wearing?"

Jana smiled. "Subedar-Major Lal Bahadur Pun. He's a retired soldier and expert bagpipe player. With a distinguished record for service during the last war. The tartans are his dress outfit. But sometimes he wears his military uniform."

That seemed to give Mr. Gopal pause, and he jotted down something in his notebook.

"And the strong-looking woman who brought us tea?"

"Mary Thomas. My ayah—well, she was my children's ayah, and then she became more of a cook and housekeeper.

A very resourceful woman, and strong-willed. Not to be tan-
gled with."

Mr. Gopal's eyebrows went up. "There was also one small
boy in the courtyard, when I came in."

"Ah yes, Tilku. He's a Nepali lad, an orphan, who was living at the Victoria Hotel."

"And what does he do with himself all day?"

Jana paused. "Oh, he runs around town delivering messages, and talks about cricket with his friends. Or he chats
with the bird, and takes him on walks."

"And the bird? Mr. Ganguly, you call him? You claim he's
psychic, no?"

Jana's first impulse was to say, Good heavens, I'm the last
person to make such a claim about an animal; underneath
this fortune-telling guise, I share the empiricism of my Scottish Enlightenment ancestors. And, after all, it had been
Mary, spreading gossip among the townspeople, who had
started that particular rumor, and the national press and All
India Radio that had publicized the story about Mr. Ganguly
inducing the police chief's son to talk. But then Jana reminded
herself that this kind of thing was helping the town build its
reputation as a special place and a destination for tourists.

She thus said, "Oh . . . at the very least, he's a sensitive
creature and a very observant one. And sometimes animals
just seem to have more of a sixth sense than humans do, you
know? For example, dogs who run and sit at the gate just
before their master comes home. And bird migrations . . .
how on earth do they know where they're going?"

Mr. Gopal thought this over and nodded. "Indeed. Well,
do tell me about how you acquired our little sensitive friend
here."

"I . . . well, it was more that he acquired me, really. It was
at the nawab's. . . . One day we just found a parrot in the

garden. He'd had his wings clipped but could still fly a little. He didn't seem very happy."

"And when was that, Mrs. Laird?"

"Let's see . . . it was in about 1956 or so, I think? Five years ago?"

"I see. What month?"

"March? April? May? Time has flown so, and so many things have happened in between, it's hard for me to remember."

Mary reappeared, and Jana asked her, "Mary, do you remember what time of year it was when Mr. Ganguly arrived at the nawab's?"

"It was very, very hot," Mary said. "Mangoes were ripe."

"You're right, of course," Jana said.

"And the nawab's daughter had just had her birthday— that was April twentieth, I think."

"Ah, yes, it's coming back to me now."

"More tea, Jana mem?"

"Mr. Gopal?" Jana asked.

"No, thank you," he said.

By now Jana was tiring, but Mr. Gopal continued, asking more and more detailed questions. Just doing his job, Jana supposed, but really, did he have to know *everything* about their day? When they all got up and when they all went to bed? What their favorite foods were? Their amusements? Which wallahs came to their house at what time in the morning?

Mr. Ganguly listened and kept shifting his gaze from Jana to the reporter, his pupils dilating and contracting. He suddenly spoke. "What's your name?" he asked Mr. Gopal. "Your name?"

"Your bird would make a good reporter himself," said Mr. Gopal.

"Yes, there isn't much that he misses," said Jana.

Mr. Ganguly persisted in his query, and Mr. Gopal gave his name. Not satisfied, the parrot leaned forward, fixed the reporter with a stern eye, and asked again.

"Oh, Mr. Ganguly, don't be tiresome," Jana said. "Here, have a nut."

With the parrot distracted, they continued, Jana feeling increasingly worn out.

The interrogation finally came to an end, and Mr. Gopal said, "May I take some photos of you and the parrot in front of the window? And of him alone on his perch?"

"Of course," Jana said.

Then, having taken a couple dozen photographs indoors, Mr. Gopal suggested that he snap the entire household outside, in front of the sign reading "Jana Bibi's Excellent Fortunes" on the gate to the house.

"Just a nice spontaneous picture," said Mr. Gopal.

"Of course," said Jana, and called the rest of the household.

"We're going to be in the magazine," Tilku said as they gathered outside. "I am going to be famous."

"*Chup.* You be quiet," said Mary. "And stand still."

Click. Click. Click.

"I believe I have captured you, Mrs. Laird. You and your staff," Mr. Gopal said, and his tone had a smugness that Jana didn't quite like.

❦ *When Mr. Ganguly Adopted Jana*

"Mother, you can never resist adopting strays," Jana's son, Jack, often pointed out.

But who adopted whom? Both in India and in Scotland, various animals had wandered into Jana's life: several stray cats; a dog or two; lizards; once, even, a fawn. She adopted

people, too, and they, her. All the members of her household
had shown up just when she needed them, and announced
that they were there to stay.

Mary, fleeing a violent husband in South India, had come
to the mission station when Jana had three children under
the age of five. She'd still been there—her pockmarked face a
badge of security—during the smallpox epidemic that had
carried off Jana's two daughters, and she'd kept Jana from
throwing herself down a well in the aftermath of those terrible days.

Lal Bahadur Pun, with his irrepressible nature, military
bearing, and super-loud bagpipes, had rid her home, the Jolly
Grant House, of a troop of rhesus monkeys.

Tilku had established himself as Mr. Ganguly's friend.
Old Munar, whose sweeping essentially just rearranged the
dirt, had been hired by Mary; he had a gentle, saintly manner, did no harm, and regularly told the others to be happy
about their own fates.

Mr. Ganguly was not the first bird to enter Jana's life. As a
child, she'd made friends with a crow, and smuggled out bits
of her lunch to it. But Mr. Ganguly was her first—and, so far,
only—parrot.

It had actually been Noor, the nawab of Terauli's youngest daughter—then ten years old—who had first noticed Mr.
Ganguly.

A flock of ringnecks visited the garden, as they did every
day, calling to each other, swooping down like an emerald
cloud, and investigating the possibilities for a feast in the
mango trees. But the parrot Noor found on the grass did not
seem to have come as part of the flock. His wings had been
clipped, not very expertly, and he was obviously used to
humans. He was potentially very elegant, with his black chin
stripe giving him the air of being in evening attire, although
he was clearly in distress. It was obvious that he had plucked

at his own breast and pulled out a few feathers, which made him look mangy and disconsolate.

"He's in party dress," said Noor. "Although a ragged party dress."

"I wonder where he came from," said Jana.

"Maybe he escaped from a fortune-teller in the town," Noor said. She reached down and scooped up the bird with her two hands. He fluttered a little but did not seem fearful or averse to being held. Then Noor held out her finger, and the bird climbed onto it.

Jana was impressed at how intrepid Noor was, but then, aristocrats were often like that, exuding a fearlessness born of always having been protected. Some people didn't know enough of the world to be afraid of it.

"I don't think he'll bite," said Noor. "Or, at least, he'll give us good warning."

Jana, too, put out her finger. The parrot climbed onto it, then up onto her arm, where he also seemed surprisingly at ease.

"He likes you!" said Noor. "I think he has adopted us."

"Do you suppose he talks?"

"Hello," said Noor to the bird, who looked up but did not answer.

Noor turned to Jana. "Can we keep him?"

"I suppose," said Jana. "If no one comes to claim him. And if he wants to stay."

"How can we test that?"

"Let's put him on the wall and see which side he seems most interested in."

The parrot showed a distinct preference for the garden side, turning his back on the fields beyond the palace.

"Shall we bring him inside?" Noor asked.

"Let's just see what he does," said Jana. "Perhaps he has a home he wants to fly away to later."

But the bird did not fly away. In fact, he stayed in the garden overnight, taking shelter under a bench. The next morning, Noor placed some bits of mango in a dish and put it in front of him. The bird looked very interested, downed the fruit in short order, and said, *"Aur! Aur!"*

"Did you hear what I heard?" Noor's face brightened with astonishment.

"I think so," said Jana.

"He asked for *more.*"

"Well, let's get him some," said Jana.

When he had eaten another helping of mango, the bird said, quite clearly, *"Shukriya,"* and then, "Thank you."

"He speaks two languages?" Noor said.

"Merci!"

"At least three, it appears," Jana noted.

By now they were convulsed with laughter, and were beginning to draw a crowd—Mary, several children from the servants' quarters, and a dozen of the palace staff.

"We should give him a name," said Noor.

One of the musicians who played in the garden at night was named Ganguly, and the name popped into Jana's head.

"Mr. Ganguly," she said to the bird. "Would you like that to be your name?"

The bird looked up, flapped his wings, and went back to the dish of mango.

"That's his name now," said Noor.

As time went by, it became more and more likely that no one would claim the bird. The palace staff made inquiries in the nearby village, and no one was missing a parrot. Mr. Ganguly's wings were allowed to grow out, the bare spot on his chest filled in, and he flapped about the garden more vigorously. He still did not fly great distances, however, or join any of the visiting flocks of ringnecks.

He allowed himself to be brought inside the palace, and sometimes perched on the back of a chair in Jana's room or on the windowsill in the room where Jana gave the children their violin lessons. He seemed to have distinct tastes in music, not liking anything slow or mournful but dancing spontaneously to lively tunes. Waltzes were not to his taste, either.

"Come, dance to this Strauss waltz," Noor would coax, without success.

Jana said, "If God had wanted parrots to waltz, I suppose he would have given them three legs."

It was Mary who first asked the question: "Do you think he knows how to tell fortunes?"

They spread some cards on the table in the music room, and Noor planted herself in a chair, with Mr. Ganguly in front of the cards.

Mr. Ganguly seemed familiar with the situation. He said to Noor, "*Nam? Nam kya hai?* Name?"

Noor and Jana and Mary all burst out laughing, and this seemed to egg Mr. Ganguly on. As soon as Noor told him her name, he walked back and forth in front of the cards, finally picked one, and handed it to her with his beak. Then he did a little bow.

When this got a round of hand clapping, he flapped his wings and gave another bow.

"What fortune has he picked for me?" Noor asked.

The card was a nine of hearts.

"What does that mean, Auntie Jana?" Noor said.

Jana had a glimmer of memory of her mother doing parlor tricks after dinner in the white-pillared house in Allahabad, delivering wittily optimistic forecasts to her elegantly clad guests. Wit failed Jana now, but she could still come up with optimism. "Nine of hearts? Obviously, that will bring you—the best of luck."

"Well, I hope so!" Noor said. She tickled Mr. Ganguly under the chin. "Good bird."

"Good bird," he repeated.

How old, Jana had often wondered, had Mr. Ganguly been when he'd arrived? How long might he live with her, cheering her up with his proclamations of "Good bird!" and "Jana Bibi zindabad!" She had read that Indian ringnecks could live to be twenty, thirty, even fifty years old, but for her small emerald-colored friend, how much of that was left? No one knew. But then, she sometimes reminded herself, none of us knows how many days and years we have left. Mr. Ganguly clearly did not worry about this, so neither would she.

Racking Engines

⚘ Jana Gets a Toothache

In her dream, Jana was taking Mr. Ganguly for a walk in the bazaar, as she often did in the morning, before the day's customers arrived at the fortune-telling salon. The parrot was on her shoulder, but to her astonishment, instead of speaking in his usual short bursts of intelligence, he was spinning out long, complex sentences—on love. In real life, Mr. Ganguly's statements on the subject amounted to a high-pitched "I love you." But in the dream, he talked of the *Kama Sutra*, Romeo and Juliet, the medieval romance of Tristan and Yseult. "How did you get so learned?" Jana asked him. "In my studies at Oxford," said Mr. Ganguly, who was suddenly wearing spectacles and a mortarboard.

"But you've only completed third standard," said Jana. "You're confusing me with my cousin," said Mr. Ganguly. "He is barely literate in English, let alone Mandarin."

Next, in the dream, Jana was in the Why Not? Tea Shop with Ramachandran and Rambir, and they were discussing whether they should use the spelling Benares or Banaras. The jolly, portly Ramachandran favored the former, but serious, lean Rambir said they should change with the times and use the latter. Mr. Ganguly burst out, "What's in a name?

That which we call a rose by any other name would smell as sweet."

"You've certainly got an educated bird," Ramachandran said to Jana.

"Yes, he outdistances me in his knowledge of literature," she said.

"And dentistry!" Mr. Ganguly exclaimed.

"What do *you* know about dentistry?" she asked him.

"An eye for an eye and a tooth for a tooth," he replied.

The scene changed suddenly, and Jana was in the Hamara Nagar jail, but a much fancier place than the glorified cowshed where she had spent a night after Mr. Ganguly had bitten Police Commissioner Bandhu Sharma. It was a palace, with high ceilings, marble floors, and Persian carpets. Someone announced, "Janet Louisa Caroline Elizabeth MacPherson Laird, you will never get out of this palace with all your teeth!" Next, she was playing the violin, but having to stop every few phrases and spit out one of her teeth into an ornate brass spittoon.

She awoke extremely relieved to find that all that had been a dream. But, oh dear, something *was* wrong with her teeth—or at least with one tooth, a molar on the left side. It was throbbing, as if there were a little rodent alive and twitching in her jaw.

She went down to the salon and found that Mary had already put the tea tray on the table next to the bay window. Jana poured herself a cup and took a sip. The hot tea, instead of being comforting, made her tooth throb some more. Hadn't Robert Burns written an address to a toothache? Using the phrase "racking engines."

"Jana mem is not in good form this morning?" said Mary, arriving from the cookhouse with hot porridge and a gravy boat full of *gur*, the unrefined sugar syrup that Jana preferred to Lyle's Golden Syrup, which she found too treacly.

"Nothing important," said Jana, ladling some *gur* onto the porridge. As soon as she took a spoonful, the sweetness set off a zinging sensation.

Mary watched her for a moment. "Headache?" she said.

Jana sighed. "No, I'm afraid it's a tooth."

Jana looked out the window and saw a few flakes of snow and her heart sank further. Last week, the burst water pipe, and now snow and, on top of that, a toothache.

"I'll get you some oil of cloves from Mr. Abinath," Mary said.

Applying oil of cloves for two days made Jana smell like mulled wine but did little to stop the toothache, which took on an evil little personality. It toyed with Jana. Sometimes it retreated for a while and lulled her into a false sense of relief, only to come roaring back when she tried to eat or drink. Finally, she faced facts. She would have to phone the dentist in Dehra Dun, reserve a taxi for the long ride down and back, and reconcile herself to the flattening of her wallet for both the visit and the transport. She sent a note over to Rambir Vohra, the editor of the Aaj Kal Printing Press, asking for the name and telephone number of his dentist and, armed with this information, walked down to the postal, telegraph, and telephone office.

Normally, she would have liked the walk; it was an easy mile from the Jolly Grant House, at the midpoint of the Central Bazaar, west to the edge of the English Bazaar, and then perhaps half a mile farther to the PTT. Along the way, she usually waved to and exchanged greetings with the *darzis* sewing cross-legged on the floor at Royal Tailors, then with Mr. Abinath, reorganizing the medicines of his apothecary, then with the other shopkeepers she knew. The shops in the Central Bazaar—more prosperous than those in the Upper Bazaar, to the east—were often a temptation, and the shopkeepers knew it, calling to her, "Laird memsahib, come in and look! Don't have to buy!" But she had no interest today in bangles, or brasswear, or carved wooden furniture, or Kashmiri rugs. With her jaw throbbing, she walked past the Giant Skating Rink, hearing the American pop tunes that, as usual, were blaring out the window.

Then on she went into the English Bazaar, which still had many relics of colonial days, including a hat shop that she doubted had made a sale in years. At the end of the town were more reminders of times past: the Municipal Garden, with its statue of George Everest, the Anglican church, and the Victoria Hotel. Not to mention the police station, lorded over by one of her least favorite people, Commissioner Bandhu Sharma. If that man had had his way the year before, Mr. Ganguly would have ended up parrot biryani! But Mr. G had redeemed himself—sort of—with Bandhu by getting Bandhu's youngest son, Raju, to speak after a couple of years' silence.

At the PTT, there was, fortunately, no competition for the phone booth—one good thing about winter. In the tourist season, she would have had to stand in line. She asked the clerk to place the call, then sat on a wooden bench and waited, the tooth going at it again—indeed, with the rhythm of a racking engine. When the call went through, she practically leapt for the receiver. The dentist, on the other end of the line, was barely audible for the interference.

"Molar?" she heard through the crackling.

"Yes," yelled Jana. "A lower one. On the left side."

"And how long has this toothache been going on?"

"Three days," she said. "Long days."

"It's not likely to get better," the dentist shouted into the phone.

"I was afraid you would say that," said Jana.

"Best to get you in right away. It just so happens," said the dentist, "that one of my patients has canceled. He was supposed to come tomorrow, but, as the Americans say, I think he has chickened out. You can take his appointment if you want."

Jana was as chicken-livered as the next dental patient, but pain made her brave.

"I'll be there," she said.

On return to the Jolly Grant House, Jana sent a quick note to Mr. Dass at the Victoria Hotel, asking him to engage the taxi.

Oddly, just making the appointment caused the toothache to recede temporarily, and Jana even wondered if that long trip to Dehra Dun was really worth the time and the expense. Then the next cup of hot tea brought the throbbing up to the racking-engine level again, and she felt relieved that she had done the right thing. Would the dentist pull the tooth? Make her stay overnight in Dehra Dun for a follow-up visit in the morning?

She flipped through her fortune-telling books, thinking she should bone up for the tourist season, which was almost upon them. She tried to learn some of the more subtle points of palmistry. Nothing stuck.

"Hopeless!" she said to Mr. Ganguly. "I haven't a shred of concentration."

Mr. Ganguly always seemed to know when things were wrong. He observed her carefully, stretching his neck toward her and fixing her with his bright black eyes.

"Not to worry," she told him. "It's only a stupid toothache. I'm going to the dentist tomorrow. I'll be gone all day, but you're not to worry. I'll be back in the evening."

"Good bird," he said.

Then she tried working on her music transcriptions. For close to a year, she had been attempting to get the tunes of the long dead MacPherson family butler in Scotland out of her head and onto paper. She had high hopes of finding a publisher in Scotland for the collection. Today, though, progress was impossible, since holding the violin made her jaw ache even worse. Why didn't I do this project long, long ago, she scolded herself.

⋅∘ℰ *The Butler's Tunes*

At least she had never stopped *playing* the tunes. She vividly remembered learning them in the kitchen of her grandfather's drafty old house. Ian the butler, his knuckles already gnarled with age, would demonstrate and then have her repeat, phrase by phrase, what he had played.

In her mission days, after supper on the verandah, she had played those same tunes for William and the children. Like so many Scottish tunes, they were named for people. In fact, the titles of Ian's tunes, put in the right order, would have made a MacPherson genealogical chart. Jana's great-grandparents appeared in "Lady Louisa's Strathspey" and "Lord Charles's Return from Calcutta," a great-uncle in "Colonel Stewart's Birthday Jig," an aunt in "Miss Caroline Cooper's Favorite Waltz." Not a few of the tunes were named for Jana herself—"Miss Janet's Delight" (a jig), "An Air for Miss Janet," "Miss MacPherson of Allahabad" (a march), and "Miss MacPherson's Reel."

Old Ian had always said that he was going to write the tunes down, but first his household duties and then, later, worsening arthritis and the general exhaustion of old age prevented him from doing so. Jana, back in India, had cried bitterly on hearing of his death, shortly after the Nazis had come to power in Germany, one piece of bad news adding to the distress of the other. That day, she had played all of Ian's tunes—a good fifty of them—in her own private memorial service, knowing that, near Glasgow, they had already put him in the ground.

Normally, in the evenings on the mission verandah, she wouldn't play his whole repertoire but would generally go on to traditional favorites: "Flowers of Edinburgh," "Soldier's Joy," "Tail Toddle," "The Mason's Apron."

"Any requests?" she would ask the family.

William, who could never remember the names of tunes, would say, "Play that fast one that goes *dum dee dum dee dum diddy dum.*" That covered a lot of the jigs, but she knew he meant "Off She Goes," so she would play that, and then "Stool of Repentance."

When she stopped playing, they would sit quietly, listening to the soft ticking calls of nightjars in the trees and the buzz of insects, the faces of the family softly illuminated by the kerosene lantern.

She had explained to William and the children the differences between a march, a reel, a jig, and a strathspey. William never remembered—it was not the kind of thing his brain seized upon—but Jack, well before his departure for boarding school at age seven, knew all the titles and which categories the tunes fell into.

Now Jack, who had inherited Grandfather MacPherson's house in Scotland and lived there, was trying to learn as an adult to play the Highland pipes. Taking up a musical instrument as an adult was like learning a language as an adult, he wrote to Jana—far more difficult than for a child, and you had to fight off a dreadful self-consciousness, to boot. But Jack was a determined sort of person and was not going to admit defeat.

"Next time I come to Hamara Nagar," he had written, "I'll be able to play in front of Lal Bahadur Pun without feeling like a rank beginner. Perhaps he'll even play duets with me."

His sisters, Caroline and Fiona, had shown musical ability

at a very early age. Now, thinking of how they would dance together in time to Jana's playing, Jana got a terrible lump in her throat. Several times after their death from smallpox, now almost three decades ago, Jana had dreamt that she had ordered two little violins from Bombay, and they had come, in a wooden box on a bullock cart, down the dusty road to the mission. In her dream, she opened the boxes, and handed an instrument to each of the little girls. Then, looking angelic in white dresses with blue sashes, they lifted the violins to their chins and played instantly, in tune, improvising new arrangements to old tunes, child virtuosos.

Then she would wake up and go help William, blind from the same smallpox outbreak, to dress and wash and shave.

William said the scourge of smallpox was God's will; Jana did not see it that way. She blamed William for not allowing the girls to be vaccinated; and she blamed herself for not having insisted, not having had a temper tantrum. Why, she could have merely snatched up the girls and taken them to the nearest town to be vaccinated, and let William splutter about God's will as much as he wanted.

Months after they had died, those thoughts went round and round in Jana's head. Gradually the torment had diminished, perhaps because she had administered so many mental lashings to herself that finally some corner of her brain decided that the punishment was enough. She also had insisted, after seeing a lot of villagers die of one dreadful disease or another, that she, William, and the servants at the mission would henceforth have vaccinations not only against smallpox but also against cholera and typhoid and any other diseases for which they had been invented. She cut off all objections with a firm "There is no other way, and I won't discuss this any further."

Laying down the law, she had been taught, was something women could do with their children but not with husbands. In retrospect, however, Jana could see that learning how to do this earlier would have been a life-saving thing.

✑ Two Taxi Rides

The next morning, she was up before dark, having engaged the taxi for seven A.M. She dressed in layers, planning to peel off her jacket and scarf and perhaps one cardigan in Dehra Dun. Mary packed her some tomato soup in a thermos bottle.

Jana gave Mr. Ganguly a tickle on his head, told him good-bye, and was off to the taxi stand at the outskirts of town, where there was a barrier saying, "No autos allowed without special permit." There, as planned, was the jovial driver who had first brought her to the town. The odd thing about Mr. Kilometres, she thought, was that he seemed jauntier—almost younger—than last year. For someone who had been driving the road for thirty years, as he claimed, he was none the worse for wear, and today he was wearing a pink plaid turban, with a pink hairnet around his tightly rolled beard.

"Mrs. Laird!" Mr. Kilometres exuberantly threw open the door to his battered taxi. "My most illustrious passenger! How are you, Mrs. Laird? Get in, please get in."

"Most of me is fine," said Jana, sliding across the cracked false-leather seats. "And yourself?"

"Tip-top. In first-class driving condition." Mr. Kilometres backed the taxi speedily into the turnaround space and, with a gleam in his eye, put it into a roaring first gear and took off. "And your good son, Mr. Laird? Far away, in Scotland, is it not?"

"Yes, he's in the city of Glasgow," said Jana.

"A very fine man," said Mr. Kilometres. "I tell lots of people, Mrs. Laird is one of my passengers, and her son, Mr. Laird, is another one. My customers are very distinguished. But Mrs. Laird is the most distinguished of all."

"You are very kind, Mr. Kilometres."

"Your son is writing frequent letters, I am sure."

"He manages to dash off a note now and then," said Jana.

"Mrs. Laird, madam, when you are dashing off your reply, please give your son my most sincere salutations," said Mr. Kilometres. "But where is the famous bird?"

"The famous bird is comfortably back home, thank you."

"My neighbor has a radio, and in the evenings, we gather to listen to All India Radio. When the announcer said, A parrot has induced a child to talk in the town of Hamara Nagar, I said, Ah! I know which bird they are talking about."

A spring in the lumpy seat was poking her, and Jana shifted her weight.

"My wife is very fond of birds," said Mr. Kilometres. "She keeps asking me to get one for her. She once had a mynah bird, but it was such a nasty fellow. It talked, but I never made any sense of what it said. My wife already has a name picked out for the bird that she wants. She says she will call it Tickle Toes. And she wants a good talker. She says she will teach it one hundred words! One hundred! That would be a lot, don't you think?"

"It would be," said Jana. "Be careful that nobody teaches the bird bad language, though. It can be very difficult to eradicate."

Mr. Kilometres laughed uproariously, to the point that Jana was worried that he was not paying enough attention to the road. He swerved around a horse-drawn tonga, squeezing a loud goose-honk out of his horn and scaring the animal to the point that it almost plunged over the side of the road. Then they rode along in silence for a while, Jana's jaw throbbing worse than ever.

"Mrs. Laird, you are a bit quiet today, I am thinking. Pulled down, in fact. Have you got an unpleasant errand in Dehra Dun?"

"Dentist," said Jana glumly.

"*Aré!*" said Mr. Kilometres in a horrified tone. "I had a tooth pulled once. My face felt as if I had been kicked by a horse."

Not heartened by this comment, Jana looked out the window and, blessedly, was momentarily distracted by the view. Tucked among the hills, far from the zigzagging road, were little villages, with terraced fields held up with stone retaining walls. In brilliant contrast against the green of the mountainside, thirty-foot-high rhododendron trees splashed brilliant patches of red flowers.

On a dusty but cheerful street in Dehra Dun, Mr. Kilometres pulled up in front of the dentist's office with a triumphant lurch.

"Good luck," said Mr. Kilometres. "I will be back to fetch you with a fresh tank of petrol."

Jana went in and settled down in the dentist's reception area. Now hungry, she realized that she wouldn't be eating for a while, and drank some of Mary's tomato soup while waiting her turn in the torture chamber. Fortunately, Dr. J. J. Sahni turned out to be a mild man with a competent air, and the chamber of horrors an unpretentious but clean room with a diploma from McGill University on the wall.

"Are you *the* Mrs. Laird?" he asked her.

"I'm surely not the only one," said Jana.

The dentist laughed politely. "No, of course not, but you are the owner of the famous parrot? From Hamara Nagar, the town of philosophers?"

"People do have a philosophical bent in that town," Jana said, as she settled herself in the chair.

"So," said Dr. Sahni, as he tilted the chair back. "Open wide, please. Aha. I see."

Jana did not like the sound of that "aha."

"We'll just take a couple of X-rays," said the dentist.

X-rays translated into rupees, and Jana gave a little shudder. But there was no stopping the process now. If there was one situation in which you did not bargain about prices, it was while leaning back in the dentist's chair. There was some whirring and clicking, and Dr. Sahni disappeared into the back room for a few moments to reappear with a reassuring expression on his face.

"I don't think we're going to have to pull that tooth," he said, "but we will have to do a bit of root-canal work. Don't worry, we'll give you a good supply of Novocain, and I should be able to complete the work in one sitting."

Out of the corner of her eye, Jana saw a long needle attached to an even longer syringe. She gripped the arms of the dentist's chair and closed her eyes.

"Now, Mrs. Laird, let's see how completely you can relax."

Not very completely, Jana feared. Soon the drilling, buzzing, and vibrating—all the things Jana had been imagining for the last three days—were coming true. Plus something she hadn't anticipated, which was a smell like burning sawdust. In between intense moments of concentration, Dr. Sahni chatted pleasantly.

"Hamara Nagar is the town whose fortunes changed dramatically, is it not? I understand you were targeted to be the site of the new government dam, but certain machinations in various ministries changed all that. I enjoyed hearing about Ramachandran's Treasure Emporium, with all its unexpected riches. Where paste emeralds turn out to be real, is it not?"

"Og og," said Jana.

"I really must go up there someday," said Dr. Sahni. "And your parrot can tell my fortune!"

Yes, do come visit, thought Jana, but leave your drill behind.

Jana tried to remind herself that modern dentistry was

one of the good things about having been born in the twentieth century. Why, lots of people had died of infected teeth
in earlier days. Just think if you had to go to some dirty old
barber and have him wrench out a tooth with a pair of pli-
ers, dosing you with brandy beforehand.

Just when she was sure that Dr. Sahni intended to drill and
poke and fuss around in her mouth forever, he was finished.

"I will give you some painkillers," said Dr. Sahni. "You
may want to take one or two tomorrow and the next day."

With the anesthetic still numbing her jaw, Jana said, "I
dou' I nee' 'em."

"Oh, I think you may," said the dentist. "In fact, take two
right now to get you back up the mountain."

Jana accepted the white tablets and a glass of water, took
two, and put the rest in her satchel.

"Wi' I ha' t' ca' ba'?" she asked.

"No, I think that tooth will be fine from now on," said
the dentist. "If you have any more trouble, give me a ring,
and I'll get you in here as soon as possible."

Returning to the waiting room, Jana extracted a large
number of rupees from her satchel and settled her bill with
Dr. Sahni's receptionist. Then she emerged into the bright
sunshine to find Mr. Kilometres waiting by the curb.

Under the influence of the painkiller, the ride back did not
seem as nerve-racking as usual. Or maybe it was just that Jana
was now getting accustomed to the way Mr. Kilometres drove.
She watched with detachment as he dodged cyclists, tongas,
and a traveling circus performer with a bear on a leash, until
he was streaming ahead with a gleam of triumph in his eyes.

"I have never collided with an animate being yet," said
Mr. Kilometres happily.

That left cars, buildings, and other solid objects, but Jana did not pursue the subject and, instead, dozed off in the back seat. By the time she woke up, they were approaching Hamara Nagar, and it was the end of the day, with the temperature falling rapidly.

At the taxi stand, Jana's knees were wobbly when she got out, but it was a great relief to be on her own two legs and breathing fresh air. She paid Mr. Kilometres and received a broad smile and a cheerful "Very best to you, Mrs. Laird, until we meet again."

"*Sat Sri Akal*," she said, taking her leave in the polite Sikh way. God is truth . . . and, she added silently, I give Him thanks for shepherding me through both the dentist's work and another one of your taxi rides.

At Abinath's Apothecary

As she walked through town, she heard some thunder rumbling around in the mountains and saw an occasional spike of lightning. She quickened her pace, being without an umbrella and hoping that she would be safely at home by the time the storm moved in. But the rain arrived just as she passed the Bharat Mata Cinema, and, almost immediately drenched, she started to run. When the hail started coming down like little bullets, she took refuge in Abinath's Apothecary, where the slogan on his sign—"Reliable Dispensing Chemist: Relief for a Suffering World"—seemed particularly comforting.

Mr. Abinath had turned on his electric light, which gave the shop, open to the street through a broad storefront, the look of a brightly lit stage set. His wares were a rainbow of color on the shelves: purple and blue bottles, silver tins of pills, stacks of sandalwood soap in yellow wrappers. When he saw her coming up the steps, a spasm of alarm crossed his usually serene and unlined face.

"Mrs. Laird, you are soaking wet!"

"I know," Jana said wearily. "I was trying to get home as quickly as possible from the taxi stand."

"And why were you taking a taxi?" Mr. Abinath looked concerned. "Why did you have to go out of town?"

"I went to the dentist in Dehra Dun," said Jana. "He performed some root-canal surgery."

"*Aré*, Mrs. Laird, you have my complete sympathy," said Mr. Abinath. "That was not a pleasant way to spend the day."

"Thank you, Mr. Abinath," said Jana.

"And how does your tooth feel now?"

"The painkiller has worn off, and I feel"—Mr. Kilometres's words popped into her mouth—"as if a horse had kicked me in the jaw."

"Well," said the chemist, his face lighting up, "I have just the thing for you. This is a potion that's good for many ailments and conditions."

"What's in it?" Jana asked cautiously. Mr. Abinath's remedies contained a wide variety of ingredients, some more reassuring to her than others. In addition to jasmine oil for anxiety, camel urine from Rajasthan for baldness, and codeine-laced aspirin for menstrual cramps, he sold asafetida for flatulence, asthma, and contraception.

"This tonic has some very special ingredients," said Mr. Abinath. "The most notable one is vitamin L."

"Vitamin L," repeated Jana in a puzzled tone.

"Vitamin L is part of my effort to develop a whole family of medicines. Would you like to hear more about it?"

"Certainly," said Jana. The hail was beating on the tin roof like machine gun fire, and both Jana and Abinath had to raise their voices.

"A, B, C, D, E—those vitamins you know about already,"

said Mr. Abinath. "But I am trying to concoct a few more. It is my ambition to come up with a vitamin for every single letter of the alphabet. I already am working on several: Vitamin G for glee. H for heartiness. I for insight. J for joy. Vitamin L is a double vitamin: love of life."

"Your vitamins are very cheerful," said Jana.

"Of course," said Abinath. "You think I am going to put sad and morose vitamins into a bottle and palm them off on an unsuspecting public? I'm also working on S for sleep and T for time, both of which are so necessary for healing."

Jana was wondering how sleep and time could be translated into vitamins when Mr. Abinath asked, "What medicine did the dentist give you?"

"Something very strong," said Jana. "A painkiller. I slept even in Mr. Kilometres's taxi ride back up the mountain."

"I see," said Mr. Abinath. "Those medicines stun the body into submission."

"I suppose they do," said Jana, "but to tell you the truth, I didn't mind being stunned."

"Here's my potion with vitamin L," said Mr. Abinath, taking a large brown bottle from under the counter. "I have tested it on my family, with excellent results. It works equally well with an aching jaw and an aching heart. Some of the ingredients are brought down from high in the mountains by nomadic traders. They tell me the ingredients together make an aphrodisiac. Others say it is a truth serum."

"Mr. Abinath," she said, "how can one medicine do all these different things?"

"It's no mystery at all," said Mr. Abinath. "It's all in the customer's expectations. You have to set those expectations at a certain level. After that, the person's brain juices start flowing in the right direction."

He continued, his face drawing up with a pondering

expression. "I'm trying to think of a catchy name that people will remember. Here is one idea. Every time I walk past the Giant Skating Rink, I hear a song floating out into the street. Those people at the Giant seem to get stuck on the same song, and play it over and over. Last year, it was 'Green Door.' This year it is 'Love Potion Number 9.' The phrase has stuck in my mind, and I keep thinking of my medicine as Love Potion Number 9. But, of course, it's not *only* a love potion."

Jana said, "Why not go them one better? How about Love Potion Number 10?"

"You've got a point there," Mr. Abinath said. "It's a long name to print on the label, though. The print will be so tiny that no one will be able to read it."

"Call it LPN10," said Jana. "Abbreviations always sound important."

"Mrs. Laird, I knew I could count on you." Mr. Abinath grabbed a pen, wrote "LPN10" on the label, and handed her the large brown bottle. "We'll both be famous for this! Although *you*, of course, are already famous."

Jana detected something wistful in Abinath's expression. Last year, when Feroze Ali Khan had gotten a lot of press as the philosopher-tailor, and Ramachandran's Treasure Emporium had become known as a repository of long-lost priceless objects, Abinath had not gotten any attention. Perhaps he felt hurt and neglected, Jana thought, and that now it is *his* turn to be interviewed by All India Radio or the *Illustrated Weekly of India*. All India Radio had made quite a fuss over the "high concentration of philosophers" in an "obscure Himalayan hill station" ("rivals the Sorbonne or Oxford University!"). Thanks to all the publicity, the town was no longer obscure, but there were evidently people here who felt they were as yet unappreciated.

The rain, Jana noted with relief, was letting up, the

evening customers coming in to get whatever medicine they needed in order to make it through the night. Jana put the brown bottle into her handbag.

"Good evening, Mr. Abinath," she said. "I'm off."

"Tell me how LPN10 works for you," said Mr. Abinath conspiratorially.

"Of course," said Jana.

ᡦ *Cozily at Home*

The lights were on in the bazaar now, and her way to the Jolly Grant House was lit quite well, though the street was glistening and she had to be careful not to slip on the hailstones accumulating in the grooves of the pavement.

When she saw her own sign, which read, "Jana Bibi's Excellent Fortunes," she felt a little rush of happiness to be home. Lal Bahadur Pun, tonight in military khakis, was at his position by the front gate, a grin of welcome lighting up his face. Eleven-year-old Tilku, also beaming, stood by with Mr. Ganguly on his shoulder.

"Good evening, madam!" Lal Bahadur Pun said, with a salute, copied by Tilku.

"Good evening, Subedar-Major. Good evening, Tilku."

Tilku handed Mr. Ganguly over to Jana, and the bird exclaimed, "Hello! Hello! Jana Bibi zindabad! Good bird! Good bird!"

"Thank you," said Jana.

"Good trip, madam?" Lal Bahadur Pun asked.

"Yes, considering the purpose. Mr. Kilometres got me back here in record time."

Mr. Ganguly screeched and hissed at the very name of the taxi driver, and gave an imitation of Mr. Kilometres's horn.

"Yes, you would have hated it," Jana said to the bird. "Did you have a good day here?"

Whatever Mr. Ganguly replied was interrupted by Mary, who arrived, wiping her hands on her sari, and announced, "Those workmen that Ramachandran recommended came and cut a hole in the wall and took out the water pipe."

"Oh my. Then what happened?"

"They said they would be back sometime with a new pipe."

"Sometime, eh? Why not tomorrow?"

"I too said, Why not tomorrow! I told them they wouldn't be paid until they came back with the new pipe. *And* put it in properly! And that if they didn't do it, Lal Bahadur Pun would go and play bad tunes next to their houses until they did."

Lal Bahadur Pun playing his pipes at top volume certainly was an intimidating proposition, thought Jana.

"I carried tins of water to your bathroom," Tilku announced. "Four of them."

"Thank you, Tilku," said Jana. "Mary, any other news?"

"I saw that Gopal man again today. The reporter. He took pictures of the whole street! I said to him, When are we going to see our pictures in the *Illustrated Weekly of India*? He said, Just keep looking, you will see."

Tilku broke in: "I saw that man, too. I was taking Mr. Ganguly for a walk on my shoulder and that man came up and offered Mr. Ganguly some nuts."

Jana frowned. "Let's not have strangers feeding him, all right?"

"Oh, Mr. Ganguly didn't take it. He turned his head away."

"Well, that's interesting," Jana said. "I've never known him to refuse a nut."

"I did something wrong, Jana mem?" Tilku's face drew up anxiously.

"No, Tilku, it's just odd. Well! Let's not stand out here in the cold talking. I'm ready for something to eat."

"Did you drink that tomato soup?" Mary asked Jana on the way in.

"Oh dear," said Jana. "I left the thermos bottle in Mr. Kilometres's taxi. I was so groggy coming out of the dentist, from the painkillers."

"Not to worry," Mary said. "He will deliver it himself or he will send it with somebody else who is coming to town. I have some more of that soup in the kitchen. You can have some now. Hot tomato soup will give you strength."

"It was a long day," Jana said. "My strength does need a little boosting, at that."

"They should put a helicopter service in; then we could ride back and forth all the time," said Mary.

"Today, I would have liked that," said Jana.

The tomato soup didn't seem any the worse for having sat in the pot all day, and Jana had a couple of bowls, and then, since she still couldn't chew very comfortably, a banana.

"Banana!" Mr. Ganguly said.

"Banana, *please*."

"Banana, please! Banana!"

The polite request coming from the bird still sounded like an order, but Jana gave him a bit. He ate it, then announced, "Bad bird!"

"Who is a bad bird?" Jana asked. "The man who saw you on the street?"

Nothing more could be gotten out of the bird that evening. He said, "Good night," which meant he wanted to go back in his cage.

"Well, then, good evening," said Jana, letting him through the door.

"Good night," said Mr. Ganguly.

Jana Takes Stock

✣ *Luxury and Austerity*

Jana mounted the stairs to her bedroom, then went into her small bathroom, with its gray plastered walls. Despite the cardboard the workmen had left over the hole they had made, she felt the cold air streaming in, and the four kerosene tins of water that Tilku had carried up were frigid to the touch. She filled the tin tub and put in the immersion heater, then waited for the water to get warm. Running hot water: wouldn't that be nice, she thought, watching the bubbles form around the rod. Then, remembering not to dip her finger into the water (she'd gotten too many electric shocks that way), she removed and unplugged the heater, stripped quickly, and lowered herself into the tub. She soaked more briefly than usual, her knees jackknifed in the tub, a hot washcloth over her chest only partially protecting her from the cold.

Once again, she fantasized wistfully about putting in new plumbing. Perhaps, if the book of Ian the butler's fiddle tunes could find a good market, she would be able to afford it. The table with the enamel bowl from Czechoslovakia served for washing her face in the morning, but it was not what you would call luxury.

The theme of luxury had been occurring to her with

increasing frequency. Imagine a scale of comfort from one to
ten, she said to herself, with one representing living on the
street, and ten, owning a Hollywood mansion with an indoor
swimming pool and a garage as long as the Louvre Museum.

On that scale, she mused, I've lived in everything from,
oh, say, a three to a nine. Quite a range of experience, and
something to be grateful for, either way. The white-pillared
house of her childhood, with its portico and deep verandah,
and its spreading gardens of roses, phlox, and cosmos, was at
least an eight.

Back in Scotland, her grandfather's castle—not really a
castle; basically, a large stone house—had been as comfortable as things were after the Great War, which, admittedly,
was not very. It never got warm, but because of its size (and
its household staff) she still gave it a seven.

The mission station she'd lived in for twenty-two years,
after making the impulsive decision to marry William and
run off to India, rated about a three. Though it had no running
water, at least it boasted a stone floor. Eventually, also, they
got a tin roof to replace the thatched one, so that rodents,
which had bothered them at first, finally were prevented from
running across the rafters and dropping pellets into the
food.

In Bombay? Her accommodations had been—oh, at least
a five. She had stayed in a guesthouse with a troupe of Shakespearean actors, then rented a beach house from friends, in
return for violin lessons for their children. Though not luxurious, the beach house had been perfectly comfortable, with
a stunning view of the water.

As for the next era of her life, the five years at the nawab's
palace, that got a nine. Her room had been enormous, with
French doors that opened onto a garden, and her bathroom
had been almost the size of the ballroom, with marble floors
and gold-plated fixtures.

And now, the ramshackle Jolly Grant House in her adopted town of Hamara Nagar? It was a constant struggle to keep it maintained. The view, the tower on the corner of the house, the fanciful verandahs and gables got a ten; the plumbing . . . oh dear, not so good. But it was home, home sweet home, and her own.

Having bathed, she emptied the water down the drain in the corner of the bathroom and toweled off as quickly as possible. Then, shivering, she dashed across the bedroom and pulled out her thick flannel pajamas from the almirah, supplementing them with a warm pullover. From the piano bench that served as her dressing-table seat, she took out a pair of heavy wool socks.

She was about to crawl into bed when her aching jaw reminded her of Mr. Abinath's potion. Where had she put it? Oh yes, the salon. She padded back downstairs, tiptoed in the dark past the sleeping Mr. Ganguly. Then she extracted the brown bottle from her satchel and went quietly back up the stairs to the third floor of the tower.

Finding her way carefully in the dark, she walked across the room and stood looking out one of the many windows. She had never had curtains made for the six-sided tower, because she did not want to cut off one inch of the view. Now, late at night, she could see the lights of the dormitories of the Far Oaks School, on a ridge across a gorge. She pictured the students, sons and daughters of missionaries and diplomats, tucked safely in their beds. The mountains in the background were a dark purple presence, barely distinguishable from the dark sky.

Feeling soothed and thankful that the long day was over, she switched on the lamp on the low side table and took a miniature brandy snifter out of the cabinet.

She twisted the cap off the brown bottle and took a sniff. Hmm, a nice flowery aroma, something like apricot jam. She

poured some into the brandy snifter and held it up to the
light, finding the liquid a clear gold color.

Nothing ventured . . . She took a sip, and found the potion
extremely pleasant. Smooth, not as sweet as it smelled, and
mild, with the suggestion of spices. Cardamom? Cloves?

She settled into an armchair and slowly sipped the potion.
With each sip, her jaw throbbed noticeably less. The racking
engines were quieting down.

So here she was, in the independent Republic of India,
fifty-nine years old, healthy, freshly released from the dentist, and not likely to have to go back to him anytime soon.
She had a home that had not yet fallen down around her
ears. She lived with an infinitely resourceful ayah, a fearless
chokidar, a cheerful messenger boy, and a mild and saintly
sweeper. And, of course, she had a parrot, an ambassador
from the animal kingdom and an endlessly amusing sooth-
sayer.

She listed other good things in her life: having tea at
the Why Not? with her neighbors and going to the cinema.
Letters (mostly informative, if a bit dutiful) from her son,
Jack, and his occasional visits to India, much as he hated
the trip. The music transcription project, which was going
slowly but might one day bring—well, perhaps not fame
and fortune, but at least some satisfaction and pocket
money. And—last but by no means least—the opportunity
to help raise the tourist appeal of the town, through putting her best foot forward as a fortune-teller. So far her performance on that front seemed to have done more good
than harm.

Yes, she had many blessings to count. So what was lacking?
Why did she have this little feeling of unfinished business . . .
of things being good but not perfect? How would she change
her life if she could? It was really too late at night to pursue

these questions very vigorously. She finished her snifter of LPN10 and drifted back down to her bedroom.

ᚺ *Reading Dr. Freud in Bed*

And now for the icy sheets! She gritted her teeth, but as soon as her feet reached the end of the bed, her face broke into a smile. Mary, bless her soul! With all the confusion caused by the workmen, Mary had still remembered the hot water bottle, and the bed was gloriously warmed up.

Jana drew the covers up around herself, expecting to fall asleep immediately, but in spite of the LPN10 and her extreme fatigue—or perhaps because of it—she found herself wide awake. After a while, she reached out and turned on the light and picked up Dr. Freud's *Interpretation of Dreams*. It was a very long book, and in the year since she had picked up this secondhand copy at Ramachandran's Treasure Emporium, she had read only about fifty pages. Now she made it through a few more, but soon her attention flagged. She started flipping through and came across a passage where Dr. Freud discussed what animals dreamt of. "Pigs dream of acorns," she read, "and geese dream of maize." Hens, it seemed, dreamt of millet.

This meant, no doubt, that Mr. Ganguly dreamt of nuts, bits of mango, and other treats. She wondered if he dreamt of lady ringnecks. Parrots were said to be sensual birds, but in her experience, Mr. Ganguly seemed more oriented toward humans than birds.

She flipped a few more pages, reading that 58 percent of dreams were disagreeable, 28.6 percent "positively pleasant." That second figure was higher than she would have suspected.

However, maybe it was just that the unpleasant ones, which made you awake trembling, were more memorable than the pleasant ones, which let you drift peacefully to consciousness.

She dozed off, waking up when the book fell across her chest. Finally, she put it on the bedside table and switched off the lamp.

When she woke, the bedroom was drenched with light, and Mary could be heard in the kitchen singing "When Morning Gilds the Skies." Jana had slept exceptionally well and, moreover, just before waking had had one of those 28.6 percent of dreams that were actually supposed to be pleasant. She was in a hotel dining room, dancing with someone on a wooden dance floor, the other dinner guests swirling around them and chatting, the air warm with champagne. An American band was playing tunes from twenty years before, the clarinets and saxophones crooning and spinning tendrils of sound, the snare drums brushing softly, the string bass keeping rhythm like a heartbeat. She was too close to the man she was dancing with to see his face, but, oh! it was all so comfortable and languorous. She leaned back into his arm and said to herself, now only half-dreaming, I want to dance forever.

Jana Overhears a Conversation

Later in the day, after writing down a nice jig by old Ian, Jana took a cup of tea up to the tower, opened all six windows, and enjoyed feeling the breezes blow through the room. Suddenly, she overheard her name mentioned in a conversation going on down on the terrace. She peeked out, and sure enough, Lal Bahadur Pun, Mary, Tilku, and Munar were having one of their spirited discussions.

"Yes, definitely, she should have one," Lal Bahadur Pun was saying.

"Why? You think husbands are always the answer?" Mary's answer was a bit testy.

Munar, the sweeper, lit himself a *biri* and, despite Mary's frown, gave Tilku a puff before he himself took a drag.

"Widows are not supposed to remarry," Munar said, in his old man's raspy voice. "They will just bring bad luck to the next man."

"Or, more likely, the next man will also bring bad luck to them," snapped Mary.

"But marriage is a good thing," said Lal Bahadur Pun, who had outlived three legally wedded wives and had had a number of unofficial ones, too. "It's good not to be alone in the world."

"Who says she's alone?" said Tilku. "She has all of us."

"Some of us are more useful to her than others," said Lal Bahadur Pun.

"I think next time Stuart-Smith sahib comes to visit, we should tell him that he should marry her," Lal Bahadur Pun said.

"No good," said Munar. "Divorced."

"It was not his fault," said Lal Bahadur Pun. "His wife in the U.S. ran away."

"That was America—what do you expect?" said Tilku. "I watched one American film once, and they all do things like that."

"When did you ever see an American film?" Lal Bahadur Pun challenged.

"I did, once!"

"*Chup!* You be quiet!" said Mary.

"I live here, too; I am allowed to speak. That is what democracy is all about. India is now a democracy."

Lal Bahadur Pun and Mary were momentarily taken aback, but Mary quickly regained her voice.

"Not for small boys," she said.

Tilku drew himself up to his full height. "Small boys know as much as old women!"

"Stop, stop, we're talking about Jana mem," Lal Bahadur Pun reminded them. "How are we going to get her a husband?"

"I'm telling you, Stuart-Smith sahib is the one," said Mary. "Jana mem's first husband was American; Stuart-Smith is American." She looked around with the air of having scored an indisputable point. "She is used to that kind of man."

"If he's American, he must be rich," Tilku said.

"Rich enough," Lal Bahadur Pun said. "But there is one problem. Eventually, Stuart-Smith sahib will have to go somewhere else, to another embassy, and, after that, back to the United States. And if Jana mem was married to him, she would have to go, too."

"That wouldn't be good," said Mary. "She might sell this house, right out from underneath us. Maybe we should make sure she *doesn't* get a husband."

"She needs a *local* husband," Tilku said. "How about Powell sahib, the eye doctor? Then she'd get free eyeglasses."

"Or maybe another American missionary sahib?" Munar said. "Those people stay in this country a long time."

"Oh, she had enough of that once," Mary said. "I was there; I know everything. William sahib was a very nice man in some ways, but that life was too hard for Jana mem. Also, I will tell you another story, believe or don't believe, but it's true. After William sahib died, this other American man came from the mission and wanted to marry Jana mem."

"So, why didn't she do it?" Tilku asked eagerly.

ᴄᶠ *A Flight from a Suitor*

Jana stepped back from the window, flooded with memories that alternately made her shudder and laugh. She thought back to her last few days at the mission station, after William had keeled over, in mid-sermon, and within minutes been pronounced dead.

During the twelve years after William was blinded from smallpox, a disloyal little thought had occasionally popped into Jana's mind: If I didn't have to take care of him, I would be free. But after his death, Jana had felt a searing, amazing grief. She *was* free now, but freedom was blisteringly painful, as if someone had taken a meat cleaver and chopped off one of her arms or legs.

The funeral was a small affair, the few Christians in the village coming with sincere tears streaming down their faces. They buried William in a tiny cemetery behind the mission wall.

The mission, financially on its last legs, was supposed to send Jana the money for her passage back to Scotland, but several weeks went by, and nothing arrived. Then, one day, a bullock cart creaked into the courtyard, and William's replacement at the mission clambered out. An American named Oral Fester, he had a few wisps of greasy hair combed over his bald head, plump hands, and a fat little belly cut into by his belt. Jana was uneasy from the first glance.

When Reverend Fester introduced himself, he took Jana's hands in a way that made her flesh crawl, and said a long prayer. The words were similar to those William would have used, but Mr. Fester had none of William's sincerity. Later that day, when Jana asked about her ticket home, Reverend Fester was evasive. The post had been delayed, he said.

That night, Jana went to bed anxious, although she kept telling herself there was nothing to be anxious about. William had never put a bolt on the bedroom door, saying that they were perfectly safe with the *chokidar* guarding the gate. But were they safe from people within the compound? Several times during the night, Jana heard footsteps on the verandah, Reverend Fester on his way to the bathroom. Her heart pounded each time the footsteps passed her door, and she held her breath until they died away, down the length of the verandah.

The next day, Reverend Fester made a quick tour of the compound. Then, late in the morning, he invited Jana to sit down at the table on the verandah where she had taught Jack to read and had eaten every meal with William.

"Mrs. Laird," said Reverend Fester, "I'm sorry to tell you that the mission is extremely restricted in its use of funds for the moment. We will be able to supply you with your steamer ticket in about two months."

He continued, giving her an oily smile: "But, of course, you may stay on here at no expense to yourself. With all your experience, I would find that very useful. You know the villagers. You know the routine of the mission."

"I think," Jana said, her mind working frantically, "that I can find accommodation with friends while I wait for the ticket. Or I can cable to family in Scotland to send funds."

"Many British folks are scrambling to leave," Reverend Fester said. He twisted the signet ring on a plump finger. "I'm told that booking passage is not easy these days."

The feeling of being trapped closed in on Jana like the walls of a cage.

"I'm sure I can manage," she said.

"Well, don't hurry, my dear." He reached across to take her hand in his, making her blood run cold. "You're completely welcome here."

That afternoon seemed intolerably long, and her mind went in circles as she desperately tried to figure out what to do. She could arrange to have a bullock cart take her to the closest telegraph station; from there she could send a cable to Glasgow. But how long would it be before a response came in? She couldn't just sit there in the telegraph office until it did.

She bathed quickly that night, aware as never before of the lack of a proper door on the bathroom. From behind the curtain, as she sponged off, she could hear everything happening on the verandah. Oral Fester first talked to Mary in condescendingly simplified English. Then he gave orders, in mangled Hindi, to the little sweeper girl who cleaned the floors.

The next day and night were equally nerve-racking. What was she afraid of? she asked herself. Reverend Fester was a man of the cloth, a God-fearing type. There was nothing to worry about. Still, she lay awake, counting Reverend Fester's trips down the verandah.

In the morning, Reverend Fester said to her, "Please consider another idea. It makes a great deal of sense to me, and I hope it will to you. I have already written to the mission, asking permission for me to marry you. I'm sure they will say yes."

"Marry?" said Jana, her voice squeaking in disbelief.

"Well, yes. You're already here. The mission knows you. They can't possibly have any objection."

"The *mission*? But . . . but . . . Reverend Fester, I don't know you . . . I don't intend . . . I can't . . ."

"I know it's a bit early since the passing of your dear husband. But life is very short and uncertain, especially in this part of the world. Sometimes we have to act more quickly than we would, given the rules of propriety that we were brought up with. In fact, I feel so confident about their answer, that I think we could go ahead, even without the mission's approval."

"I . . . Reverend Fester . . . it's impossible, really . . . I—"

"I'm not much older than you, and healthy, and my own dear wife has been in her grave for two months. Don't you believe that it is Divine Providence that has brought us together?"

More like the devil! Jana almost blurted out.

"I hadn't planned to marry again," said Jana, urgently.

"Neither had I, dear lady, neither had I! But this seems—preordained."

Preordained. William, proposing marriage long ago in the Willow Tearoom in Glasgow, had also thought it was God's will, but at the time, William had been so fresh and natural that he had only amused Jana, not scared her. She had not shared William's faith, but, until their views clashed on the subject of vaccination, she had found it benign. Later, of course, when her two daughters fell to smallpox, unprotected by the vaccine that William dismissed as blasphemy—the discharge from a sick cow—she felt differently. Her only consolation was that she'd already sent Jack back to boarding school.

Reverend Fester reached for her hand, and she snatched it away.

He was not going to be deterred. "Think about it," he said. "Sleep on it."

Her stomach churning, she nodded. But after supper, she called Mary, and the two of them walked down the path from the mission, toward the village.

"Mary," Jana said, "we must leave here as quickly as we can. Can you get a bullock cart to wait for us just before dawn?"

"I can do," Mary said confidently.

"Pack your own duffel, and I'll get my things together.

Then we'll get up as quietly as possible and be gone by the time he wakes up. And, right now, keep Reverend Fester away from the house while I get some money from the cash box."

Mary proved to be an excellent actress, diverting Reverend Fester's attention with a cock-and-bull story about there being a mad dog outside the gate.

The next morning, it was four o'clock by Jana's old watch when Mary came and shook her shoulder.

"Jana mem, bullock cart is waiting down the road."

With her suitcase in one hand and the violin case in the other, Jana sneaked around the back of the building, so as not to wake the sleeping dogs in the front. Mary, her duffel bag on her head, was close behind.

But when they got to the gate, the dogs suddenly started up a loud barking. Jana and Mary ran down the dirt path, Jana's suitcase and violin case banging against her legs, Mary keeping the duffel on her head only with difficulty. They could hear people stirring in the building, and then Reverend Fester calling, "What's happening? Who's there?"

Jana heaved her suitcase and violin case up onto the bullock cart, clambered up, reached for Mary's duffel, and then gave Mary a hand. Mary landed in the cart with a thud, the driver gave a shout to the bullocks, and they set off. In the dark, Jana could smell the dust they raised, feel every lurch of the cart, and hear every creak of the wheels.

But now, Oral Fester, in his pajamas, was gaining on them, easily outstripping the lumbering bullocks.

"Stop! Mrs. Laird! Mrs. Laird! I order you to stop."

"I'm sorry, Mr. Fester, we're not stopping."

Oral Fester tried to leap onto the moving bullock cart, but Mary grabbed her umbrella and threatened to give him a poke. "Fester sahib, we are not stopping! Don't try to make us."

Oral Fester marched along beside them for a good quarter

mile, arguing, even threatening to send the police after them. "I shall report you to the mission," he warned. "You'll never get your return passage." Then he tried pleading: "Please see reason, Mrs. Laird. Just tell me what you require to stay."

"Reverend Fester," cried Jana, "nothing will persuade me to stay. Nothing on earth that you can say, promise, or threaten! So turn around, please, and go back to the mission."

Again he tried to climb onto the moving cart, but even if the cart had been still, his tubby frame would have made it difficult. Jana, her temper finally snapping, leaned out and put her face as close to his as possible.

"LET US GO! You . . . you *badmash*! You fatso! God will strike you dead if you try to come after us."

Stunned and disbelieving, Reverend Fester stood in a cloud of dirt from their cart. Jana and Mary watched for a while, and then Jana turned her back on Reverend Fester and the road behind them.

As they got farther along, Jana heaved a sigh of relief, and they put first one furlong, and then another between herself and the mission. It was good-bye to one long section of her life. Her youth, her marriage, her bearing children and the few years while she'd raised them . . . all that was behind her. Forty-five years old, and suddenly free. Free, she thought, but except for Mary, alone.

"Where are we going, Jana mem?" Mary asked.

"Bombay," said Jana. "We're going to Bombay."

It's Not Easy Being Rambir

✎ Rambir and Ritu at Home

Rambir cleared a space on his cluttered desk and started on the layout for the next week's paper. He always found this part of his job restful. He did not much like dealing with the machines in the back room—neither the press, which he called Old Clackety-Clack, nor the mimeograph machine in the corner, which he called the Purple Pestilence. The typewriter in the other corner might have been a Royal, but Rambir thought of it as the Peon.

Really, he knew he should get *more* machines. A new press, which would work reliably and not overheat, and a Teletype machine, so he could get stories as they were breaking from Reuters or the Associated Press. And he needed a phone line to the office, and possibly even one to his home. But all that would cost money, and money did not flow into the Aaj Kal Printing Press in huge amounts. Perhaps, one day.

In the meantime, there was the pleasure of doing things by hand. He loved the cutting and pasting, the scissors and gum pot of the layout process. He liked planning which story would go in which column, where to put photographs, whether this or that advertisement should have a single line or double line as a border.

Over the course of the afternoon, he did several drafts of the layout, tossing many pieces of scratch paper in the wastebasket, before he decided that he would pack it in and go home.

After padlocking the door, Rambir made his way to his flat a few streets back from the main street of the Central Bazaar. The building dated from the early part of the twentieth century, its four stories built into the hillside, so that to Rambir, who lived on the top level, it looked like a cliff dwelling of swallows. The landlord and his many relatives occupied the first three floors.

Today, as he usually did, Rambir approached the building from the lower level, although this meant that he had to climb three steep exterior flights of stairs. He could have walked another quarter of a mile on the winding road, around to the higher level. But today he preferred the faster, if more athletically demanding, route.

As the building was color-washed yellow inside and out, Rambir called it the Jaundice House. Ritu called it the Daffodil House, and, of course, she was right to look on the bright side, but that was Ritu, the eternal optimist. In spite of its green shutters and corrugated red roof, the building had seemed drab to them when they'd moved in, so she had hung several baskets of geraniums from the beams of the verandah, giving it cheerful splashes of red. Sometimes they sat on this lofty porch and took in the spectacular views.

"This flat is a bargain," Ritu would say on those occasions. "Where else would you get a view like this?"

"The view's fine," said Rambir, "but the flat's pretty small. Tiny, actually."

Rambir's point of view regarding the proper size for a residence had been formed by the enormous house he had grown up in, with its large internal courtyard, its many high-ceilinged rooms, its expansive sprawling gardens, and its row of servants' quarters. Everything else after that had seemed cramped and impoverished to him. Whereas Ritu's family had been squeezed into a couple of rooms, with a latrine shared by several other families. From her point of view, just having a nest of their own was quite wonderful. A sitting-dining room, a bedroom, a sliver of kitchen, and your own bathroom, not to mention running water—what more did anyone need?

The smell of onions and garlic frying greeted Rambir as he got to the third staircase. He quickened his step. Ritu and the new cook-bearer were already cooking, and that was a good sign. It meant that they would eat at a reasonable hour. Last week, when the previous cook-bearer had quit, pleading old age, Ritu herself had done the cooking, and the timetable had been ragged, to say the least. Typically, Ritu would start cooking rice, figure it would cook itself quite nicely without her standing over it, and go to the sitting room to correct papers. The rice would burn, and Ritu would start all over again. By that time, the vegetables and dal would be cold, and she would have to heat them up, and then they'd get overcooked.

Ritu had many, many talents, but cooking was not one of them. Rambir had drawn a sigh of relief when they had found (or, to be more accurate, *Ritu* had found) a new cook-bearer willing to work for the small salary they could offer. Ritu had great managerial skills, Rambir had to admit. The new cook-bearer, Krishan, was eager to please, and Ritu was getting a good effort from him. She knew when to smile, when to frown, when to praise, and when to withhold praise. People responded accordingly.

Rambir peeked into the kitchen and saw Ritu checking the dal while Krishan was making chapattis.

Ritu turned and smiled at Rambir. "Hello, darling. We're going to eat in a very, very few minutes."

"That's good," said Rambir.

Krishan finished up the stack of chapattis while Ritu went into the main room, cleared away Rambir's editorial notes and her own exam papers off the dining table, and laid out plates, forks, and water tumblers.

"You got a letter," she said to Rambir. The handwriting on the envelope was his brother Jai's, much like his own slanting script, although their teachers in school had tried to make them write straight up and down.

"I'll look at it after dinner," he said, with a nonchalance that both of them knew was false.

When they sat down to eat, it was nine o'clock; Rambir was ravenous, the food was good, and he took three helpings. No matter how much he ate, he stayed thin, fretting away the calories, while the happy-go-lucky Ritu tended to put on weight. She had wasted very little of *her* life fretting, concentrating on improving things for herself and others.

After dinner, Ritu cleaned up, the new cook-bearer having left at the beginning of the meal. In the meantime, Rambir settled on the sofa, and, feeling the usual mixture of hope and anxiety, he slit open Jai's letter. Out came a couple of pages, and a half dozen small black-and-white photos.

"He's sent me the photos of little Ranjit's birthday party," Rambir said.

All Rambir's siblings and their spouses were in the picture, with their children, and Rambir's parents in the center of it. Jai was just a year younger than Rambir, but they looked so much alike they could have been twins.

Jai was the only one of Rambir's siblings who had defied their father's ban on communication with Rambir, but he hadn't quite worked up the courage to actually make the trip from Delhi to Hamara Nagar to see Rambir in person. Jai liked Ritu and had sympathized with Rambir's decision to marry her in spite of his parents' adamant opposition. But sympathy didn't make a huge difference in the world, Rambir had decided. Ritu and Rambir had gone alone to the registry, signed their names in a large book, and, afterward, without the presence of friends or family, garlanded each other with marigolds on the steps to the registry building.

"Oh, do let me see the photos," said Ritu, coming back into the room. "Oh, look, how sweet Jai's baby is!"

Rambir's heart twisted, and he thought back to the night, five years earlier, when he had taken Ritu to the hospital, her sari stained with blood from her third miscarriage, and heard the doctor's stern words: "This is the last time. Mother Nature has spoken. You can't do this again."

Rambir had been doubly stricken. He had entertained the hope that, once they had produced a grandchild for his father and mother, all would be forgiven, but it appeared that the easy way—the cinema plot way—to reconciliation was not going to open up.

How had Ritu recovered, if not quickly, so completely? How was she able to carry on, go to teach her classes? But that was Ritu, all bubbly smiles on the surface, all steel underneath. If he had a chance to start over, Rambir asked himself, would he do things differently? No, he would not. The break with the family, the move to Hamara Nagar, and the purchase of the Aaj Kal Printing Press had made him a stronger person, much more adult than he would have been just staying in Delhi and taking orders. Ritu, he knew, *was* the right person for him. He'd never loved any other woman, and he couldn't imagine being married to anyone else. The only problem was that sometimes he wondered how on earth *she* could possibly love *him*.

He looked again at the photos. Jai had mentioned that their father had some heart trouble and now walked with difficulty, and yes, both parents looked much older than he remembered. Rambir had a sudden chill. He did not want to go to the door one day only to see a runner standing there with an envelope from the PTT office. He did not want to open a telegram to find that it was all over, and that Jai, not Rambir, had been the one to perform the farewell rituals.

"Dear," said Ritu, brightly.

Rambir felt a twinge of apprehension. When Ritu said "dear" like that, it meant she was going to bring up a topic that he wouldn't be comfortable with. Such as "Dear, my old girls' reunion at Isabella Thoburn is coming up; you won't suffer too much without me for a few days, will you?" Or "Dear, do you think we might buy a radio?" It was always something perfectly reasonable. But Rambir didn't like it when Ritu was away, and he didn't like spending money on things that weren't absolutely essential.

In the end, Ritu *had* gone to her reunion, and he had survived, and they *had* bought a radio, and now he couldn't imagine getting through a day without listening to All India Radio.

"Dear," she said, "I've been invited to go to a conference on science education in modern India."

"Where is the conference to be held?" Rambir asked.

"It's in Pune," Ritu said brightly.

Pune! Way down there? Why, it was a couple of days by train, thought Rambir. He tried to smile, and to wipe what Ritu called "your worried look" off his face.

"They'll even pay for the train fare," said Ritu.

That did away with one of the objections he could have raised.

"And provide accommodations."

There went another.

"That—that sounds like an honor," he said.

"I think it is," she said, her eyes shining. "They want me to present a paper. They imagine that I have something to say!"

"You do have things to say," said Rambir bravely, "and you should say them."

"I think I'll talk about the work my girls do in physics. How they seem to enjoy labs so much and do so well drawing up their reports. Do you know, Ramachandran's twin girls are both very gifted in this area! I've been telling them they should aim for university degrees in science. They roll their eyes and say, What would Mums and Dads say? They just want to marry us off! I tell them, It would be a leap of faith for you, but look, women can be scientists. Think of Madame Curie. And look at India's own Anna Mani. On her eighth birthday, her parents wanted to give her diamond earrings, but instead, she asked for a full set of the *Encyclopaedia Britannica*. Making girls passionate for learning is what I want to do."

"I'm sure you'll give a very stimulating paper," said Rambir. "When is the conference?"

"In May."

"Awfully hot to travel in the plains," he said.

"I know," she said, "but people have survived traveling in May." She studied his face. "I won't go if you don't want me to."

He took a deep breath. "Go!" he said. "I'll be able to boast about my brainy wife!"

"Are you sure?" she asked.

"Of course I'm sure." He was sure. He was also dismayed. But, he figured, it was Ritu's patriotic duty to go and, therefore, *his* patriotic duty to let her—to encourage her to—do so.

"Krishan will take very good care of you," Ritu said. "By the time I leave, I'll have him thoroughly trained. And everything else runs like clockwork. Krishan will oversee the sweeper, so everything will be kept spick-and-span. The *dhobi* knows when to come and pick up the dirty clothes. You'll be fine."

"Of course," said Rambir, "I'll be more than fine! I'll be tip-top!"

"Or—" Ritu had a sudden idea. "You could come with me! And on the way home, maybe we could spend a day or two in Delhi."

And try to visit your parents were the unsaid words hanging in the air. Ritu had come up with that idea before.

"I can't leave the paper for that long," said Rambir. "And I don't think a stay in Delhi would be very—fruitful."

"We could drop in on them . . . surprise them . . . maybe catch them with their guard down?"

"They hate surprises," said Rambir. "It would be a catastrophe."

"Oh, dear. Well, all right then, you stay here and keep the home fires burning—and the presses rolling."

She glanced at her watch. "Oh! Oh!"

"What?" Ritu's exclamation made Rambir jump.

"We're missing Radio Ceylon!"

Ritu, whose mind labored with formulas and scientific truths and measurements and experiments, was completely capable of shutting her mind down and turning into a giddy schoolgirl, having fun with cinema and American and British pop songs.

She clicked on the radio, and an unctuous voice flowed into the room: "For Usha, with oceans and oceans of love, and a kiss floating at the crest of every wave."

Ritu burst into her silvery laugh. "Picture that! Kisses like little rafts? With flags on them, of course. A veritable armada of kisses!"

Rambir laughed too, grateful to live with someone who could make him laugh.

The song was one of Ritu's new favorites, "Love Potion Number 9." In it, the singer, unlucky in love, took his troubles to a gypsy, who made him up a magic potion on the spot. Then he fell in love with everything.

"I just love the story of it," Ritu said. "Just fancy this man kissing the lamppost and the policeman. What would Bandhu Sharma do if someone suddenly kissed him?"

Rambir laughed again. Ritu was working her magic, making him feel relaxed and safe, and as if he could actually enjoy life.

"I'm going to send in a dedication for you," Ritu said suddenly. "To Rambir, my knight in shining armor. My prince. My companion on the road of life."

Rambir shook his head, as if refusing the second helping of some delicious sweet he really wanted to eat. Having one's personal life blasted all over the subcontinent on Radio Ceylon? Quite embarrassing, wouldn't that be?

"Oh, come now," said Ritu, reading his mind. "No one will know which Rambir and which Ritu they're talking about."

✒ According to His Needs?

The next morning, his mood was once again gloomy.

"Darling, don't fret so much," Ritu said, kissing him before he went out the door to work.

The wind was fierce. Flakes of snow blew down the street, a sudden optical illusion making it look as if they were rising from the pavement. Rambir did not like it when it snowed; no one had proper footwear for such an event, rickshaws slid about, and horses stumbled and sometimes even lost their footing. It plagued his conscience to see the charcoal carriers plodding by with bare feet, stooped over under their bundles.

" 'To each according to his needs,' " he muttered. Oh, that was so far from being accomplished! Perhaps it would happen someday, but no time soon. Even with Mr. Nehru, even with independence. In the meantime, what could one do? Just try to prick people's consciences, he decided. This resolve made him feel better about the choice he had made to take over the ailing press, put out the English-language weekly newspaper *Our Town, Our Times,* and speak his mind on many topics. How many people in this town worried one bit about the people in Algeria wanting their freedom? Not many, but a few more this week than last, thanks to him. And how many applauded when a new nation in sub-Saharan Africa came into being? Ghana, or Senegal, or Togo? Intellectuals in Delhi and in Calcutta certainly did, but here in the hills? The need for enlightenment was great in this town, Rambir felt, and he wanted to fulfill that need.

Rambir turned his key in the padlock, and the door to the office swung open. "Must do something to spruce up this building," he muttered to himself, seeing the peeling paint on the door and the window frames. Inside, he opened the shutters, and the white winter light came into the room.

Today, he had to write his editorial.

A reader had written in to say that India needed the atomic bomb, because the Chinese would undoubtedly have it before long. Rambir felt his stomach turn over. Must our country emulate the superpowers, he asked himself? It was bad enough for humanity that the USA and the USSR—and Britain and France—had their bombs. India's role should be that of a moral superpower, above the fray. Had not Mahatma Gandhi himself said that mankind must adopt nonviolence, or face certain suicide?

Rambir, unlike his pious parents, had no beliefs that he would call religious, but sometimes the Hindu vision of great ages turning struck him as very apt. Creation giving way to destruction, destruction giving way to creation. We are indeed in the Kali Yuga, he thought, the age of strife. What other age would produce nuclear weapons? Rambir could just imagine the mushroom-shaped cloud, the blinding light and deafening noise, the waves spreading outward from a point of impact.

He briefly looked at an old newspaper article about Premier Khrushchev pounding his shoe on the table. Was this how world leaders should act, like children having a tantrum? And then he pulled out a copy of the American President Eisenhower's farewell address. "In the councils of government, we must guard against the acquisition of unwarranted influence, whether sought or unsought, by the military-industrial complex," he read. Yes, former president Eisenhower was quite right: one should beware.

He picked up his pencil and wrote: "The Soviets and the Americans, they are Brobdingnagians in a world of Lilliputians! But are they giants for evil or giants for good?"

The Interpretation of Dreams

✑ Jana's Mailbag

The postman was at the front gate, reaching into his sack to pull out a thick stack of letters for Jana. She'd been getting much more mail lately than she used to. She came back into the house, settled herself comfortably in the bay window, and started slitting open the envelopes. She did not recognize the handwriting of any of the senders.

The first letter was from Bombay, with the return address saying, "R.K. Films." Jana rolled her eyes at the idea that a famous cine-studio would be writing to her. The letter offered to give Mr. Ganguly a starring role in a feature film and said that someone would come and pick up Mr. Ganguly at the earliest convenience.

"Hardly!" Jana said. Although, she thought, Mr. Ganguly would be an appealing film star.

Then she opened several requests for money. One was from someone who claimed to have been Jana's ayah in Allahabad when Jana was a little girl. It was in English, with elaborate script and flowery language, obviously written by a professional scribe, and Jana could see no evidence that the woman had been her beloved nursemaid.

Next, an animal welfare society in Nagpur asked for a

contribution, as did a veterinary hospital in Bombay and a bird-watchers' club in Delhi.

Jana sighed. Get a little bit of fame, and you pay the price.

There was also a letter written in aggressive block capitals in black ink, with a skull and crossbones drawn at both the top and the bottom of the page. "Madam, you are a frod! You know nutthing of palm-reeding, cards, or anything else. Take your stupid bird and go back to whare you cam from!"

Good heavens, she thought, a poison-pen letter. She shuddered and tossed it in the wastebasket.

Next, she unfolded a letter typed on official-looking stationery from a legal firm in Bombay. The tone was ominous.

"Dear Mrs. Laird," she read. "It has come to our attention that you may be in possession of stolen property, the penalty for which is a not insubstantial fine and/or period of incarceration. Our client is the rightful owner of the example of *Psittacula krameri manillensis* that you expropriated at some time on or before May 1, 1955. We hereby inform you that if you return the parrot, pay reasonable damages to our client, and renounce any claim to ownership, we will not take legal action. Otherwise, we will sue for one lakh of rupees, plus all legal expenses . . ."

Jana also threw *that* letter in the wastebasket. It's a completely bogus claim, she said to herself, but she found her stomach turning over. It had to be bogus. And yet—Jana herself did not know exactly where Mr. Ganguly had come from, and the small possibility that this claim could be valid struck fear into her heart.

"Mr. Ganguly!" she said to the bird. "Ever since you made the town famous by getting little Raju to talk, people are becoming quite desperate to acquire you. And squeeze money out of me."

Her bird was thinking more about needs of his own. "Nut."

"Nut, please," she corrected him.

"Nut, please."

"That's a good bird." She gave him a groundnut, which he shelled and ate.

"Where did you come from?" She studied his brilliant green feathers, his bright red beak, and the formal-looking black ring around his neck. Granted, he was a common ring-neck parrot, one of millions, but he was a very fine specimen. He was valuable and important to her, but not for the money anyone else thought he was worth. What other bird could have such a personality? she asked herself. He was a good judge of character, sociable, chatty, and occasionally more insightful than most humans.

"Would you kindly tell me your history?" she asked. "Before you came to my garden, that is."

But as extensive as his vocabulary was—in several languages—it was not adequate to tell her his history.

✂ *Tea at the Why Not?*

Mr. Joshi of the Why Not? Tea Shop poured three glasses of scalding tea and boiling milk and carried them over in his bare hands, making Jana wonder how he could possibly tolerate the hot glasses. He put the tea down on the table and then fetched and plunked down a sugar bowl, too.

"I know you like to add your own amount of sugar," he said. "Mrs. Laird adds a bit, Mr. Ramachandran adds a double amount. Editor sahib here does not even sweeten his tea. Together, you work out to average."

"When we were at university," Ramachandran said, "I used to take all Rambir's allotment of sweets and sugar in the canteen."

"Yes," said Rambir, "the girls called us Sweet V.K. and

Sour Rambir. Like a Chinese dish. I didn't think it was very complimentary."

"No, that wasn't exactly fair," said V. K. Ramachandran. "You're just serious and straightforward. Not sour; there is a difference."

In the corner, Mr. Joshi's nephew was tending a conical pan of bubbling oil, and Mr. Joshi checked on his progress and then brought over a plate of piping hot samosas. "If a samosa goes for an hour in my shop without being eaten, that is a bad sign. Here, all is cheapest, freshest, and best. I don't believe in serving stale food. Unlike some others."

They all knew that he meant Mr. Motilal of the Superior Tea Shop. Mr. Joshi added, "Some people want to squeeze every single last anna out of the customer, and others want to squeeze out every single last smile."

Jana tucked away that phrase to tell Kenneth Stuart-Smith so that he could put it in his *Globe-Trotter's Companion*.

"How is your good wife, Mr. Ramachandran?" Mr. Joshi asked.

"Tip-top," said Ramachandran. "Absolutely tip-top. Giggling and cooing at the new baby. That child is the lord and master of the universe! You would expect the other children to be jealous, but they too giggle and coo. Our house sounds like an aviary full of doves."

Mr. Joshi laughed politely at Ramachandran's joke and returned to the back of the shop, where the next batch of tea was boiling away.

"How are your lovely daughters, Asha and Bimla?" Jana asked Ramachandran.

"They too are tip-top! Except, of course," added Ramachandran, "that they're always worrying about their physics homework. They have such a hard teacher! But very brilliant, of course. Rambir, you must tell your wife that her students are completely in awe of her. Completely in awe."

Rambir smiled with pride.

Ramachandran continued: "Your wife, my dear fellow, is a model citizen as described in our constitution." He turned to Jana. "Did you know that, Mrs. Laird?"

"I can well believe it," said Jana, "but tell me more."

"Rambir," said Ramachandran, "you are better versed in the constitution than I am; you know all about Part this and Clause that. Duties of the citizen, and so forth."

Rambir could quote the constitution chapter and verse. Jana saw him trying to restrain himself from doing so and, finally, failing. With his pride breaking through his modesty, he said, "I think it's interesting that what she tries to do is right there in Part IV-A, 51A, Clause H. One of the duties of the citizen is to develop the scientific temper."

"She certainly does that!" agreed Jana.

"And another—in Clause J—is to strive toward excellence in all spheres of individual and collective activity so that the nation constantly rises to higher levels of endeavor and achievement."

"You do that, too," said Jana. "You both are exactly the type of citizen that a modern nation needs."

"You're so correct, Mrs. Laird," Ramachandran said, helping himself to another samosa. "In college we used to talk about these things—you know, role of government, role of the citizen. Those were revolutionary times, of course. But once we were independent, a lot of people just turned to advancing their own comfort. Not my friend Rambir!"

"I wonder," said Jana, "I wonder if I'm doing *my* bit. One gets caught up in one's own concerns."

Rambir said reassuringly, "Mrs. Laird, of course you are! You, too, are trying to promote the ideals of Clause H, one of which is humanism."

Jana drew a deep breath. "I'm glad you see it that way. But what is humanism, exactly? And is it as difficult as science?"

"More so, I would say," judged Rambir. "Treating one's fellow man as one's self, is it not?"

"You're getting that mixed up with morality," Ramachandran said.

Jana, feeling that the conversation was drifting toward abstraction, brought it back to Ritu. "Is she burning the midnight oil, as always?"

"She is," said Rambir, "and she's been invited to give a paper at a conference in May. She'll have to travel all the way to Pune."

"By herself?" said Ramachandran, in alarm.

"She says she's not at all nervous. She'll travel in the women's compartment. Safe as houses, they tell us."

"Mary and I have done that several times," Jana said. "She will be fine."

"My girls want to cut their hair to look just like Ritu does," said Ramachandran. "That sort of geometric look, with the hair going this way, on the diagonal." He demonstrated with his hand. "But my wife told them they can't, they have to keep their hair in nice tidy plaits. Like Mrs. Laird, here! Padma tells Asha and Bimla that they must emulate Mrs. Laird."

"They can emulate me in hairstyle—if Padma says so," Jana said, "but please, not in their professional lives. Asha and Bimla can actually *do* physics. They will have real professions."

"Yes, yes, they can be physicists," said Ramachandran, with a casual wave of the hand, as if he were talking about some hobby they could keep up, like stamp collecting. "Just like Ritu. Such a sensible girl. Except for whom she married, of course."

He gave a jolly laugh and looked at Rambir. "Now, that must have been a moment of madness."

"I'm thankful that she was capable of a moment of

madness," said Rambir. "She's had very few of those in her life, and I'm glad I was the beneficiary of one of them."

Jana watched the interaction between the two friends, amused, and then they turned their attention to her.

"Mrs. Laird, isn't this your anniversary?" Mr. Ramachandran asked.

"Anniversary? My birthday is on Republic Day, January 26. And my wedding anniversary is in February."

"No, no, no, the anniversary of your arrival in Hamara Nagar."

"Actually, you're right," said Jana. "Mr. Dass at the Victoria would have the record of the day I checked in at the hotel."

"It was around the time that Rambir and I were sitting at this very table, looking out on this very street, and discussing how we were in danger of being submerged by the waters of an infernal dam."

"But we're not drowned yet. We're still here," said Rambir.

"Indeed, we are still here! And Rambir is still writing his editorials on the perils of the atomic age." Ramachandran's tone managed to be teasing and awed at the same time.

"Someone's got to do it," said Rambir. Changing the subject, he asked Jana, "And what do you hear from that fellow, the American? Mr. Smith?"

"Stuart-Smith," Jana said. "I had a letter from him just the other day. *The Globe-Trotter's Companion* is already out! The publisher did a rush job on it, to have it for this year's tourist season. Apparently it's selling quite well."

"Oh, yes, Stuart-Smith," said Ramachandran. "A good fellow. Grew up in India, so he doesn't spew out as much nonsense as those fellows who fly over the subcontinent and then write a book about it. *Two* books if they've flown over in the daytime."

"Quite, quite." Rambir rolled his eyes.

"Anyway," said Jana, "there's a complimentary bit on *us* in the book. Hamara Nagar is referred to as 'the home of the philosophers.' The samosas at the Why Not? get special attention."

"Deservedly," said Ramachandran. He pointed to the last one and looked at the others inquiringly; they shook their heads, and he popped it into his mouth.

"That's good news," Rambir said. "But it's not safe to rest on our laurels. Don't you think we should continue to improve the standing of the town as a destination for tourists from all over the world? Why should people focus on the Louvre and the Sistine Chapel and the Parthenon when they could come here? Let's push Hamara Nagar as . . . as . . ."

Rambir searched for an idea, but Ramachandran, finishing his samosa, beat him to it. "The home of dreams," he said grandly.

"The home of what?" said Rambir.

"Dreams."

"What do you mean, exactly?" asked Jana.

"I'm not even sure." Ramachandran laughed so loud and so abruptly that the people at the next table jumped. "The phrase just popped into my head. Phrases do that, don't they! It's a nice one, don't you think?"

"What a coincidence," said Jana. "You know, I've been thinking about dreams lately. And reading Dr. Freud's *Interpretation of Dreams*. Have you read it?"

Neither Ramachandran nor Rambir had.

"It's a very odd book," said Jana. "Rather full of paradoxes, for my taste. But I understand one ought to be up on those things."

"I've got it!" Ramachandran turned to Rambir. "Our friend Mrs. Laird here can write a column on dreams for the newspaper. The column can be called 'What Do Your Dreams Portend?' Like astrology, only more personal. My wife is always telling me her dreams. Of course, I say to her, My dear, *I* am your dream—your dream come true! What else do you need to dream about?" He chuckled loudly at his own joke.

Jana saw that Rambir was taken aback.

"A dream column?" he said, skeptically.

"I know," Ramachandran coaxed, "that you generally like the newspaper to have a serious and elevated tone. But we have to consider popular appeal. We must be flexible. We are asking the broader world to take notice of us, and so we must accommodate ourselves to the tastes of the broader world. You have increased your readership, is it not?"

"Well, yes," admitted Rambir, allowing himself to look proud about it. "We have subscribers from out of town, in Mussoorie and Dehra Dun, and even half a dozen in Delhi itself."

"Delhi, excellent. Today, half a dozen; tomorrow, two dozen; next month, a hundred; next year, a thousand! If they find you on the cutting edge."

"I really don't think dream interpretation is the cutting edge," Rambir said. "My readers want meat. They don't want macaroons."

"Nonsense, my dear fellow—they need both meat *and* macaroons. Variety, variety, that is what you need."

Rambir sighed. "I suppose you're right. A flexible attitude is required."

Ramachandran beamed. "Good fellow. Well, how about it, Mrs. Laird? You could answer readers' questions about their dreams."

"Who will write in with questions?" Jana asked.

"Everyone," said Ramachandran. "Although, in the beginning, we'll have to put in a few ourselves. What do they call it? To bootlace the thing?"

"Bootstrap," Rambir said.

"At least not bootleg!" said Ramachandran.

There was a moment of silence while the three considered the new idea. Rambir said thoughtfully, "I have this dream all the time. I'm swimming at the Gymkhana Club pool in Delhi."

"And?" said Ramachandran.

"That's all," said Rambir. "Just swimming."

"There, Mrs. Laird, that's not at all a complicated dream," Ramachandran said. "You can figure out some nice simple interpretation. Excellent for a beginner."

"Did you swim at the Gymkhana Club as a child?" Jana asked Rambir.

"No," said Rambir, "we weren't particularly welcome. My father was one of the first Indian members to join after independence. I've actually never swum in the Gymkhana Club pool. And—this is a confession—I don't even know how to swim."

"Do you wish to learn?" Jana asked.

"Well, theoretically, yes, but there wouldn't be any pool to swim in here in town anyway."

Jana turned to Ramachandran. "What about you, Mr. Ramachandran? Have you a beginner dream for me?"

Ramachandran thought for a moment and took his last noisy swig of tea. "I have a dream about finding jewelry for the emporium and discovering that it is purest gold."

"Finding gold," said Jana. "That's your dream, you say?"

"Yes," said Ramachandran. "Again, that shouldn't be any trouble for you in your column, should it?"

"I guess not . . ." said Jana.

Mr. Joshi came up with a plate of little rhomboid-shaped white sweetmeats with flakes of silver leaf on top.

"Not for me, thank you," said Jana and Rambir, in one breath. Ramachandran looked wistfully at them and finally shook his head.

"Well, I've got to go finish my editorial," said Rambir.

"Yes, you go save the world," said Ramachandran. "The world certainly needs saving, although whether it *deserves* it is something else."

"Don't poke fun at Rambir," said Jana. "The world needs more conscientious citizens like him."

"I wouldn't dream of poking fun at my old college chum, would I? But he does work too hard, and I try to keep things light with him."

"Mr. Ramachandran is right. Rambir, you mustn't overwork," said Jana. "You and Ritu will end up in adjacent hospital beds."

"Not to worry," said Rambir.

Jana thought she detected a note of wistfulness or anxiety in his voice. Perhaps it was just too many hours at the press.

"And *I've* got to go work on my music manuscript," said Jana.

"Oh yes, the one that will bring you wealth and fame," said Ramachandran.

"Thank you, Mr. Ramachandran. I hope that some people will get pleasure out of my old butler's tunes."

"Well, off we go, is it not?" said Ramachandran.

"It is," said Jana.

ᴄᏰ *Jana Works on Her First Column*

Writing a weekly column about dreams. What had possessed her to say yes?

"Mary," said Jana, "I am out of my mind."

"What is the problem, Jana mem? Headache? Too tired?"

"No—worse," said Jana. "Mr. Ramachandran and Rambir

sahib want me to write a column for the newspaper about dreams."

"Very good!" said Mary.

"You think so?"

"Yes, yes. All the ladies will be reading it. At least Mr. Ramachandran's wife will read it, is it not? Don't you think?"

"Assuredly," said Jana, "since in the beginning probably most of the dreams will be hers! I already have one of Mr. Ramachandran's dreams to write about. And one of Rambir's."

"My mother always had dreams," said Mary. "She would tell all us children about them and then predict the future on the basis of them. One bad thing, then another bad thing. She never said anything good would come."

Mary's mother had been an impoverished sweeper from South India, and Jana was not surprised to hear that she'd expected little from life. Mary, in escaping from her hereditary profession and her violent husband, was the exception to the rule that people of humble beginnings could expect a life of misery.

"I personally always dream that I am eating mangoes," said Mary. "And when I dream of mangoes, I go and buy them in the bazaar. So, my dream comes true."

"Because you make it come true," said Jana. "The self-fulfilling prophecy. Your mind reminds you that you want something, and then you go get it."

That seemed to her to fit with Dr. Freud's contention that a dream was a fulfillment of a wish. To her mind, he had vastly overstated the case, and yet some dreams certainly were the fulfillment of wishes, Mary's mango dream among them. Of course, Dr. Freud would probably say that Mary had wanted to be impregnated by the mango seller, or some such nonsense.

Jana was now actually reading *The Interpretation of Dreams* during the daytime, figuring that she'd never finish it if she continued to read two pages a night and promptly fall asleep before she got to a third. Now, with the book in hand, she settled into the window seat in the salon for some serious study.

She had bought the book secondhand at the Treasure Emporium, and the former owner, a Mr. S. S. Bannerjee, had written on the flyleaf, "Acquired by me on December 15, 1937, discarded by C. G. Jung on his visit to India."

On the endpapers was a handwritten index of sorts. S.S., as Jana was now thinking of him, had apparently been interested in making a dream dictionary. Under "fruits," he had penciled in "apples," "pears," "cherries," "grapes," and "plums." "Mangoes," "lychees," and "papayas" did not appear. Ah well, thought Jana, Dr. Freud had not lived in the tropics.

Another category S.S. had made in his index was "bodily functions," and there were several of these, from sex to elimination. Dr. Freud was a bit of a dirty old man, Jana decided, or maybe S.S. was.

Her mind turned to Rambir's swimming dream. It was a dream of regrets, Jana figured. Rambir was longing for his lost childhood, and for being the apple of his parents' eye, and for the privileged life he had lived in Delhi.

Consulting S. S. Bannerjee's index, she noted to her delight that swimming was included. Swimming, she read, along with flying, hovering, and other such activities, referred back to childhood games involving movement. "I guessed right," she said to herself. But then she read on: swimming, in particular, signified the desire to return to the childhood pleasure of wetting the bed. Pleasure? She could not remember wetting the bed in her own childhood, and to the best of her memory, her own children had never acted as if bedwetting were a pleasure. In fact, on the rare occasions when they did wet the bed, they woke her up, sobbing.

In any case, how could she insult Rambir with such an

interpretation? And his readers would definitely be disgusted. No, this was not going to go into a family newspaper. Save that kind of thing for the obscure scholarly journals read by half a dozen people with thick eyeglasses. She'd just have to make up something more acceptable.

Swimming . . . at one with the creatures of the sea . . . moving through a medium different than you usually did . . . propelling yourself like a fish through water, with joy and freedom. Swimming—an expression of power, but also of calm, and happiness, and soft, flowing well-being. She jotted down these notes. Then, in a burst of inspiration, she came up with the following for the newspaper column:

"You seek harmony and good relations in whatever you do, which will serve you well in life. The dream of childhood means that you will regain something lost. Simplicity, swimming is simplicity itself. You know what you want. You have only to keep this in mind; don't get distracted by distractions."

Jana crossed out "distracted by distractions." What else, she scolded herself, would one be distracted by? Instead she wrote, "knocked off course by distractions." She finished with "Take heart! You have the right instincts, and you are on the right course."

Next, she turned to Ramachandran's dream: acquiring tinsel for the Treasure Emporium and finding that it was gold.

Obviously, Ramachandran's dream harked back to the unexpected good luck he had had the year before, when moldy old books had turned out to be first editions signed by the authors, and banged-up cigarette cases the former possessions of world-famous leaders. Of course, he had given away some precious gems before realizing their worth. The costume jewelry he had given Jana for her fortune-telling outfit had turned out to be real emeralds in settings dating from the fall of the last Mughal emperor.

Ramachandran had not begrudged her the emeralds, Jana reflected. In fact, since giving them to her had been part of the cycle of good luck that he had initiated, he seemed reconciled to the fact that he had lost items of value by inattention.

So, what was she to say about Ramachandran's dream? Again she flipped to S. S. Bannerjee's penciled index, and then gave a gasp, half of amusement, half of dismissal. My! Gold, Dr. Freud said, represented feces. So that's where the expression "filthy lucre" comes from, Jana thought. Trust Dr. Freud to take something good, like swimming or gold, and turn it into something revolting. Well, she could not throw Ramachandran's dream back into his face by talking about excrement.

She thought a while, then wrote: "You have made an acquisition of something valuable. This says something good about you. Think about what is good, what is merely convenient or comfortable, and what is dispensable. Perhaps you have overlooked things in the past. But you have learned from your mistakes, and you are well on your way to fame and riches. Gold is only the half of it. Platinum, diamonds, silver, rubies—all will come through your door. But fame will come, too. And not only because you are rich, but because you are a generous man with an expansive nature."

That really did describe Ramachandran, she thought. He *was* a generous man with an expansive nature—and an expanding family and an expanding waistline. Might one put in a plug for personality improvement in one's dream analysis? Say, in a tactful way, Lose weight and get one of those operations that prevent you from having more children?

She considered writing, "Your dream signifies that you have *arrived*—others are just now realizing your importance. But you should remember how important moderation is to well-being. Remember that everything you put in your mouth is consecrated to the god of your body, the temple of your soul. Would you overwhelm the god at a temple with too many offerings at one time?"

As for moderation in the bedroom, she felt like saying, "The blessings of family have been showered upon you! Count them and be satisfied!"

She sighed. These admonishments would be both ignored and resented.

She copied her column onto clean paper, and was relieved to have finished her homework for the day.

"Hello!" Mr. Ganguly, on his perch near the table, had gotten bored.

"Yes, I know," said Jana. "It's not that interesting sitting and watching someone write. Come on, let's go for a walk. We'll go up to the press and give this to Rambir."

"Walk! Good bird! Jana Bibi zindabad!"

With Mr. Ganguly on her shoulder, she went out the door and through the courtyard, where bright sunshine greeted them. Once in the street, she headed up to Aaj Kal Printing Press with a sense of well-being. "We must count our blessings," her husband, William, would say, even after he went blind. "There are still the gifts of the other senses."

Yes, there were, particularly from one's ears. She paused for a moment and closed her eyes and heard, with even greater clarity, the cawing of crows, the tinkling of mule bells, and the chants from the temple.

The clock tower sounded its hourly chimes. Kenneth Stuart-Smith had noticed that the clock chimed two minutes later than the time announced on All India Radio, but he had turned this lapse in punctuality to advantage in his write-up in *The Globe-Trotter's Companion.* "What is a minute or two in the great sweep of history?" he'd asked. "Hamara

Nagar goes on its own time, which the traveler looking for charm will come to love."

Jana opened her eyes and waved across the street to Royal Tailors, where Feroze Ali Khan's cousins were busily stitching away inside, listening to the radio as they worked.

She loved this street, this bazaar, this mountainside, this part of the world. Certainly, there were other places with mountain views. There were other places with friendly neighbors and peaceful little marketplaces. But somehow, fate had drawn her here and it felt right, and even if it seemed a bit daft, as her son sometimes said, it was daft in the right way. It was her sort of daftness.

A Mystery

Surprising Information from Rambir

"Rambir, here's my contribution to the newspaper."

"Oh, thank you, thank you, thank you! I'm so grateful that you didn't wait until the last minute."

Sinking into the chair Rambir offered, Jana took in the clutter and confusion of the office, the banging and clattering noises coming from the press in the back room, and the dark circles under Rambir's eyes.

"Editor sahib," she said sternly, "you've been burning the midnight oil again."

"Yes," said Rambir. "I didn't mean to, but some contributors sent me last-minute changes late yesterday afternoon."

"You should be more firm about deadlines," Jana said. "If they don't get their material in on time, it has to wait until next week!"

"I know that's a good principle," said Rambir wearily, "but I really want the paper to be as up-to-date as possible. I also had a last-minute idea for an essay."

Rambir's essays. They were well informed and passionate, Jana admitted, and of course people should be concerned about the United States and USSR threatening each other and the world with nuclear bombs. Certainly the civil rights

movement in America was worth mentioning, and libera-
tion movements in Africa. But usually, Jana felt, Rambir's
high-minded outrage could wait until the following week.

"You mustn't work yourself into an early grave," said Jana.
"Everyone appreciates your efforts, but we'd rather have you
healthy than have an error-free newspaper. Surely *today* you
can relax for a moment?"

"No, I have several small printing jobs. All three schools
have student concerts this weekend, so I have to get three sets
of programs out the door by tomorrow morning. And the
problem is, my helper has fallen ill. He is always falling ill."

"Perhaps there's too much pressure for him, too," Jana
suggested.

"Oh, pressure," said Rambir dismissively. "The trouble is
that he drinks."

Jana grimaced.

"Yes, so he's either got a stomach problem or liver problem or headache or whatever. I've told him, he's had his last
chance. Next time he shows up drunk or too hungover to
work, that's the end. He doesn't go home for the day. He goes
home for good."

Rambir made a gesture of despair. "Why can't I seem to
hire good employees? There must be some people willing to
work for an honest wage, in a reputable establishment?
Maybe the problem is that there's nothing interesting to
steal here. If one worked in a restaurant, one could steal food.
If one worked in Pahari Provisioners, one could steal cooking
pots. But who wants to steal words?"

"That kind of cynicism doesn't sound like you," Jana said.
"I think you really are too tired, Rambir."

"I'm sorry, I'm ranting," said Rambir.

"Ah!" A sudden idea occurred to Jana, something that
might solve two problems at once. "Why don't I send Tilku
down to help you? He really should be learning a trade. I

worry about that boy. He likes being a messenger boy because he can run around all day, and chat with people, and not answer to anyone. But really, he could do better."

"Well, I could try him out for a week or two," said Rambir, not sounding very convinced.

"Yes, nothing ventured, nothing gained," said Jana. "Really, the boy should go to school, but he's quite adamant that two years was enough."

"How old is Tilku?" said Rambir.

"He thinks he's eleven," said Jana. "He isn't sure when he was born or even where. Probably in Nepal. He can't remember his mother and father. He says that I am his mother and his father and that Mr. Ganguly is his brother."

"He's a lively little chap," remarked Rambir. "He has an intelligent little face. And bright eyes."

"He *is* bright," Jana said. "I expect he'll think it's rather fun running a machine like the printing press."

"Very well, then," said Rambir. "If he's willing, do send him along."

"Oh, excellent," said Jana. "I hope he works out."

Meanwhile, Rambir had peeked at Jana's manuscript and was smiling. "Only one thing," he said. "I'll have to give Ramachandran and myself fictitious names."

"I already did," said Jana. "Look down at the bottom of the page. Ramachandran is 'Curator of Surprises' and you are 'In the Swim.' But, of course, you can edit as you please."

"Let me think about those names a bit," said Rambir.

She was on the verge of leaving when Rambir said, "I forgot to tell you one thing. My journalist friend T. S. Malik said he was really looking forward to meeting you and interviewing you. We were students together . . . there must be a picture somewhere around here." He managed to locate a group photo and pointed out himself, Ramachandran, and another earnest-looking young man.

"Oh?" Jana was puzzled.

"Yes, for the *Weekly*."

"But—someone's already come from the *Weekly*," Jana said. "A month ago. When we had that cold snap, remember? I'm sure I told you about that."

Rambir looked sheepish. "I must have been distracted."

Jana let that pass; Rambir was often so preoccupied with the state of the world that he missed what was going on under his own nose. She continued: "It was a fellow named Gopal. At least he *said* his name was Gopal. He stayed a long time and asked tons of questions and took a lot of pictures. He should be able to write a *book* about us."

"That's odd," said Rambir. "My friend said he was coming *next* week."

"Well, maybe the *Weekly* changed things at the last moment," said Jana. "And sent Mr. Gopal instead of your friend."

"That's so strange," said Rambir. "I could have sworn that he said next week . . . Did the *Weekly* tell you in advance when they were coming?"

"Of course," said Jana. "They sent a letter several weeks ago. At that point, they gave me one date . . . but then I got a telegram moving the date up, a few days before Mr. Gopal actually came."

"Hmm. Well, it's done with, then."

"I'll let you know if I hear again from the *Weekly*," Jana said. "But I think they have ample material on us already."

Jana continued on her errands, picked up her dress shoes at the *mochi*'s, and got home to find a telegram on the table of the salon. She slit it open and was astonished to read, CONFIRM INTERVIEW PHOTO SHOOT TOMORROW MARCH 30. REGARDS T. S. MALIK ILLUSTRATED WEEKLY OF INDIA.

That's odd, thought Jana. Apparently the right hand doesn't know what the left is doing.

✑ Second Reporter

Jana didn't bother, the next morning, to get into her green silk fortune-telling costume; nor did she have Mary braid her hair or ask Lal Bahadur Pun to dress in his tartans. When this Mr. Malik arrived, she would explain that Mr. Gopal had already done the needful regarding interviewing. It was too bad to have Mr. Malik travel up the mountain road for nothing, but these mix-ups did happen.

At eleven A.M., Jana was in the courtyard when a man arrived at the front gate, with a porter carrying his photographic equipment. He was definitely the person in the photograph Rambir had shown her, although he now had some streaks of gray in his black hair. Another skinnymalink, thought Jana. Were all journalists thin by nature, or did chasing after stories keep the pounds off? Unlike Mr. Gopal, Mr. Malik was accompanied by a porter carrying a tripod and a couple of camera cases.

"Mr. Malik," Jana said, after introducing herself. "I'm so sorry you had to make that long trip."

The reporter gave a start and his eyebrows shot up in puzzlement.

"But I'm very glad to be here," he said. "I've been looking forward to meeting you and the parrot and hearing about all your experiences."

"But surely . . ."

"Is there a problem, Mrs. Laird? You don't wish to be interviewed? Some people are quite shy, I know."

"No, Mr. Malik, I'm not shy, but don't you know that the *Weekly* sent someone else over, a month ago, to do the interview and the photo shoot?"

"What?" An astonished line formed between Mr. Malik's eyes.

"Yes, young Mr. Gopal. Aren't you—he isn't—don't you know each other?"

"I know all the other staff reporters," Mr. Malik said. "And I doubt they would have put a stringer on this story without telling me. I don't know anyone named Gopal whom we would have sent. In any case, this story was my responsibility. I wouldn't have handed it over to just anyone."

"You'd better come in," Jana said.

She led him into the salon, where he looked around much the same way Mr. Gopal had done. "Very lovely, Mrs. Laird," he said. "Oh, you appear to be having some work done?"

"A pipe froze and burst a month ago," Jana said. "The workmen were doing quite well, but then all four got sick—flu, I think—and after that, they had to go to a family funeral. They'll be finished repainting soon, I hope."

They sat at the table in front of the bay window, Mary brought tea, and then Mr. Malik questioned Jana over and over about Mr. Gopal's visit.

"Could he be someone from another newspaper trying to steal the story?" Jana said.

"Did he show you any credentials?" Mr. Malik asked.

"Well, no—I was expecting someone from the *Weekly,* so I took his word that he was who he said he was."

"And how old was he? What did he look like?"

"Oh—thirty, I would say, perhaps thirty-five at the oldest. Rather like you in height and build. Black hair. Dark brown eyes."

"That doesn't narrow it down much. Any peculiarities, mannerisms?"

Jana searched her memory. "I don't think Mr. Ganguly liked him. He kept saying 'Bad bird' for a couple of days after Mr. Gopal was here."

"That doesn't give us much to go on. Do you have any hunches?"

"Well, I've been getting letters from people claiming in one way or another to be the real owner of Mr. Ganguly. I'm wondering if one of them might have sent Mr. Gopal on a reconnoitering mission. Or perhaps Mr. Gopal was one of these people."

"Did he bring a photographer with him?"

"No, he was all alone. And now that you mention it, he *didn't* have much in the way of photographic equipment on him," said Jana. "Just a little Kodak, with a simple flashlamp. At the time I thought that perhaps on a long-distance assignment they travel more lightly."

"In any case, he took a lot of photos of you and the bird."

"He did. And he asked a lot of questions! Oh my goodness, the questions he asked. All about our daily life and timetable and where we liked to walk and . . . perhaps I gave him too much information."

"Perhaps," said Mr. Malik.

Jana, feeling a knot of anxiety tighten in her chest, looked hard at Mr. Malik. Could he, too, be an impostor? But no, he was the man she'd seen in Rambir's photo, although twenty years older now.

"Meanwhile," said Malik, "we still need the information on you for the *Weekly*. Would it be awfully exhausting to go through the whole process a second time?"

Jana sighed. It did sound like a tiring proposition.

"Would you want me in full regalia?" she asked.

"Oh, as you are now is perfect," Malik said. "Jana Bibi at home, in her leisure moments."

"All right," said Jana.

The real photo shoot ended up taking less time than the fake one of the previous month. Mr. Malik then got Jana's history, as well as a few thoughts on the town, on fortune-telling, and on the new directions Jana's fortune-telling was going to take, including the interpretation of dreams.

Afterward, Malik gave Jana his card (which Mr. Gopal had not done) and a certificate entitling her to a free subscription to the *Weekly* for a year.

"Well, I'm off to say hello to Rambir," Malik said.

"You should pry him out of his office for lunch at the Victoria, or somewhere," Jana said.

"Yes, I know, he is overconscientious! He's always been like that. But I'll see if I can get a good meal and a bottle of beer or two into him."

"Good luck, Mr. Malik!" Jana laughed.

She watched Mr. Malik and his helper depart, confident that *they* were who they were supposed to be, but apprehensive about the unsolved mystery.

Always Something to Worry About

✑ *Tilku on the Job*

At Aaj Kal Printing Press, the machines in the back room were silent, and Rambir sat scribbling at his desk, cursing his employee, that useless fellow who had chosen drink over work. Then there was a tentative tap on the door.

"Yes? Come in?"

A Nepali boy of eleven or twelve, dressed in a multicolored sweater and khaki shorts, argyle socks, and tennis shoes, peered cautiously into the room. "Sahib?"

"Yes?" said Rambir. "What do you want?"

"Laird memsahib sent me up to work."

"Oh, yes!" Rambir remembered the conversation with Jana. "You are . . ."

"Tilku, sahib. I am Tilku."

"Oh yes, yes, yes, of course. Well, Tilku, I have some work for you. Do you think you can learn some new work?"

"Ye-es, sahib," said Tilku uncertainly.

"Do you know how to read?"

"Yes, sahib! Hindi and English!"

Aware that Tilku had only two years of schooling under his belt, Rambir was skeptical. "How much English?" he asked.

"Many letters! *P, T,* and *T*—postal, telegraph, and telephone!"

"You'll need to know a few more than that before you can be moderately useful. How about writing?"

"I can write my name," said Tilku. "In Hindi. Do you want to see?"

"No, I believe you. Okay, tell me what you *do* know how to do."

Tilku took a deep breath, and his chest swelled. "I know where *everyone* lives in this town and can run there in no time flat! I can tell time by the clock tower. I know how to take care of parrots."

Well, one thing you could say about the boy: he put his best foot forward.

"So, you want to work here at the press."

"I don't *want* to work," said Tilku, with disarming candor. "But Laird memsahib said you needed a boy, and she thought I should do it."

"All right, fair enough," said Rambir. "Come into the machine room."

In the back room, Tilku's eyes widened in alarm at the sight of the wheels and rollers and levers of the printing press.

"Does it bite, sahib?" he asked cautiously.

Rambir laughed. "No, it does not bite. See, here's how you put the paper in. And here's where it comes out. You have to make sure that the paper doesn't go all over the floor. We're printing three hundred of these booklets. After printing, they have to get stapled and folded."

He showed Tilku the stapler, a device that looked something like a sewing machine.

"You slide the booklet in here, and press down here."

"*Achcha,* sahib. I can do that."

"Then you fold and press."

"*Achcha,* sahib."

They did a trial run of the booklet, and Rambir examined it carefully, finding some errors and making some substitutions in the movable type. Then he cranked a flywheel, the machine groaned and clacked and squeaked, and the printed pages started emerging.

At first, Tilku seemed interested, but as the pages piled up, his attention began to flag. Finally, the pages were ready to collate, staple, and fold.

"Ready to go to work?"

"Yes, sahib."

"Place the first page here," Rambir told Tilku. "The second page here."

Rambir demonstrated, then watched while Tilku assembled a booklet, stapled it, and folded it.

"That's the idea."

Having gotten Tilku launched, Rambir went back into the office and returned to work on his editorial. With the sound of the presses running in the background, he found it much easier to concentrate. After an hour, he went back into the pressroom. Tilku looked exhausted, but he had stapled a good stack of booklets. Rambir checked a few, to make sure there were no pages upside down. Alas, three booklets were defective.

"These must be redone," said Rambir, grabbing a staple puller.

"That thing looks like tiger fangs," said Tilku, apprehensively.

"Nonsense," said Rambir. Impatiently, he extracted the staple from a set of pages, scratching a finger in the process. Tilku shot him what looked to Rambir like an "I told you so" glance.

Annoyed, Rambir said, "Now you do the others." He examined the cut and sucked the blood off, then once more turned his attention to Tilku.

After a moment's hesitation, Tilku managed to remove the offending staples and reconstitute two booklets without mishap. He set the staple puller on the table, visibly relieved.

"Payment, sahib?" he asked hopefully.

"Payment is on Friday," Rambir said.

Tilku's face fell.

"Just think," Rambir said, "if you get five days' wages all at once, how rich you will feel."

Tilku forced a smile.

"See you tomorrow. Early, right?"

"How early, sahib?"

"Seven o'clock," said Rambir.

"Very early, sahib," said Tilku.

"The early bird," said Rambir sternly, in English, "gets the worm."

"Bird, sahib?"

"Never mind," said Rambir. "Just an expression."

Ritu's Strange Symptoms

When Rambir got home, Ritu was lying in the bedroom, a wet washcloth over her eyes.

"What's the matter?"

"Oh, nothing. Some silly thing. It's almost gone now."

"*What's* almost gone?"

Ritu let out a long breath. "Really, it *is* gone now, totally."

"Would you please tell me? Do you want me to call Dr. Chawla? Or run down to Abinath's?"

"No, no, I'm fine, fine, super fine. Krishan's made a lovely thing with lots of vegetables, and we'll eat very soon." She took the washcloth off her eyes, smiled determinedly, and went into the bathroom to hang it up.

"You don't look quite like yourself," Rambir said as they settled at the dining table. "And I insist on knowing what's the problem."

Ritu shook her head and took a bite. "It was a silly thing. I think I had been correcting papers too long. I was looking at one, and all of a sudden the letters started to dance, and I couldn't quite make out what was on the page. Then I saw these funny little sparkly things. Like bits of tinsel. Or Diwali sparklers. They were actually rather interesting."

"They don't sound interesting to me!" My God, Rambir thought, my wife has a brain tumor. "I'm getting Dr. Chawla this minute."

"You don't have to do that, darling. The Diwali sparklers have gone away. Everything is, as the British say, tickety-boo."

Ritu! If there was an earthquake and the house was falling down about them, she'd say everything was tickety-boo.

"All right, promise me," he said. "Even before you go to school tomorrow, you are to stop off at Dr. Chawla's."

"I promise, darling."

Rambir finally picked up his fork, and Ritu said, "What's in that little bowl, chutney? Oh, that man Krishan was quite a find, wasn't he? I didn't even tell him to make it!"

Rambir started to pass her the chutney, but she said, "Take some first, take some first."

He took some and tasted. The chutney was tangy, with just the right bite.

"How is it?"

"Excellent," he said. "Haven't had chutney this good for years. My mother used to make something like this."

She tasted it, too, and smiled. "Oh, so good!"

As they continued to eat, she said, "I got my train reservation today. For the conference."

"If you go," he said.

"What do you mean, if I go?"

"You have to make sure that you're all right," he said. "Ask Dr. Chawla if you should travel."

She rolled her eyes. "All right. I'll ask him. But I know he'll say yes. He'll just tell me not to correct so many papers in one day."

Pakoras and Old Goat

◆ *No Tea Shops in Outer Space*

The month of April came gently in, with its warm days and soft, fragrant breezes, and the inhabitants of Hamara Nagar looked down on the plain below, which shimmered feverishly in the heat and dust.

"We are lucky to be here," Mary said, changing her tune from just a few weeks earlier, when she likened the cold to a hellish dungeon that no one should be forced to live in.

By midmonth, tourists were starting to take over the town, and Jana, Ramachandran, and Rambir considered themselves lucky to get their favorite table at the Why Not? They settled in for a late lunch and tea, looking out at the flow of passersby in the street: European ladies with sunburned bare arms, Japanese couples snapping photos of each other on the steps of the open-fronted shops, Tibetan merchant women in long black dresses and colorful striped aprons.

"I have been teaching my nephew to make *pakoras*," Mr. Joshi said, bringing over a plate of them.

Jana, Ramachandran, and Rambir were taken aback by the look of the fritters, which were certainly not dainty, but rather lumpy and misshapen. Jana glanced over at Mr. Joshi's nephew, who was standing in the corner, watching them anxiously for their reaction. She took a bite and found she could say, with all honesty, "Utterly delicious! Nice and crispy!"

"He's a good boy, he is learning," Mr. Joshi said. "He will carry on when I am gone."

"I hope that's not for a long while, Mr. Joshi," Jana said. "Your health is good, is it not?"

"It is good," Mr. Joshi said, "but one always has to plan for the future. It is galloping down on us every day. The time will come when I will not be able to make tea, just sit in the corner and look at everyone else laughing and talking and not know what they are laughing and talking about. Someone else will have to make tea for *me*. And bring me a *pakora* or samosa. Which I will want to be very fresh and tasty."

"Quite," Jana said.

Mr. Joshi withdrew to behind the counter, where he busied himself with the boiling water and milk. Meanwhile, Rambir told Ramachandran and Jana the latest world news.

"The Soviets have put a man into space," he said.

"Probably served him right," said Ramachandran. "What had the fellow done?"

Rambir's gaunt face broke into an amused guffaw, and Ramachandran looked proud at having drawn a laugh out of his too-serious friend.

Jana thought with wonder about the Russian man hurtling around in his spaceship. First that *Sputnik* thing, a little Jerusalem artichoke going round the earth, sending out radio beeps, and then the Americans put *theirs* up, and now this.

"I'm not going into space myself," said Ramachandran, "until they have a nice tea shop on the moon. Life is better here."

Rambir turned to Jana. "What news, Mrs. Laird?"

Jana said, "Your friend Mr. Malik came and interviewed us and took pictures. A very nice man."

"Yes, I can vouch for that," Rambir said. "And did he clear up the mystery of the other man?"

"He didn't, actually. He was just as mystified as we were."

"Somebody trying to scoop the *Weekly,* no doubt," Ramachandran said. "Getting into your house by hook or by crook."

"Crook is the thing I worry about," Jana said.

"I haven't seen a story on you in any other magazine," Rambir said. "And a reputable magazine wouldn't have resorted to such silly cloak-and-dagger stuff. Although journalists *can* go to extremes to get a story."

"Have you had any other unusual occurrences?" Ramachandran asked.

"No," Jana said. "Life goes on. The workmen are repairing the damage caused by the burst pipe."

She turned to Rambir. "Did you get any more dream letters for me to answer?"

"Oh, thanks for reminding me." Rambir handed over a letter written neatly on lined school paper.

" 'What does it mean,' " Jana read aloud, " 'when you dream about a lot of kangaroos, koalas, and wide-open spaces?' "

"*Elementary,* my dear Watson," Ramachandran said. "The person is dreaming of Australia."

"That is certainly my impression, too," Jana said.

"So, what will you answer?"

Jana fueled her thoughts with a swallow of tea. " 'You feel penned in and are longing for adventure. You are struggling to accommodate your desires with the demands of your humdrum existence.' "

"How do you know the person has a humdrum existence?" Ramachandran asked.

"It's a given, I would say," Rambir said. "Why would you write in to a newspaper about your dreams if you had an *exciting* existence?"

"Well put," said Jana.

"So, have you any advice for this person?" Ramachandran asked.

"Dangerous to give advice," Jana said. "What if they take it seriously and it is the wrong advice, and they go and mess up their life?"

Rambir seemed to agree with that concern, but Ramachandran flipped his hand in the air and said, "Put it in terms that *everyone* should hear."

"All right," said Jana, closing her eyes and waiting for inspiration to come from somewhere, like an arrow from Cupid's bow. Then she opened her eyes and looked around at the crowd of customers munching happily on Mr. Joshi's snacks.

"'Listen carefully to your own heart,'" she said, "'but also look carefully at your own life. Life can seem very long one day, very short the next. Might there be adventures closer at hand than those you envision? Perhaps you'll soon make a new friend who might be helpful to you. Consult others, but, in the end, rely on yourself.'"

"That's perfect, Mrs. Laird! Rambir, there's nothing wrong with what she's saying, is there?"

Rambir could come up with no objections.

"It's a bit of a formula, I suppose," Jana said. "Think of this, but also think of that. Be brave, but also be cautious. Look to the left, but also to the right."

Ramachandran said, "Excellent advice! Especially for crossing the street."

Rambir asked, "Is there any piece of advice you can give without a *but*?"

Jana thought again, trying to find lessons from the hardest times of her own life.

"Oh, yes," she said. "Two words: Don't despair."

Mumford Stein

"Well," said Ramachandran, "I'm off! Got to go see what's up at my house. And tickle the baby! One gets an irrepressible urge to tickle a baby, doesn't one?"

"Yes," said Jana, "please tickle him for me, too."

Ramachandran looked at Rambir as if expecting him to commission a bit of tickling, too, but Rambir seemed distracted.

"Lost in thought?" said Ramachandran.

"No, actually . . . I was trying to remember what it was I'm supposed to pick up before going home. Ah, now I remember. Batteries!"

"Oh!" said Jana. "I need some, too. For my electric torch."

"In that case," Rambir said, "I'll accompany you up to Pahari Provisioners."

They took their leave of Ramachandran and went uphill to the small store crammed with cooking pots, army blankets, enamelware from Czechoslovakia, and other essentials. Hira Lal, the shopkeeper (whom everyone called Mr. Pahari), seemed to want to set a record for getting the most merchandise into the smallest space possible.

Even before they went up the shallow steps from the street, Jana could see that Mr. Pahari was waiting on a bearded young man, European or possibly American. The man was dressed in a faded cotton jacket, canvas trousers, and hiking boots. As they got closer, Jana heard that he was talking in rapid-fire Hindi that sounded to her like a backcountry dialect. He was discussing the merits of plastic versus metal pipe, and other things apparently related to rigging up a simple water supply.

For a moment, Mr. Pahari disappeared into the back room to search for an item, and the man, who looked to be in his late twenties, turned and saw Rambir and Jana, and gave a polite nod and smile.

"Excuse me," Rambir said to the young man, in English, "are you an engineer?"

"Me? An engineer? No, no, just doing a little rough-and-ready irrigation project."

An American, Jana thought. Even without the accent, you can tell by the energy level.

Mr. Pahari returned, victoriously brandishing an L-shaped plastic joint, and the young nonengineer soon completed his purchases and stuffed them into a rucksack.

"Namasté, editor sahib. Namasté, Mrs. Laird," said Mr. Pahari. "Oh, Mr. Stein. Don't go," he called to the young man, who had already stepped out onto the street. "Come and meet some people who can tell you about the town. Mr. Rambir Vohra, our newspaper editor, and Mrs. Laird, our European fortune-teller and resident violinist."

The young man stepped back up. "Call me Mumford," he said breezily, and there were handshakes all around.

Mr. Pahari said uncertainly, "Mr. Stein is a . . . a college professor."

"Well, not yet," said Mumford Stein. "But one day, I hope. I'm doing doctoral research in anthropology."

"Oh, here in town?" Jana asked.

"No, in a village maybe twenty miles from here."

"That sounds very interesting," Jana said. "I lived in a mission station next to a tiny village for twenty-two years. I would like to hear more about your experiences."

"Be delighted to tell you," said Mumford Stein. "Only I have to get back tonight, and I've got a long way to walk."

"Walk?" Rambir asked. "Twenty miles?"

"Yes," said Mumford Stein. "Sometimes I use a pony or a mule, but once it gets dark, I'd rather trust my own legs."

"Have you already walked twenty miles from the village *today*?" Jana asked.

"No, no, I came yesterday and treated myself to a night at the hotel. Sometimes when you've been out in the village for months, you need a hot bath. And I had to get a cholera booster and, oh, see a movie . . . just other things you do in the big city."

Detecting some irony in his tone, Jana said, "And where are you from?"

"Chicago," he said.

"That's a bit bigger than Hamara Nagar, I understand."

"A bit," said Mumford Stein cheerfully. "But it's got the essentials. Hamara Nagar, I mean. Tea shops, bookstore, post office, cinema, hardware store. Much more than that gets to be frills. Well, one night of luxury and back to the cowshed!"

"I admire your spirit," Rambir said. "All that walking, and hard conditions, and being away from home. I actually can't imagine it."

"Oh, just part of the whole experience. If you're going to write about village life, you need to spend time in villages. Kind of unavoidable."

With a cheerful departing namasté to Jana and Rambir, he strode away at a fast clip, leaving them behind, slack-jawed.

"A force of nature, that young man," Rambir said.

"Reminds me a little of my late husband," Jana said. "An enthusiast. Except that this one is of the secular variety. Nice young fellow, I'd say. Well, my dear editor sahib, please say hello to Ritu."

"Of course I will."

They went down the steps into the street, Rambir heading for the Jaundice/Daffodil House and Jana home to the Jolly Grant House. It had been quite a sociable day already, and she still had a dinner engagement to look forward to.

⤳ *Dinner with a Divorced Man*

The Victoria was buzzing with conversation in a number of languages. Jana's favorite grizzled old bearer came over to wait on them, and they exchanged polite inquiries and reassuring replies on health.

"Beer, sahib, memsahib?" the bearer asked.

"What are those people drinking?" Kenneth asked, gesturing to the next table.

"New beer, sahib. Ophrysia by name. Local brew."

"Is it any good?"

"I don't drink alcohol, sahib, so I don't know. *They* like it."

"Let's give it a try," Kenneth said.

Jana nodded in agreement.

"Ophrysia," mused Kenneth, when the bearer had disappeared. "That's an evocative name for me." At Jana's puzzled look, he explained, "A quail that used to be common in these parts. Feared to be extinct, however. As a kid, I always hoped to see one alive."

"Did it go extinct from hunting?" Jana asked.

"I presume so."

They chatted, comparing notes as they often had, about their respective childhoods in India, hers as the daughter of a senior British raj official and his as the child of American missionaries, or, as he called it, a mish kid. The bearer returned, showed them the picture of a quail on the bottles, and poured the beer.

"Cheers," they said simultaneously, clinking glasses.

"What do you think?" Kenneth said, after they had each taken a sip.

"Not bad. Something to mention in the next edition of *Globe-Trotters*. How's that going, by the way?"

"I'm working on it. If you can call sampling beers and going on hikes working, that is." He grinned. "I have to squeeze it in between crises at the embassy."

"That seems to suit you," said Jana. "You look very well."

Indeed, he looked far more rested than he had last year, when both of them were staying at the Victoria. At the time, she had just acquired the Jolly Grant House and was fixing it up, and he was worrying about his teenage daughter, Sandra, and going through a divorce. Now he looked, as the phrase went, ten years younger, with fewer lines in his forehead, good color in his face, and, somehow, less silver in his hair. Jana had always assumed that divorce would show on a person in a negative way, like the sallowness of a liver condition, but here was Kenneth Stuart-Smith, robustly healthy and happy, divorced, and rather glamorous for it. Otherwise, he was the same Kenneth, his thoughtful blue-gray eyes inspiring confidence.

It was the first time, to the best of her knowledge, that she had ever had dinner with a divorced man. On a few occasions, in Bombay, she'd had dinner with a self-reportedly widowed man, only to find out that the wife was not only alive and kicking but having the husband followed around by a private detective. Jana got more than one letter from these betrayed wives, to her very great shock. Happily, Kenneth Stuart-Smith's ex-wife, who had run off with an automobile dealer in Boston, was not going to do any such thing. She was well out of the picture.

Meanwhile, the bearer was waiting to take their order.

"Menu, sahib, memsahib," he reminded, gesturing to the single printed (and worn-looking) sheet on the table.

Jana and Kenneth studied the menu, which they knew was a fiction, or at least an optimistic approximation of reality.

"What is the fish?" Jana asked.

"Oh, sorry, memsahib, no fish this week." The bearer looked so apologetic that Jana chuckled.

"Special biryani?" asked Kenneth.

"Tomorrow night, sahib."

"I see. Well, what is there to eat tonight?"

"Mutton curry," said the bearer firmly.

Jana and Kenneth looked at each other; said, in one breath, "Old goat"; and burst out laughing.

"My daughter's favorite," said Kenneth wryly. "All right, friend, bring it on."

Although they had not ordered it, the bearer first brought mulligatawny soup, and Jana took several spoonfuls, out of politeness. Then came the main meal, with the old goat and an off-white mashed substance that was probably potato, although possibly some other root vegetable. The boiled carrots were more recognizable.

"There's something on your mind," said Kenneth.

"Oh, it's a mystery, actually. It has to do with the reporter—a reporter—who came from the *Illustrated Weekly of India* to interview me. But he turned out not to be from the *Weekly*. A second reporter came a month later. So now I'm quite nervous. The first fellow got all sorts of information about me and the household and took dozens of pictures, and I have no idea why!"

"Hmm," said Kenneth thoughtfully. "Have you any idea who he might be?"

"No," said Jana. "I threw out the telegram saying that he

was arriving, so we don't even know where it came from. And of course, *we* didn't take pictures of *him*. Mr. Ganguly seemed a bit upset, though, and talked for a couple of days about a bad bird."

Kenneth let out another long "Hmm."

"The second man who came was the genuine article, I'm quite sure. Rambir knows him."

"And did he—the second fellow—have any idea why someone would impersonate a reporter from the *Weekly*?"

"No, he didn't, but he told me—and later he also told Rambir—that he would keep in touch if he found anything out. Meanwhile, we haven't seen the first batch of pictures appearing in any publication. The impostor snapped photos of me in my best battle garb . . . and lots and lots of Mr. Ganguly."

"I'd take some extra precautions if I were you," said Kenneth. "You've got Lal Bahadur Pun, of course, and he's a pretty fearsome fellow. But you might need a second *chokidar*. There are some nights when Lal Bahadur Pun is off playing for weddings."

"Yes, that is a gap," said Jana. "One of his friends often fills in, but, yes, I should get some reserves."

"Could the phony reporter want something in the house?" Kenneth asked. "Your jewelry? The emerald necklace that everyone now knows is real? Or—could it be Mr. Ganguly he was most interested in?"

Jana felt her face twist in dismay.

"Maybe Tilku shouldn't take Mr. Ganguly on walks," Kenneth suggested. "Tilku's not very big, you know, and he could get distracted or talked into going somewhere with a stranger, and then he and Mr. Ganguly could get kidnapped."

"Birdnapped," said Jana gloomily.

"Yes, we don't want that happening."

Jana thought out loud: "Could the false reporter have just been a—well, a fan who wanted to get close to Mr. Ganguly or me, and take pictures? One reads of cinema stars and singers and so forth who have sticky fans. You know, people who wait forever at the dressing-room door just to get a one-second glimpse of their idol."

"That's possible," said Kenneth, obviously not convinced. "That would be the most benign situation, I suppose. Have you gotten any fan mail?"

"Mostly I get requests for money. Oh!" She remembered the poison-pen letter. "I got one nasty note."

"Did you save it?"

She sighed and shook her head. "And also one legal-sounding letter saying I had stolen Mr. Ganguly and to give him back."

"Did you keep that one?"

Jana, exasperated at herself, shook her head.

"Don't throw out anything like that for a while," said Kenneth. "And now I'm doubly convinced that you should take extra precautions to guard the house."

"I wish I trusted the police chief more," said Jana. "You know, Bandhu Sharma, who put me in jail when Mr. Ganguly bit him. We're on polite terms since Mr. Ganguly got his son to talk, but he probably wouldn't be on my side."

Kenneth thought for a while, then said, "You know, there *is* an international gang that specializes in abductions of valuable animals. They're like art thieves: they know who the customers are, how to deliver and keep things underground. One of the operators is nicknamed D.P."

"D.P.?"

"Dubla-Patla. Lean and scrawny."

"Oh, no," said Jana. "That Mr. Gopal was a *very* thin fellow. But, of course, hardly unique for that. Who *are* the customers?"

"Some individuals, bird fanatics, the like. Collectors. Eccentrics with private zoos. If an animal fell into their hands, that would be the least grim situation—for the animal. At least . . . it *might* be well treated."

"The least grim?" Jana said. "And the most?"

"Oh . . . a situation where the animal was used for research—a pharmaceutical company testing new drugs, for example. A nuclear laboratory testing the effects of radiation on living creatures—canaries in the mine, so to speak. Plus, more than a few governments are trying to use animals for spying and military purposes. Porpoises are trained to look for submarines, dogs and cats have radio transmitters and receivers embedded under their coats."

"That's disgusting!" Jana said.

"There's a long history of it. Think of it. In all our past, humans couldn't have carried out warfare without animals. Elephants, camels, dogs . . ."

Jana shuddered. "Oh, of course. And *horses*. I remember my grandfather telling me that hundreds of thousands of horses died in the Great War."

"We make other creatures do our will," said Kenneth. "Birds are certainly not immune. We were *still* using pigeons to carry messages during the invasion of Normandy."

"But why would someone want Mr. Ganguly? He hardly even flies. When he does, he gets himself into trouble."

"He's got a reputation," Kenneth said. "The Soviets—and others—have long been interested in psychic phenomena. Seems odd for supposedly hard-boiled materialists, but there you have it. Maybe they think they can use Mr. Ganguly to figure out whether informants are lying or telling the truth. An avian lie detector."

"That sounds completely harebrained!"

"Just because a scheme sounds harebrained doesn't mean someone isn't trying to carry it out at this very moment."

Jana picked up a forkful of boiled carrot but realized she suddenly had lost her appetite. She put it down.

Kenneth lowered his voice. "We shouldn't talk about this here."

Jana looked around the dining room, where the hotel guests were chattering, eating, and toasting each other noisily, and where loud laughter and the clink of forks on plates provided a background of sound.

"Don't worry—no one heard us over this din," Kenneth said.

Hurriedly, Jana changed the subject.

"I saw a picture of your new American ambassador," she said. "Rather a tall, lanky fellow, isn't he? Towers over all the Indians. Sometimes I wonder whether that's good manners, to send someone so tall to a country with so many short people."

"Oh, he's doing well; he's quite popular, even with short people," said Kenneth. "An amusing man, actually. And, of course, it's a change to have a Democrat out here. He's quite the Kennedy man. It's less stuffy at the embassy than it was."

Halfway through the meal, Jana spied the Victoria's manager, Mr. Dass, across the room giving instructions to a couple of the bearers. The line between his eyebrows warned Jana that all was not well.

"He seems to be in a tizzy," she murmured to Kenneth.

"A Dass tizzy is a serious thing," Kenneth said. "Sometimes I can't help thinking of him as Dizzy."

Mr. Dass's state of anxiety was amply confirmed when he came over to their table. Over the last year, Jana had come to realize that he was chronically afraid that someone would criticize him for doing the wrong thing—or the *right* thing, for that matter. Today his "multifarious responsibilities" (as he put it) wore heavily on his thirty-year-old shoulders.

She asked, although reluctantly, because she feared the

explanation would be all too long, "Is there something wrong, Mr. Dass?"

The answer came in a torrent of words.

"Oh, Mrs. Laird, Mr. Stuart-Smith, I am so glad you are here and I can talk to you! You understand me. Mr. Stuart-Smith, you wrote such good things in *Globe-Trotter's Companion* that we have a fifty-eight percent increase in reservations this year. Fifty-eight percent! I have had people of all nationalities asking for rooms for a month, sometimes *two* months. Indians *and* foreigners. Americans, British, French people, Dutch, German, Japanese, and Iranians. It is becoming a veritable United Nations right here. People from all walks of life—schoolteachers, lawyers, businessmen, writers, philanthropists. And coming for many different purposes: hiking, honeymooning, communing with God and nature . . ."

"Why, Mr. Dass, it sounds as if things are going swimmingly," said Jana.

"Yes, But now . . ." Mr. Dass wrung his hands. "The owners are talking about selling the Victoria to some rich Bombay people."

He stopped to let the message sink in, and then continued with another torrent of words:

"Will they come in here and fire us all? You can imagine how this is affecting my wife. And myself. The Victoria Hotel has a long history, and I was proud of our standards. But this young man from Bombay came to scout out the situation. He took one look and kept repeating, This is so archaic! Why are there no telephones in the rooms?

"He thought that up here in Hamara Nagar, we should have the same amenities as they have in Delhi and Bombay and Calcutta. So he was making notes on a pad of paper, and he was taking measurements in the bathrooms.

"Then he went into the dining room. He thought there

ought to be a bar where one could purchase European and American cocktails. Manhattan. Beefeater gimlet. Old-fashioned. So what do they want, old-fashioned or modern?" Mr. Dass flipped his hands upward in a perplexed gesture.

"They even want us to change our uniforms. They say we look like relics. Relics. What do they want, suits with bubbles over our heads such as those Soviet cosmonauts wear?"

Jana broke in, trying to sound reassuring: "Mr. Dass, why on earth would they replace you? You know everything about this hotel from top to bottom. So much knowledge is loaded into your head. Perhaps they'll even give you a rise in salary."

The idea that something good could come from the change had not occurred to Mr. Dass, and for the moment the flood of words abated.

"Mr. Dass, please don't worry," said Jana. "Most things we worry about don't come to pass."

"Many things *I* worry about *do* come to pass," said Mr. Dass darkly.

When Mr. Dass had left, Kenneth said to Jana, "Poor Dizzy! He is a first-class worrier. I hope he doesn't worry himself into a nervous breakdown."

Jana said, "My father always said that worrying was a sign of intelligence. Now I wonder if it's better to be stupid."

"One treads a fine line," said Kenneth.

The sweet—a cake in the form of the Victoria itself, with some mango fool on the side—was definitely better than the main course.

"Excellent ending to the meal," Jana said. "And what a lovely evening! Thank you so much."

"I'll walk you back to the Jolly Grant House," Kenneth said.

They made their way through the dark streets. Both the English Bazaar and the Central Bazaar were closed for the night, the storefronts covered with corrugated metal shutters

and secured with large padlocks. At the Jolly Grant House, a
couple of lights burned brightly, one in Jana's bedroom, the
other in the salon. Mary, as was her habit, had turned them
on before retiring to her own room on the lower level. Lal
Bahadur Pun was at the gate, a blanket over his military uniform against the chill of the evening. From a hundred yards
down the street, Jana heard him stamping occasionally on
the pavement with his stick, a warning to would-be intrud-
ers not to even consider trying to break in.

"Evening, sir, madam!" he said as Jana and Kenneth drew
near.

"Good evening, Subedar-Major," Kenneth said. "All quiet
tonight?"

"All quiet, sir!"

Then Kenneth and Jana explained how it was going to be
necessary to be extra vigilant from now on in guarding the
house. Lal Bahadur Pun's face took on the stern expression
that made monkeys flee at the sight of him, whether or not
he was carrying his bagpipes.

"No one will get in this house," he said. "I have two,
three friends, also retired army, who can help."

Jana immediately felt less anxious. If anything could make
you feel safe in life, it was having a cadre of Gurkhas standing
guard.

"And keep your ears open in the bazaar, also," she said.
"If anyone seems to be asking too many questions about us,
and about Mr. Ganguly, please tell me immediately."

"Of course! Not to worry, madam!"

Jana Finds a Cousin

⁘ *Some Purchases at the Treasure Emporium*

A week went by, with no further puzzling occurrences. Mr. Ganguly stopped talking about the mysterious bad bird, and Jana started to let down her guard.

What bad thing could possibly happen here? The sun smiled down upon the town, and the breezes from the forest smelled deliciously of pine. Tourists were everywhere, clutching copies of *Globe-Trotter's Companion*. Rug sales at the Kashmiri Palace boomed. Muktinanda could barely keep up with the demand for cricket magazines and the *Illustrated Weekly of India*.

Jana's fortune-telling business was now so brisk that people had to wait in the courtyard.

"I need some benches for them to sit on," she told Mary, and so, after closing one afternoon, she put Mr. Ganguly on her shoulder and walked next door to the Treasure Emporium. Ramachandran, too, was seeing a big increase in customers. Some of his minions (now in colorful new uniforms) were running back and forth from the storeroom; others were wrapping packages and carrying them to the door. Others still were fetching tea or Coca-Cola for the clientele.

Ramachandran's twin daughters, Asha and Bimla, just

out of class for the afternoon, rushed to greet Jana, and immediately started playing with Mr. Ganguly and giving him groundnuts.

"Good bird," said Mr. Ganguly, first to one and then to the other.

"You girls do spoil him," Jana said.

"We like spoiling him," Bimla said.

"Did you come to visit or to shop?" Asha asked.

"To shop, actually," Jana said. "I need some seating for the courtyard. A nice bench to put against the wall so that people can be comfortable while waiting to have their fortunes told."

"Dads!" Asha penetrated the circle of people around Ramachandran, finally extricating him and pulling him over toward Jana. "Auntie Jana needs something for her customers to sit on."

"We have just the thing for you," Ramachandran said happily. "This bench was recovered from a nineteenth-century mansion that was being torn down. I can give you a very tiny price."

The tiny price was more like a medium-sized price, Jana thought. At her uncertain expression, Ramachandran said quickly, "And I have a little gift for Mr. Ganguly, as well! No charge."

The gift was a music box with a painted wooden parrot on top.

"Look, Auntie Jana!" Bimla wound the key, and the bird started to turn. The music played a cuckoo-like call, and Mr. Ganguly imitated it, revolving 360 degrees as the wooden bird did.

"Good bird!" said Mr. Ganguly. When the music stopped, he demanded, "More! More!"

Somehow, Jana always came out of Ramachandran's Treasure Emporium with more treasures than she had planned to pick up, and today was no exception. Now Ramachandran was pointing out a painting of a large blue-and-red parrot—perhaps a macaw, she thought, although the artist did not seem to be strong in ornithology. The bird's stance was atypical, to say the least, as it was lying on a couch with its eyes shut.

"The Dreaming Parrot," Ramachandran said. "Just perfect for the fortune-telling salon."

Mr. Ganguly looked at it and said, "Dead bird," which sent Asha and Bimla into peals of laughter.

"The artist is a struggling young painter," said Ramachandran. "I know you like to support young artists, Mrs. Laird."

"Oh, all right," said Jana, and before she knew it, one minion had wrapped up the music box, another the painting, and two more had started out the door with the bench.

"Immediate delivery," said Ramachandran. "The bench will be set up in your courtyard before you get home. But don't go yet—here is someone I want you to meet."

Another Scot at Ramachandran's

Jana had seen Miss Miriam Orley—a tiny Anglo-Indian woman who taught at the Far Oaks School—in the bazaar, and also at events at the school. Each time, Miss Orley had been wearing a burgundy suit. Not the same burgundy suit; she owned a range of them, varying in style, and Jana remembered their tailor, Feroze, mentioning that he had been sewing for Miss Orley for many years. Evidently, she kept adding to the collection, not getting rid of the old ones.

Today, at the Treasure Emporium, along with the requisite wine-colored suit, Miss Orley was wearing a pleated pink blouse with a rosebud at the collar and a pearl brooch. Her hair was very white in front but gray in back, and arranged in tidy marcel waves. She was obviously a repeat customer at the Treasure Emporium, because Ramachandran and his daughters all greeted her warmly.

"Namasté," Mr. Ganguly called.

"Namasté to you," Miss Orley said. To Jana, she said, "What a lovely bird. May I give him a bit of a tickle?"

The woman obviously knew how to handle birds, touching him lightly on the neck without trying to pat his feathers.

"Mrs. Laird, do you know Miss Orley?" said Ramachandran. "She teaches Latin. *Gaudeamus igitur,* and all that!"

"Mr. Ramachandran and I share an enthusiasm for Latin expressions," Miss Orley explained to Jana.

"We haven't formally met," Jana said, "but I have seen you at the school and in the bazaar."

"You're the lady with the fortune-telling salon," Miss Orley replied. "I've been so curious."

"Well, please come and see the place," said Jana. "Come for a cup of tea."

Meanwhile, Ramachandran had sent one of the girls back to his Rare Book Corner, and she had returned with a large, leather-bound volume.

"My dear Miss Orley," said Ramachandran. "We got *The Complete Works of Robert Burns* from a man in Dehra Dun who was cleaning out his parents' house and selling everything he possibly could. I thought of you immediately!"

"Mr. Ramachandran, you are so thoughtful!"

Jana was wondering why this little Anglo-Indian lady was a Burns fan, but Miss Orley turned and said to Jana, "I'm a bit of a Scot, you see. As you are, I'm told."

"By heritage," said Jana. "I'm actually an Indian citizen and have lived here—or in the country, anyway—for almost all my life."

Ramachandran had now come up with another book for Miss Orley, one about Scottish regiments in India.

"Let's see if they have anything about the Thirty-eighth King's Own Scottish Borderers," said Miss Orley, and she turned the pages carefully, reading the captions under the line drawings of soldiers in formal jackets and kilts, with bear hats that added a foot and a half to their apparent height.

"My great-great-grandfather was one of the Thirty-eighth," she said. "He came out to India with his twin brother. The twin went home, but the other brother never left. He married an Anglo-Indian girl and settled not far from here."

Jana started. "Twins? What was their name?" On hearing "MacPherson," Jana felt a jolt of excitement. "My great-great-grandfather just might have been the other brother!"

Miss Orley's eyes lit up, and she let out an "Oh my!" and a surprised little laugh.

"So," continued Jana, "we may even be cousins of some sort . . . fourth or fifth, or however you count them. I'll have to ask my son back in Scotland to dig a bit in the family archives."

Well, Jana thought, this was an interesting day! It was not often that you ran into a long-lost—or, rather, a never-heard-of—cousin while browsing for knickknacks in the bazaar. On the other hand, if it was going to happen, it would happen in the Treasure Emporium.

"In fact, why don't you come have that cup of tea right now?" she urged Miss Miriam Orley. "Have you got to get back to the school for any reason?"

"I'm on duty in study hall tonight, but I'm free for the moment. I won't interrupt your work?" Miriam Orley asked.

"No, not at all. I've already told enough fortunes for the day. That's why I came up to the emporium to take a break."

"You're so kind. I would very much enjoy a cup of tea."

Miss Orley had old-fashioned manners, Jana noted, guessing that she was one of those people whose religion was thank-you notes and careful reciprocation of small favors.

They waited while Ramachandran had one of his minions wrap up the two books, which Miss Orley had indeed decided to buy, and then Miss Orley and Mr. Ramachandran exchanged gestures of namasté and also said, "*Vale,* Mr. Ramachandran" and "*Vale,* Miss Orley."

Good-byes and *vales* completed, Jana led Miriam the few steps down the street to the Jolly Grant House.

"The house," Jana explained as they went in the gate to the courtyard, "was built by my mother's father—not the MacPherson side of the family; that was my father's side. The Grants felt much more of an affinity for India—at least in this century."

"And how long have you been here?" asked Miss Orley.

"In this house? About a year. I got a letter out of the blue saying I had inherited it. So I moved in—once I got rid of the monkeys and had it fixed up, that is. It's not an enormous house; my grandfather used to put guests in what's now the Treasure Emporium. He liked having guests in a separate building. He said he could tolerate them longer and they had a better time, being independent."

"Aha," said Miss Orley. "My parents had much the same approach. They had a guest cottage in their compound, too."

A revealing little piece of information, Jana thought, reinforcing her suspicion that Miss Orley came from a background of relative wealth. This was confirmed when Miss Orley went on: "They had a villa over on Maharajah's Hill."

"Oh, that must have been lovely," said Jana.

"It was," said Miss Orley. "They had to sell it long ago, though."

And? Jana burned with curiosity to ask what had happened, but checked herself. If Miss Orley wanted to tell her about the decline of her family fortunes, she would do so, but all in good time.

"Please ignore the repairs going on," Jana said.

"Oh, but this is enchanting," Miss Orley exclaimed as they passed through the front hall, into Jana's salon. "It combines the exotic, the familiar, and the comfortable! One gets a feeling both of adventure and of safety, which of course are often contradictory."

"Upstairs," suggested Mr. Ganguly.

"Oh, yes, we'll go up," said Jana, and she led Miss Orley up to the tower room.

"What a panorama!" said Miss Orley.

"Yes, you can see everything from here. It was used as a lookout tower during the war, in case the Japanese got up to this corner of the world. They—the Japanese—never seemed to consider it worth their effort, however."

Miss Orley put her eye to the telescope. "Oh, this is quite the spyglass! Was this here during the war?"

Jana laughed. "No, afraid not. It's on loan from Mr. Powell, the optometrist."

"Oh yes, of course. Niel. He's a distant relative of mine."

"Really." Jana thought it over. "Perhaps he's a relative of mine, too, then." A phrase from her school days flittered briefly through her mind—something about making the whole world kin.

"Unlikely," said Miss Orley. "He's on my mother's side."

"A very nice man, though," said Jana. "And he fitted me for an excellent pair of specs."

"Niel, oh certainly, he's a good egg." Miss Orley continued to peer. "I can see the school very well. In fact, I can see the windows to my own suite, in the girls' dormitory."

"What's it like to live with a gaggle of girls?" Jana asked, thinking it would be exhausting.

"It's entertaining, most of the time," said Miss Orley.

"And the rest of the time?"

"Well, it's always interesting. Sometimes a bit heart-wrenching. Some of the girls make it a habit to come to my apartment and have a good cry when they get their hearts broken. That's not infrequently. Oh! I can see one of the girls hanging so far out the window, she's going to fall!"

Even with the naked eye, Jana could see this, too. Although she couldn't be heard at this distance, she opened the window, leaned out, and yelled, "Get back inside!"

"Hic et nunc!" Miss Orley yelled. "Here and now!" She explained to Jana, "That's what I tell my students when it's time to put down their pens and hand in their tests."

The girl pulled herself back inside, and Miss Orley said, "Oh, there she goes. That's a relief. That would have made a good photo, though. An action shot! It makes me want a tele-photo lens. Photography is my new vice."

The idea of this proper-looking lady having any vices struck Jana as funny, and she smiled.

"It's on the late side for tea," she said, wishing she had some sherry to offer Miss Orley. Then an idea struck her. "I've got a—I suppose you could call it an apricot liqueur. It might be quite good with soda water."

She got two little cordial glasses out of the sideboard and poured a small bit of LPN10 into them, then added soda, and handed one of the glasses to Miss Orley.

"Cheers!"

Miss Orley took a sip. "Quite delicious!"

Jana said, "I should tell you that it's Mr. Abinath's latest concoction—Love Potion Number 10, LPN10 for short. It helped quite a lot after I had a tooth worked on."

Miss Orley laughed. "Love Potion Number 10. Makes one think of those Hollywood film stars who keep marrying and marrying, apparently trying to get it right."

Finding formality excessive, considering they were probably distant kin, they decided to call each other by their first names.

"Janet—or Jana?" Miss Orley asked.

"Either will do," said Jana.

Miss Orley chose Janet. For herself, she said, she wasn't partial to pet names. "My family used to call me Mimi, and I only partly succeeded at getting them to say Miriam. But that *is* what I prefer."

Jana lifted the bottle of LPN10, Miriam (as now established) held her glass forward, and Jana poured a few more drops.

"So," Jana said, "you teach Latin. That sounds impressively brainy to me. Tell me how that came about."

"Oh, my parents were very advanced. They never anticipated that I would *have* to support myself, but they did believe that girls should be able to do something useful and make a contribution to society."

Miriam, it turned out, had gone to Isabella Thoburn College, in Lucknow, and, although she didn't actually say so, Jana suspected she had been a top student. Oh my, she thought with alarm, she *is* brainy. She's had far more formal education than I have.

Although an avid reader, Jana sometimes felt self-conscious about her own lack of higher education. She had failed the audition for the Glasgow Athenaeum as a violin student and, after that, had never felt brave enough to apply for admission to any college or university in Scotland. In any case, her grandfather MacPherson had felt that she had already had plenty of education for *his* purposes, which were to use her as his unpaid secretary. What an irony, Jana reflected. Had my parents lived and had I stayed in India in 1919, I too might have been able to do more studies. "What did you study in university?" had become a question that Jana dreaded, and she was relieved that Miriam, perhaps by chance, perhaps by tact, did not pose it.

Instead, Jana continued to ask Miriam about her own history.

"You said your parents had a house on Maharajah's Hill. Does that mean you grew up here?"

"Yes and no. We came here in the hot weather. My family actually came from Allahabad. My father worked for the railroads."

"Allahabad? Really? That's where we lived when I was small, too. I remember riding in a carriage to the cathedral."

A funny expression crossed Miriam's face. "I, too, remember riding in a carriage to the cathedral. Just once, though."

"Allahabad must have changed a lot," Jana said. "I haven't been back in years. And your relative, Mr. Powell? Did he grow up there, too?"

"Niel? Actually, no. He lived most of his life in Calcutta, until his . . . well, he lived there while Celeste was still around."

"Celeste?" Jana had never heard Mr. Powell mention anyone by that name.

"His wife. She ran off with a Panamanian businessman."

"Goodness," said Jana. "I can't see him married, somehow. I would have sworn that he was the quintessential bachelor."

"He seems that way, doesn't he? If you mention marriage, he gets a dark look on his face and says, Marriage is hell."

"Poor man," said Jana.

"Now, *you* were married, I believe," Miriam said.

"Yes, to an American. A missionary, actually. He died just about the time of independence. I've had to muddle through alone, since. And yourself—you've never been married?"

"No."

"Never tempted?"

"Oh, that's a different story," said Miriam. She looked at her watch. "Good heavens! I've got to get back to the dormitory and preside over dinner and study hall! Much more pleasant to stay here drinking this delicious apricot concoction, I must say."

"I'll get some more from Mr. Abinath, and we can do it again," said Jana.

"That would be lovely. Oh—and do you like cinema?"

"I used to go to the Bharat Mata every once in a while."

"I usually go to the Europa," said Miriam. "Hindi films aren't really my cup of tea. The European part of me is stronger when it comes to my preference for films and music."

"I actually love both Hindi films and foreign ones," said Jana. "But I haven't been to the Europa in ages. So do let's go sometime."

With Mr. Ganguly on her shoulder, she saw Miriam down to the gate.

"You don't need an escort to the school?" Jana asked.

"Good heavens, no! Well, good-bye."

"Namasté," said Mr. Ganguly. "Good bird."

"I was going to say the same to you," said Miriam.

For She's a Jolly Good Fellow

When Miriam had gone, Jana carried the cordial glasses down to the kitchen building and found Mary making vegetable soup and Lal Bahadur Pun telling her about conditions in Burma during the war.

"I just had a nice visit with Miss Orley," Jana said.

"She is a very good lady," Mary said. "When I see her at

church, she puts money in the collection plate. She does not take it out."

"Do many people take money *out* of the collection plate?"

"I have seen that," said Mary, with a frown.

Jana said, "Miss Orley and I discovered that we may be cousins. Not close. But an ancestor of hers was probably the brother of an ancestor of mine."

Mary mulled that over. "Both of you are good ladies, so maybe this is one family resemblance."

"I talked to the *chokidars* at the Far Oaks School," said Lal Bahadur Pun. "They say Miss Orley is a very generous lady. She gave one of them school fees for his daughter. And another had a wife who got very sick. Miss Orley paid the doctor bill. She doesn't even want people to know she does all these things."

"That's awfully nice to do for strangers," Jana said.

"Oh, they're not strangers. Some of the school servants, she knew in childhood. They worked in her parents' home."

"She can't have a lot of money now," Jana observed. "At least I don't think so."

"It's not always the rich people who give money away," said Mary. "Often it's the people who aren't rich but are nice."

"She has a heart like a big memsahib," said Lal Bahadur Pun. "Not like one of these people who suddenly get rich and think they can be big shots by ordering people around."

"Also," said Mary, "she has an old aunt she always goes to see. That old aunt has a bearer, Jacob John, and Orley memsahib pays his salary."

"Mary, how on earth do you know all this?"

"Jacob John comes from Madras! He speaks Tamil. I spoke to him at church."

"There aren't many secrets here, are there?" Jana said.

"You want to know something, you ask, you find out. That's not difficult, Jana mem," Mary said.

Bit of a fishbowl, this town, thought Jana. It puts pressure on a person to live in an inspectable way. Also, with a shiver, she remembered the information Mr. Gopal had gotten about her, and she wondered if he had gone around collecting even more information from the townspeople.

"But there still must be secrets," observed Mary. "If something really *is* a secret, we wouldn't know about it."

This was irrefutable. The reality one knew about was one thing; what was under the surface was another, and who knew whether it was good or bad?

"At least we can say that people agree that Miss Orley is a very fine lady," Jana said.

"Oh, very fine, very fine!" chorused Mary and Lal Bahadur Pun.

Jana Tells Tilku to Persevere

It was quiet in the house without Tilku around during the day, and Jana missed his company on walks to the Municipal Garden with Mr. Ganguly. When she did see him, he looked glum, not at all like his normal exuberant self.

"Is the boy eating properly?" she asked Mary.

"Oh, he eats like a soldier," Mary said. "Not to worry about how much he eats."

When Sunday came, the bells chimed down at the All-Saints Church, and Mary departed for the service, dressed in a bright yellow sari. Jana took a cup of tea up to the tower and listened to the morning sounds, special and more peaceful on Sunday. Hymns from the little church floated up into the air, making her smile. After William's death, Jana had ceased to be a churchgoer, but hearing people singing together always lifted her heart.

Also, it was good to keep the Sabbath, she thought . . . *a* Sabbath, any form of Sabbath. A time when you did something different, more restful than during the rest of the week. She looked down onto the courtyard and saw Tilku alone, smoking a *biri,* his shoulders slumped. If she'd scolded him once about smoking, she'd scolded him a dozen times, and if Mary were there, she would be giving Tilku what for. But now scolding didn't seem like the answer. There was something so pathetic about the boy sitting on the wall, smoking alone, without even old Munar to talk to.

"Tilku!" Jana called.

Tilku jumped, and looked up to the tower.

"Do you want to take a walk? With me and Mr. Ganguly?"

"Oh, Jana mem, yes! Yes! He can ride on my shoulder?"

"Of course."

They went on Jana's favorite walk, down the street, through the Central Bazaar, and into the English Bazaar, and turned into the Municipal Garden. Mr. Powell, walking his dachshunds, waved at them from across the garden, and Jana watched as a group of children played on the spinning table, jumping on and screaming as it went faster and faster. They walked by the golden rain tree, the same tree that Mr. Ganguly had gotten stuck in last year, when he'd escaped from Bandhu's jail. Tilku had climbed the tree and rescued him, to the applause of the spectators.

Jana now asked, "Do you like the work at the press?"

Tilku's grimace answered the question.

"Editor sahib is so strict," he said. "Worse than teachers at school. And being inside—that's not for me, Jana mem."

Jana, picturing Tilku standing by a clattering machine, felt her heart sink. How could she have thought that this was a good idea? And yet . . . maybe, in a while, the boy would grow to like it better.

"Tilku," she said, "editor sahib is giving you a good opportunity to learn something and earn money. Please give it your best effort."

"I am trying hard. *So* hard, Jana mem. But—it feels like—being in a cage. In prison!" he said melodramatically.

"It's not a prison, Tilku," Jana said. "You aren't a prisoner. Do keep trying, just for a while, and we can think about it again later."

"All right, Jana mem," Tilku said, in a voice that sounded anything but all right.

"Bath!" squawked Mr. Ganguly.

Jana and Tilku looked at each other and laughed, and Tilku put Mr. Ganguly down into the birdbath, where he splashed ecstatically, throwing droplets so far that they had to step back.

"I wish . . ." Tilku began, with a faraway look on his face.

"What do you wish, Tilku?"

"Jana mem, I wish I was a bird."

"Why, Tilku?" said Jana, her heart twisting at his sad expression.

"They are free. They fly from tree to tree."

"Lots of birds aren't free," Jana said. "In fact, Mr. Ganguly isn't free."

"He's more free than I am, Jana mem," said Tilku. "Or, at least, he is happy."

Romance for Jana?

✑ All in a Day's Work

How had it gotten to be noon already? For that matter, how had it gotten to be 1961? Jana stared, discouraged, at the music paper spread all over the salon table. She was experiencing a mental block about the ending to one of old Ian's marches. Why had she not thought to write those tunes down when it would have been so much easier, when she had been gone from Scotland for only a few months, rather than letting it go—not a few *years,* but *decades.* "Better late than never," she said aloud to herself and then to Mr. Ganguly. "Do you hear that, my friend? Better late than never."

Mr. Ganguly was eyeing the music paper, obviously considering it something he could shred with relish.

"Oh, no, you don't," said Jana.

Well, some mornings were more productive than others.

"Walk?" she said to the parrot.

"Jana Bibi zindabad!" squawked Mr. Ganguly. "Good bird!"

"I knew you'd think so."

Jana put away the ink bottle, the pens, and the music in the almirah.

As always, the walk cleared her head and made her troubles seem insignificant. Lunch on the terrace further improved her mood, so that she was amply ready to interpret dreams and to tell people that whatever card Mr. Ganguly picked from the deck of Hindu gods and goddesses, it was for the best.

That afternoon, business in the fortune-telling salon presented some new twists. The first couple was an anomaly, Jana felt. Most people consulting her about their love life were worried young women who had plucked the petals off daisies—*he loves me, he loves me not*—and, having landed on *he loves me not,* were searching for a second opinion.

But when the doorbell jingled and a young Indian couple walked in, unrequited love clearly wasn't *their* problem. They were obviously so dizzily, euphorically, ecstatically in love that Jana instantly fell in love with *them.* Mr. Ganguly, delighted to see a beautiful young girl, made a volley of kissing noises in her direction.

"We're having an argument," said the husband, while the wife smiled silently, showing a pair of irresistible dimples.

The young man went on: "We're arguing about who fell in love first, she or I."

"Well, that certainly is something to argue about," Jana said. She added to herself, Would that all arguments were that benign.

"The manager at the Victoria Hotel told us there was a fortune-teller with a psychic bird in the Central Bazaar, so here we are."

This time the bride echoed him: "Yes, here we are."

"And when did you meet?" said Jana.

"Last year this time."

"Love match?" asked Jana, and the girl giggled.

"No, no," said the young man. "Our parents brought us

together and left us in a room for an hour to look at each other to see if we agreed to the marriage."

"And?" said Jana, picturing the two young people sitting side by side, barely daring to glance at each other, searching their brains for something to say.

"I maintain," said the man, "that I was in love first. But she says she was."

Hearing a word he recognized, Mr. Ganguly broke in: "I love you!"

"Well, let's see," said Jana. "You had your horoscopes matched, I presume."

"We did."

"And did that reveal anything?"

"That we'd have a long, happy marriage!" said the young man.

"And many children," the young woman burst out, and then blushed deep red.

"Well, we've got the basics in order, then." Jana spread the cards faceup and moved Mr. Ganguly from his perch to the table, where he inclined his head politely to the couple.

"Mr. Parrot," said the young husband, "*tota sahib*. Who was in love first, myself or my wife?"

Mr. Ganguly turned away, as if deep in thought, then faced them again and picked the card with Rama and Sita. He walked over to the bride and bowed, then to the groom and did the same, then laid the card halfway between them.

"I think he might be suggesting the answer," said Jana. "Could it be that Cupid's dart—so to speak—struck you at the selfsame moment?"

This answer seemed to satisfy them both.

"I wish you both all the joy and blessings the world has to offer," Jana said.

"Thank you," they said in unison.

"Kiss, kiss!" said Mr. Ganguly.

The young lovers both colored at that, but from the pause in their footsteps when they went into the hall to go out the door, Jana deduced that they had taken his advice.

"Whew!" said Jana, when they had gone. "They must have each drunk a bottle of Mr. Abinath's Love Potion Number 10. I hope they go and spread the happiness around."

It seemed to be two-for-one day. The next customer was again not a single customer but another couple, this time French, and as they entered the hall, they were chattering to each other at top speed, with a fair number of *ooh-la-la*s and *mon dieu*s thrown in. Jana strained to understand, summoning up what remained of her schoolgirl French. When Mary showed them into the salon, she was able to give them a smile and a "Bonjour, madame! Bonjour, monsieur!"

That was a mistake, since they assumed she was fluent and continued to speak French. It turned out that they didn't want their cards read, but their stomachs filled.

"Where can you find a decent meal in this town?" said the husband.

"Decent?" said Jana.

"Well, a drinkable wine or beer, meat that doesn't taste like old shoe, vegetables that don't give you diarrhea, fish that doesn't give you hepatitis . . ."

"Where are you staying?" Jana said.

"At the Victoria," said the wife.

"Aha," said Jana.

"We've had their mutton curry three days in a row," said the husband. "My jaw is sore from chewing. We're ready for some variety."

"There's Kwality Restaurant," Jana said.

The wife rolled her eyes, and the husband grasped his stomach.

"Kwality! A chain! Leave that to the Americans," he said. "We ate at Kwality in Delhi and Kwality in Dehra Dun, but when we got to this town, we thought we'd find some little authentic bistro sort of thing, with local specialties and the like."

"They have ham banjos at Kwality," Jana said.

"Banjos *de jambon*?" the husband said. "What are those? Banjos?"

"They're round little fried ham sandwiches," said Jana. "You know how banjos—the musical instrument—are round?" She mimed strumming a banjo.

"I'd sooner eat a real banjo," the wife said. Turning to her husband, she asked, "Should we go over to Mussoorie and see what they have?"

Jana said, "It's the same in Mussoorie. They have Kwality, too."

The couple had started to look glummer and glummer.

"If you want local specialties," Jana mused, switching to English in exhaustion, "you should try the tea shops. The Superior is bigger, but the Why Not? is friendlier. And the owner is always trying to improve his repertoire. You won't get a banquet, but you'll get all sorts of good snacks. The samosas and *pakoras* are made before your eyes, so you know they're fresh."

"*Très bien*," said the husband. "We will try that," agreed the wife.

As they went out the door, Mr. Ganguly called, *"Merci! Au revoir!"*

To Jana, turning and flapping his wings, he said, "Nut! Nut, please!"

"I guess the conversation made you hungry," she said, and gave him one.

• • •

It was getting late in the afternoon, and Jana decided that they could close down for the day, but the doorbell tinkled again. However, it was only Asha and Bimla, Ramachandran's daughters, out of school for the afternoon and paying one of their social calls.

"Hello, Auntie Jana," they said in unison. They looked so much alike that Jana could not tell them apart. Long black braids, expressive round faces, large dark eyes—they looked like South Indian movie stars, except that they wore school uniforms and carried book satchels and hockey sticks.

Unlike Jana, Mr. Ganguly *could* tell the girls apart. He called them Ah and Bee, which at first had led everyone to think that he was engaged in some sort of spelling game.

Today, he said, "Namasté, Ah! Namasté, Bee!"

"You're so c-u-u-u-te! Auntie Jana, he's so cute, isn't he?"

"Can he really tell you apart?" Jana said.

"Let's test him," said one of the girls, sitting down at the table.

The other went into the hall, and Jana said to Mr. Ganguly, "Who's this? Ah or Bee?"

"Ah! Ah! Good bird."

"Thank you, sweetie," the girl sitting at the salon table said. "I'm glad you think I'm a good bird."

"Did he get it right?" Jana asked.

Laughter exploded from the hall, and the girl at the table said, "Wouldn't you like to know?"

"No, really, *did* he get it right?"

"He did," said the girl at the table. "Bim, come on back."

Bimla came back, and Jana stared at the two; she still could detect no difference, no moles, birthmarks, freckles—nothing.

"How does he do it?" she said. "What *is* the difference between you two?"

"We actually don't know ourselves," one girl said. The other rushed to add, "But whatever it is, he picks up on it."

"Would you do me a favor?" Jana said. "When you come to see me, perhaps, Asha, you could wear a flower behind your right ear, and, Bimla, you, one behind your left? When you come in, you can each take a flower from the vase in the hall."

"At home, Mums makes us wear different colored hair ribbons on our plaits," said Asha. "But at school, we have to wear school colors! So the teachers never figure us out."

Mary brought in tea, with half the cake she had made the day before.

"Hip hip hooray for Mary!" Asha—if she was to be believed—said.

"Hip hip hooray for Mary!" Bimla—if *she* was to be believed—repeated.

Then the two, showing identical appetites, polished off the cake in record time.

"Thank you, Auntie Jana! We have to run. We have a *physics* test tomorrow, and we have to *study*."

"Good luck!" Jana said.

"Yes, our teacher, Mrs. Vohra, keeps telling us that Quantum will be very disappointed if we don't do well."

"Quantum?" Jana asked.

"Oh, sometimes she draws this funny man on the blackboard with a balloon coming out of his mouth with formulas and things in it. His name is Mr. Quantum Physics."

Jana chuckled. "It sounds as if she keeps you interested." Her own experience with science had not been so lucky.

"Oh, she does, she does," Asha said. "But she marks the tests *really* strictly! Good-bye, Mr. Ganguly! You're so lucky, you don't have to take physics tests."

When they were gone, Jana felt as if a whirlwind had blown through the salon, but it was a whirlwind that made her smile.

A Letter from Lily

The postman came toiling up the street, his large bag of letters over one shoulder and a walking stick in his hand. He looked too old to be delivering letters, but he claimed that he was completely fit and healthy, and would not stop delivering the letters until God's will decided it. He was a favorite in the neighborhood, since a lot of good things came by mail: pensions, wedding invitations, letters from faraway relatives. Jana figured that his popularity kept him alive.

"Salaam, memsahib," he said cheerfully. "By the grace of God, you have got two letters."

Jana took the envelopes; one was from N. G. Powell, at Sharp Eyes Vision Care, and Jana wondered why Mr. Powell would be writing to her. The other was light blue, expensive-looking, and postmarked Bombay. Jana recognized the handwriting immediately. Lily! How nice.

She went back into the house, settled into the sun on the window seat, and slit open the letter from Mr. Powell.

"Dear Mrs. Laird," she read. "I understand that you have met my cousin Miriam. I do hope you will be able to come for a little celebration of her seventieth birthday at my house, the Lookout, Maharajah's Hill, Sunday, May, 7th, at 4:00 P.M. The school is giving her a big assembly, with speeches by the teachers and students, but I thought she'd like a smaller family gathering, too. It's a surprise, so please don't tell her about it!"

How nice of him to invite me, Jana thought. And now she

could also satisfy her curiosity about the big houses on Maharajah's Hill, or at least one of them.

Next she turned to see what Lily had to say.

"My dear Jana," Lily wrote. "We were so glad to get your Christmas card, and about the same time, we heard about Hamara Nagar on All India Radio! Our Jana, a celebrity! With a psychic parrot, no less!

"The Bombay social whirl continues, and as you must remember from your time here, it's quite exhausting. I kept saying to Cyrus, let's go see Jana up in the hills and have a nice rest. Well, you know Cyrus on the subject of rest. There will be time to rest when we're dead, he says. He's working on some new business ventures with his cousin Max, who is spending much more time in India than in Paris these days, now that Cécile, poor lamb, has passed on.

"Anyway," the letter went on, "Max and Cyrus are building up their hotel business. They heard of this opportunity in Hamara Nagar—a hotel that is just crying out for renovation. So we get to see you after all!"

Oh my goodness, thought Jana. The Victoria. So *that's* who's planning to buy it. Well, an infusion of Bombay money probably wouldn't hurt the old place at all. It might even raise it on Jana's scale of luxury—from, oh, five and a half to seven? Eight?

And an infusion of Lily-style entertainment into Jana's life wouldn't exactly be bad, either. In Bombay, Lily had made sure that Jana did not work too hard at her various teaching and music-playing jobs, by encouraging Jana to get out and have fun. "Come, we'll go and each have a lovely manicure!" Lily would say. Or "You've got to have my dressmaker make you up some clothes. How about a nice silk dress? You think it's expensive, but I tell you, good silk wears like iron. It's the cheapest in the long run!"

Yes, it would be good to see Lily. And Cyrus; the two of

them together made such an amusing couple, trading off repartee. And—be honest, Janet Louisa Caroline Elizabeth MacPherson Laird, she said to herself—it will be good to see . . . Maximilian King. Or, as the *Times of India Directory and Year Book Including Who's Who* listed him, Maximilian-Jamshed Shershah King, aviator; chairman, board of directors, Timeless Hotels, Inc.; president, French-Indian Business Alliance.

How many times had she actually met Max? Only a handful, really. She knew much more about Max from Lily and Cyrus than she did from talking to him in person. But that was to be expected. People didn't just come up to you and say, My mother was French and my father was a prominent businessman from Bombay and I received both the French Légion d'Honneur and the Victoria Cross and have my pilot's license and am fluent in six languages and have made a fortune in importing and exporting. Not to mention that I am an accomplished amateur on both the cello and the string bass. The only problem is, I am devoted to my wife, Cécile, who is in a wheelchair. And to my two children, Henri-Jehangir and Freny-Christine, who, despite their East-meets-West names, are much more French than Indian and, I'm sad to say, not very interested in their Parsi heritage.

Jana sighed and tried to remember. Which year was it that she had gone with Lily and Cyrus and Max to the New Year's Eve party at the Bombay Flying Club? Oh, 1953, it must have been. Max was on a quick business trip from Paris, and Lily had talked them all into wearing costumes for the fancy dress ball.

"Let's go as minstrels," Lily had suggested. "I'll take my viola, and Jana, you take your violin. Maybe Max can borrow a bass from the band. Not for the grand march, of course!" Cyrus, who didn't play an instrument, was given a tambourine to shake.

The four of them had made a huge hit, sitting in with the band and playing a few numbers, and even winning the fancy dress prize. Standing next to Max, playing in time with him—well, thought Jana, that had been even better than dancing. Although there had been plenty of dancing, too.

And then . . . Well, Jana asked herself, how much importance should one attach to one teeny-tiny kiss? There had been mistletoe hanging everywhere at that party, and on the stroke of midnight, there'd been a lot of kissing—some of it very chaste and proper, some uproariously drunken. Jana had hugged Lily and Cyrus, and then she and Max had turned to each other and, perhaps aiming for each other's cheeks, had ended up exchanging a soft—but long enough to feel, and to remember the feeling for weeks—kiss on the lips.

Jana fetched her own writing paper and fountain pen from the almirah.

"Dear Lily," she wrote. "How lovely it will be to see the three of you!"

On the way home from posting the letter at the PTT, she wondered whether Maximilian King had changed much since she'd seen him. And what should be her first words to him? Condolences on the death of his wife, she supposed, although saying, "I'm so sorry" seemed like rank hypocrisy. "I'm so glad" would hardly do, though.

Maybe the answer would come to her in a dream. Before getting into bed that night, she remembered old Munar's advice that she concentrate on what she wanted to dream about before going to sleep. Awake, she conjured up the New Year's Eve party at the Bombay Flying Club. Couldn't she dream of that, and dancing, and playing in the band next to Max?

She fell into a sound slumber, and awoke the next morning utterly unable to remember a single second of any dream.

✑ *Jana and Miss O Go to the Cinema*

Jana always noticed what was playing at the Europa, but usually she wasn't tempted. Who chose those films? she wondered. Apparently someone with a taste for the gloomy and macabre. In recent weeks they'd shown *On the Beach*. The film was about the last few weeks of human life on earth after a nuclear catastrophe, with poisonous radioactivity spreading around the globe and killing every last creature. I can get that message from Rambir's editorials, she decided.

Then there was *A Night to Remember*. The giant poster on the theater wall showed the *Titanic* with its prow sticking out of the waves at a slant, and people in the water waving fruitlessly for rescue. Ten years old at the time the *Titanic* went down, Jana had lost a school friend in that disaster and didn't need to be reminded.

Next came *The Curse of Frankenstein*. No, thank you, thought Jana, no clanking, deformed monsters.

But now, according to a note that arrived from Miriam Orley, *An Affair to Remember* was playing, and Miriam wrote, "I understand that Cary Grant and Deborah Kerr are quite delicious."

The exchange of notes resulted in their deciding to go to the five P.M. show on Thursday, Miriam not being on duty either at dinner or in study hall. Jana sent Tilku down in advance to get two balcony tickets.

Jana and Miriam had a light meal at the Jolly Grant House at four o' clock, then walked down to the theater and got there in time to settle comfortably into their seats and look around at the other cinema-goers.

"This was quite an elegant cinema at one time," Miriam said.

"I don't remember," Jana said. "It wasn't here when I was ten."

The Europa's rise and fall had taken place in the half century since that time. The tattered velvet upholstery had surely started out plush and luxurious, and the threadbare carpet must have once been thick and firm underfoot. Now the theater was desperately in need of renovation. I'd put in new seats with foam rubber cushions, Jana thought. She shifted her weight to avoid being poked by a spring that reminded her all too much of Mr. Kilometres's taxi.

Besides the seats, the roof was crying out for attention, as was the lighting. The shell-shaped lamps on the walls cast funny shadows on the ceiling, and several bulbs had burned out, resulting in patches of darkness. The red velvet curtains were missing many of their gold tassels.

In the "VIP" seats in the balcony, Jana and Miriam looked around, nodding and smiling to people in the crowd they recognized. Mr. Powell, alone a few rows back from them, waved and smiled, and Mr. Dass of the Victoria Hotel, sitting with his shy little wife, gestured namasté. Well, good, thought Jana, at least poor Dizzy gets *some* recreation.

Editor Rambir's wife, Ritu, was also there, with a few people—most probably, Jana guessed, other teachers from St. Margaret's but not Rambir, who evidently could not be pried away from his work.

Otherwise, there was a fairly sizable crowd of people that Jana did not know, probably tourists. Behind her, she overheard snatches from some young British people talking enthusiastically about trekking.

"We seem to be getting a different kind of British person here now," Jana murmured to Miriam. "A jollier bunch than before independence."

"Oh, India's becoming frightfully popular with young

Brits," said Miriam, "and it appears to be mutual. People were thoroughly gaga over the queen."

Finally, the lights went down and the curtains swished open. Jana sat back in her seat and felt herself relaxing. Going to the cinema was like having a nice glass of Mr. Abinath's LPN10 . . . a respite from having to concentrate on the tasks of everyday life. She realized that Miriam, too, was relaxing in her seat, and the room itself seemed to let out a slow, contented breath.

They watched a newsreel of Prime Minister Nehru dedicating a dam, and Jana thought, Fine, but thank heavens the dam's not here! Then came a newsreel of the royal visit of Queen Elizabeth and Prince Philip to Pakistan and India. Jana marveled at the young queen's hats. "She shook fifty thousand hands in five weeks," the narrator of the film announced.

"She did a good job, didn't she?" whispered Miriam.

On through the cartoon, in which Mickey Mouse and Minnie fell hopelessly in love, to the feature film. *An Affair to Remember*—well, I should say so, Jana thought. She got completely swept up in the story. Wouldn't it be romantic to meet someone on shipboard, the way Deborah Kerr and Cary Grant had? And terrible to be separated by a stroke of fate? But wonderful to be reunited. Jana thoroughly enjoyed crying at the end.

"*Amor vincit omnia*," said Miriam, who also seemed to have enjoyed having a nice little weep.

Wiping their eyes with their handkerchiefs, they stood for the national anthem and then filed out. On the way home, and later that evening, Jana's thoughts turned to Maximilian King, whom she would soon see again, in his newly single state.

Medicine for the Heart?

ᴏᶜ *Rambir at Abinath's*

"Cheerio," said Ritu, her satchel slung over her shoulder. "I'm off to try to persuade a bunch of giggling schoolgirls that for every action there is an equal and opposite reaction."

"You're terrifying," Rambir said. To the air on the verandah and the mountains beyond, he announced, "My wife is absolutely terrifying."

"You're adorable." Ritu turned to her own imaginary audience. "My husband is absolutely adorable."

"What time will you be home?" Rambir said.

"Oh, six, I suppose," she said. "After classes, I have to supervise the Girl Guides. And then go to a teachers' meeting. I'll beat you home, though. Don't be *too* late. Just click the padlock on that office door and *leave*."

"I won't be late," Rambir said. "Don't forget to make that appointment with Mr. Powell."

"I won't," she said.

He watched her back disappear down the three flights of stairs to the street. In her salwar kameez, with her satchel, she looked like a schoolgirl herself, with all the energy of her pupils, or more.

Ritu's blind spots and flashing lights, Dr. Chawla had told

her the week before, were a sort of migraine, not a brain tumor.

Rambir had felt both a huge relief and a touch of irritation when Ritu had said, "I told you it was nothing, silly!"

"And does he say you can go to the conference?" Rambir would have been delighted to have someone tell Ritu not to travel, although not for such a dire reason as a brain tumor.

But Ritu had said, "Of course I can go to the conference. He says not to eat chocolate, and some other things. Or drink red wine."

"Which you don't drink, anyway."

"No," she'd said cheerfully. "I'll stick to tea! He also said to get my eyes checked. It's been a while. You know, darling, my specs are *dreadfully* out of fashion."

"What's wrong with them?" Rambir said.

"Darling, they so plain and boxy! I might get some with a cat's eye shape. Wouldn't those be cute?"

Now, at the bottom of the stairs, she turned and looked up to him, and blew him a kiss. He smiled and waved, then went back into the flat and got his things together in his battered attaché case to take to the office.

Before starting work, though, he had a quick errand to do. He walked briskly down the street of the Central Bazaar, past Royal Tailors and several more shops, then went up the two shallow steps into Abinath's Apothecary. He was greeted by a courteous "Namasté, editor sahib. How is your health? Not overworking as usual, I hope?"

"You sound like my wife," Rambir said. "And Mrs. Laird."

"We worry about you. You should take some rest."

"Rest is for old people," Rambir said.

"Rest is for everyone. Oh well, I know I'm talking to the air. What may I sell you today?"

"Aspirin," said Rambir.

"If you got more sleep, you would need less aspirin," Abinath said.

"But that wouldn't be good for your sales, would it now? 'Tis an ill wind that blows no one any good."

Abinath, used to this kind of comment from Rambir, swallowed any offense he might have taken, and got down a tin.

"Here. Aspro," he said.

"Aspro. Sounds like a brand for tennis shoes."

"Editor sahib, you know it is bona fide aspirin," Abinath said. "Acetyl . . . salicylic . . . acid."

"Thank you. Something with a name like that, I can trust," Rambir said. "It's more . . . scientific-sounding."

"Of course, of course." Abinath seemed to be hesitating about something, and then, like a boy who holds his nose and jumps into the river for a swim, he said, "Editor sahib, I'm thinking I should place an advertisement in your newspaper for my new medicine."

"Oh? Have you got it written up?"

Abinath handed him a piece of paper with an advertisement he had obviously designed himself, perhaps with the help of one of his school-age children. It had pictures of birds, animals, flowers, curlicues, and symbols that might have been Tibetan, Masonic, or God knows what else. In italics was the proud declaration: *Secret formula passed down through generations. LPN10, for long life, super vitality, and success in all endeavors, particularly of the heart.*

Rambir reminded himself that he was not required to *approve* of the advertisements people put in his newspaper. Print them, pocket the money, and be thankful for the extra cash—that was all he had to do. "What does LPN10 stand for?" he asked.

"It's a code name," Abinath said.

"LPN10 . . . let me guess. Liquid Power Nectar 10."

"Okay, editor sahib, since you're interested, I'll tell you. Love Potion Number 10."

Something straight out of a Bombay film studio, Rambir thought.

"I detect some skepticism on your part," said Abinath. "And I have the answer. Take this sample bottle and try it yourself. And your lovely lady-scientist wife, have her try it, too!"

"She likes that song 'Love Potion Number 9,' that keeps floating out into the street from the skating rink," Rambir said. "Now, this medicine of yours. Is it really a love potion?"

"The name is merely shorthand," Abinath said. "It's a love-of-*life* potion."

"You know, Mr. Abinath," said Rambir, "my lady-scientist wife, as you call her, will ask what sorts of *tests* have been made on this medicine."

"Tests? Put your mind at ease; it has had extensive tests. I gave my wife a double dose and my children a half dose each. And let me tell you, we are the happiest, healthiest, strongest family in the town. In the province, I dare say. Here, do take this sample."

Rambir took the sample bottle, unscrewed the cap, and sniffed.

"Quite a nice smell," he said. "Fruity, I would call it."

"Fruity, indeed! But don't just smell, drink."

"I'll take it home and try it there," said Rambir.

"Very well," said Abinath.

✑ Rambir Writes to His Dad

He had a long day at the press. The boy, Tilku, was neither very enthusiastic nor very talented at stapling brochures or stacking and folding the newspaper. Old Clackety-Clack kept stopping, and Rambir had to make frequent adjustments to get it going again. When Tilku had left, Rambir looked at his watch. He had an hour before Ritu would get home. He needed to edit several more stories, but instead he decided to use the time to dash off . . . well, not *dash* off a letter. That was hardly the spirit in which he wrote to his father.

When he was first married, he had written to his dad, popped the letter into the mail, waited a week or so, then written another letter, not keeping track of how often he tried for a reconciliation. After a while, he had begun a log, and now, over the last five years, he had written eighty-seven letters. None had been answered. He knew the address was still right, and he personally watched the man at the post office bring down the postmark stamp—*thump*—on the envelope and put the letter in the outgoing box. One letter might have gotten lost, or two, but eighty-seven? Not likely.

Now he picked up a pen to write the eighty-eighth.

"My esteemed papa-ji," he wrote. "This brings you my respectful greetings from Hamara Nagar. I am sitting in my office, looking out the window into the street. The evening crowds have begun to throng. I will soon be going home to partake of my evening meal. As I have mentioned, Ritu and I rent an apartment in this town—a small one, but it is on the top floor of a well-constructed building, and it has a view of the mountains. Having a long view like that makes me take a long view of the past and the future."

He started to write, "I think of our family," but stopped. His father had told him, in no uncertain terms, that Rambir was no longer to consider himself a part of the family. The words "our family" might well enrage his father, to the point that he might not read any further, but instead throw the letter in the wastebasket. Of course, that's what he probably did with all the letters Rambir had written, anyway. How to keep his father reading?

Long view . . . past . . . present . . . future . . . continuity . . . tradition . . . loyalty . . . These words went through Rambir's head. Hadn't he already pleaded, "Papa-ji, I feel tremendous pain for having given you distress; my life will not be right until I can come and see you, take the dust from your feet, and hear you say that I am indeed your son"?

He wanted to pour out his feelings on the page, make his father hear the cry from the heart. Instead, he ended up with the usual dry recitation of his life and Ritu's. The paper had increased in circulation. He was making plans to purchase a modern copying machine. Ritu's students, writing in their underground student newspaper, had rated Ritu "both the most demanding and the most rewarding teacher" at St. Margaret's. Rambir had been named businessman of the year by the newly formed Hamara Nagar Rotary Club. The government had decided on a different location for the proposed dam, and the town was enjoying renewed prosperity with the increased tourism.

Which was the right approach? Tell his dad good things, which might, just might, make him proud? Or tell him about failures and disappointments (there were always a few of those, after all), which would enable his father to say, "I told you so" and feel self-righteous and smug? He'd tried one; he'd tried the other.

Say what is in your heart, he told himself. But his heart had a lot of scar tissue over it, making it hard to get the truth out. He sighed, then signed the letter, "Your faithful son, Rambir."

Printed Matter

✑ From Muktinanda's to the Book Depot

Jana went up to Muktinanda's Stationers and School Supplies to get some new pen nibs and a bottle of ink. She found Muktinanda, an angular man who reminded her of a long pair of calipers, putting cricket magazines and *Filmfare* on the rack. At the sight of Jana, Muktinanda's face lit up.

"Mrs. Laird! The *Weekly* is here, with the photo essay about you! Just take a look."

Muktinanda laid a copy of the magazine on the counter and flipped the pages until he found the story. "Here you are!"

The story was the work of the second reporter who had come to the Jolly Grant House. Jana, in her workaday clothes, was in front of the bay window with her violin raised to play, and Mr. Ganguly, on his perch, was lifting his wing as if to say hello. The rest of the household was also pictured.

Muktinanda read aloud the title of the piece: "'India's Varied Citizens Come in All Sizes and Shapes.' Quite nice pictures, don't you think?" he added.

"I'll need several copies of the magazine," said Jana. "Let's see: one for each person in the house, and one to send to my son, Jack."

Muktinanda looked apologetic. "Oh, Mrs. Laird, I only have this one left. A young man came and bought all the rest. I saved one for you, but I forgot that you might want more."

"What young man?" said Jana. "What did he look like?"

"*Aré*, I can't remember very well, Mrs. Laird. Thin. Face a bit . . . shifty. That's it. I didn't like the looks of him much. He bought the magazines and disappeared as quickly as possible."

"I'll have to see if the Book Depot has any left," Jana said.

She paid for the nibs and the ink and the magazine, took her leave of Muktinanda, and continued down the street, disquieted. Why on earth would someone buy up all the issues of the *Illustrated Weekly of India*? She would have to write a quick note to Kenneth Stuart-Smith and post it as soon as possible. She had not heard from him since they'd had dinner at the Victoria, when the weather was still cold. It had since turned lovely, and she would have expected him to be back in the hills, ready to do some hiking and information-gathering. Where was the man, anyway? Had he found out anything more about the animal-kidnapping gang? She mused on such questions all the way to the English Bazaar.

The bookstore was right next to Sharp Eyes Vision Care. When Jana was ten, a young British man used to be behind the counter; he called her Miss Janet and gravely recommended titles—*The Wouldbegoods, Little Women, Girls of the Hamlet Club*—which she then bought with her pocket money.

Until recently, the store had been called the Britannia Book Depot, but now, Jana noticed, there was a big new sign saying "Hindustan Book Depot" and, behind the counter, an earnest-looking young woman in a camel-colored silk sari. Booksellers are booksellers, thought Jana. No matter what guise they appear in, they are eager to get books into hands, stories into hearts.

"Good morning, madam," said the young woman, her English fluid and impeccable.

"Good morning," said Jana.

"Are you looking for something special?"

"A couple of things," Jana said. "Do you sell the *Illustrated Weekly*?"

"Of course, madam," she said. "But this week, we haven't got any. Someone seems to have stolen them right out from under our nose."

Jana felt her stomach knot up. "How strange."

"It was, rather. We tried to get more, but they're nowhere to be found. There was a large section on film stars. Maybe people want those pictures to hang on their walls, you know."

"Maybe," said Jana. She tried to persuade herself that it was something as simple as that.

"Can I help you with something else?" the young woman asked.

Strange occurrences or not, one's errands must be done. "A gift, actually," Jana said. "A birthday gift."

"For a girl or a boy?"

"A woman about to celebrate her seventieth birthday."

The young woman thought a minute, then said brightly, "A book of poetry, perhaps?"

"Yes, that's a good idea," said Jana. A book of poetry was a good gift for a seventy-year-old lady.

The young woman in the camel-colored sari went back into a storeroom and returned with a slim blue volume.

"Poems. By a young woman poet," she said. "Someone who lived around here. She was a teacher at one of the boarding schools. I don't know if she's still alive." She handed the book to Jana, who looked at it and burst out laughing.

The book was called *In Search,* and on the back inside cover, there was a very small black-and-white photograph of the author—Miriam Orley.

"Something is funny, madam?"

"No, no," said Jana. "I'm glad you showed this to me."

Jana studied the photograph. The young Miriam Orley had jet-black eyes and black hair, which she wore waved in fashionable finger curls that framed her luminous face. Her skin was creamy and unlined. And instead of the suit the current Miss Orley wore these days, for teaching and everything else, she had on a stylish black dress with a white lace collar.

Jana turned the book over in her hand, opened it, felt the pages. Someone had obviously put a lot of love into its creation. The paper was heavy and creamy, still closed along the folds. It was an unread copy—the pages had not yet been split. Jana was amazed that the young woman had found it in the back room. It must have been sitting there for years!

"The publication date is 1935," said Jana. "It's amazing that it looks as new as it does." She sniffed at it. "And it doesn't even smell particularly musty, even after twenty-five monsoons. Truly incredible."

"We keep this building as dry as possible, for the books," the young woman said.

Jana searched in vain for a price. "How much does it cost?"

The woman turned the book over, looked puzzled, and examined a few other books of poetry. "Two rupees, eight annas, I would say. Shall I wrap it up for you? Pink tissue paper, with white ribbon?"

"Actually, no," said Jana. "I'll keep this one for myself. So I still need another book for the gift I came to get."

"Poetry, again?"

Jana considered the question. "No, I think not, after all." Hadn't Miriam told her that she was interested in photography?

Jana browsed the shelves, the young lady in the camel-colored sari searching at the same time, but it was Jana who first spied a serious-looking volume called *Principles of Photography.*

"Oof! This must weigh ten pounds," Jana said. Truly a heavy book! It would be a compliment to give someone such a book, she thought; it would acknowledge the depth of that person's interest in the subject.

Jana left the store with the two books in her satchel. They seemed like odd bedfellows—or bagfellows, she thought, feeling rather clever at thinking up this term. One was bulky and heavy and the latest word about technology, incongruously gift-wrapped in pink and violet tissue paper. The other was slim and old-fashioned, its contents still sealed behind uncut pages.

I still wish I could find the *Weekly,* Jana thought. I don't like unexplained strange occurrences.

A Glimpse into a Soul

The satchel strap was cutting into her shoulder, and when Jana came to the bench on the lookout point halfway back to her house, she decided to sit and rest for a while. She took out Miriam's book of poems and opened it. Because of the unsplit pages, she could read only every eighth page, but that was enough to make her wildly curious about the rest. The poems, which she had expected to be sweet little pieces about flowers and birds, were tough and fiery, and seemed to tell a story. Eager to know more of the story than these glimpses, Jana stuffed the book back into her satchel and hurried home, changing the satchel from one shoulder to the other as she went, and sometimes holding it with both arms across her chest.

She found the house quiet, Mary apparently out on errands. Mr. Ganguly's cage was empty, which gave her an anxious start, until she looked out the window and saw Tilku playing with him on the terrace below. Already home from work at the press, Tilku was putting Mr. Ganguly through his tricks: playing dead, waving his wing as if to say hello and good-bye, dancing on Tilku's arm while Tilku sang film songs. Oh, she thought, they look so happy and innocent.

Meanwhile, Miriam's poems were waiting to be liberated from the unread book. Jana found the paper knife in the almirah and slit the pages, trying to take care, and getting annoyed at herself for creating an occasional ragged edge. Then she sat in the window seat and started reading.

Jana's experience with poetry had been mainly during her school days, when she was required to memorize lines. Some of these lines still came back to her—some scraps of Shakespearean sonnets, a passage from *As You Like It*, bits from Alfred, Lord Tennyson. Frequently, lines had gotten scrambled in her head. She *knew* that "The Charge of the Light Brigade" went "half a league, half a league, half a league onward," but somehow it had become "happily, happily, happily onward." On the whole, she had to admit, poetry just wasn't her cup of tea.

But Miriam's book of poems was, as Jana had thought, a *story*. Disguised? she wondered. Miriam's own or someone else's? The story was about a woman who had trusted a man too much, been overtaken by his charm, and then been abandoned. The writing is very powerful, Jana thought. It makes *me* feel first carved up by grief, then exploding with rage, then, finally, wiser but profoundly sad because of . . . because of what? Because of the loss not only of love but of innocence, Jana decided.

So much emotion in so few pages—it made Jana uneasy. She felt as if she'd eavesdropped on one of Miriam's conversations or stumbled on her wounded, or naked, or, even, committing some sort of *crime*. But, surely, Miriam *wanted* people to read these poems, or at least had wanted it at one time; otherwise she wouldn't have allowed the book to be published. It was brave of Miriam, Jana thought, to let other people glimpse into a corner of her soul. I don't think I could have done this myself, she admitted. I wouldn't have wanted to call attention to my own pain. I wouldn't have wanted to draw sharks to the blood in the water.

She put the book down on the table, feeling admiration and even gratitude not only toward Miriam but also toward all the other poets of the world, writing in their different languages, confessing their different sorrows.

Tilku Invalided Out

✑ *A Close Call*

There was an ominous thump in the back room, followed by a chattering noise. Old Clackety-Clack was having one of its seizures, when it hiccuped and coughed up paper unpredictably into the air rather than depositing it politely in the rack. Tilku was standing next to the machine, staring dumbly at the flying paper.

"Turn the thing off!" Rambir shouted above the din. Then, seeing that Tilku had no idea what to do and looked utterly terrified, Rambir darted over and flicked the necessary switches and levers. The machine came to a shuddering halt. Rambir made a few adjustments, telling Tilku to watch carefully.

"This time, you start the machine," Rambir said.

Tilku took a deep breath, his face screwed up with anxiety.

"I don't think this machine likes me, sahib."

Rambir snorted. "Machines don't have likes or dislikes. Come on, all you have to do is turn this flywheel." *Our Town, Our Times* was already behind schedule! Rambir seized the wheel and gave it a whirl, and the whirring, clacking noise burst forth again. Tilku, startled, lost his balance, brushed against the machine, and let out a shriek. Rambir lunged forward, pulled Tilku back, turned the press off, and stood there, his own heart pounding.

"You wretched boy!"

A mixture of fear and relief registered in Tilku's face.

"Sorry. Sorry, sahib. Sorry."

"Here, let me see what you've done to yourself."

Tilku's shirt was torn, and Rambir saw a red patch on the boy's arm.

"It's hot, sahib, and paining." Tilku held his injured arm with the other one, his face contorted.

Rambir looked at his watch. So much for the rush printing job. Old Dr. Chawla would still be in his surgery at this time of the afternoon, and Rambir would have to take Tilku to have the arm looked at. What if the kid had broken it?

"Okay, Tilku, let's lock up," he said.

At Dr. Chawla's clinic, on the second floor of the Kashmiri Palace, Rambir, who had written several editorials decrying child labor, found himself embarrassed to explain how Tilku had hurt himself.

"We should X-ray the arm," Dr. Chawla said, and he took Tilku into an adjacent room, while Rambir sat on the wooden bench in the waiting room. He heard some whirs and thumps, and Dr. Chawla brought Tilku back into his office and called Rambir in.

"My niece is developing the film now," Dr. Chawla said. "So we'll know if that arm is broken."

"I don't think it's broken, Doctor sahib," said Tilku, who had brightened up considerably with all this attention. He lifted his arm above his head.

"How old are you, Tilku?" Dr. Chawla's eyes crinkled under his bushy eyebrows. He looked like the epitome of what he was: a benevolent Sikh grandfather.

"Eleven, Doctor sahib. I think."

"And how about school?"

"I finished school, Doctor sahib," Tilku said.

"I don't want to interfere with your business," Dr. Chawla said to Rambir, "but this boy hasn't quite the size or strength—or perhaps the attention span—to operate a big machine."

Dr. Chawla's niece, a young woman in a salwar kameez, poked her head in to say that the X-ray was ready, and the doctor stepped out momentarily, then quickly reappeared.

"Young man," he said to Tilku, "you're right: your arm is not broken. But we'll put some antiseptic and a bandage on that burn."

Tilku winced as Dr. Chawla dressed the burn.

"Hold still now," said the doctor. "There! Brave boy."

When Dr. Chawla had finished, Rambir paid for the X-ray and the office visit, and he and Tilku went down the staircase in silence, to the street.

"You are angry with me, editor sahib?" Tilku asked.

"No," said Rambir, "but I'm thinking that this work might not be the best for you after all."

"Jana mem told me to stay and try my hardest."

"You tell her I said that you did a good job, and finished up the work very nicely."

"No more work, sahib?"

"Not now," Rambir said.

With a dazzling smile, Tilku gave Rambir a quick salaam and took off down the street toward the Jolly Grant House.

Rambir Picks Up Ritu at the Eye Doctor's

As he watched Tilku disappear down the street, Rambir, exhausted from the effort and guilt of the day, remembered with a start that he was supposed to pick up Ritu at Sharp

Eyes Vision Care. He turned and walked briskly back to the English Bazaar, and found Ritu sitting in Mr. Powell's waiting area, her pupils enormous, her eyes running, and the skin around them stained with yellow ointment. When she saw him, she jumped up and, even though holding his arm, almost tripped as they went down the steps into the street.

Glancing at his watch, Rambir saw that he had kept Ritu waiting almost an hour. "I *am* sorry," he said. "We had a bit of an accident at the press. My fault for taking on an eleven-year-old! I told him not to come back. You should have seen his face! Total joy, like a soldier being invalided out of the army."

"Was he badly hurt?"

"No, fortunately. Dr. Chawla told him he was a brave boy and bandaged him up. What did Mr. Powell say about your eyes?"

"They're fine—nearsighted as ever, that's all."

"That's good," Rambir said. "And how was school today?"

Ritu let out a laugh. "Oh, pandemonium all day long. We had a lab on inclined planes, but it was interrupted by a crow flying in the window. Poor fellow seemed quite confused, not the slightest bit interested in the lesson."

"Are you tired? We could take a rickshaw," he said.

"No, honestly, let's not spend the money."

They stumbled along toward home, Rambir guiding Ritu around horse and cow patties in the street.

"I wrote him again, today," said Rambir. He did not have to tell Ritu who "he" was.

"Maybe you'll get an answer this time," Ritu said.

If she had said that once, she had said it a hundred times. She also said, not for the first time, "What if we just appeared one day on the doorstep, in Delhi?"

"All the servants have strict instructions not to let me in," said Rambir.

"Yes, but in the surprise of the moment, might he not relent? Just out of curiosity?"

"You don't know my father," said Rambir. "He does not like surprises."

"But your mother, she must want to see her oldest son. Doesn't she?"

"She probably does," said Rambir.

"Your father must feel very guilty," Ritu said firmly.

Rambir gave a sick laugh. "Why on earth would you think that? That's the opposite of what he thinks. You've never even met the man! He feels highly self-righteous and correct about sticking to principle."

"Way down deep," Ritu persisted, "he feels guilty about the way he's treated you, and he *wants* to make up. But all his training about caste and this and that are putting him in a bind."

"You've never even met the man," Rambir said again.

"Ah, no," said Ritu, "but I've met his son."

Warnings

✑ *Mr. Dass Learns About the Kings*

The day after her shopping expedition to get the books, Jana had an unexpected visitor to the salon. Mary ushered in Mr. Dass from the Victoria, and instantly Jana recognized the signs of a Dass tizzy. The line between Mr. Dass's eyebrows was twice as deep as usual, and his face was twisted with worry bordering on panic.

She quickly seated him at the table in the bay window. Mr. Ganguly looked down at him from his perch and, recognizing a human in distress, flapped his wings and squawked, "Not to worry! Not to worry!" Jana had never been sure how the bird figured these things out; did the smell of anxiety tip him off? She didn't think he had much sense of smell, though. Maybe it was the choked-up tone of Mr. Dass's voice.

"Tea, Mr. Dass?" she asked.

"No, no, I can't really stop long. I just had to tell you some news. I have found out the name of the prospective buyers of the hotel," he blurted out. "They are two cousins—a Mr. Maximilian King, of Paris and Bombay, and a Mr. Cyrus King, also of Bombay."

Mr. Dass uttered the words *buyers, Paris,* and *Bombay* with the same degree of alarm. When Jana burst into a smile, his distress was compounded by puzzlement.

"Dear Mr. Dass, I *know* them," said Jana. "Don't worry! They're both very nice men, very progressive and humanitarian, with a sense of humor. I think they'll be wonderful employers. Don't you worry the slightest little bit."

"Not to worry!" chimed in Mr. Ganguly.

Mr. Dass looked skeptical. "Rumor has it that they are very tough businessmen," he said. "They've been buying up all sorts of hotels and tearing them down and erecting great big modern structures in their place."

"But," said Jana, "I understand that they are planning a chain of hotels with a historical flavor. Working from photographs, and so forth. I understand completely what they are trying to do! When repairing the Jolly Grant House, I wanted it to *look* like it did when it was first built.

"But," she went on, "I also wanted it to be modern and comfortable. Granted, in that regard, I haven't made much progress. I still want to put in a new bath and kitchen and some degree of central heating."

Mr. Dass still looked worried, and Jana went on:

"Also, just keeping an old building standing sometimes means tearing out some things and replacing them with others. It's like dental surgery. You don't *like* going in there with drills and picks and whatnot, but if you don't do it, rot and decay will set in and you will lose the whole structure anyway. Destruction and rebirth—all part of life," she continued. "The phoenix rises from the ashes."

"Phoenix?" Mr. Dass asked.

"The bird. The mythological bird."

"Good bird!" added Mr. Ganguly.

"Or," Jana said, "to take an example from Hindu philosophy: Lord Shiva destroys, and then he creates again!"

Rather than comforting Mr. Dass, Jana could see that she

was overwhelming him. She leaned back in her chair and said, trying to sound soothing and calm, "Mr. Dass, don't worry. Take this one step at a time."

"One step? One step? How can I do that? These people are coming at a quick march! They have already sent architects to measure the rooms. Timed how long it takes to flush a toilet! Sent two cooks to inspect the kitchen—a Parsi chef and a *French* one!"

It sounded as if, gastronomically, things would pick up nicely under the new regime, and Jana couldn't entirely suppress a smile. This was unfortunate, and Mr. Dass reacted quickly. "You are *smiling,* Mrs. Laird. *Smiling?* I thought you would understand how worried I am."

Jana rushed to reassure him: "I do understand, Mr. Dass, I really do. But things are going to be all right. I promise. Are you really sure you don't want a nice cup of tea? And a biscuit with guava jelly?"

"No, no, Mrs. Laird, these days I can't eat and can't sleep."

"Even *tea*? Just a tiny cup?"

"Well, since you are insisting, all right."

Mr. Dass ended up drinking not one, not two, but three cups of tea, with plenty of milk and many lumps of sugar. After this, he seemed, if not exactly serene, at least more optimistic.

"Thank you, Mrs. Laird," he said. "I will now go back to the hotel and try to face—developments."

A Tune Is Missing

When Mr. Dass had gone, Mary came and took away the tea things, and Jana puttered around the salon. She had not made much progress on the music transcriptions lately. She took the half-completed scores out of the almirah and put them on the table, counting up the number of tunes. Now there were nineteen. Thirty-one more to go.

But wait—hadn't she already written down a little air that old Ian had called "Does One Bow to Fate?," suggesting that he didn't think you should? Where *was* that piece of paper? She was sure that she had transcribed the tune. It was a lovely, haunting little thing. Even Mr. Ganguly, who usually hated laments, had seemed captivated by it, listening quietly with his head cocked. Jana could clearly remember making a clean copy of it, back in the wintertime, probably before the pipe had burst. And now it was gone. Oh, dear. In a moment of distraction, maybe she'd crumpled up the final copy as well as the rough one.

She took her violin out of the case, tuned it briefly, and played the air. Again, Mr. Ganguly listened without a squawk of protest. She grabbed her pen and quickly wrote down the notes, this time producing a perfect copy without even doing a rough draft. With a feeling of accomplishment, she signed her name to the bottom of the sheet and dated it.

Then she played the tune again, and it put her in a reflective mood—rather a strange one, in fact. Where was she to go from here, what was coming next in her life? She had tried to calm Mr. Dass down; now could she follow her own advice? Could she take one step at a time, assume that things were going to be good?

High Society in Hamara Nagar

✑ *Mr. Ganguly Spots a Big Bad Bird*

Jana put the final bar sign on a brisk march that old Ian used to call "Full Speed Ahead." Then she realized she had left out a measure. Blast! Another piece of staff paper wasted. Enough of this for the day.

"Mary," she called, "I'm taking Mr. Ganguly for a walk. If anyone comes asking about us, get their name and remember what they look like."

Tilku, now gleefully unemployed, with the burn on his arm healed, came too, stopping occasionally to chat with his cronies in the street, and then running to catch up to Jana. They were just past the Giant Skating Rink, when they heard a noise. First it was a faraway growl, then, coming closer, a roar punctuated by a clacking noise similar to that of Rambir's printing press. Looking up, Jana saw a helicopter overhead.

Mr. Ganguly made his extreme displeasure known.

"Big bird," he shrieked. "Bad bird!"

Jana chuckled. "It is a very big bird, isn't it!"

"Jana mem!" Tilku's eyes were bright. "Look, there!"

There was a bend in the road, and the helicopter disappeared from sight beyond a patch of forest.

Now Jana and Tilku and Mr. Ganguly found themselves

part of a stream of people all going in the direction of the Victoria Hotel. Shop attendants flowed out onto the street, their bosses protesting hopelessly, until they, too, finally slammed their doors shut and joined the crowd. Schoolchildren pushed forward in clumps, rickshaw pullers ran with their empty rickshaws, and otherwise perfectly respectable people seemed to have taken leave of their senses, scurrying forward like leaves driven by the wind.

"What is it? Where are you going?" Jana called to a woman she recognized, who flung a response over her shoulder and kept running. Tilku hurried up to some Nepali workmen and got a few impatient words out of them.

"Helicopter is landing," he said, returning to Jana. "They are all going to watch. In the courtyard of the Victoria."

But when they got within sight of the wall surrounding the Victoria, they saw the town's four policemen trying to keep the crowd back. The helicopter was in view again, and the sound was louder than ever.

"It's coming closer!" a man shouted. "It's going to land on our heads!"

"Don't be an idiot," someone else called. "It's landing just now inside the gates."

Jana could imagine poor Mr. Dass having an Olympic-sized tizzy. Hearing the sound of hooves on the pavement, she turned to see Police Commissioner Bandhu Sharma on a white horse, with a couple of grooms running before him and pushing the crowd aside so that Bandhu could approach the gate and dismount.

The commotion was deafening as two Victoria Hotel gatemen opened the gates for Bandhu, then tried to close them. But it was too late; a dozen people had already slipped through, and more were surging in. The helicopter had landed. The gatemen finally succeeded in slamming the gates shut and keeping them bolted. Jana barely had time to catch a glimpse of someone in an aviator jacket and dark glasses, sitting in the middle seat of the helicopter, with a woman on one side and a man on the other.

Meanwhile, Bandhu's horse, terrified by the noise, reared up and whinnied, threatening to charge into the crowd, until finally the two grooms got him under control and led him away.

Jana could not hear much of what he was saying, but it seemed that Bandhu was welcoming the people who had just dismounted from the helicopter. Meanwhile, Tilku managed to climb up onto the Victoria's wall, in spite of all the other little boys trying to do the same thing and whacking at each other.

"Jana mem," Tilku called down, "Commissioner sahib is garlanding the helicopter sahibs! And Dass sahib is also garlanding them. Jana mem, they are covered with marigolds!"

The King party, as it turned out, had just been officially welcomed to Hamara Nagar.

An Evening with the Kings

The note from the Victoria arrived at the Jolly Grant House in midmorning.

"Dearest Jana," it read, "we're here and we're so eager to see you! We came yesterday afternoon in the company helicopter, with Max at the controls! I must tell you, this is the *only* way to travel. Except that we drew such crowds everywhere. We sent on the staff in advance, by road, and got a special permit to have an automobile within the town limits."

What that had cost, in terms of rupees and string pulling, was anyone's guess. Jana continued reading.

"So, if you'll come to dinner and dancing tonight at the

Victoria, we'll send the driver to get you. I hope you aren't busy!"

Invitations from Lily, Jana remembered from her Bombay days, tended to come at the last minute, and if a note could sound breathless, this one did. She stifled a slight feeling of hurt at not having been informed in advance of the helicopter arrival and, grabbing a pen, wrote back, "Lovely! I accept with pleasure."

That night, she dressed in her Mughal-wedding-style fortune-telling costume, which Feroze Ali Khan had so lovingly made. With the curly-toed slippers, and—Why not? she thought—the emerald necklace. The risk was being overdressed, of course, but knowing that Lily and Cyrus liked dressing (even out in the provinces), she felt that excess would be better than looking like a Scottish matron in a wool skirt and cardigan.

Promptly as promised, a Mercedes-Benz 220SE, shiny and black, appeared in front of the Jolly Grant House, driven by a man in a smart green uniform. Turning around in the street in front of the gate had proven impossible, so the driver had turned into an alley downhill, then backed up. Lal Bahadur Pun, visibly impressed, and Mary, less so, relayed the driver's message: "Madam's car is ready to take her to the Victoria Hotel."

A car was such a rare sight in town that there were almost as many people gathered around it as had swarmed to see the helicopter the day before. Lal Bahadur Pun, joined by Tilku, bellowed at them, swinging his stick to little effect. Finally, he yelled to Tilku to run and get his bagpipes from his room. Then Lal Bahadur Pun's most aggressive pest-eradication melodies kept the crowd sufficiently at bay so that Jana could slip into the back seat of the car.

Sliding across the soft leather upholstery, she looked up

and saw faces staring in the windows, all around. She felt like a goldfish on display in a fishbowl. It was startling to her how, suddenly, her own house and her own neighborhood felt not like safe, familiar territory but like a circus tent with the crowds pressing forward to see the performers.

"Madam is ready to go?" the driver asked.

"Yes, carry on," she said.

The driver leaned heavily on the horn and yelled out the window. When the crowd did not disperse, he moved the car forward anyway, scattering people right and left. There was really no place to run, and the onlookers pressed themselves up against the shops, until finally the car was out of the Central Bazaar and on the wider and less crowded street of the English Bazaar.

"Quite an undertaking, isn't it?" Jana said to the driver.

"Oh, madam, every place we go has been like this. Crowds, crowds, crowds. I came on the road in front of the fuel truck. They had to refuel the helicopter at the air force station at Sarsawa, and then they stopped for lunch in Dehra Dun. Each time, people found out, and a huge crowd formed in no time flat."

"How many cars had to come, in addition to the helicopter?"

"I brought Mr. Maximilian King's French cook and accountant and lawyer in this car. Two of Mr. Cyrus King's bearers and Mrs. King's ayah came by train from Delhi and then by taxi from Dehra Dun . . . some fellow who calls himself Kilometres drove them."

"Aha," said Jana. "But how did everyone get to Delhi from Bombay?"

"Oh, company plane, madam. We all came in the company plane. Timeless Hotels now has headquarters in Bombay and an office in Delhi, with *many* cars in each place, and one helicopter in each, also."

So, this was how the Kings moved from one place to another.

Suddenly curious, Jana asked the driver, "Do people enjoy working for the Kings?"

"Oh, yes, yes, madam. How else would we get to see all of India?"

"They seem to be building quite an empire."

"Oh, this is the new empire," the driver said. "Everything is bigger and better than in the days of the British sahibs."

"It certainly seems so," said Jana.

"The King party is in the southern wing of the building," Mr. Dass told Jana, after the driver had deposited her at the front door of the hotel. "They're using the Bombay Room as their sitting room. It used to be called the Viceroy Room. I'll have a bearer show you there."

"That's not necessary, Mr. Dass," Jana said. "I know this hotel like the back of my hand."

She made her way across the courtyard to the wing where the most expensive rooms were. It was not the wing she had stayed in the previous year, but the one on the opposite side. Approaching the door to the Bombay Room, she could hear male laughter, and American big band music being played on a gramophone. She tapped lightly on the door. In a few seconds, it swung open.

"Cyrus! Max! She's here!" cried Lily King, opening her arms wide and kissing Jana on both cheeks. "Jana! Welcome, welcome. You're looking gorgeous, not a day older, absolutely *smashing*."

Jana's first thought was that—thank goodness—she'd made the right wardrobe decision. The exotic formality of the fortune-telling outfit was perfectly in keeping with the Kings' evening attire. Lily, who often wore full-skirted dresses custom-made in Bombay or Paris, was tonight in a sari of mauve shot silk that shimmered gold, depending on the light. The men, approaching behind her, were both splendid in white dinner jackets. Jana noticed, as never before, what superb shiny heads of hair they had—all jet black, Lily's lustrous and shoulder-length, the men's thick and healthy and well trimmed.

"You're here," said Maximilian King and Cyrus King in unison.

"I am," she said, "and here *you* all are."

"Yes, that's established!" said Lily, and they all laughed and smiled, and Jana kissed the air next to the cheeks of both men.

It had not taken long for the Kings to make themselves completely at home. In the corner, a bar had been set up with an ice bucket, a martini shaker, bottles of whisky, soda water, flagons, highball glasses, and champagne flutes. The room overflowed with elaborate bouquets of flowers, and on the coffee table were issues of the latest American and British magazines: *Vogue, Punch, Life, Time,* and the *Economist.* Goodness, the airmail postage! was the thought that flickered through Jana's brain. But there was also a copy of Rambir's paper, and the issue of the *Illustrated Weekly of India* with the story about Jana in it.

"We just read about you," Lily said.

"Our celebrity," said Cyrus.

Max said nothing, but he exchanged smiles with Jana, and she felt as if something—a magic little strand—was joining them, through the air, without their having to touch.

"Cyrus, you can pour Jana some champagne, you know how!" said Lily.

The smell of champagne was already in the room, and, in fact, the very air seemed bubbly and festive. For Jana, it was like being a child and entering a room and seeing a birthday cake and balloons and streamers, and a table heaped with brightly wrapped presents—for her. Everything came in a rush: jokes, little explosions of laughter, stories, references to funny things that had happened in the past. Glamour, fun, witty and slightly wicked conversation—this is what I have been missing, she thought.

"Come, come, sit here on this sofa with me," Lily said, and the men settled in the armchairs on the other side of the coffee table.

"Isn't it lovely to be together. And, you know, if this works out, we'll be here a lot." Lily turned to Cyrus. "Won't we, darling? Tell Jana all about the project."

Cyrus said, "We've been looking at many of the old hill stations for our line of hotels. In Mussoorie, we've found a site where we could build a brand-new one. In Simla, we're going to take over Fonseca's. We've also been to Nainital, Sattal, Almora, and some places closer to Bombay."

"We'll gut this place and refurnish it," said Lily. "Get rid of this dowdy old furniture. Can't you see everything sleek and Danish modern? Built-in closets, full-length mirrors, that sort of thing."

"And telephones in every room—absolutely essential!" said Cyrus.

"And the name. We've got to be country-oriented," Lily said. "It can't be the Victoria."

"We actually don't have to change the name much," Cyrus said. "We're thinking of the Victory Hotel. That would make it easy for the people in the bazaar to remember."

"They'll continue to call it the Victoria, never fear," Jana said. "They're still calling the Far Oaks School the Company School, from the days of the East India Company. But, of course, you do need to update the guidebooks."

"Oh, *guide*books, right." Max picked up one of the books on the table beside him; Jana saw that it was *The Globe-Trotter's Companion.* "I'm glad that fellow gave this hotel a good write-up. Gives *us* a leg up in promoting the place. But, I must say, he wore rose-colored glasses. I mean, calling a shabby little place like this a 'charming relic of the olden days' is almost *comical*. The oldest wing doesn't even have flush toilets. Think of it: thunder buckets, in this day and age!"

Jana felt a sudden chill, as if he'd tossed cold water in her face, and a wave of protectiveness for her friend Kenneth Stuart-Smith.

"It *is* a relic," she said. "But I rather love it. And I don't think 'charming' is stretching the truth. It's quite comfortable, too, don't you think?"

"My dear, you were a missionary wife for too long," Lily said. "You wouldn't know luxury if you fell on top of it! And the author of this book—I think his standards are pretty low, too. Now, if we buy this hotel, we'll want it to rate four stars in *Michelin,* and get into the top category in *Fodor's.* We want to bring it up to international standards."

Max said, "All in good time! We don't need that to happen tonight! Tonight, we're having a wonderful evening together. I propose a toast. To our friend Jana—may her fortunes always be excellent!"

They raised their glasses to her and drank. Jana lifted hers, too. "And I say, to you, may our friendship continue forever."

"I brought you a little present," said Lily, handing Jana a wrapped package.

It was a framed photograph of the four of them, taken at the New Year's Eve party at the Bombay Flying Club, holding their musical instruments and a placard that said, "First Prize," against a backdrop of balloons and streamers and people dancing.

"I found the picture and thought it should be framed and hung on a wall," Lily said. "And then it occurred to me that it should be *your* wall."

"That's so kind," Jana said. "That was a nice evening, wasn't it?" She glanced at Max.

"An extremely jolly evening," he said. "I remember it well."

There was a light tap on the door.

"Yes?" Cyrus said loudly.

A bearer opened it and announced anxiously, "Sahibs, table is ready in the dining room."

Lily chuckled. "See? Out in the provinces, they want you to eat early so that you can get up early and go trekking, or something dreadful like that."

Max said, "Now, Lily, remember that we're going to accommodate trekkers in the new Victory Hotel. Even *you* would like the luxury trekking I have in mind: porters carrying everything, good food, large tents, furniture, bathing facilities . . . all the creature comforts, to make the splendid mountain views all the more enjoyable."

In the dining room, they were the last to enter. The other diners were already on the dessert course, while the Kings' table stood in splendor, fresh flowers colorful against the heavy white table linen, the serviettes folded into the shape of swans. In the corner, the small string band was transitioning from the Blue Danube to the Emperor Waltz.

Mr. Dass, on the verge of anxious tears, led them to their table and seated Lily and Jana next to each other. Max moved to the chair on Jana's other side, and Cyrus sat down across the table. As Mr. Dass retreated to the doorway, Jana heard Lily murmur to Cyrus, "The staff will need some retraining, of course. We've got to have people with more pleasant expressions than that."

Oh, poor old Dizzy, Jana thought.

"Not a bad room," said Cyrus, looking around. "Good proportions and all."

"Yes, I love it," said Jana.

"Oh, sweetie, you are so cute," Lily said.

"I *do* love it." In fact, Jana thought the Victoria's dining room in its current, unrenovated state perfectly presentable. The ceiling was high, the windows long and elegant, the wooden floor not too wavy. Nice round tables, in different sizes. Serviceable chairs. What would one want to change here?

The first thing one would want to change, according to Lily, Cyrus, and Max, was the food.

"We sent our cook to tell the kitchen what we need and see if the current staff can keep up with a more demanding clientele," Lily said. "They're doing some experiments tonight."

Again Jana felt a spasm of protectiveness, this time for the old cooks and bearers she knew had been working at the hotel for so long. How insulted they must have been by this invasion, she thought. She could almost see them quitting en masse—and sending Mr. Dass not into a mere tizzy but a bona fide heart attack. Not that any of them could afford to quit, of course.

She took two sips of water and one of her favorite bearers noticed immediately and stepped forward to refresh her water glass. As the bearer poured, his hands trembled, a drop of water spilled onto the tablecloth, and a look of panic crossed his face. Jana gave him the tiniest little motion of her head and a glance out of the corner of her eye to reassure him.

She was ready for the usual menu of old goat and unidentifiable vegetables, and also for the bearer's apologies for all the things that weren't available. However, tonight, things happened differently. No menu at all was presented.

"They're doing our request," said Lily. "What we want is to combine the best of the world's two most delicious cuisines— French and Parsi."

"That does sound good," Jana said.

When the soup came, it was not the usual mulligatawny but a smooth carrot bisque served with a swirl of sour cream in the middle.

"Our cook's favorite little artistic flourish," Lily chuckled.

Jana tasted it, and was surprised at the effect on her—delight, curiosity . . . how could a mere mouthful of something make you sit up and take notice? "What's that spice?" she asked.

"Oh, a bit of ginger. Our fellows brought their own spices just in case they didn't have what they needed here."

"Mmmmm," said Jana, and took another sip. It had been a long time since she had tasted anything new. The Victoria, the Why Not?, and Mary's competent but not very large repertoire had made up the way she thought about food.

The meal followed with the Kings' new version of old goat. It was falling off the fork, succulent, flavored with spices that seemed one moment to be separate, distinct, and surprising, another moment to blend and reconcile in perfect harmony.

"What did they *do* to it?" Jana asked in amazement.

"Oh, no doubt they've been marinating the meat since yesterday," Lily said.

"We're calling it *dhansak à la King*," Cyrus said.

The meal continued. Jana, her head already reeling from the champagne they'd had before dinner, sipped the red wine Max had brought from France. The men got absorbed in talk of their business plans. Lily smiled indulgently and turned her full attention to Jana.

"So, what's this year's project?" she asked.

"Dreams," Jana said.

Lily looked puzzled. "No projects this year? Just dreaming about things?"

"No, no," Jana said, "the interpretation of dreams. This is our approach for this year, to keep those dam people away."

Lily's eyebrows went up.

"D-A-M," Jana explained. "We feel we can't relax our vigilance. Ramachandran—of the Treasure Emporium, remember? And our newspaper editor, Rambir Vohra, want to make Hamara Nagar the home of dreams."

Lily broke into Cyrus and Max's conversation.

"Darlings, listen to Jana. Maybe she's got the name for this hotel. Instead of the Victory, the Home of Dreams! Wouldn't that be charming? So, Jana, what's your part in this?"

"To answer letters to the editor in the newspaper. And in my salon, in addition to palmistry and cards, I'm offering the interpretation of dreams."

"Lovely! What a sweet idea," Lily gushed.

"I've been brushing up on my Freud," Jana said.

"Very brainy of you," said Lily.

"Actually, brushing up isn't exactly the way to put it, since I've never read anything by him before. But one hears constant mention of the Freudian slip, the Oedipal complex, and that sort of thing. So, when someone tells me their dream, I try to figure out what they are *hiding* from themselves."

"Oh my, oh my, that sounds so very interesting and exotic." Lily leaned forward, and her eyebrows went up. "I have this dream I'm *always* dreaming. Tell me what you think it means."

The two men looked benignly amused.

"Well," said Jana, then stopped. "You'll take this with a grain of salt, won't you? It's strictly for fun."

"Oh, I know, I know," said Lily. "Not that that's bad, mind you! Fun is very important in life. It's serious, if you know what I mean. A necessity."

Cyrus broke in: "Well, come on, Lily, my pet, tell Jana your dream." To the others, he said, "Lily is always waking me up in the middle of the night to tell me her dreams. She gets a groggy audience. By morning, I really can't remember what she told me. Or sometimes I incorporate it into my own dreams. I don't know what I've dreamt and what she's dreamt."

"That sounds romantic," said Max. "The marriage of true minds, and such. You don't even know whose dream is whose. The root-balls to two plants are entwined. Jana, these two are such lovebirds, even after—oh, it must be thirty years by now."

Meanwhile, Lily had been thinking about how to start. She smoothed her hair behind her ears and held her chin in one elegantly manicured hand. "I've had this dream three or four times already. I'm riding on an elephant. The elephant picks me up with its trunk and dumps me in the river! Next I'm swimming with some exotic river animal—a kind of dolphin, I think. I go up onto the shore, dripping wet, and there's my mother, who's been looking for me everywhere. I say to her, Mother, here I am."

Jana took a deep breath, Dr. Freud's ideas popping into her head while she searched for something one could politely say at the dinner table. Elephant? Trunk? That had to pertain to sex. Dolphins, too. And yet, maybe Lily's inhibitions were showing up, in the form of her mother. Was Cyrus the elephant? Max? Some other man?

"Lily dear," said Jana, thinking fast. "Your dream is so marvelous!"

Yes, that was the kind of thing to buy time with while you figured out what to say next. Jana took another sip of red wine, smiled (mysteriously, she hoped), and continued:

"You seem exhilarated about something, yet also worried. Riding on an elephant says to me . . . that you have a huge challenge ahead of you, full of risks."

Stalling further, she said, "What color is the elephant?"

"White," said Lily.

"Aha, a white elephant. That means something that's

cumbersome, not useful, that perhaps has been hanging around the house for a while."

"Max, how about you?" Lily said. "Any dreams for Jana?"

"I always have trouble remembering my dreams," said Max. "I only remember one childhood nightmare. I used to dream that I was falling out of the sky."

"You grew up with pressure," said Lily. "Between Parsi high standards and the competitiveness of the French exam system, you learned to be a high performer. But it took its toll. It was *pressure*."

Jana was grateful to Lily for having done her work for her.

"Lily must be right," Jana said. "But you seem to have survived quite nicely."

Not only survived. Max was lean and fit-looking, no doubt from frequent games of squash and tennis. His clear eyes, his bearing, his strong, well-groomed hands—everything about him exuded health and assurance.

He did not talk as much as Lily and Cyrus but seemed to be taking in everything and weighing it, his lips curving slightly upward in an amused half smile. Every now and then, he gave a little nod.

"Shall we dance?" he now asked Jana. The string band was playing a fox-trot, and people had moved to the floor and were dancing and laughing. Jana, dancing with Max, remembered from the New Year's Eve party at the Bombay Flying Club the feel of his hand pressed confidently against her back, and the way he guided her so skillfully around the floor. Yes, she was deciding, if I do end up getting a husband, it has to be someone who can dance this way.

"Are you playing the cello or the bass fiddle these days?" she asked.

"Only rarely. At family parties, and the like. One gets very busy, you know. And you?"

"Oh, I play mostly for my parrot to dance to."

Max laughed. "Lucky parrot." The band changed from one tune to the next, and Max adapted his pace and steered her in a new direction on the dance floor.

"We heard you yesterday, coming in with the helicopter," Jana said. "My parrot commented that it was a very big, bad bird."

Max chuckled. "Oh, it is that. Would you like to take a ride in it?"

"Oh my, yes," Jana said. "That would be very exciting!"

"I know Cyrus has gotten me into some golf game tomorrow, so we'll fly down to Dehra Dun for that," Max said, "and afterward, we'll have to wait a few days for another fuel delivery to the hotel. But perhaps in a week or ten days' time?"

"Perfect," said Jana.

Cyrus and Lily were also dancing, and she could see them looking over at her, smiling collusively.

The band played the last dance, and then the national anthem. Glancing at her watch, Jana saw that it was near midnight. By this time of night, she had generally long since put Dr. Freud's book down on the night table and turned off the light.

"A nightcap, anyone?" Lily asked.

"Not for me," said Jana.

"We've got to get up tomorrow and hit small balls with long clubs," Cyrus said.

"That sounds violent," said Lily.

"You two look tired—you should toddle off to dreamland," Max told Cyrus and Lily. "I'll see Jana home. Have you got a wrap of some sort?"

"Yes," said Jana, "back in the Viceroy—I mean, the Bombay Room. And also, the photo Lily gave me."

"We'll say good night here, darling," Lily said, and she and Cyrus both hugged Jana.

In the Bombay Room, the glasses had been washed, the bottles lined up neatly at the bar, the ice bucket removed, the magazines stacked, and the pillows plumped and lined up in an orderly row on the sofa. On the table, neatly folded, were Jana's green-and-gold stole and the photo.

Max unfolded the stole and held it out wide, then put it around Jana's shoulders with a gentle, deft movement. She gave a little shiver.

"Cold?" he asked.

"No, not at all." She turned her face to him and smiled.

"Your eyes are exactly the same color green as that shawl," he said.

Even without her glasses, she could see that *his* eyes were a very dark brown, almost black.

"So. The driver will be at the gate," Max said.

They crossed the courtyard, now deserted; only a few lights showed through the windows of the hotel.

"Things close up early here," Max said. "It's very quiet compared to Bombay. Let alone Paris."

"I've been in quieter places," Jana said. "Try a mission station, for example."

Max's face twisted in mock horror. "I don't think I will," he said.

The hotel *chokidar* at the front gate stamped his stick when he saw them coming. The sound was loud enough to bring the driver of the Mercedes-Benz out of the driver's seat (where, Jana knew, he had been dozing) and into an immediately alert, on-duty position beside the car.

"Good evening, sir, madam."

Jana slid onto the soft leather seat, Max beside her, and the car pulled away. They were both out of conversation, but it was comfortable and dreamlike, the car gliding through the dark streets, past the Municipal Garden, between the closed-up shops of the English Bazaar, and into the narrower main street of the Central Bazaar. Max put his hand over hers companionably on the seat, and she was conscious of his warmth, and the piney smell of his skin.

"Sir, we must turn and back up here," the driver said.

Seeing Max's puzzled look, Jana explained: "There's no room to turn in front of the Jolly Grant House. Either we back up, or you can drop me at the gate and go another half mile or so to where there's another turning place."

"We'll stop here, and I'll walk you the rest of the way."

They slid from the cocoon of the back seat into the quiet street.

"Look up," Max said, and she lifted her eyes to an astonishing expanse of stars.

"You can see so many more stars here than in the cities," Max said.

"We're closer to them here."

"Yes, I suppose so."

He guided her back to the Jolly Grant House, one hand at the small of her back.

As they got closer, she started to worry. The euphoria of the champagne and the dancing and the dinner chatter had worn off, and she was wondering. A question popped into her head, one that a Far Oaks schoolgirl, worrying about a new boyfriend, had asked Jana. When do you kiss? Too soon, and it would seem too eager. Too late . . . and . . . well, too late would be too late.

The usual daytime crowds of curious people were safely in their homes, and the bands of children. But . . . there was the driver, watching them from behind . . . and now she could hear Lal Bahadur Pun thumping *his* stick at the front gate, and also at the gate, she saw, stood the second night watchman, complete with Gurkha knife at his belt. The schoolgirl's question of when to kiss was moot.

"Good evening, sir, madam," Lal Bahadur Pun said.

"Good evening, Subedar-Major," said Jana. "Any unusual happenings tonight?"

"Nothing. Thieves don't dare come now. They'd get their heads chopped off."

"Twice," said *chokidar* number two.

"The prospect would frighten anyone off," Jana said.

The mood of the evening was now altered. Jana held out her hand, and Max clasped it in both of his.

"Don't forget the helicopter ride," he said.

"How could I?"

He turned and walked down the street to the waiting car. Jana watched from the gate, then said good night to the watchmen, went through the courtyard, let herself in, and bolted the front door behind her. She peeked into the salon, which was dark, with Mr. Ganguly's cage covered for the night, and then went quietly up the stairs.

For the first time, her bedroom looked to her, if not Spartan, a bit humble, and sparsely furnished. That was what a touch—just a touch—of glamour could do to make you question an otherwise comfortable existence.

The platform bed, with the cotton quilts plumped up, still looked inviting, though, and she got into her summer nightgown and slid between the sheets, wondering whether that bed would be big enough for two people.

Lily Comes for Lunch

The next morning, Jana felt not the slightest bit tired from her late evening and all the champagne and rich food. She swung her legs out of bed, heated her bathwater, and scrubbed in the tin tub, humming "Tuxedo Junction."

When she went down to the salon for breakfast, Mary and Mr. Ganguly both seemed to be waiting like school hall monitors for her to give an account of herself.

"Nice evening, Jana mem?" Mary asked. "King sahib and memsahib are in good health?"

"Yes, they are," said Jana, spreading her toast with butter and guava jelly.

"And the other King sahib? Come down to earth from flying the helicopter?"

"Ye-es," said Jana, finding the question a wee bit impertinent. "They were all very pleasant and showed me a very nice time."

"*Achcha,*" said Mary. The word could have meant just about anything: Is that so? I see. . . . What *did* Mary see? Then Jana remembered that, in Bombay, Mary had never warmed up to the Kings and their friends. Jana wasn't sure why. Maybe the Kings had not paid much attention to Mary. As for Max, Mary had barely met him.

"You remember that Mrs. King is coming for lunch, right, Mary?"

"Of course, madam," said Mary, in her most formal and least approving tone. "What time?"

"Oh, I said one, but I wouldn't count too much on punctuality."

It was closer to two when Lily arrived by automobile at the gate of the Jolly Grant House, and Mary, her face impassive, showed her into the salon. Lily's chirps of appreciation were gratifying to Jana.

"Oh, I do love the *atmosphere*! And this is . . . Mr. Ganguly?"

The parrot was generally on his best behavior for well-dressed women with sparkly jewelry, and he now squawked, "Namasté! Hello! *Bonjour!*"

"The same to you," Lily said. "He's a very brainy bird, isn't he?"

"He likes you," Jana said. "Come along, Mr. Ganguly, let's take Mrs. King up to the tower."

She transferred the bird from his perch to her shoulder, and then led Lily up the stairs into the tower, where the windows were open to the breeze.

"It makes you feel as if you're in a tree house!" Lily said. "Or on a ship sailing along." She peeked through the telescope.

"Oh, my word. You can see little boys herding cattle along the mountain paths."

She crossed the room and looked down into the street. "And an endless parade of people! Without even having to go out of the house."

"Mary's going to bring us some lunch," Jana said. "You don't mind picnicking in the tower, do you?"

"Mind?" said Lily. "Good heavens, no! It's such an adventure!"

They settled into the armchairs, and Mary came with a tray of chicken salad, cheese straws, cauliflower and eggplant curry, fragrant rice, and fruit salad.

"Ah, this looks like a first-class lunch," said Lily, helping herself to everything, which made Mary thaw out and give a hint of a smile.

"Did you sleep well?" Jana asked.

Lily shrugged. "I may have had a bit too much champagne, because I woke up in the middle of the night. Or perhaps it was the *beds*. I think they last got new beds at the hotel during Queen Victoria's time. And you? Did you sleep well?"

"I did, actually," said Jana. "That was a lovely evening. You were so kind to ask me."

"Kind? Good heavens, what nonsense. We were *all* thrilled to see you again. We were worried when we heard that you were popping off on this Himalayan adventure. But you seem happy. Are you?"

"Of course!" Jana said. "I'm quite settled."

"Any music students yet?" asked Lily.

"I was teaching a little boy to play harmonium, but he lost interest. Or, rather, his parents lost interest. But it's all right. Between the fortune-telling salon and the music transcriptions and trying to keep this house from falling down, I have more than enough to do."

"And men," said Lily, with relish. "How about the men in your life?"

"Let's see," said Jana. "There's Lal Bahadur Pun, the *chokidar,* and Munar, the sweeper, and Tilku—he's eleven years old—and, of course, Mr. Ganguly."

The bird, now on his perch, brightened up at the sound of his name.

"I don't mean your *household,* silly," said Lily.

"I know you don't," Jana said, with a laugh and a shrug.

"I meant romance!" Lily's dark eyes gleamed as she got into her favorite subject.

"Don't you think I'm a little old to be worrying about such things?"

"What nonsense!" Lily said. "Who's ever too old? I think you could use a husband."

You and my entire household, Jana thought.

Lily continued: "Actually, you don't have to look. There's one right under your nose."

Jana felt her face growing very red, which she tried to stop, the effort only making her blush more furiously.

"You know who I'm talking about." Lily chuckled. "We just had to watch the two of you dancing together last night."

"Isn't it a little soon after Cécile's death? It seems immoral, somehow."

Lily gave a peal of laughter. "Oh, Jana, you are too deliciously innocent."

"Well, if not immoral, then at least in poor taste."

"Absolutely not," said Lily dismissively. "You should see the ladies in Bombay. They are drooling, trampling on each other in their haste to get close to Max. There are a couple of cinema actresses who have pursued him *relentlessly*. And fathers keep sending him letters proposing matches with their eighteen-year-old daughters."

"Well, I'm afraid *my* father is long out of commission for that," Jana said.

"Cyrus and I will act as your parents," said Lily. "And as Max's."

Jana laughed. The idea was doubly funny; Cyrus and Lily, ten years younger than herself, and five years younger than Max, would be odd parents to either.

"No, really, don't laugh," Lily said. "Shall I bring up the subject?"

"Good heavens, no. I would think that someone as—well, urbane as Max"—once again Jana felt the blood rising to her cheeks—"wouldn't want or need an intermediary. He didn't have one for his French wife, did he?"

"Maybe not," Lily said. "But that was in France. If you're thinking that good manners have anything to do with it, think again. This is the jungle. If you're not going to let someone else do it, my advice to you is: Pounce! Don't dally a minute longer!"

"You make me feel like a cat in wait for a mouse. I'm not actually a very pouncy person," Jana said.

"If you don't pounce," said Lily, "you will be left by the wayside. You have to rethink things. I know that you were brought up to believe that gentleman should make the first move in a romance."

Jana felt the blood throbbing in her temples. She imagined Max with a large sign next to him saying, "Available only while supplies last."

"Don't fret," said Lily. "Max is taken with you. He's like

an apricot hanging on the vine. Give the branch a tiny shake, and he will fall willingly and with a daft smile on his face into your outstretched hands. She who hesitates is lost!"

The Men of the Bombay Years

During the Bombay years, Lily had occasionally tried a bit of matchmaking, but Jana had resisted her efforts. On her own steam, she had met plenty of men. She had learned how to tell which ones were likely to have wives. But there was one situation in which she had fallen completely under the spell of the man's charm and had disregarded all the warning signals, even the dent on his ring finger. Jonathan Lawrence.

He was a businessman from London who had persuaded her to spend two weeks with him in the Andaman Islands, where he was going to buy into a vanilla plantation. Two glorious weeks! An early honeymoon, he called it. They stayed at the plantation owner's sprawling house, and in the mornings, when Lawrence was going over the plantation's records, Jana took tonga rides around the island. The warm breezes, the smell of spices wafting through the air, the turquoise water, the long, lazy evenings—everything seemed such a wonderful dream.

They had flown back to Calcutta and Lawrence had put her on the plane for Bombay, saying that he would be in touch immediately. And then he never had. Not once, and her own letters to him got returned, marked "Addressee no longer at this address." Later, by chance, she saw his picture in the international edition of the *New York Herald Tribune*, along with a woman identified as his wife. They were attending a big conference in Paris.

Among the men who were *not* dreadful, in those years, was a sweet, Anglo-Indian gentleman, long retired from a respected career as a chartered accountant. Aldus Turnduff was the president of the Symphony Lovers' Club of Bombay, and his grandchildren were violin students of Jana's. While Jana gave them lessons, Mr. Turnduff would listen from the next room. Afterward, he would beg Jana to play for him, "a tune or two, my dear." She was happy to oblige, although the adoration made her uncomfortable.

Then one day she received a letter from him proposing marriage, assuring her that all his children and grandchildren approved, and that she would want for nothing. He signed it "your humble suitor."

Mary, her eyes narrowing, guessed what the letter was all about. "Too old," she said.

She's right, Jana thought. Mr. Turnduff was lovely, kind, utterly infatuated with her. But in no time flat, she'd end up being his nurse, and she'd had enough of that with William.

Flattered, touched, sad at the thought of hurting him, she let several days go by before penning a kind but firm rejection. She heard nothing back; and then, the following week, a mutual acquaintance told her that Mr. Turnduff, while presiding over the monthly meeting of his beloved club, had put his hand over his heart and gotten a stricken look on his face. He'd sat down in his chair, and had tried to catch his breath and go on with the proceedings, but had expired before the ambulance came.

"He died of a broken heart," the acquaintance said, more melodramatically than necessary to make Jana feel extremely guilty.

"Sweetie, let *me* introduce you to some men," Lily had said. But none of these introductions had resulted in anything.

A Fashion Problem

The next morning, while she was still mulling over everything Lily had said, Jana got another note on Lily's expensive blue notepaper. It was peppered with exclamation points, so that Jana could almost see Lily bubbling over with enthusiasm and clapping her hands.

"I don't know why I didn't think of this yesterday," wrote Lily. "Let's have a nice little picnic! Just the four of us! We can kill two birds with one stone. Teach the hotel staff what a real picnic is, and let you and Max have a chance to sit and talk quietly, *en plein air! Très intime!* And, by the way, no nasty little soggy sandwiches in crumpled wax paper and bottles of warm lemonade! We'll have real food.

"And—I'll be able to wear the darling little safari suit I got made up for our game-hunting trip in Kenya."

Lily was not to be deterred from her matchmaking, Jana realized. She supposed she ought to be grateful, but the idea of Lily's machinations behind her back made her nervous. Moreover, for a picnic, she had nothing approximating a "darling little safari suit."

Could Feroze Ali Khan make her an outfit in time? She decided to pop across the street to Royal Tailors, where Feroze's cousins were working away, cross-legged on the floor with their old Singers humming in front of them.

"Where is Feroze sahib?" Jana asked.

"Playing with those twin babies," the cousins told her.

"Would you ask him to drop by the Jolly Grant House today, if he has time?"

Lots of *achchas* and affirmative head wiggles reassured her that they would. Feroze would come to her rescue, she was sure. Not that he would like this project much. She knew that Feroze thought trousers for women were ugly, even though he and his workers had made up hundreds of pairs for school-girls for their sports day marching competitions. And Royal Tailors even provided *shorts* for girls' running races, the workers making lewd comments, and Feroze telling them to mind their own business and get the seams straight.

Having left a request for Feroze to stop by, she dashed down to Fab-Fab, where the owner, Keram Chand, was sitting on the platform in front of his shelves of cloth.

"You look worried, Mrs. Laird," he said.

"Well, I have a bit of a wardrobe emergency," she said. "I need to have some picnic clothes made up."

"Picnic is requiring new clothes? Yes, I see. Like trekking, no?"

"Not really like trekking," Jana said. "More like . . . well, a combination of trekking and a garden party. So the fabric needs to be heavy cotton, I think."

Wham! Wham! Wham! Bolts of cloth came flying down from the shelves, Keram Chand pointing out the virtues of each one.

"Khaki color is good for trekking, Mrs. Laird."

"Yes . . . but . . ."

"Nice light green?"

She always gravitated to green. And Lily's darling little safari suit would have to be khaki, she thought, and it would be better to have something different.

She fingered the cloth. Would it shrink, and would the color run? Would it hold up in the tender hands of the *dhobi,* who got the clothes clean by slapping them on the rocks down at the *dhobi ghat*? She hoped so.

Feroze arrived at the Jolly Grant House in the early afternoon, bearing a couple of Sears, Roebuck catalogs and old copies of *Filmfare,* from which he and his customers drew inspiration for their styles. Jana was happy, as always, to see his familiar figure, dignified in his straight trousers, high-necked coat, and astrakhan hat.

"Salaam, Feroze sahib, how are you?"

"Thanks to your prayers, I am fine," Feroze said.

"And your good wife?"

"She too, God be praised."

"And your two adorable babies?"

"They are growing and crying and now giving small-small smiles."

Jana gave a big-big smile at the thought of Feroze, not much younger than herself but husband to the beautiful young Zohra, tickling their twin babies. He did look rejuvenated, certainly happier than he had at this time last year, and apparently having adapted successfully to the fame that had come with his interviews on All India Radio. The philosopher-tailor, they had called him, which, Zohra had told Jana, had temporarily challenged his ability to philosophize. By now, Jana hoped, he had resumed jotting down his thoughts in the small notebook where he also kept his customers' accounts and measurements.

"Feroze, I am invited to a picnic and must have some picnic clothes."

"Very good, Mrs. Laird," Feroze said. "What kind of costume do you require?"

"Cotton trousers and a cotton jacket, using this cloth I bought this morning down at Fab-Fab."

Feroze seemed to be struggling to conceal his disappointment that this, unlike the last project, was not his idea of fashion. He made a head gesture that could signify just about anything: It's all right, it's not all right, we'll make do, I'll reserve judgment, anything you say, Laird memsahib.

"You have my measurements," she said, "same as last year's."

They took the Sears catalogs over to the window, where the light was better, and examined the women's sports clothes section. There were women dressed in flippy little skirts, swinging golf clubs and tennis rackets. Women dressed in bathing costumes and rubber caps decorated with rubber flowers, leaping off diving boards. Finally, they found what they wanted in the pictures of women standing next to their husbands cooking on outside fireplaces. "Back Yard Barbecue," the page announced, and showed ladies' trousers with little waist-length jackets.

"American ladies are picnicking often, I am thinking," Feroze said. "Husbands are cooking, and wives are giving orders?"

"Perhaps," Jana said. "You never know who's really giving the orders."

"That is true, Mrs. Laird, in our households as well. You want these pockets?"

"Pockets would be practical," Jana decided.

"And little flaps on the shoulder?"

"A bit military for my taste," Jana said. "I wish Zohra had time to embroider a nice flower on the pocket."

"An appliqué would be better," Feroze said. "I think she can do that."

"And first of all, the *dhobi* should wash the cloth, in case it shrinks. Or in case the color runs." Jana had learned that lesson the hard way.

"Extremely true," said Feroze.

The details were decided, and Feroze took the cloth and promised to return—Inshallah—in ten days with the finished product.

When the outfit came back from Royal Tailors, it was roomy, and Jana even had to roll up the trouser legs. The cloth had the salty smell of human hands, and it scratched Jana's skin. Somehow, the effect was not one of a "darling little safari suit," but more of a factory worker's uniform spruced up for inspection. However, the appliqué on the pocket, a parrot in bright green, made Jana smile.

"What do you think, Mary?" Jana asked.

Mary's eye scanned the outfit from top to bottom. "Looks like men's clothes, Jana mem," she said.

"I don't think Feroze approved much of it, either," Jana said. "But I believe it's the right thing for—oh, safaris, and picnics, and the like."

Mary made a stern, skeptical face, which only caused Jana to burst out laughing.

"And helicopter rides," Jana added.

Magazine Advice

In the days after Lily's note, Jana had trouble concentrating on her work. The fortunes she told to eager tourists seemed to fall flat. Her interpretations of dreams sounded literal and obvious to her, and she had trouble remembering much more about palmistry than that a strong thumb indicated a strong will. Only Mr. Ganguly was in form, welcoming customers with cheerful namastés and salaams and *bonjours,* picking the appropriate card from the deck of Hindu gods, telling ladies they were beautiful, marvelous, and saying, without even being taught, "Come again, see you later," when they left.

One evening, Jana went to bed early, hoping to get a good night's sleep. But she woke up, Lily's advice on pouncing still going through her head. After lying in the dark for a long time, she switched on the bedside light and picked up a copy of *Filmfare* that Zohra had passed to her. Reading *Filmfare* was

a guilty pleasure, but slightly less guilty, she felt, if you'd borrowed rather than bought it.

She flipped through the pages, looking at the pictures of
starlets in glittering saris and reading the gossip. Then, the
title of an interview with a rising leading lady caught her
eye: "Radhika Talks About How to Catch a Man."

"If you're lucky and your parents get you a good one, this
article is not for you," it said at the top of the page. "But if
you're on your own and looking to be wed, read on."

Above all, the star warned, "Don't be too *nice*. Be fascinating! Be elusive! Play hard to get! Have temper tantrums!"

This went against everything Jana had ever been taught
or had tried to be. She remembered her sister, LouLou, having
a temper tantrum when LouLou was three and Jana was six.
Jana had watched in complete puzzlement as LouLou beat her
heels on the floor and screamed. That must *hurt,* Jana had
thought, the effort involved in having a temper tantrum
seeming a bad bargain to her. Jana usually had better luck
with her mother's directive: "Ask nicely, and we'll see."

Ask nicely . . . how would that work in getting yourself a
man? Better or worse than pouncing or having a temper tantrum? Oh bother, she thought, put the magazine down, and
turned out the light. To her relief, she found herself drifting
off to sleep.

Mr. Ganguly in Jeopardy

·⚭ *An Intruder*

Jana sat bolt upright in her bed, her heart pounding. A nightmare, she thought, but then she realized that she really *was* hearing shouts and scuffling in the courtyard below, and Lal Bahadur Pun yelling to the new co-*chokidar*. Then running footsteps sounded in the street and faded away.

Wrapping her dressing gown around herself, she went out onto the bedroom verandah and called down, "Subedar-Major, what's happening?"

The two night watchmen, grim-faced and puffing, came over near the house and looked up at Jana.

"A man was making a noise on *that* side," said Lal Bahadur Pun, pointing to the far end of the wall. "In the street. So we ran over to see."

"And then," said the second *chokidar*, "another man—very quietly—tried to come over the wall on *that* side." He pointed to the other end of the wall, where the shadows were deeper.

"But I saw him out of the corner of my eye," Lal Bahadur Pun said.

"He didn't get in, did he?"

Lal Bahadur Pun looked chastened. "The wall is very low, madam. He had jumped into the compound. But as soon as he saw me, he turned around and leapt back over the wall. I ran over and climbed over the wall myself and chased him down the street. I got almost close enough to give him a good whack with my stick. But then he disappeared. I decided I needed to come back here to stand guard. Maybe someone was just trying to lure me away, I thought. So I came back."

"What did he look like? How was he dressed?"

"Just a *goonda*," Lal Bahadur Pun said. "Low-life man. I didn't see his face. He moved very quickly."

"If he thought he was going to get into the house," Jana said, "he was very stupid."

"No one will get in, madam," said Lal Bahadur Pun firmly. "Please go back inside. You can sleep."

I rather doubt that, thought Jana. She stood on the balcony, from where she had a good view of the street. It was absolutely dark and deserted, the storefronts shuttered up. She listened for human sounds but heard nothing except some owls calling softly to each other, far away.

"Madam, please, there is no danger," Lal Bahadur Pun said.

"All right," said Jana. "We'll talk about this in the morning."

She went back inside but could not get to sleep. Was the intruder trying to get at Mr. Ganguly? At one point, she got up, went out to the verandah door, and looked out. Lal Bahadur Pun and his friend were patrolling, occasionally meeting near the front gate to mutter to each other. Close to dawn, when the town was starting to wake up, she heard the clip-clop of mules on the street and, finally, fell asleep.

Miss O's Birthday Party

With all the turmoil, Jana had almost forgotten about Miriam Orley's seventieth birthday party, and now she wondered whether she should take Mr. Ganguly with her. He always was popular at parties. She worried, though, about the three-mile walk through some patches of woods that were way too quiet, even deserted. She pictured would-be kidnappers lying in wait to snatch Mr. Ganguly off her shoulder.

In the end, she decided to take a rickshaw there and back. With four strong men surrounding her, Mr. Ganguly in his carrying cage unobtrusively on the seat beside her, and the top to the rickshaw raised, she would feel safe. Moreover, she would ask Lal Bahadur Pun to get rickshaw pullers person-ally known to him as reliable.

So here she was now, rolling speedily through the Cen-tral Bazaar, the men shouting at passersby to get out of the way. Soon they turned off the bazaar road, onto Maharajah's Hill.

Jana did not know this part of town very well, and had not been here since the year before, while searching for Mr. Ganguly when he flew out the door of Bandhu Sharma's jail. There were several villas built in the nineteenth century, a few from the early twentieth. Most of the houses were large and white, with filigree stone white walls edging the road. The exceptions were some pastel-colored bungalows with red corrugated tile roofs and a gray stone structure reminiscent of a medieval European castle.

Mr. Powell's house, identified on the gate as dating from 1928, was one of the smaller, less ostentatious ones. Spot-lessly whitewashed, spare, and angular, it had a flat roof and a pebbled courtyard. With Mr. Ganguly's cage in one hand and the birthday gift for Miriam in the other, Jana climbed out of the rickshaw and agreed with the men on a time to come back for her.

An old bearer heard her from the house and came hob-bling out to take Mr. Ganguly's cage. Then he led Jana around the back of the house to a courtyard, where a table had been set up for the birthday lunch.

"Mrs. Laird, how good of you to come."

Mr. Powell, in his off-duty attire of windowpane shirt, dark green tie, and neatly buttoned brown cardigan, still conveyed the same sense of order, calm, and propriety as he did in his workaday high-necked white jacket. His two dachshunds now came scampering toward Jana, giving her shrill barks of welcome. Mr. Ganguly went into a threat position, puffing up his chest and, to the best that he could in the carrying cage, opening his wings.

"Albert! Victoria!" Mr. Powell said. "Here! Lie down! Stay!"

The dogs retreated to a position at the edge of the courtyard, their two bodies close, like sausages in a pan.

"You can take your parrot out of his cage if you wish," Mr. Powell said. "The dogs won't bother him."

"Oh, the parrot! I've been hearing so much about him," came a voice from the corner of the terrace, and Jana turned to see a tiny, fragile-looking old woman sitting in a wooden armchair under a sun umbrella. She was dressed in a lavender, blue, and green floral print, with a light blue cardigan and a filmy white scarf around her neck, and her snow-white hair was neatly combed. The face had once been beautiful, Jana thought, and the bones were still regally shaped. She wore stylish sunglasses, the kind Jana had admired at Sharp Eyes Vision Care.

"Mrs. Laird," Mr. Powell said, "I must introduce you to Miriam's aunt Sylvia. Mrs. Laird, Mrs. Sylvia Foster."

Jana, with Mr. Ganguly now on her shoulder, stepped across the courtyard and took the woman's outstretched hand. She held it gently for a moment, half-afraid that a normal handshake would crush the fragile bones.

"I'm Janet, Mrs. Foster. Or Jana, if you prefer."

"I will call you Jana," Aunt Sylvia said. "And bring your parrot a little closer. I have very little eyesight left, but I detect a lovely flash of green."

Mr. Ganguly had decided that the tiny yet oddly pretty person in front of him was French. *"Bonjour, madame,"* he said.

"Oh! He has lovely manners."

"Especially when he likes someone," Jana said.

"What is his name, again?"

"We call him Mr. Ganguly," Jana said.

"I had a parrot once," said Aunt Sylvia. "Perhaps sixty years ago now. Doesn't seem possible. We called it Lucky."

"Sometimes he calls himself that," Jana said. "Perhaps he hears me saying I'm lucky to have him. Would you like to hold him?"

"I'll have to rest my arm like this," Aunt Sylvia said. "But see if he'll stay on it."

Jana gently transferred the bird from her own shoulder to Aunt Sylvia's forearm, where he sat, apparently at ease.

"He seems very calm and happy in your presence," Jana said.

"Oh yes, birds do," said Aunt Sylvia.

Just as Jana was wondering whether other guests would be coming to this party, a young Anglo-Indian man and woman who looked to be in their twenties arrived and were introduced as Mr. Powell's niece and her husband. Slim and stylish, they reminded Jana of the Duke and Duchess of Windsor in their younger days.

"Maureen . . . and Cyril," Mr. Powell said. "Mrs. Laird."

"We've *heard* about you!" Maureen said. "And your parrot!"

"You're very kind," said Jana, and shook hands with both.

"This is all the family we have here," Mr. Powell explained to Jana. "The rest have all gone—to the U.K., to Australia, to Canada. Or died."

He said it matter-of-factly. Why, Jana wondered, had *he* had not emigrated, too?

"And where's the birthday girl?" Maureen asked.

"I asked her for a little later than the rest of you," Mr. Powell said. "She thinks she's coming for her regular Sunday afternoon tea with Aunt Sylvia. Oh, thank you, Jacob John."

Aha, thought Jana. Jacob John. The bearer Mary had told her about: Tamil-speaking, from South India, devoted to Aunt Sylvia—but paid by Miriam. He shuffled back and forth with trays of cucumber sandwiches, Marmite sandwiches, cake, *pakoras,* samosas, peanut brittle, and éclairs. Then he set up the pitcher of lemonade and brought out a huge teapot covered with a cozy.

A distant crunch of rickshaw wheels on the gravel could be heard.

"She's here!" Mr. Powell said.

A moment later, Miriam herself was on the patio. When she saw all the people and the table piled with presents, she let out a cry and brought her hands to her mouth.

Mr. Powell, who had a surprisingly strong bass voice, started singing "Happy Birthday to You," and the rest joined in; even Mr. Ganguly added some piercing, though generally in-tune, notes. Miriam beamed, looking twenty years younger than her true age.

"Cousin Miriam, forever young," said Mr. Powell. "Age cannot wither her! Many happy returns of the day."

The party lasted until the shadows grew long. Jana felt it was bittersweet, the gaiety tempered by nostalgia and mourning for days gone by. It was clear, however, that these people, in earlier times, had known how to party. Mr. Powell started telling stories of fancy dress balls in Calcutta, New Year's Eve celebrations, dances at various clubs. Miriam told stories of Christmas parties at the Coral Club, when Father

Christmas arrived on a camel or an elephant and distributed presents out of a huge red-and-white satchel.

Jana noticed how the other guests refilled Aunt Sylvia's teacup and brought her favorites from the buffet without needing to ask what she wanted. Mr. Ganguly stayed with the old lady the entire time, Aunt Sylvia from time to time tickling him under the chin.

After the party, Jana and Miriam shared a rickshaw to the Central Bazaar.

"A lovely party," Miriam said, briefly leaning back on the cracked leather seat and closing her eyes. "It was kind of you to come."

"Not at all—it was an honor," Jana said. "I didn't know you had an aunt. How old is she?"

"Sylvia?" Miriam calculated for a moment. "She will be— ninety-two next birthday."

"Good heavens," Jana said. "That means she was born in . . ."

"In 1869," said Miriam.

"Oh, my."

"Yes. The same year as Mohandas K. Gandhi."

Jana sighed. "But Sylvia, unlike Gandhi, is still here."

"Yes, that's the benefit of being obscure, isn't it, now? The assassins leave you alone."

Jana pondered this sober observation for a moment and then said, "Mr. Ganguly seemed to be having a lovely time with her."

"Yes, she's a sensitive soul. There was no doubt some little current of understanding between the two of them that the rest of us weren't privy to."

Jana laughed. "She seems to be perfectly compos mentis."

"Oh! More than most people half her age," Miriam said.

"She puts me to shame with her memory. Her eyesight's very bad, of course. But her hearing is quite remarkable, and she never forgets a song."

"I wish I could say the same thing for myself! I'm quite struggling to remember the tunes our butler taught me when I was twenty!"

"Oh, Aunt Sylvia remembers everything. She's a walking encyclopedia of news events, too. Except for the walking part. She can get from her bedroom to the patio and back."

"Everyone seems very devoted to her."

"Oh, they are, they are."

Jana wondered whether Miriam's own devotion to Aunt Sylvia was one of the things that had kept her from taking the plunge and emigrating, as so many others of her family had done.

"It's close to the end of the term at Far Oaks, isn't it?" Jana asked. "Does that mean exams and so forth?"

"Oh yes," said Miriam wearily. "My least favorite part of teaching. Actually, my enthusiasm for the work itself is beginning to wane. I felt rather guilty when they gave me the party last week. All these people acting as if they wanted me to stay on *another* forty years. That would bring me up to age one hundred and ten."

Jana chuckled. "It does seem as if one could take one's retirement by age one hundred, at least."

Miriam was silent for a while.

Jana said, "You've never thought of joining your relatives abroad?"

"Oh, I have, certainly. . . . Maureen and Cyril will doubtless leave before long. But while Sylvia's still alive . . ."

"She seems very happy at Mr. Powell's."

"Yes, of course, but I'm her closer relative and her favorite."

An unspoken comment hung in the air: *Perhaps there's not much longer to wait, anyway.*

"If I tell you a secret," Miriam said suddenly, "can you keep it?"

"Of course," Jana said.

"I have . . . a pen pal in Australia."

Miriam paused, then launched into an explanation: "Five years ago, I organized a pen pal exchange between my Latin students and those of a teacher in Perth. Of course, the teacher and I had to write to each other several times to get things set up and to match up the students. After that, however, we never stopped writing. I actually sent him— something I had written."

"Your book of poems!" said Jana.

"How did you know about that?" Miriam's eyebrows went up in surprise.

"Quite by chance, I found a copy at the Book Depot. I bought it, actually. The poems are *very* good," Jana said.

"I wrote them long ago," Miriam said with a sigh, "then kept them in a drawer for several years before seeing if anyone wanted to publish them. I don't know what on earth compelled me to send the book to Marcus . . . Oh, that's his name. Marcus Phillips. Somehow, we've gotten on a first-name basis. It's funny, how one gets to know someone in letters. Better than in real life, sometimes, I suspect."

Miriam continued: "He was—and is still—a widower, and when we set up the pen pal program, he was on the verge of retirement from teaching. He's since done that, and bought a bed-and-breakfast place outside the city. He says he's enjoying it immensely, and only one thing is lacking."

The rickshaw was rolling along, somehow inviting confidences between the passengers. Mr. Ganguly also seemed to be listening, his head cocked and one eye fixed on Miriam.

"Jana, he wants me to come to Australia and *marry* him." With a start, Jana realized that Miriam was probably the one who wrote into the newspaper asking the significance of kangaroo and koala dreams!

She wondered what this Australian suitor of Miss Miriam Orley's could possibly look like, and, as if reading her mind, Miriam pulled an airmail envelope out of her handbag.

"I just received this," Miriam said, extracting a photo.

The man was so comically odd-looking that Jana had trouble suppressing a laugh. *Gnomish* was the word that came to mind. Marcus Phillips was mostly bald, with a head that actually came to a point, and ears to match. He did have an amiable expression, though, and an innocence about him that Jana found endearing.

"I think he's quite nice-looking," said Miriam, which made Jana smile and nod, "but then, I'm a bit prejudiced in his favor because he writes so beautifully. His letters are so interesting, and he can be quite funny. And, of course, he taught Latin."

"By definition, a civilized man," Jana said.

Miriam took this gentle ribbing well. "I really don't know what to do. Just suppose I scrape the boat passage together, and give notice to the school, and go all the way out there—and don't like him? Then what?"

Jana took a deep breath. "I've been in the same kinds of situations myself," she said. "I gave notice to the nawab and packed up all my things and dragged Mary and Mr. Ganguly up here . . . but what if the Jolly Grant House had been uninhabitable? What if I'd disliked the town? Sometimes, one takes a leap of faith. Besides, maybe going to Australia is worthwhile in itself. If Mr. Phillips turns out to be not your cup of tea, there might be other reasons to stay in Australia once you get there."

Miriam shook her head. "I just don't know. Seems like a big step, at my age."

"Will it be a smaller step next year?"

Miriam let out her breath. "No, I suppose you're right."

Jana looked at Mr. Ganguly and wondered if he would suddenly come out with *"Carpe diem!"* or *"Tempus fugit!"* But he was slumped in his carrying case, seemingly trying to blot out the ride. He really did not like wheeled transport, motorized or otherwise.

"There is one more little thing," Miriam said. "My parents died deeply in debt, and I felt I had to pay back the creditors to preserve the family honor."

"You could send money orders from Australia."

"I want to wrap things up here first," Miriam said.

There was a pause, and then Jana asked, "How long do you think it would take you to finish paying off the debts?"

"I hope to have it done in a year or two," Miriam said.

"What were the debts for?"

"My father had borrowed from all his friends, in order to set up—of all things—a saloon. The venture failed miserably."

Miriam was paying for debts incurred for a saloon? Jana felt a wave of irritation. She also remembered what Mary and Lal Bahadur Pun had told her about Miriam paying the school fees of the children of some of the school servants. A teacher's salary would not permit one to be very much of a philanthropist, Jana thought, and pay off family debts at the same time. Was Miriam being a martyr? Her parents certainly didn't care now whether she paid off their debts. They were in a place where assets and liabilities no longer counted. Wasn't it about time that Miriam lived her own life?

"I think you should start making plans to go to Australia," said Jana firmly. "Here and now."

"Hic et nunc," piped up Mr. Ganguly, *"hic et nunc."*

"That's extraordinary," said Miriam. "Where did he pick that up?"

"I believe he heard you say it, at my house."

"Couldn't have been more than once or twice," Miriam said.

Jana returned to press her—and Mr. Ganguly's—point: "See—we both think you should go to Australia sooner rather than later."

Miriam sighed. "But there's also Aunt Sylvia."

They fell into silence. Miriam put the picture of Marcus Phillips back into her handbag. Jana looked out at the scenery sliding by, the white mansions, the patches of forested hillside. Mr. Ganguly closed his eyes and offered no more opinions until they got back to the Jolly Grant House. Then, when they had descended from the rickshaw and Miriam was headed back to the school, he gave a good-bye flap of his wings and called, *"Hic et nunc."*

✂ Kenneth in Town, Bearing Gifts

Kenneth Stuart-Smith was not only back in town, he was back with offerings bought at the American embassy commissary in Delhi: a case of olives, half a dozen tins of Australian butter, and a case of anchovies.

"Very good, sahib!" Mary said.

Stuart-Smith had also brought presents for the rest of the household, which he distributed in the salon. There was a tin of ghee for Mary, a pack of *biris* for Munar, a shirt for Tilku, and a very loud whistle for Lal Bahadur Pun. The din in the room rose as everyone tried to tell Stuart-Smith what had happened the night of the attempted break-in at the Jolly Grant House.

"We should get a couple of dogs," Tilku said. "Some really fierce ones."

Mary did not like dogs, having been bitten as a child. She

pointed out, "If we have dogs in the courtyard, then we will have to keep them chained up in the daytime when customers are coming in."

"Yes, it's not really the best thing to attract the tourists," Jana said. She turned to Kenneth. "You were right: we did need an extra *chokidar* on guard at night. But even though we hired one, someone had the cheek to try to get in. There was a team of two men, and one of them acted as a decoy to draw attention away from the house while the other came over the wall. I'm convinced that it's Mr. Ganguly they want."

"Definitely the thief is wanting Mr. Ganguly," Tilku said.

Mary interrupted him. "I have an idea," she said. "You know how a hunter uses a decoy? I think *we* should use a decoy. We will lure the thief—or thieves—in and make them *think* that they have succeeded in kidnapping Mr. Ganguly. But really, they will be taking away *another* bird—which we are passing off as Mr. Ganguly. Then after that, they'll go away and not bother us anymore."

Mary continued: "In the meantime, we take Mr. Ganguly to a different location. When the other bird is stolen, we make a big announcement in the papers. Then we let a little bit of time go by and we fetch Mr. Ganguly and say we have gotten another bird."

"There's a problem with that plan," Kenneth Stuart-Smith said. "Mr. G has become so famous that once we get him back here, it will be all too obvious that he is the real Mr. G. Then the whole cycle of attempted kidnapping will start all over again. Plus, if people do believe that you no longer have Mr. G, your fortune-telling business will suffer. Who knows, maybe tourism in the entire town will suffer without one of its major attractions."

Jana said, "It also wouldn't be fair to the decoy bird. Who knows what the birdnappers would do to *him*?"

"We'll just—" Mary and Lal Bahadur Pun broke in together. "We'll just have to catch the thief! In the act of stealing the decoy! And get the decoy back, too."

"I think that's right," Jana said thoughtfully. "We must catch the thief."

"Where could Mr. Ganguly stay?" Tilku asked.

"I think he could stay with Miss Miriam Orley," said Mary. "She is a kind lady, and she can keep a secret. He already has a name for her. He calls her Hic et Nunc. I'm not sure what that means."

"It means *ekdum* in Latin," Jana said. "Yes, he does like Miss Orley. But think of him being in the dormitory with all those girls, and the school bearers and sweepers who work in the dormitory. Somebody will notice right away, and before long the news will be everywhere."

"Maybe Mr. Ramachandran can let him stay at his house," said Mary. "His children could keep the bird occupied."

"Oh no, not safe at all, with everyone coming and going," Jana objected.

"Editor Rambir?"

"Too busy. Mr. Ganguly would be alone in the flat the whole day. He needs company." Jana thought some more. "I'll mull this over," she said. "We may be on the right track."

In the meantime, Lal Bahadur Pun suggested, they could get a couple more men to be on guard at night.

A Scheme to Protect Mr. Ganguly

"I like Miss Orley's aunt," Jana said to Mary. "And the bearer you told me about, Jacob John. You know, Mr. Ganguly really seemed to take to Aunt Sylvia. Indeed, he put up rather a fuss when we left. Perhaps he could stay with her while we have the decoy here. Do you think Jacob John and she could take care of him? They're in such an out-of-the-way place, on Maharajah's Hill. You can't hear much from one house to the next. If—when—Mr. Ganguly screeches, it's not going to attract much attention. What do you think?"

Mary considered the idea and came up with another advantage: "And I can get the news from Jacob John, at church. In Tamil, so no one will understand!"

"Well, I would visit, too," Jana said. "I can sneak over there without everyone in the bazaar figuring it out. In any case, it's not going to be for a very long time."

"He'll need a sleeping cage," Mary said. "I'll ask Jacob John if he can make a temporary one out of some screens."

"That might work for a short while," Jana said, although she hated to think of Mr. Ganguly's sleep being disturbed. "Well, then. It only remains for us to get the decoy. The fake Mr. Ganguly. Where *can* we find another bird?"

They were working on this question when the sound of a bagpipe floated up from the terrace below.

"Maybe Lal Bahadur Pun has an idea," Jana said. Mary went to the back verandah and called down. The tune stopped with a little sigh, and a few moments later Lal Bahadur Pun was in the salon.

"There is a big village fair a few miles out, starting tomorrow," he said. "All sorts of peddlers go there. There might be bird sellers, or fortune-tellers who would be willing to get rid of their birds. Mary and I can go to the fair and see what we can find."

"It has to be an Indian ringneck, male," said Jana. "Make sure it has the black ring around the neck. And try to get an intelligent one. One that talks as much as possible."

It was a tall order for a shopping commission. But neither

Mary nor Lal Bahadur Pun was the type to be daunted for long. Jana remembered what they had been through. Given their life experiences—Mary literally up from the gutter, and Lal Bahadur Pun a survivor of the jungles of World War II—this was actually rather a small assignment.

The Temporary Bachelor

⁕ *Krishan Takes Leave*

The cook-bearer—Krishan, right, that was his name—was standing there looking anguished and apologetic, and Rambir wondered what could possibly be the matter.

"Sahib," Krishan said, "you see . . . my father." His face twisted. "He is gone."

"I'm sorry."

"Yes, sahib. He has gone to be reunited with God."

The phrase tugged at Rambir's own heart. What if his own father died suddenly, and went to be reunited with God—or wherever one went—and had never been reunited with *him*, Rambir?

"And I am the oldest son," Krishan said, with an air of being both proud and burdened by this fact.

"Yes, I too," Rambir said. (For what it's worth, he added to himself.) "I quite understand."

"So now, sahib, I must go to my village."

Yes. Rambir could see the funeral pyre on the banks of a stream, the mourners wailing, Krishan saying his good-byes, putting the torch to the sticks.

"Of course, go," he said hurriedly. "For how many days, do you think?"

"One week, sahib. Maybe ten days."

Rambir gulped. It *had* to be while Ritu was away, didn't it. When it rained, it poured. Now come, come, he told himself sternly, life and death are not scheduled for *your* convenience.

Krishan was still waiting for an answer.

"Achcha," Rambir said. And then: "Wait." He went into his bedroom, got some bills from his wallet, returned, and handed them to the cook-bearer.

"To help pay for the rites," he said.

Krishan acknowledged the gift with a mournful namasté.

"Sorry to inconvenience . . ."

"No problem," said Rambir quickly, "no problem."

"Sahib needs breakfast?"

"I'll get something at the Why Not?" Rambir said.

❧ *Ramachandran as Cheerful as Ever*

"So, old shoe," said Ramachandran, "you are a bachelor this week."

"Yes," said Rambir, "and I'm starving!"

"Didn't your new cook-bearer make you any breakfast?"

Rambir shook his head. "His father died. He had to go back to his village to perform the rites."

"Oh, that's sad," Ramachandran said sympathetically. "And when is Ritu coming home?"

"Not for almost two *weeks*," Rambir groaned.

"Aha. The cat's away! But the mouse is not playing, ho ho!"

"No, hardly," Rambir said. He was offended by the very suggestion—even a joking one—that he would do something dishonorable behind Ritu's back.

"Sorry, old chap. You know I was only ragging you."

Mr. Joshi had arrived with their tea, and his eyebrows went up in surprise when Rambir asked for potato *parathas,* a chili omelet, and a double order of toast and jam.

"Hungry this morning, editor sahib?"

Rambir frowned at this personal remark, but Ramachandran said, "Yes, yes, let's get some nourishment into this man here. He's wasting away from overwork and bachelordom."

"Bachelorhood," Rambir corrected.

"Dom, hood . . . same principle applies."

Mr. Joshi retreated to the back of the shop and barked at his helper to fry up that omelet *ekdum.* In the meantime, Ramachandran was still pursuing the same theme.

"So, bachelor life is not to your taste."

Rambir took a big gulp of his tea and said, "Bachelor life is . . . not so easy for a married man to go back to. It's too . . . too *quiet* in the flat."

Mentally, he added, Must you plunge in the knife and twist it? You have all the comforts and pleasures of a traditional family life. *Your* wife isn't in constant demand by the rest of the world. All she does is produce babies, which slip out of her like eggs from a chicken.

"Well, come to our house," Ramachandran was saying, "and we'll give you some good South Indian food."

"How's the new *puja* room coming?" Rambir asked.

"Oh, workmen milling about here and there, spilling buckets of plaster and putting up the wrong color of paint."

"In other words, normal progress."

Ramachandran's laugh, Rambir thought, was generous, given that the remark was not so very humorous. Rambir said, "Well, when it's done, Padma can do her morning devotions in style."

Ramachandran beamed proudly. He's always so cheerful, Rambir thought. Ramachandran had been cheerful in their days at Benares Hindu University, when he was sixty pounds thinner, and a socialist and a freedom fighter, and had argued fervently, on the debate team, "Resolved: that love marriages produce more happiness than arranged ones" and "Resolved: that family planning must be instituted immediately on all levels of society."

In fact, Ramachandran's good cheer had failed for only about ten minutes, when, just before receiving his degree, he had gotten a letter from his parents ordering him to give up his "little flirtation" with a fellow student and come home and get married. The cheer had returned, in force, when his parents had sent a photo of the wife they had found for him and told him the size of the dowry. Ramachandran had remarked to Rambir that he was beginning to see the wisdom of traditional ways.

Mr. Joshi was back, with the first installment of Rambir's breakfast. Rambir attacked the chili omelet, and then devoured the toast. When the *parathas* arrived, he dug voraciously into them, as Ramachandran watched in some amazement.

"So, how's the press today?" Ramachandran asked.

"Pressing," said Rambir.

"Cheer up, old chap! Ritu will be back before you know it. Everything will be fine. Soon, soon, mark my words."

"Not soon enough," Rambir said.

✂ *Clean Clothes*

That evening, when Rambir returned from the press even later than usual, the *dhobi* was on the back steps to the flat, and Rambir drew a sigh of relief that the man had waited for him. He unlocked the padlock and let himself and the *dhobi* into the flat, where the man untied his bundle and put the clean laundry on the dining table.

"Count clothes, please, sahib," the *dhobi* reminded him.

Rambir went through the stacks of shirts, singlets, trunks, and socks.

"Forty-six?"

"No, sahib, fifty-three pieces."

Rambir, at first puzzled, realized that he was supposed to count each sock separately.

Did Ritu pay the *dhobi* monthly or weekly? And how much? Rambir saw from the man's expectant expression that it was weekly.

"Let's see, I owe you . . ."

"Two rupees, eight annas, sahib."

Was that high or low? Rambir had no idea, but the man seemed honest, and Ritu generally had good instincts about the people she hired. He reached into his pocket for the money.

"This week's clothes, sahib?" the *dhobi* asked, obviously not in the slightest deceived by Rambir's attempts to hide his ignorance of the whole laundry process.

"Oh, right. Just one moment." Rambir made a pass through the flat, getting his towel from the bathroom, a tea towel from the kitchen, and his socks, shirts, and undergarments from the corner of the bedroom.

"Count again, sahib" was the *dhobi*'s next reminder. "Each piece, one."

"Forty-seven," Rambir said.

"I am taking forty-seven now, I will bring back forty-seven next week," the *dhobi* said firmly.

"Right."

The man turned his back to go, and something about his knotted calves showing below his *dhoti* and his sharp elbows sticking out from under his shawl made Rambir give a start.

The man was going about in such thin, ragged clothes! And, of course, he had washed the clothes in a mountain stream that must have been barely above freezing.

Rambir thought of the fiery editorials he had written on social issues. "How does such a benighted policy benefit the common man?" he would thunder. Right, here was one of those common men he was always talking about. But did he have any idea what this *dhobi* thought about anything? What his life was really like?

"You're going home now?" he asked the man.

"Yes, sahib."

"Where is that?"

The man named a village five miles outside town, and Rambir realized that he would have to walk along a stretch of road where there were reputed to be leopards.

"Do you have an electric torch?" said Rambir.

"No, sahib, I know the way, and my eyes are very good in the dark."

"I see. Well." What could he say to this man? He looked at the pile of neatly ironed shirts the *dhobi* had brought back. In fact, everything was ironed, socks and underwear as well. The man had taken the dirt and wrinkles and ink stains, the evidence of the fatigue of Rambir's workweek, and he had returned order and control, so that Rambir could begin the next week's work. There was *energy* in clean clothes, some-how. Clean laundry . . . a clean slate . . . Rambir's mind started working on a thought piece for his newspaper.

"You have done good work," Rambir said finally.

The man looked bewildered.

"Sahib requires?"

"Nothing else," said Rambir. "Just . . . just go safely on that road. You have a family, no?"

"My wife and three small ones."

"May they be safe and in good health," Rambir said.

"Namasté, sahib." Still frowning with some puzzlement, the *dhobi* picked up the bundle of dirty clothes, and made his way out the door.

As he watched the *dhobi* disappear, the image of Krishan also came to Rambir's mind. By now, his cook-bearer must have walked the twenty miles of rocky road and steep trails to his ancestral home. Rambir remembered pictures he had seen of remote rural villages: small stone houses, chickens wandering in and out, cattle sheds nearby. Was Krishan exhausted and heartbroken, dutifully comforting his ancient mother? Or was he relieved, gossiping with his friends, getting drunk on home brew? The lives of others were such closed books.

Rambir Makes Dinner

Even philosophers, even newspaper editors have to eat. By now, it had been many hours since the meal with Ramachandran at the Why Not? Tea Shop, and, of course, there was no nice hot plate of rice and dal and vegetable curry waiting for Rambir. His stomach was gurgling and squeezing, and the choices were dwindling. He could go to the Victoria for bland Western food, or to Kwality for more interesting Chinese fare, but the expense stopped him in his tracks. The Why Not? and its rival, the Superior, were by now shuttered up for the night. I should have jumped on Ramachandran's invitation! he thought. Too late now. It's all right, he decided. I shall fend for myself!

Feeling vaguely heroic, he steeled himself to enter the kitchen. The tiny room always caused him anxiety. Ritu thought it was fine, and Krishan accomplished miracles in it without complaint, but to Rambir, it was alien territory. There was a sink with a cold-water tap, a table holding a kerosene stove, a shelf on the wall with a couple of cooking pots, and a small stand with a drawer containing some utensils.

He'd make tea and rice and . . . what would he put with the rice? He looked into the pantry, which was not a separate room but a recessed rectangle in the wall. On the top shelf were tins labeled in Ritu's tidy handwriting: "Rice," "Tea," "Sugar," "Salt," "Atta." On the next shelf, there were three smaller tins with colorful labels, things Ritu had bought at Pahari Provisioners: pineapple juice, tomato juice, and peas. Emergency rations, she called them. On the bottom shelf was a rectangular tin of Britannia biscuits. Plain ones, not even the ones with apricot jam centers.

Rice and—a curry of peas? But what else would go into it? An onion—he knew that—and some garlic, and some spices. Aha! There was the mortar and pestle, on the lower shelf of the stand that held the fridge. But nothing for the mortar and pestle to grind up.

Besides, rice involved boiling water, and that involved using the stove. He knew you had to do something to the wick. Was there enough kerosene in the stove, anyway? What a nasty smell that stuff had.

Rambir opened the tin labeled "Tea" and peered at the tea leaves. They looked like dried scraps of debris. How much of this unpromising material did you put in the water, once you'd persuaded it to boil?

Perhaps he could live without tea this evening. Meanwhile, he would subsist on emergency rations. He managed to find the tin opener—which looked to him quite unfriendly, practically lethal—on the shelf below the fridge, and he bravely opened the tin of tomato juice and the tin of peas. He drained the water from the peas into the sink, put them into a bowl, and poured the tomato juice into a glass. Then he went into the sitting-dining room, sat down at the head of the table, and ate his meal of cold, metallic-tasting peas and tomato juice.

Now, for a sweet. Britannia biscuits, with no tea? Washed down with *water*?

"For the want of a nail, the shoe was lost." Rambir had recently written an editorial about the need to coordinate practical and theoretical education. With a sudden flash of insight, he *felt* the truth of what he had been saying in that piece. He now chastised himself: I didn't even know the real meaning of what I was advocating.

Still, what about all the English poetry he knew? Wasn't that of *some* use? Well, yes, yes, it was a comfort to quote English poetry when faced with a practical problem. But, he concluded, it would be even better to have the skills to solve the problem.

❦ *Listening to the Radio*

By now, it was ten o'clock and time for the late evening news. Rambir turned the dial on his Motorola, and the silvery tones of Roshan Menon flowed into the room. Roshan Menon's voice reminded him of Ritu's, smooth and elegant, with precise diction. Ritu, despite her humble origins, had picked up that polished way of speaking. He pictured her in the classroom, lecturing about the laws of gravity. "For every action . . . there is an equal and opposite reaction." Ritu would make such a statement sound like poetry.

After the news, Rambir fiddled with the dial, looking for the BBC or the Voice of America. As if from outer space, squeaks, fizzes, crackles, and squeals streamed into the room.

Finally, he heard English being spoken, and realized that he was listening to Radio Ceylon's Friday night hit parade.

Without Ritu there with him, the lovelorn dedications seemed even sillier than usual—in fact, downright painful to listen to. "To darling beautiful Sushila, with all my love, from your faithful swain, Ranjit." "Premila, my sweetie pie, you put honey in my life. Your Vikram."

"Now for the last request of the evening," said the announcer. "Our program goes by so quickly, doesn't it? Well, that's just the way life is. You hear your favorite songs a few times, and then it's done. Anyway, here comes the favorite of the week! Love Potion Number 9! From the United States of America!

"And here's a nice dedication. To the beautiful and brainy Ritu: Forbidden fruits are the best. I've slid down the inclined plane of love. This song is for you, with thanks, from . . ."

At this point static interrupted the broadcast, and Rambir could not hear the name of the person. Could it be mere coincidence? There were plenty of people named Ritu in the world. But beautiful and brainy? And *inclined plane*? He felt sick to his stomach, a chill suddenly invading his entire body.

New Birds for Old

✤ Nasty

Loud screeching from the salon awoke Jana. She pulled on her dressing gown and went downstairs to find Mary distraught, with blood trickling from a wound on her hand. A saucer was upside down in the cage, with spinach and boiled rice scattered on the removable tray underneath.

"I was going to give him food and water, Jana mem, but he bit me!"

Jana said, "But yesterday, we didn't have any trouble."

The fake Mr. Ganguly had been quiet, even lethargic, when Mary and Lal Bahadur Pun had brought him back from the fair. They'd put him into the cage, where he'd promptly fallen asleep.

Jana grimaced. "Maybe the people who sold him to you drugged him in some way. Oh dear. This creature looks as if he's going to be pretty useless for fortune-telling. They told you he was a fortune-telling bird?"

"Yes, Jana mem, they swore he was very good, very gentle, loves people."

"I don't see much evidence of *that*. Did you see him telling fortunes?"

"I saw him, Jana mem. He picked up the card, handed it to the customer, went back in his cage. All completely pukka. Unless this is not the same bird! The man could have quickly changed birds when my back was turned."

"Maybe that happened," said Jana. "Here, let me take a look at that bite."

The wound looked superficial, but Jana said, "I think you'd better soak it and put Merthiolate on it."

Mary grimaced but went off to clean up the bite.

Jana sat down next to the birdcage and talked quietly to the bird: "I'm very sorry you seem upset this morning. I'm sure things will be better during the day. Especially if you have a wee bit of breakfast, and some nice, fresh water. But you'll have to let us put it in the cage."

During this whole speech, the bird fixed her with a suspicious beady eye.

"Now I'm going to open the door. Don't be upset."

Carefully, she released the latch.

The instant the door swung open, the bird immediately shot out of the cage. Jana jumped back, dodging the bird as it flew, screeching, around the room. It lit briefly on the statue of Saint Francis, then flapped back to the top of the cage, went down to a corner of the room, and up to the back of a chair. It next landed on the table, puffed up, and deposited some droppings, and then, before Jana's appalled gaze, and just as Mary returned to the room, flew out the window and into the forest, without a backward glance.

"He's gone," Jana said.

"Better that way," said Mary. "We need to find a very calm, quiet bird."

"He left us his calling card," Jana said, pointing to the mess on the table.

"Oh! Dirty creature!"

"Maybe it's just as well that he's flown off," Jana said.

"But now we need another bird! And how can we open for business this afternoon?"

"We'll just have to say that—oh, that Mr. Ganguly is in a bad mood, and Tilku has taken him for a walk. I'll have to push the dream analysis, since we can't do Mr. Ganguly's cards and don't have the tarot cards, either."

Mary's jaw set. "Breakfast now, Jana mem? You need strength. Otherwise you'll get pulled down."

"I'm feeling pulled down already!" Jana said. "Here we are with no Mr. Ganguly, and now this decoy plot is getting off to a bad start."

"Not to worry, Jana mem. Lal Bahadur Pun and I will find another bird—today!"

Aloo

Through the ayah network, Mary and Lal Bahadur Pun found a bird, the pet of an old lady who said she could no longer take care of it. It was the right species, and the right sex, but neither Mary nor Lal Bahadur Pun looked very confident or proud of their acquisition. Moreover, his wings had been clipped, something that Jana did not do with Mr. Ganguly, so until the feathers grew out, an observant thief would notice the difference immediately.

Just as the other decoy bird had seemed to be at the beginning, this bird was placid, and allowed himself to be transferred in and out of the cage.

"We'll give him a good night's sleep and see how he is in the morning," Jana said. "I hope he doesn't turn fierce on us like the other one."

The next morning, the bird sat quietly in the cage. He

allowed Jana to slide in a dish of food without lunging or threatening to bite. He ate all his breakfast. He seemed altogether a mannerly, amiable creature. Relieved, Jana took him out of the cage, allowed him to climb up to her shoulder, and walked around the house, showing him the different rooms. She returned to the salon and put him on the perch, where he seemed completely content.

When Mary came in with the account books, she asked, "How is this bird, Jana mem?"

"He seems rather sweet, really," Jana said.

"Hello," Mary said to the bird. "Namasté. Salaam."

"He isn't talking yet," Jana said, "but I don't think that's really cause for concern."

Mary, however, persisted. "You, bird, what's your name?" She asked but was met with silence.

"How are you?" said Mary. "How many languages do you know?" When the response was still indifference, she asked the same questions in Hindi, with the same result.

"Maybe he only knows bird language," said Mary.

"We haven't even heard that out of him," said Jana. "Nary a self-respecting screech. But, Mary, leave him for now. He'll come around."

Actually, although Jana missed Mr. Ganguly's opinions, it was an advantage not to be interrupted by requests for "Nut!" or "Walk!" when she was sitting at the table trying to do her music transcriptions.

Two days later, though, when he still hadn't made any sound whatsoever, she started to worry. Then, on the evening of the second day, he uttered a pathetic little meow.

"This bird thinks he's a cat," Mary said.

"The old lady said he could talk?" Jana asked, disbelieving.

"She swore he could," said Mary. "And she said that they understand each other perfectly and that the bird reads her mind."

The bird impostor sat on Mr. Ganguly's perch, and Jana wondered if he would respond to fiddle tunes, which always made Mr. Ganguly dance. She took her violin out of the case, all the while watching the bird, which followed her with his eyes. Then she started playing a jig, "Miss Margaret Brown's Favorite," and this time the bird did seem to sway to the music.

Then, on a hunch, Jana went around the corner and played, out of the bird's view. "Mary," she called, "is the bird dancing?"

"Just sitting, Jana mem."

Jane came back into the room, and the bird again followed her with its gaze. She pretended to play, bowing vigorously but not actually touching the strings, and the bird swayed back and forth. She quickened the movement of her arm, again without making a sound, and the bird moved to the same rhythm. He was trying to copy her gestures.

"Mary," she said, "I think I've figured it out. This bird is deaf. Go behind him and give a big shout."

As she expected, the big shout produced no reaction at all. Mary looked discouraged and embarrassed, indeed. "Maybe he can still do cards," she said.

Jana got a pack of fortune-telling cards from the almirah and spread them on the table, then put the bird down in front of them.

"Now pick one up, there's a good bird," she said.

The bird picked up a card and held it for an extended moment, appearing to think it over. Jana and Mary clapped, but apparently too soon: the bird walked to the edge of the table and dropped the card off.

"No!" Mary said, dismayed.

Jana reached under the table and picked up the card.

"You can bring a horse to the water, but you can't make it drink," she observed.

"Here, take this." She held the card out to the bird, which

took it in his beak, transferred it to one claw, and ripped it in two.

"This bird has as much personality as . . . as . . ." Mary searched for a word. "As a potato. I'm calling him Aloo."

"But remember to call him Mr. Ganguly when other people are around," Jana said hurriedly.

Nonetheless, she started thinking of him as Aloo, too.

What's in a Bird's Brain?

Aloo did permit himself to be carried about on people's shoulders, so Jana took him for a walk, making sure people saw her going along at a good clip and not stopping for any conversations. Normally, Mr. Ganguly would call out greetings to his favorite humans, and she did not want people wondering why he was in an antisocial mood.

There were other differences. Though his wit was slower than Mr. Ganguly's, his digestive system was faster, and the cape Feroze Ali Khan had made for Jana to protect her clothing soon had droppings on it. With Mr. Ganguly, the cape had been a precaution, rarely if ever really necessary. But Aloo did not seem to have that same sense of delicacy.

In his place, thought Jana, I probably wouldn't, either. After all, the poor little fellow hadn't volunteered for this masquerade. I bet he'd rather be with his old owner, she reflected. Or perhaps with a flock of parrots somewhere, swooping down on orchards, holding conventions in the trees, and complaining about the generally dreadful nature of the bipeds with which the avian kingdom had to share the planet.

Jana thought of the flocks of parrots that used to come to the nawab's garden. She had sometimes imagined the conversations the birds must be having.

"Oh, look at that fat man and his fat wife, they can barely wobble! Have you ever seen such an ungainly species? They can't even run very fast, except for a very few of them."

"As for flying, they are pathetic. They have to climb into a shining silver tube, which then goes up into the air with an enormous amount of smell and noise. Then the tube comes down, and other bipeds all act as if the tube is giving birth. Clapping, saying, Hooray, they're here at last."

"And have you seen their feathers? No, of course you haven't, because they don't have any. They have to steal *ours* to put on their hats."

Jana thought of the ostrich feathers her mother's generation had worn, and was glad those fashions were gone. Then she continued the bird conversation in her head.

"These bipeds can be friendly, but many are deadly dangerous. They climb trees and steal eggs!"

"And they will try to teach you some of their so ugly language! Will they learn *our* language? No, they will not. You can screech at them all day, trying to teach them something, and they will just complain about how you are noisy."

"Sorry, little friend," she said to the passenger on her shoulder. "When all this is over, we'll try to find you a home where you can be happy."

Flight

⌇ A Ride

A couple of days before the planned picnic, Jana was interrupted from her work by the arrival of a messenger from the Victoria Hotel, bearing a note from Max.

"Shall we test out the helicopter tour this afternoon?" it asked. "Neither Lily nor Cyrus wants to go, so we have an extra seat if you wish to bring someone else."

Jana knew exactly who would love going up in a helicopter. Tilku, fired from his job at the press, was once more happily running errands and was currently out on a commission. Jana went out into the street and within ten minutes, she saw him trotting along. She waved him down and told him of his opportunity.

"Helicopter?" Tilku's eyes shone.

"Shh!" Jana said. "Don't tell anyone. We have to sneak into the Victoria as if nothing is happening. Otherwise, we'll have an enormous crowd, the way they did when they arrived."

"Helicopter?" Tilku was still dizzy and disbelieving.

"Yes. With King sahib. Go quickly, wash up, comb your hair, and put on your good clothes. And wear your shoes!"

"Yes, Jana mem!" Tilku dashed off.

Jana searched for a piece of cardboard and printed out a

sign that said, "Closed for the Afternoon" and hung it over the "Jana Bibi's Excellent Fortunes" sign.

"Okay, Tilku, off we go," she said.

Keeping a helicopter takeoff a secret had been a fond illusion. When Jana and Tilku arrived at the Victoria, there was already a feeling of anticipation in both the Central Bazaar and the English Bazaar. People were heading toward the gates of the Victoria. By the time they got there, Mr. Dass had put on several watchmen, who let Jana and Tilku through but closed the gate to the rest.

The helicopter was sitting behind the hotel, on a large grassy area sometimes used for weddings or big parties. A fuel truck was parked near the helicopter, which looked like a large soap bubble attached to a Meccano set. The bubble, however, was not soap; but bluish plastic, giving it a science-fiction look.

The crowd had given up on the front gate and had rushed around the hillside, to the back of the hotel. As there was no level place to stand, they resorted to scrambling up and down the slopes, and getting into the trees for a good look. Mr. Dass called the watchmen from the front gate and they rushed into the back area, waving sticks and threatening anyone who tried to climb over the wall. The monkeys in the nearby trees took fright and retreated farther back into the woods.

Max came out of the hotel, looking handsome in an aviator jacket, and Jana's heart gave a little jump.

"I've already double-checked everything," he said, "but one more time, just to be sure."

He went over the whole aircraft, with a helper. The fuel was pronounced adequate, everything in order, and then Jana was allowed to board. Max got into the middle seat, and Tilku scrambled up on the other side of him.

"Buckle yourselves in," Max said.

The doors to the bubble had been taken off and, Jana learned, were to remain that way.

"It will get too hot if we keep them on," Max said.

Tilku's face was completely transformed.

"Pilot sahib," he said, pointing to the controls. "What are these things?"

Max then explained to Tilku what the different dials, sticks, and pedals did. This was a new side to Max, one she had not seen before: the side that understood machines, planned out a flight, and then, gravely, explained things to a child.

"Seat belts fastened?" Max said.

"Mine is," said Jana.

"Yes, sahib!" said Tilku breathlessly.

"Keep your hands in and your belts fastened at all times. We'll go straight up, and then we'll head across the town and out to the hills."

As they rose, the noise of the whirring blades meant that conversation, if any, had to be carried on at a shout. Tilku fell silent for a while, but soon he started asking questions, and Max explained everything clearly and comprehensively. Tilku was undaunted—even enthralled—and his eyes shone as he absorbed such concepts as centrifugal force, torque, and nautical miles.

They headed over the town, over the Municipal Garden, over the Giant Skating Rink, over the bell tower of the All-Saints church, the single minaret of the mosque, the peaked roof of the temple.

"Our house, Jana mem!" Tilku cried as the Jolly Grant House came into view. They gazed down on the red corrugated roof. Next door, the Treasure Emporium looked like a cement-walled warehouse from the air. They headed away from the center of the town, crossed a frighteningly sharp

ravine, and then flew over the playing field, classroom buildings, and dormitories of the Far Oaks School.

It seemed completely dreamlike to Jana. They were floating, soaring, swimming through the air. Is this how birds
feel? she wondered, looking down on the world of nature
and of human beings.

They were perhaps ten miles as the crow flies from the town
and had just passed a village of small stone houses with
thatched roofs when Tilku spotted someone who had spotted *them.*

"Look, Jana mem! Somebody down there is *hurt!*"

Jana looked out her side of the bubble and saw that Tilku
was right. Two white men, apparently hikers, had met with
some sort of mishap, or at least one of them had; he was lying
on the ground on his side, his legs drawn up beside him. The
second man, at the sight of the helicopter, had started waving frantically and yelling; Jana could not hear the words,
but it was clear from the man's expression that he was calling, "Help!"

"Max, can we do anything?"

Max scanned the landscape, searching for a landing site,
but the terrain was exceptionally craggy, without any large
enough horizontal places. It was Tilku who first saw the slight
patch of meadow roughly the size of the grassy area behind
the Victoria Hotel.

"Pilot sahib! You can land—over there."

Max hovered over the patch, while the unhurt hiker who
had been standing and waving came breathlessly toward
them, breaking into a run where the terrain would allow.
Jana saw that it was the young anthropologist she had met in
town at Pahari Provisioners.

"My friend . . . he just collapsed . . . couldn't go any

farther," Mumford Stein yelled above the sound of the helicopter blades.

Max brought the helicopter down, amazingly precisely, on the grassy spot. Then, with Tilku and Jana close behind, he followed Mumford Stein back to the injured hiker.

"Can you get him back to town?" Mumford asked.

"We'll have to get him into the chopper first," Max said. "And it doesn't look as if he can walk even a step."

"Can you and I carry him?" said Mumford. "Making a chair of our arms? Bob, can you get yourself up enough for us to lift you?"

The other hiker's face was gray, with little beads of sweat forming on his upper lip. He said, with labored breath, "I think so."

With muttered instructions to each other, Max and Mumford Stein got the trembling Bob to his feet, locked their arms to make a chair, and let the man ease himself down and put his arms around their shoulders. Then, careful not to trip on the rough ground, they carried him back and hoisted him up into one of the passenger seats in the helicopter.

Jana and Tilku followed them, Tilku saying anxiously, "Jana mem, only two passengers can fit in the helicopter."

"I know, Tilku. Don't worry, it will be all right."

With the patient now settled and his seat belt buckled, Max turned to Jana. "We could have Tilku sit on your lap. Or one of you can go back with me now, and I'll return for the other—and Mumford, if he wants to come back to town."

Jana said, "Take Tilku. Mumford and I will be all right here until you come back."

"We could just walk back," Mumford suggested to Jana.

Max shook his head. "Nonsense! It would be at least twenty miles by the path. I'll be back in no time flat. Come on, copilot."

Tilku, a blinding smile on his face, needed no further

prompting. He jumped into the second passenger seat and buckled his seat belt. As the helicopter rose into the air, he waved out the opening in the bubble to Jana, then turned his full attention to Max.

❧ Tilku Brags

The next day, Jana looked out the tower window and saw her household assembled for the usual morning gossip session. Something, however, was new: Tilku was lording it over Mary, Lal Bahadur Pun, and Munar, all of whom were momentarily at a loss for words.

"If you want a good helicopter for these parts, you choose a Hiller UH-12B." Tilku paused and looked around to see what effect this pronouncement had on the others. "Cruising speed, seventy-one knots. Many important people fly in Hillers. Prime Minister Nehru, for example."

"Oh," said Mary, recovering some of her usual aplomb. "So now you are friends with Prime Minister Nehru, eh? He told you he likes Hiller-Biller helicopters the best. Next week you'll have a ride around with him, is that it?"

Tilku was unaffected by this sarcasm.

"If I had a helicopter, I would deliver messages to Dehra Dun in no time flat!" he said. "But people would have to pay a lot more than two annas."

"You have to go to school to fly helicopters," Lal Bahadur Pun said, "and you don't like school."

That stopped Tilku in his tracks. He turned toward Lal Bahadur Pun with anxiety suddenly draining his small face.

"Yes!" Mary backed up what the Gurkha had said. "You have to read and write and do calculations. You think just any little boy off the street can grow up to be a helicopter pilot? Think again."

Old Munar said kindly, "Don't worry, son—if you are a good boy in this life, you will be a helicopter pilot in the next. And an excellent one, too, I am sure!"

"I won't wait until then!" Tilku set his small jaw. "I'll show you all! I'm going to fly helicopters, *soon*. I'll be in the Indian Air Force."

"Okay, okay," said Lal Bahadur Pun. "We will call you pilot sahib. Or Captain Tilku."

Lal Bahadur Pun was still joking, but Tilku's face lit up at the very sound of these titles. Summoning up confidence and resolve, he drew himself up to his full—if still small— height.

"You will see," he said. "You will see."

En Plein Air

·◌❦ *Fancy People*

It was the morning of the picnic. From her bedroom verandah, Jana saw half a dozen porters trudging by, the first carrying what looked to be a rolled-up carpet. The second man had bolsters and pillows lashed to his back with crisscrossed rope. The third carried several kerosene stoves; the fourth, an ice chest; the fifth, a wooden crate. The sixth balanced on his head a wooden rack containing metal pots and pans.

It was a gorgeous day, the best May had to offer. The air felt warm and hospitable, there was a very slight breeze, and the sky was enormous, a pale ever-expanding blue. Jana bathed quickly in the tin tub, then put on the outfit Feroze had made.

She studied herself in the dressing table mirror. No, this was not Feroze's most successful dressmaking effort. It was country-made, not sophisticated. She remembered a cartoon she had seen somewhere, probably in the *Illustrated Weekly*. A dentist was standing next to a patient with a long hypodermic needle, saying, "You don't mind if I give you some local anesthetic?" And the patient was saying, "Spare no expense! I can afford imported!"

The Kings could all afford imported clothing—Italian

shoes, British woolens, Irish linen—as well as the best Bombay had to offer, and here was Jana in her locally made not-quite-safari suit.

It's a *picnic,* she reminded herself. Not a performance. And yet she had butterflies in her stomach, like the butterflies she had felt before the disastrous violin audition at the Glasgow Athenaeum so many years ago.

It was only a picnic, but it was also an audition of sorts, Lily's engineered opportunity for Jana to have some more time with Max. The day of the helicopter ride, she'd barely had a chance to exchange two sentences with him, with Tilku peppering him with questions, and the wounded hiker being rescued, and Mumford Stein sitting in the helicopter on the way back. Mumford talked a blue streak, and by the time they touched down on the grassy area behind the Victoria, it was too late for Jana to do much socializing with Max. Cyrus came out to meet them with a fistful of business letters and telegrams to discuss, and Jana felt that it was time to beat a tactful retreat to the Jolly Grant House and a hot bath.

Nonetheless, she felt she'd learned something about Max on that day—about his competence, his ability to handle an emergency, the sheer skill it took to ease the helicopter down into a small space. Also, she had been touched by his kindness with Tilku, the way he'd turned his whole attention to the boy and made him feel important.

Max had brushed off the rescue, saying that it was pretty tame, compared to some other rescues he'd been involved in during the war, and he'd also apologized for their outing being disrupted.

"You needn't apologize," she'd rushed to say. "I thought you were—utterly splendid!"

Now, as she settled down to breakfast in the salon, Mary asked, "No lunch today, Jana mem, right? Any dinner?"

"If I know the Kings' idea of a light lunch, I probably won't want to eat for a week," Jana said.

Mary's face grew stony, as it often did when the Kings were discussed.

"Very fancy people," Mary said. "Always causing some big *tamasha*. Can't just sit and be quiet and nice."

Her ayah, Jana reflected, was expressing a minority view; for most people, causing a big uproar wherever you went was something altogether admirable.

"They're great fun, Mary," Jana said.

Mary looked unconvinced. "Okay, Jana mem."

Later, Mary brought the account books, and Jana noted that the bills were higher than usual.

"Prices have jumped in town," Mary said pointedly. "I went to buy cashews and the man said, Sorry, big scarcity. Bombay people have bought them all up. And ghee. So expensive, also! How can I cook?"

"Well, perhaps we don't need to eat cashews this week," Jana said. "Mary, can you help me after breakfast with my hair? Those little feeder plaits that come like this?" She drew a line from her temple to her ear. "No one can braid hair like you."

"Okay, Jana mem," said Mary, still grumpy but momentarily appeased by the flattery.

A Picnic

"We'll take ponies," Lily had said.

Riding would never have been Jana's first choice. She had suggested walking to the picnic site, which was only three miles outside town, but Lily's reaction to that was a predictable "Good heavens!" Cyrus and Max, Lily added, would feel that walking was a waste of time and a bore. Very well; if the rest of them were going to ride, then Jana would grit her teeth, be a good sport, and follow suit. A childhood mishap with a runaway pony had left her uneasy with horses, although she had been required to submit to several years of riding lessons. It would be all right, she told herself firmly, especially if the *syce* trotted along beside her and kept the horse under control. So, when the stamping and harrumphing of horses outside the Jolly Grant House gate announced the arrival of the party to pick Jana up, she squared her shoulders and prepared to leave.

"Don't let anyone in the house," she said to Mary and Lal Bahadur Pun. She gave Tilku eight annas for lunch in the bazaar and said, "Don't spend it on cigarettes!" adding, to old Munar, "Don't allow the boy to smoke cigarettes on the terrace. Or anywhere else, for that matter."

In the street, the assembled picnic party did not dismount but waved hello from on high. Cyrus and Lily were in front and, behind them, a European couple that Jana did not know. She did not see Max. Lily leaned down from her saddle and said, apologetically, to Jana, "Max was held up. He got a telegram, and he had to go down to the PTT and place a quick phone call to Bombay. It has to do with another possible investor in the hotel project. He'll be along afterward."

Jana's heart sank. One could wait forever at the PTT for a phone call. They could just forget Max's presence at the picnic. Lily saw her expression and said, "I shouldn't expect him to be held up too long. They said that things were going very smoothly today with the trunk lines. Oh!" She turned around in the saddle and waved at the two Europeans. "Jana, meet Renard and Odette de Lisle . . . from Brussels."

Jana warily went up beside the fidgety horses and got handshakes from the Belgians. Then she put one foot in the stirrup and swung her other leg over the saddle, relieved, when she landed, to find herself in the right position and her seat firmly planted. She said to the *syce*, "Slowly, slowly, okay?" and got a reassuring *achcha* in response. The horses started off, and Jana was glad to find them going at a deliberate pace. Cowardly enough for me, she said mentally.

When they got to the picnic site, she took in with amazement the preparations that had already been made: the Kashmiri rug spread out, defining an outdoor dining room, the bolsters and cushions and low tables. A small distance away, a number of cooks were working busily, stirring things in pots over the kerosene stoves, frying in conical pans, chopping, mixing, conferring, and scolding one another.

On the ledge above, a troop of monkeys looked down, kept at bay only by the boy who was posted to threaten them with a big stick; and somewhere in the distance, the tinkle of cowbells could be heard.

Lily looked uncharacteristically concerned about something, murmuring occasionally to Cyrus and then summoning up a brighter look when she talked to Jana and the Belgians. Renard and Odette, Cyrus explained in an aside to Jana, had gotten interested in the Victory Hotel project and might even invest a sizable amount of money in it.

"We thought we could make a royal picnic one of the offerings of the hotel," Lily told Jana. "Don't you think this is a wonderful spot for such a thing?"

They walked over to the edge of the lookout point and took in a majestic view: steep chasms and gorges, ranges of purple and brown mountains, and beyond, shimmering in the bright air like huge diamonds, snowcapped mountains.

"We'll have to install a railing here," Lily said.

"Oh, surely not," said Jana, the image of a railing on this

untamed and beautiful spot creating a jarring image in her mind.

Lily, meanwhile, had found something else not to her liking. "There's a lot of noise here today," she said.

Indeed, shouts were rising into the air and the sound of slapping, and Jana looked down to where, a couple of hundred feet below, a number of *dhobis* were doing their work, raising sheets and pillowcases above their heads, then beating them against the rocks. Others were rinsing pieces of clothing in the stream. The Belgian couple looked inquiringly, and Lily said, "I suppose we'll have to get them to do the laundry somewhere else."

Where? Jana wondered.

"In any case, we won't use these primitive methods at the hotel," Lily went on, still speaking to the Belgians. "We'll automate. We can't have customers complaining of *dhobi* itch and sand flies!"

And the *dhobis*? Jana wondered. Where were they to go? Would they be hired to run the machines?

The meal, when it was ready, was like many Jana had enjoyed at the Kings' house, and at the various clubs they belonged to in Bombay. First, while the main dishes were still cooking, there were little delicacies. The party settled on the Kashmiri rug, leaning against the bolsters, while the bearers circulated with trays of tiny cocktail kebabs, roasted cashews, stuffed taro leaves, spiced chicken livers.

"Some *amuse-gueules* to excite the appetite," Lily said to the Belgians.

There was one exhilarating taste after another. Jana took a miniature toast slice spread with smoked fish pâté and felt chilies and shallots and lime tickle her mouth. Then she tried a mixture of crumbled bits of chickpea wafer, chopped onions, lots of coriander, and some hot chutney, which she scooped up with a freshly made puri.

Between rounds, another bearer circulated with small finger bowls and hand towels. Jana started to feel stuffed, and the meal had not yet begun.

"When we get in full swing with the new hotel, we can fly in seafood from Bombay to Delhi and have it brought up here by helicopter," Lily said. "We think people will take to pomfret steamed in banana leaves, with the most divine mint-and-coconut chutney."

One course flowed into the next.

"Eat, eat," Lily kept saying, as a mutton *dhansak* appeared, and juicy chunks of chicken served in a gravy of ground cashews and chilies and cloves and cardamom. There would be a lull, and Jana would think, Well, that's all now, and then a side dish would be offered: spicy cauliflower, Brussels sprouts, artful little pumpkin crescents, fried plantains, a green-mango-and-coconut salad, and then a cucumber-and-ginger salad.

"Save room for the sweets," Lily said, contradicting her earlier order. "We've got lots of mangoes and melons and pomegranates, and a trifle, and, oh Lord, I can't even remember what I asked them to make. Cashew wafers, I think."

"Ophrysia, anyone?" Cyrus asked. Ophrysia beer seemed to be the only local thing about the picnic. The Belgians sampled it and nodded approvingly, which made Cyrus smile and gesture for some more.

They'd almost finished the sweets when they heard Max arriving, leaving his horse at the edge of the clearing. He loped over to the party, a triumphant look on his face.

"It's in the bag," he announced. "They're good for thirty percent of the development costs. They particularly like the idea of expanding the project into the town, perhaps putting the helicopter pad in between the Central Bazaar and English Bazaar, and having a regular tour bus from Delhi for the second-string tourists."

Jana said jokingly, "You mean people like myself."

"Jana!" said Max. "So glad you're here with the de Lisles, so that we can get your opinion on something. Do you think you can be in charge of the entertainment facilities at the hotel? Find some more fortune-tellers, book the acts for the sideshows? Mix some classical Indian dance acts with some folk things? Bharatanatyam one night, Manipuri dancers the next? You probably even know some people who would be eager for employment."

Jana was taken aback. This was not at all the kind of outing she had anticipated. She looked over at Lily, whose face seemed to telegraph the thought *I'm sorry, things got a bit away from me.*

Only there was more. Lily was looking at Max very anxiously, as if she didn't want him to talk anymore. But Cyrus blurted out, "And . . . the other thing? Is that—in the bag, too?"

Max gave him a grin, and nodded.

"Congratulations!" Cyrus exclaimed. "You cradle robber, you! Sly dog, you kept it from us for so long. Congratulations to you, and our best wishes to the lucky girl."

There was a long moment of silence. Jana felt her whole body temperature dropping. In fact, everything in her body seemed to be plunging down, her stomach falling, her heart, the blood in her veins and arteries pulled toward the ground by a strange force of gravity. Lily was looking at her, pleading with her eyes: *Forgive me.*

The Belgian couple unwittingly came to the rescue with a flurry of questions and congratulations, and they raised their glasses for a toast. Jana fought to keep composed.

"Congratulations," the Belgian couple said and, forcing herself to smile, Jana raised her glass and said, "Yes! Of course! Congratulations."

⸱ᴕ The Dream Editor

The shadows were lengthening; it was time to ride back to town. Walking toward the horses, Lily stayed close to Jana's side and murmured, "I didn't have time to tell you. I really didn't know before this morning that Max might get engaged. I'm so sorry."

"What are you girls whispering about?" Cyrus asked. "Girl talk?"

"Yes, just girl talk," Jana said, forcing a laugh.

When the whole party mounted up and started back toward town, Jana was at the front of the line, and for once she was not afraid of the animal beneath her. She was grateful for it. She dug in her heels, as she had been taught, and the horse responded with an obedient trot and then, as the road allowed it, an easy canter. The others were soon left behind. She made it back to town in record time, arriving at the Jolly Grant House in tears of relief. Lal Bahadur Pun was at the gate, and she dismounted and handed him the reins.

"The *syce* will be by soon to get him," she said.

Tilku opened the front door to the house.

"Did you get yourself some food?" Jana asked.

"I ate very good things in the bazaar," he said.

"Did anyone come here today?"

"Just the postman, Jana mem. I put the letters on the table."

"Mary not back yet?" Jana asked.

"No, Jana mem."

The house was almost in darkness. Jana went into the salon and turned on a light; it was not bright enough to dispel the gloom. Aloo sat in the birdcage, silent. Before, when she'd felt sad or lonely, there was at least Mr. Ganguly to tell her she was a good bird, or a bad bird, or to demand that she play "Miss Margaret Brown's Favorite" for him to dance to. Now she felt completely friendless.

She sat down, put her head on the table. Past hurts and humiliations rushed through her mind, the effect like that of flesh opening under imperfectly healed scabs. The disappearance of the British businessman who had taken her to the Andaman Islands came to mind and, oddly, the rejection of her violin audition at the Athenaeum. Thank you for applying, but we don't want you.

And also, she felt like—what was that word the Americans used?—a sucker. Ha, ha. *Fooled you,* jeered voices in her head. And she'd had a new outfit made for that damned picnic!

She got up, went outside, crossed the courtyard to the kitchen, poured a tumbler of water from the clay pot, and brought it back to the salon. Idly, she slit open the letters on the table. They were variously addressed: To Auntie Jana . . . to Mrs. Laird . . . to Jana Bibi . . . and, in the case of several, to the Dream Editor, *Our Town, Our Times,* Aaj Kal Printing Press.

She read one after the other. Dear Auntie Jana, Dear Jana Bibi, Dear Dream Editor. Please interpret this dream for me. I am flying. I am swimming. I am dancing . . . I am talking to a bear . . . a fox . . . a jester . . . a teacher . . . a boy in my class at school. What does it mean?

Some were more involved. "I got a letter from an old boyfriend and it suddenly turned into a handkerchief." "I dreamt I was very hungry and standing outside the Why Not? and watching the people eat samosas, but there was none for me." And, then, finally one that said simply, "I am dreaming that a handsome prince will come riding on horseback and ask my parents for my hand in marriage. Will he come?"

The letters, with their different styles and handwriting, their various symbols and situations, all seemed to convey the same thing to her. The writers were imploring not *tell me what my dream means* but *tell me if it will come true*. Will my love come, and when?

I should write my own dream inquiry, she thought. But it would be a little different.

It would not be about dreaming at night. It would be about dreaming during the daytime. She stood and walked around the salon, talking to herself.

"Dear Dream Editor, I was having foolish fantasies about a man who was younger, and richer, and came from a different world. But that dream disappeared like a little wisp of smoke from a candle."

What would she answer to such a letter?

First she tried a scolding: "Is this the worst thing that ever happened to you? Of course it isn't!" Of course it wasn't. It couldn't even compare to the deaths of her daughters, Fiona and Caroline. *That* was the standard of almost infinite pain, next to which any other loss seemed unimportant.

Then she had another thought. Perhaps the Dream Editor would answer, "It's for the best. Just consider: he comes from a different world, one that tolerates you and patronizes you but one you aren't a part of. And, furthermore, he's trying to change *your* world, take over your territory."

That should make a girl angry, she told herself, and for a moment, she did work up some ire. It had been too long a day, though, and she was too tired, and she really couldn't summon up the energy for righteous wrath. She sank into a chair and tried thinking of reasons why Max probably wasn't very attractive after all.

"Perhaps he snores!" she said, and managed to let out a choked little laugh.

None of this was working. "I really don't care that much," she told herself, but a tear trickled down her cheek. Crybaby, said a voice from her childhood, but the voice did not check that tear, or the next. Soon they were flowing freely.

"Oh, all right then, have a good cry," the Dream Editor said. "Go right ahead, just cry, cry, cry your eyes out. But then, please go ahead with your life."

How long did Jana cry? She did not know. But it felt as if a dam had burst. The tears that had been held back during the congratulations to Max and the small talk afterward now tumbled out, unchecked. She dimly heard the nighttime call to prayer from the mosque, but she kept on crying. Gradually, the sobs turned to sniffling, and then even the sniffling died out. She took a deep breath and got up out of her chair. She turned off the light in the salon, turned on the light for Mary in the front hall, and went up to bed.

An Aunt and a Niece

✎ *Jana Visits Aunt Sylvia*

"It's so good of you to put him up," Jana said.

Mr. Ganguly was perched on the arm of Aunt Sylvia's chair, apparently very happy. In fact, when Jana approached, Mr. Ganguly was standoffish toward her, even turning his back.

"We've been having a lovely time," Aunt Sylvia said. "We've done some music. I played the piano for the first time in years. It was horribly out of tune, though. Mr. Ganguly objected! I played "Blue Bells of Scotland" and he repeated it, only a lot more in tune! Oh my, what's this?"

Jana was holding a medium-sized brown bottle and a package wrapped in white tissue paper with yellow ribbon. She handed Sylvia the bottle to examine. "This is Mr. Abinath's potion for all-around health and happiness. I've found it's quite good with soda."

"Well!" said Aunt Sylvia with enthusiasm. "Let's have a dose and see if it brings us around." Jacob John, who had been hovering nearby, went to fetch a couple of small glasses and a bottle of soda water.

"And this," said Jana, "is something I found at the Book Depot."

Aunt Sylvia untied the ribbon and took off the paper to reveal a book of pictures of Allahabad at the turn of the century. Her face lit up. "Oh! Look! This wasn't far from where we lived!"

A picture of the cathedral, dated February 1901, revealed a memorial service for Queen Victoria.

"Oh," Sylvia said, "the queen! Of course, I know Elizabeth is the queen now, but for me, *the* queen is Victoria. We loved her—at least my family did. And she loved India, too. She had curry introduced to the royal menus, and she studied Urdu with her Indian clerk."

"She did?" Jana said. "I didn't know that."

"Yes, she quite favored him, much to the irritation of her other advisers. Hmm, 1901 was when she died . . . Let's see: I would have been thirty-two and Miriam would have been about ten."

Aunt Sylvia turned the page to find another photo of the cathedral, this time with a wedding party coming out of it. She pointed it out to Jana, who said, "Those look like a lot of happy faces."

"Yes, they do look happy, don't they? I wouldn't show this picture to Miriam, though. I wouldn't want to remind her of that dreadful business with Nigel Skinner."

"Nigel Skinner?"

Jana listened, realizing that she was at last hearing the story behind Miriam's poems.

"Oh, yes, Nigel was the young man she was going to marry. Nigel and Miriam were the *darlings* of the Coral Club. *What* a beautiful couple they made! She, with that creamy skin, and he—oh, a veritable Adonis. Only problem was, he thought so, too."

Aunt Sylvia tickled Mr. Ganguly and continued: "Everyone was so excited about the wedding, and Miriam's parents had laid on such a . . . well, the only word is *tamasha*. Enough food for an army, and everything set up in a giant tent. The guests all amassed, counting on a wonderful party and a jolly good tuck-in! Miriam had the most beautiful wedding gown. And then . . ."

Aunt Sylvia took a sip of her LPN10 and soda. "Then . . . nothing! She waited and waited. The man . . . had . . . done . . . a . . . bunk! The next anyone heard of him was ten years later, when someone in the family saw him in Calcutta."

Feeling slightly disloyal to Miriam for being so interested in this story, Jana leaned forward to hear more of it. "That must have been dreadful for Miriam."

"Oh, without a doubt. We all worried about her. And her parents never recovered from the humiliation, either. Her mother had a nervous breakdown, and her father took to drink. *Serious drink,* that is. I think the scandal is what killed them. The ridiculous thing is that Miriam feels guilty about that! Still! As if she'd let them down!"

Sylvia shook her head, Mr. Ganguly copied her, and Jana shook hers, too.

Sylvia went on: "Miriam left Allahabad shortly afterward and got that teaching position she still has at the Far Oaks School. I don't think she should have closeted herself away like that, but there you have it."

Jana asked, "Aunt Sylvia—if I may call you that—you know about Miriam's pen pal, don't you?"

"Well, I do a little," Sylvia said. "Not that people tell me everything, but my ears are still pretty sharp. My impression is that she's dithering. Just dithering." Aunt Sylvia waved one hand. "Of *course* she should pack up and go to Australia! How can anyone doubt it? She hangs on here because she thinks *I* need her. It makes one morbid, to feel that people are waiting for you to die, sacrificing and delaying their own lives for you, when all you want is for them to get on with their own. Miriam thinks I'm too old to make friends, that I'll be too lonely, that I can't get along without her. Well! I make new friends, don't I? You're one of them, aren't you? Mr. Ganguly's one of them, too."

Mr. Ganguly said, "Auntie Sylvia zindabad," moved up her arm to her shoulder, and nuzzled her neck.

"There's a good boy," Aunt Sylvia said.

Jana looked at Aunt Sylvia's hands; they were free of rings. Jana hesitated, then asked, "Aunt Sylvia, were *you* married?"

"*Moi?* Oh yes, I've had three husbands. Lovely men, actually. The first one was killed in the British Tibetan campaign, in 1903. He got an asthma attack from the high altitude. The second one died in the so-called Great War. Great—I'm sorry, my dear, I'm getting a little cynical. It seems ridiculous to call any war *great*, but there you have it. By the third husband, I was getting superstitious. Any man I married seemed to get himself killed. But the third one said he was game. It was just before the great stock market crash of 1929. I was on the verge of sixty at that point."

As I am now, Jana thought. "And children? Did you have any?"

"Four sons, all killed in one war or another. I thought I had donated enough manpower to such things, but apparently, it's never enough."

Aunt Sylvia took a sip of LPN10. "Now, as I was telling you, two years after I married husband number three, *he* popped off, too. Apoplexy, brought on by bankruptcy. He was a jute merchant, and his business was ruined in the Great Depression. There's that word again, *great*. The Great War, the Great Depression. People use great as a synonym for *evil*, I think."

Aunt Sylvia sat for a while in silence, then said, "So those were enough marriages for me, at least for a while. Although lately . . . I've been wondering."

Jana's eyebrows went up inquiringly.

"I've been wondering if I shouldn't give it another try.

Just to see if I can find a man who will outlast me. Someone too old to be conscripted or volunteer!"

"Really? You're serious?" This venerable lady, nearly ninety-two, walking down the aisle . . . or maybe being rolled down it in a wheelchair?

"Why wouldn't I be serious?" Sylvia said. "You only live once. What's standing in my way? There are no children worrying about somebody stealing their inheritance—and, in any case, no inheritance to steal. And somehow, I don't fret anymore about whether things are going to *turn out* all right. They *are* all right. It's taken me a long time to grow young."

Aunt Sylvia gave Jana a wicked little smile. "As for you, I understand that your husband—just one?" Jana nodded. "He's long dead, so my advice to you is to get busy and find yourself another!"

Would people never stop giving her that advice? "I don't think it's in the cards," Jana said, wincing at the thought of Max King.

"Ah well, perhaps you'll change your mind. You're still a girl. But I do think Miriam should seize her opportunity. Nice men who own bed-and-breakfasts don't grow on trees."

Mr. Ganguly, at this mention of Miriam's name, opened his beak and pronounced, *"Hic et nunc!"*

"What's that he said?" Aunt Sylvia asked.

"Hic et nunc," said Jana. "It's Latin for 'here and now.'"

"So, he agrees with me!" said Aunt Sylvia.

"Actually, it's how he refers to Miriam. It's what she says to her Latin students when she wants them to put down their pens and hand in their exam papers. Boys and girls! Finish your work! *Hic et nunc!*"

"I see," said Aunt Sylvia. "But still, I think he gets the translation." She turned to Mr. Ganguly. "So you think Miriam should take off and go to Australia—*hic et nunc*?"

The bird flapped his wings as if in vigorous assent.

"As I said!" Aunt Sylvia exclaimed.

They had another round of LPN10 and soda, and Aunt Sylvia said, "Miriam thinks she should hover over me until I depart this vale of tears. But I have no intention of departing it yet. In addition to this matter of the last husband, I have some things I would like to say to the so-called leaders on this planet. One shouldn't hand in one's dinner pail until one has spoken one's piece!"

"Hand in one's dinner pail?" Jana asked.

"Kick the bucket! Make a final exit! Throw in the towel!"

Well, that's one way to thumb your nose at the Grim Reaper, Jana thought. Use every slang expression possible.

"You could write a good, strong letter to the editor of the paper," Jana said.

"I could," said Aunt Sylvia.

"Or," said Jana. "Perhaps you could talk to him directly. I know him; he's a conscientious fellow. Maybe he would come over and discuss it with you. You could dictate your message to him. Then he could print it in the newspaper—and even send it via telegram to larger newspapers. Perhaps the Associated Press would pick it up."

"What a good idea!" Aunt Sylvia's weak old eyes, tiny-looking behind the glasses, suddenly brightened with enthusiasm.

"Well." Jana glanced at her watch. "Aunt Sylvia, I'll go now, so I won't have to walk back in the dark."

"Yes, dear, you go. And thank you for the lovely book and the marvelous potion. It should put whisky and soda quite out of fashion!"

"Mr. Abinath would like that," said Jana. "I think he felt neglected last year when they were handing out fame."

"Next round, he might get his share of fame—and fortune."

Jana turned to her parrot. "Now, Mr. G, I will be back. Be a good bird and do what Aunt Sylvia tells you."

Mr. Ganguly gave Jana what felt to her like a frosty look, turned to Aunt Sylvia, and said, "I love you." And as Jana was leaving the room, he cried, "Good-bye! Bad bird!"

Oh my, thought Jana, it seems I'll have to be prepared for Mr. G doling out a few more punishments in the future.

✑ "Gaudeamus Igitur"

The next day, Jana got a note from Miriam, who had slipped on the path from the dormitory to the classrooms and sprained her ankle.

"I hobble around but can't go far," Miriam wrote. "So I'm sitting here with my leg up, organizing photos. Come for tea if you have the inclination to get out of the house."

Jana remembered Aunt Sylvia's comment about Miriam "closeting herself" away at the school and felt that this was a case of double-closeting: Miriam confined to her little suite, going through old photos. She looked out the tower window, across the gorge to the Far Oaks School girls' dormitory, at Miriam's windows. We should have rigged up a Morse code system with mirrors, Jana thought. Then we could have conversations at will.

She briefly considered taking Aloo with her but decided that was pointless, the bird's messiness, lack of conversational skills, and deficient charm making him not a good visitor. Instead, she put on her walking shoes, grabbed her satchel, and set out.

The walk to the school was about two miles, just enough to be refreshing. Jana passed the classroom building, the high school boys' dorm, and the little girls' dorm. In front of the little boys' dorm, she paused and watched the boys play. Some chased one another with loud shouts; others bunched in tight circles, shooting marbles, and Jana was reminded of pictures of electrons buzzing furiously around the center of an atom. Next came the high school girls' dormitory, where Miriam had her own small apartment.

Following Miriam's instructions, she made her way down a long verandah, where girls were drying their hair in the sun or shaving their legs in buckets and then tossing the water down the hillside. Others were buying pastries and peanut brittle from a box wallah who was vending them out of his tin footlocker. Jana got a few curious looks, as well as some cheery hellos from girls who had come into the Jolly Grant House of a Saturday. She went up an outside staircase, found the teachers' wing, and knocked on the door of Miriam's place.

"Come in," Miriam called, and Jana opened the door to find her hobbling around on crutches. A small teakettle was already boiling on an electric hot plate, and there were nice floral dishes and teacups and a platter of macaroons laid out on a table.

"I was hoping you'd come," Miriam said. Then, waving at the pastries, she added, "Box wallah's special. The man lies in wait on the verandah just as the girls are coming back from class. Usually I try to resist temptation, but sometimes I cave in."

"I would, too," Jana said.

While the tea was steeping, Jana noticed a number of enlarged photographs on the table.

"May I look?" she asked. There were close-ups of people in the bazaar: Feroze's tailors bent over their sewing machines, a street vendor roasting corn, a cow helping itself to tomatoes from a vegetable stand. Jana smiled at these, and went on to a number of photos taken at the school. Such simple things, but caught at just the right moment, capturing a flash of emotion: the intense concentration of a girl at the piano, the triumph of a boy shooting a basketball, the energy of those little boys Jana had seen playing marbles.

"So this is what you meant by organizing photos," Jana said. "I pictured you repairing old family photo albums."

"No, these are my latest attempts at shots of everyday life. I found that book you gave me on photography *very* helpful, by the way."

"I'm glad," said Jana.

"Photography is becoming an addiction," Miriam said. "I keep entering the contests the *Illustrated Weekly* holds. Haven't won anything yet, but hope springs eternal. *Dum spiro, spero.* While I breathe, I hope!"

A burst of laughter sounded from the verandah.

Jana gestured to the window. "You *can* hear the girls from here, can't you."

"Yes, you certainly can!"

Now, a loud rendition of "Gaudeamus Igitur" was floating up through the window.

"I teach it to the freshmen in Latin I," Miriam said. "It's always on the final exam. So they've been practicing."

"I remember that one," Jana said. "I learned it in Latin class myself. Things stick in your brain when you learn them at fourteen or fifteen."

Phrases returned, amazing her after so many years. *Pereat tristitia* . . . perish   sadness . . . *pereant   osores* . . . perish haters . . . *pereat diabolus* . . . perish the devil.

"I got in trouble once," Miriam said, "by revealing to the class that it was a drinking song, not a hymn, and that they should sing it lustily. Parents complained about the word *lust.* Perhaps they thought that if you don't use the word around young people, the thing itself will go away."

More laughter sounded from down below. The girls practically bellowed, *"Vivat membrum quodlibet!"*

"Long live all our male classmates," Miriam said. "Loosely
translated."

There were a few more verses in unison, and then a single
voice arose, singing in a parody of a very old person. Jana
realized suddenly that the girl was imitating Miriam and,
horrified, wished she could jump up and close the window.

Miriam, however, just shrugged. "I take that as a sign,"
she said.

"Of *what?*" Jana asked.

"That it's time to retire from the oh so noble profession of
teaching. When they start to make fun of you, it's time to go."

"But . . ." Jana searched for a way to minimize the insult.
"They learned the song well. And they seem to enjoy singing it."

"They do, they do. And I used to enjoy teaching it." Miriam sighed. "Now I'd rather snap pictures. The camera
doesn't make fun of me. Or if it does, it's my own fault. Bad
pictures? Throw them out and try again. One day, I'd like to
put together a book of photos. What do they call them? A
coffee-table book. So heavy you can hardly lift it."

"You put together a book of poems once," Jana pointed
out. "You can put together a book of pictures."

Miriam smiled. "Maybe so. More tea?"

Jana held out her cup, added milk and one lump of sugar,
and finished her macaroon.

"Things have changed," Miriam said. "I used to love
teaching, love the students. Every Christmas, I'd get dozens
of cards from old students—from Canada, from the States,
from India. I used to think that would be enough for me,
forever. I talked to the principal the other day. He tells me,
You can retire, you've more than earned it. You can stay
right in your apartment here at the school, room and board

provided. Security forever, a cocoon. I've been thinking it over."

"I can see how one might be tempted," Jana said. "You *could* spend all day long on your photography. And never have to mark papers again."

Miriam laughed. "Yes, that would be a relief! But somehow . . ."

"There's still the idea of . . . Australia," Jana said cautiously. "Have you heard from Mr. Phillips lately?"

"Oh, I can't go," Miriam said shortly. "I can't leave Aunt Sylvia. How can you go off and leave your ninety-two-year-old aunt?"

The question hung in the air for a moment, and then Jana decided she'd plunge in and answer it.

ᴄʃ *A Brochure*

"I'm walking again," Miriam wrote a few days later to Jana, "although not large distances. Dr. Chawla says to build up gradually. But I'd like to get into town and stop at your house and say hello, and go over to Aunt Sylvia's."

"Take a dandy into town," Jana wrote. "There's no shame in being carried, if you're wounded."

Miriam did not take a dandy. She said she didn't like being jolted about, and that the swaying motion of the chair made her seasick. She walked from the Far Oaks School, in the afternoon after her Latin IV class, and arrived at the Jolly Grant House out of breath and white around the lips. Jana settled her on the window seat in the salon, propped her leg up on a chair, and revived her with some undiluted LPN10.

"So much for doctor's orders," Jana scolded.

"I know, I know." Miriam took something out of her suit

jacket pocket and handed it to Jana. "I just wanted to show you this in person. And get your reaction."

It was a brochure, folded three ways. On the top panel, a color photo showed a low brown brick bungalow, surrounded by gardens established in reddish soil. There were planter's chairs on the wraparound verandah. Jana read aloud: "Welcome to the Take-It-Easy Bed-and-Breakfast, your home away from home in Perth. Reasonable rates, hearty breakfasts, well-appointed rooms, and sympathetic hospitality. Stay a week, a month, or a year. Our guests return to us with a sigh of relief."

The inside panels contained information on rates, meals, and amenities, plus the same photo of Marcus Phillips that Miriam had shown Jana that day in the rickshaw. The photographs of the rooms, Jana felt, weren't very revealing; in one, a huge wardrobe dominated the picture, and in another, she couldn't see much more than the ceiling fan.

"He needs a little help with the photography," Miriam said wryly.

"I know just who could provide that," Jana said.

"Oh, I don't know what to do!" Miriam burst out. "If I believed in fortune-telling and all that nonsense, I'd ask you to spread out your cards!" She stopped, with a horrified expression on her face. "I'm so sorry, that was rude."

Jana laughed. "My deck of tarot cards got ruined, anyway, and I'm still looking for a replacement. And Mr. Ganguly's stand-in isn't much good at picking the cards of the Indian gods. What's left? Tea leaves? Clouds? Palmistry? Here, let me see your hand. Although remember that your fate isn't written in your palm or, as an old ayah of mine used to say, on your forehead. It is written in your heart and your head."

"Oh, take a look—I suppose it can't do any harm." Miriam held out her hand, palm up.

"Let's see the backs of both hands." Jana held out both her own hands, and Miriam laid hers to rest on top of them.

They were not youthful hands; the blue veins stood out prominently, the knuckles were enlarged, freckles and white spots marred the light brown skin. And yet there was a beauty to them that brought a lump to Jana's throat. If hands could speak, these did—of sensitivity, and of intelligence, and, though Jana didn't know quite why she thought so, of originality.

She told Miriam to turn her hands over. The palms were much younger-looking, the lines nowhere near as deep and numerous as Jana would have thought.

"What do you see?" Miriam asked.

"I see what I already know," Jana said. "Here's someone with talent and passion. And longing."

Miriam's face twisted. Jana, worried that Miriam might burst into tears, realized she had hit too close to home; she looked away and took a breath. The moment passed; Miriam regained her composure, and Jana examined the lines in her palm. She found herself smiling and giving a quiet chuckle.

"Why are you laughing?" Miriam asked.

"There's a little line some call a marriage line, right here. You've got a good, deep one."

"That's ironic," Miriam said.

"A lot of life is."

Mary came in, to ask if Miriam wanted to stay and have soup with Jana.

"Thanks, Mary, I've got to get back," Miriam said. "But tell me what you think of this picture." She showed Mary the picture of the bed-and-breakfast.

"Looks like a pukka house, madam," Mary said. "Nice and strong, won't leak during the monsoon."

"There isn't much monsoon where this house is," Miriam said.

Miriam looked at her watch again and got up and started to move toward the door. "I've never actually traveled by air before," she said. "In fact, I've never been out of India."

"Are those reasons to do it, or not to do it?" Jana asked.

Miriam let a sharp breath out. "It would be harebrained to go off to marry someone without ever having heard the sound of his voice."

Jana turned the brochure over.

"Look, there's a telephone number given here. You could call."

"I wouldn't have any idea how!"

"The clerk at the PTT will know how. He places the trunk call for you, then you just wait until he says to pick up the receiver." Miriam hesitated, and Jana said, "I'll go with you. You'll see, it won't be difficult. Let's do it on Saturday."

◦⧸ *A Phone Call*

On Saturday morning, Jana bustled about and got dressed with more dispatch than usual, not lingering over her tea. Miriam arrived at about nine, still hobbling, and with a mixture of anxiety and determination on her face.

"What time is it in Australia?" Jana asked.

Miriam had put this question to the geography teacher at the school and learned that Perth was two and a half hours ahead of New Delhi.

"Only two and a half time zones," Miriam said. "That doesn't seem so bad."

"Yes," Jana said, "not like trying to call America or something."

At the PTT, they had to wait their turn in back of several

tourists, and by the time they got to the clerk, Miriam looked uncertain. Jana determined to keep her on course.

"Trunk lines not so busy today," the clerk said. "That is good luck for you ladies."

"Oh, we can speak now?" Miriam said.

"No, no. I can *reserve* now, is what I am telling you. I will find out what time they can return the call."

There was another long wait. Miriam and Jana sat on the wooden bench in the PTT, listening to ringing noises and the clack of the telegraph machine in the next room. People came and went, bought stamps and air letter forms, sent packages off.

In about half an hour, the PTT clerk looked over brightly and announced, "Success!"

"You've got Australia?" Miriam asked eagerly.

"I have booked the call! Come back in six hours."

Six hours! Miriam and Jana looked at each other, first in dismay, then in resignation. They discussed walking back to the Jolly Grant House and returning in the afternoon, but Jana thought to ask, "Might the call come through earlier than expected?" and they got an ambiguous wag of the head in reply. "Maybe earlier, maybe later."

"We can't sit here for six hours!" Miriam said. "Well, perhaps *I* can, but I really can't make *you* do that." She looked down at her ankle, which was swollen again from the walk.

"We'll take turns," Jana said firmly. "I'll sit here for a while; you go take a rickshaw to the Victoria and see if Mr. Dass will get some ice for that ankle and let you sit on the verandah. I'm sure he will. He might even get the kitchen to make us a picnic lunch."

Miriam, visibly brightening, allowed herself to be persuaded to carry out this plan. She went and returned in an hour, the ankle better for having been iced. Mr. Dass did indeed make them a picnic lunch, and sent a thermos of tea and two cups, and another thermos at three P.M. The lunch included none of Lily King's delicacies; it was much as she remembered picnic lunches packed by the Victoria in her childhood: thin cheese sandwiches, on the soggy side, and a banana and a tangerine for each of them. When you were hungry enough, it all tasted wonderful.

They were just starting on the second thermos when the PTT clerk announced that the call would come through shortly. Miriam jumped up, spilling her tea.

"I am saying *soon*, madam, not *immediately*," the clerk said. "Anytime now." With a puff of annoyance, Miriam sat down and dabbed at the tea stains with her handkerchief.

"Anytime now" became four P.M, and then five. The PTT was threatening to close, and Jana felt frantic. If this effort failed today, would she get Miriam here a second time? She checked her satchel, found a ten-rupee note, and went up to the clerk. "This call is very important, understand?" she whispered. "And you can also come and have a free fortune told, anytime." Bribery was against her principles, but then again, one had to consider circumstances, and reward people for extra effort.

Finally, at seven P.M., with the doors to the PTT closed and locked, and Miriam and Jana exhausted, hungry, and thirsty, the clerk pointed to the phone booth and said, "You can pick up now, madam. Please talk loudly."

Miriam took a deep breath and squared her shoulders. "Wish me luck," she said to Jana.

A moment later, Miriam put her head out of the booth and called to the clerk, "I can hardly hear a thing."

"Madam, I told you to talk *loudly*."

"But I *am* talking loudly," Miriam protested. "The problem is that I can't *hear* very well."

"You must *listen* loudly also," the clerk insisted.

Miriam stepped back into the booth. Through its glass door, Jana saw her apparently listening as loudly as she could. She could also hear Miriam's responses, delivered as if Miriam were trying to yell at a volume that would be heard in Australia.

"VERY WELL, THANK YOU, AND YOURSELF?"

She hasn't much privacy, Jana thought. I must try and close my ears. Fighting back her desire to eavesdrop, she walked across the room and studied the official government pronouncements tacked up in a glassed-in case. The clock on the wall was ticking audibly, something she'd never noticed when the noise of PTT customers filled the room during business hours. Lord knows how much this is going to cost Miriam, she thought. A lot of rolls of film, that's for sure, if not a telephoto lens.

At the end of fifteen minutes, Jana heard Miriam bellowing her good-byes and saw her hang up the receiver. The clerk, with unheard-of speed, calculated the cost, wrote up the bill, took the money from Miriam, stamped the receipt, and hustled them out the door.

Miriam and Jana stood in the street. People hurrying home swerved around them, and cinema-goers pressed by into the nearby Europa for the evening show.

"So, what did he say?" Jana said. "What did *you* say? Did you *like* him?"

Miriam was silent for a long moment. Then she tried to say something a couple of times, but instead burst into tears. Oh no, thought Jana, the call was a disaster. She reached into her satchel for a clean handkerchief, which Miriam accepted and dabbed at her face.

At last, quieting down to a sniffle, Miriam turned to Jana and took a deep breath. She said, "I think . . ." She sniffed some more, managing to get out "He's . . . he's very nice. I think he's . . ."

"He's *what*?" asked Jana.

"He's just as nice as his letters," said Miriam, half-laughing, half-crying. Finally, her face broke into a simple, astonished smile. "And I think he sounded . . . reliable."

Pounce on him, then, Jana thought. Aloud, she said, "That's very good news."

Around the Hairpin Bends

❦ *A Different Kind of Picnic*

"Not much going on here at the Victoria," Kenneth Stuart-Smith wrote in his note. "The folks from Bombay have departed—at least temporarily. Dizzy has been mumbling about a stay of execution. So—how about lunch down at the falls? We can talk in private there. The kitchen will fix box lunches. I can hire ponies, if you want."

Another picnic, another pony ride? Jana's first reaction was a firm no. But having a sandwich with Kenneth, seated on a rock, would not entail a lot of drama. Besides, she said to herself, noting the irony, now I even have riding clothes to wear: the not-quite-safari suit. Moreover, since her hurried departure from the picnic with the Kings, she had lost her fear of horses, so even the zigzagging steep trail down to the falls held no terrors.

She sent the messenger from the Victoria back with a note accepting, with thanks.

The zigzag path to the falls was quiet and secluded, seemingly a hundred miles from the bustle of the town. After a ride down without mishap, Jana and Kenneth spread their jackets on a ledge and sat on them, watching the waterfall pounding down into a swirling water hole. As expected, the hotel's cheese sandwiches drooped in the hand, but this time, along with the bananas, chocolate bars rounded out the menu.

"At least here we won't be overheard," Kenneth said. "I have to bring you up-to-date on the gang that's been stealing animals. They've been revving up their activity in northern India."

"Birds in particular?" Jana asked.

"Parrots have been especially vulnerable. A seventy-five-year-old macaw with near-total recall of people's faces disappeared from a Calcutta household."

"An old parrot?" said Jana. "Remember the Dr. Dolittle books? Dr. Dolittle had a parrot called Polynesia who was a repository of wisdom, because she was so old and had seen so much."

Kenneth said, "They *do* live a long time, and have good memories. But apropos of how Mr. Ganguly might be in danger, I remembered how you said he could tell Ramachandran's twins apart. He might fetch a good price as someone who can detect an impostor."

A chill went down Jana's spine.

"The latest word from the Indian intelligence services," Kenneth continued, "is that several members of the gang are in Dehra Dun right now. And that our scrawny friend, D.P.— Dubla-Patla, remember?—is poised to do a bird snatching in Hamara Nagar."

"Is he—are they—*violent*?" Jana asked. "Tilku takes the fake Mr. Ganguly for a daily walk in the bazaar. Mary is supposed to trail him at all times, but still, I worry. About Tilku, that is. Mr. Ganguly is parked safely at Aunt Sylvia's."

"I think Lal Bahadur Pun should trail Tilku, too," Kenneth said, "so that he can step in, in an emergency. No one's going to tangle with a retired Gurkha with a knife as sharp as a razor blade."

"Yes, that sounds like a good idea."

"We've got the Dehra Dun police on the lookout," Kenneth said. "So if D.P. captures Aloo and heads on down the mountain road, there will be people lying in wait for him."

They finished the picnic and got back on the horses for the uphill trip home. Though saddlesore from the unaccustomed riding of the last weeks, Jana felt confident about her horsemanship, and also assured that Kenneth would soon help bring this whole saga of the bird thief to a close.

When they got back to the Jolly Grant House, Kenneth asked, "Will all your household be here tomorrow after breakfast?"

"I should think so," Jana said.

"That's good. We should give them a briefing. I've got the picture of D.P. for them to look at, as well as photos of other members of the gang. Mary and Lal Bahadur Pun must be told to trail Tilku any time he goes out. And Tilku must be told not to get into any vehicle—car, bus, anything—with a stranger. If someone approaches him and demands Aloo, he's to hand over the bird and then get out of there as soon as possible."

"We'll tell everyone what they need to do," said Jana. "Thanks, Stu." Somehow, without even realizing it, she had given him a nickname.

ᘓ *To the Chase*

The next morning, Jana carried her tray of eggs and toast and tea up to the tower. She ate her breakfast pensively, wondering what the meeting with Kenneth would produce. Finishing one cup of tea, she poured herself a second from the small pot, and polished off the last of the toast. Now she was fortified for the day's events. She went to the window and looked out at the enormous pale-blue sky, then glanced down at the courtyard, where Tilku was sitting on the parapet with Aloo on his arm.

"Namasté," Tilku shouted, trying in vain to penetrate the bird's unhearing consciousness. "Now you say it, too." Hope springs eternal, Jana thought.

After bringing the tray down to the kitchen, she went to the courtyard and waited for Kenneth on the bench. When he arrived, she led him into the salon and called for the rest of the household.

Mary had just returned from buying cooking oil in the bazaar. Munar stopped his sweeping and came in from the terrace. Lal Bahadur Pun, surprisingly fresh after two hours of sleep, emerged from downstairs, just as Kenneth was laying out the photos of the bird-snatching gang. They all pored over the pictures. They recognized the impostor reporter who had come to the house earlier, and Kenneth pointed out a taller and even skinnier man, whom he called "D.P."

"Tilku must look at these," Lal Bahadur Pun said.

"But where *is* he?" Jana said. "Where are Tilku and Aloo? I saw them not twenty minutes ago on the terrace."

Mary's face twisted in alarm. "They were here when I left. I told them not to go out until after Stuart-Smith sahib talked to us."

"Oh dear." Jana felt a spasm of alarm. "Maybe he wasn't paying attention."

"Sometimes he likes to disobey my orders," Mary observed. "Or maybe he thought he could do his morning walk quickly-quickly."

Kenneth grimaced. "Typically, where does Tilku walk when he takes Aloo around town?"

"He makes a big loop," Mary said. "He goes to the Municipal Garden and comes back through the English Bazaar. Then he walks south to the edge of town, to the taxi stand at the barricade."

"That's where I left my car," said Kenneth. He patted his pocket for his car keys. "I'm thinking it would be good to go down there and sit quietly and observe. We'll see if Tilku comes, and if anyone approaches him. Jana, are you game?"

"Of course." Jana quickly went to find her walking shoes, sunglasses, and a scarf.

"I should get word to the police in Dehra Dun to watch for a man with an eleven-year-old boy and a parrot," Kenneth said. "Subedar-Major, you go over to the PTT and call them." He wrote down a couple of names and codes on a piece of paper, and a phone number.

To Mary, he said, "Mary, you cover the English Bazaar and the Municipal Garden. If you see Tilku, bring him back to the Jolly Grant House immediately!"

"Of course, sahib!" Mary said smartly.

Kenneth added one more instruction: "Munar, you be in charge at the house until Lal Bahadur Pun gets back."

"I will be in charge," said Munar, although there was a quaver in his voice.

By now, Jana had her walking shoes on, and a moment later she and Stuart-Smith were on their way out the door. They went at a quick pace, practically a trot, through the bazaar, and down the road to the taxi stand.

It was a busy day. Taxis were arriving up the long road from Dehra Dun and disgorging tourists, and a babel of languages could be heard. The gate to the town was closed, as usual, the sign still warning, "No autos permitted without special permit." Several automobiles were parked in the small flat area downhill from the barricade: Mercedes-Benzes, old Peugeots, American station wagons.

Kenneth pointed out his car, a blue Ford sedan, and they hurried to it; he got into the driver's seat, and Jana slid onto the bench from the passenger's side. They looked at each other, both uneasy, and watched in silence as yet another taxi disgorged its passengers and a rickshaw gobbled them up and rolled off. Jana recognized several of the porters who were waiting for people to hand over luggage to carry, and she hoped none of them would see her. She was grateful for the scarf and the dark glasses, although she knew they wouldn't provide much camouflage for anyone who knew her well.

Ten minutes later, a familiar goose honk sounded, and Jana's heart sank. There was Mr. Kilometres, his taxi bulging at the seams with an American family with numerous children. When he came to a stop and jumped out to open the doors, people of all sizes gushed forth like champagne out of an uncorked bottle.

Worse, Mr. Kilometres instantly recognized Jana. Immediately after he'd gotten paid and said good-bye to his passengers, he bounded over with a wave and a cry, carrying a thermos bottle. "Mrs. Laird! So good to see you! My wife washed your thermos!"

Jana took the thermos but held a finger briefly to her lip, then spoke quietly to him through the window.

"Mr. Kilometres, we're here on a delicate matter. I can't talk now."

A hurt expression flitted across his face, so she tried to soften the blow.

"Secret," she whispered. "Government work."

The expression was immediately replaced with a look of

collusion. Mr. Kilometres strolled casually back to his taxi, took out a rag from the boot, and started dusting the car off.

"Maybe this is a wild-goose chase," Jana said to Stuart-Smith. "Maybe we're sitting here for nothing."

"Wait—isn't that Tilku now?"

Jana's pulse quickened. It *was* Tilku, a hundred yards uphill and obviously unaware of their presence, with Aloo, the impostor bird, on his shoulder.

"He's still got the bird," whispered Jana. "So no one's approached him yet."

For a while, Tilku sat on a retaining wall, and talked to tourists, allowing them to tickle Aloo under the chin. Jana was starting to think that this operation would all come to naught, and that they should call out to Tilku and just walk him home.

But suddenly, they saw a tall, bony man walk up to Tilku.

"That's certainly D.P.," Kenneth said. "He looks as if he'd slice you open if you bumped into him. Thin, but strong as steel."

"The human razor man," said Jana.

The razor man had engaged Tilku in conversation and started making chirruping noises at the bird. Then he took a piece of paper out of his pocket, unfolded it, and handed it to Tilku, who scrutinized it, nodded, and wiggled his head in agreement.

"Come on, Tilku, hand over the bird!" Jana whispered.

"I'm a little concerned," Stuart-Smith whispered back. "They're talking more than they should be. I'm afraid D.P. may be getting too much information out of Tilku."

Tilku was now handing Aloo to D.P., and Aloo obligingly climbed up the man's arm, onto his shoulder.

"Oh good, he's made the transfer," said Jana.

But then she watched in alarm as Tilku followed the man to a dark gray Hindustan Ambassador. Perhaps he's just say-

ing good-bye, she thought. The man opened the back door
and took out a traveling cage for a bird, put Aloo into it, and
placed it on the back seat. Then, to Jana's horror, Tilku got
into the car, and the man slammed the door and jumped into
the driver's side.

"Stu, Tilku's going with him!" Jana said.

Kenneth turned the keys in the ignition. No response. He
tried again and again, with the same result. A glance at
the fuel gauge brought a groan.

"Someone must have siphoned off all the gas."

Jana thought quickly. "Maybe Mr. Kilometres can take
us." She jumped out of the car, and the next moment, she and
Kenneth were dashing toward Mr. Kilometres.

At their few breathless words of explanation, Mr. Kilometres cried, "Jump in, jump in," and as Jana and Kenneth
scrambled into the back seat, he leapt into the driver's seat
and turned the key in the ignition.

"Following, correct, sahib?"

"Yes, follow that gray Hindustan," Stuart-Smith said.

"I know, I know! I saw that film. Not to worry."

The gray Hindustan was an eighth of a mile down the
road by now, but Mr. Kilometres was already gaining on it.

"He has kidnapped Tilku and Mr. Ganguly? Oh, the das-
tard! But never fear, we will rescue them."

The skinny man turned out to be a skillful mountain
driver, even a match for Mr. Kilometres. Jana closed her eyes
and clutched the strap above the door, praying that they
would not go sailing into the blue on the next bend. She was
dimly aware of Kenneth hanging on to the front seat with
one hand and the other handle with the other hand. Mr.
Kilometres kept up a constant commentary.

"Oh, that fellow came close on that one. He thought he'd
pick up speed! But we'll gain on him, never fear. Oh! Why
don't they clean up that rock slide? It's been there for two

months! Someone's going to have a puncture. *Aré,* this brake
is a little sluggish . . ."

With each new observation by Mr. Kilometres, the possibility of a new disaster sprang to Jana's mind. She opened her
eyes, saw the landscape hurtling past, and wondered whether
they would be alive at the end of this ride to tell the tale.

Waiting for Ritu

✑ A Room and a Viewpoint

Normally, Rambir would have let Ritu take a taxi from the station to Hamara Nagar, but he was so unnerved by the dedication for Ritu's favorite song, "Love Potion Number 9," on Radio Ceylon, that he decided to go to Dehra Dun himself and meet her train. For the three days before Ritu was due to come in, he worked until the wee hours of the morning, slapping together the news stories and the advertisements. The final layout of the paper was haphazard, and Rambir was sure that there were typos and missing words and errors on every page. But still, it was finished ahead of time. The fellow he had hired to replace Tilku would just have to cope, on his own.

"Just print the bloody thing!" Rambir told him. "And get it out!"

As luck would have it, Rambir managed to get a lift to Dehra Dun with some King employees who were catching the night train to Delhi. Since Ritu was coming in the morning, this meant that he would have to spend the night in Dehra Dun. It would be another expense, for which he gave a sigh, but that way, he would be sure to be on the platform when Ritu stepped off the train. Then, he figured, that Kilometres fellow could drive them back up the mountain.

At the Dehra Dun railway station, he asked if there was a vacancy in the retiring room and was turned away. "Sorry, sahib," the official said. "Only passengers can sleep in the retiring rooms. Go across the street to the Coziest Possible Hotel."

At Rambir's blank look, the man explained. "That's its name."

Rambir stepped back out of the station, dodged a fortune-teller, and wove his way through the tangle of bicycles, bullock carts, buses, and cars. He saw no hotel called the Coziest Possible. After asking directions several times, however, he found himself a couple of streets down, in a narrow alley. Looking up, he finally saw the sign on the second floor of a dingy yellow building. In a mixture of Hindi and English script, it said, "Be our cozy guest tonight, wake up happy, wise, and bright!"

"Kind of an irresistible promise, isn't it?" The voice at his elbow was familiar. Rambir turned and saw Mumford Stein, a rucksack slung over one shoulder. The anthropologist had shaved off his beard and had just had a haircut, to boot, which made him look younger and more respectable than at their first meeting.

"Mr. Stein! What are you doing in Dehra Dun?"

"Oh, it's a real pain in the neck. Or mouth. I got this awful toothache and had to come down to the dentist. He's just finished working on me, and, unfortunately, he says I have to return tomorrow."

"My sympathies. Are you staying at this hotel?"

"I was just going in to ask if they had room. I stayed here once before, on my way in. The price is right."

"Is it—clean?"

"Oh, sure," said Mumford. "They hose it out on a regular basis."

Rambir felt himself grimacing.

"Just kidding," Mumford said. "It's fine. Rudimentary, but fine."

"How do you even get in?"

"Follow me," said Mumford. He led Rambir around to the side and up a staircase, to a room the size of the average *paan* shop in the Upper Bazaar of Hamara Nagar, a few feet square. Rambir saw nothing that spelled "hotel lobby" to him—no counter, mailboxes, armchairs—and no obsequious clerk.

"Don't worry," said Mumford. "Someone will have seen us."

Sure enough, in a few minutes, a man in kurta pajama, barefoot and chewing *paan,* came through a curtained doorway in the back of the room.

"*Namasté, bhai sahib,*" Mumford said. "Any rooms to be had today?"

There was one left, with two beds.

"Bathroom?" Mumford asked.

"Down the hall. Very clean, all best, don't worry."

"What do you think—care to share the last room?" Mumford said.

Rambir gulped. This place has to be utterly loaded with germs and cockroaches, he thought. But here was this American, from the land of chrome and tile bathrooms, declaring it acceptable.

"I'm game," said Rambir, and followed Mumford down a narrow, ocher-walled hall.

The room had two webbed charpoys and a few hooks on the wall where one could hang clothing. The door boasted latches, inside and out.

"This is fine," Mumford said. "I'm getting hungry. Are you? Let's go in search of grub."

He stashed his things in the corner, gestured to Rambir to do likewise, and took a padlock from the outer pocket of his rucksack.

"You seem to be a seasoned traveler," Rambir commented.

"Yeah, I've been all over the world," Mumford said

casually as they went back into the hall. "Took the Orient Express from Paris to Istanbul . . . and the train from Moscow to Vladivostok. Hitchhiked through East Africa. Crossed the Atlantic in a sailing boat." He closed the door, looped the padlock through the latch, and clicked it shut.

"You sailed across the ocean *alone*?"

Mumford shrugged. "It wasn't that big a deal. I had good weather all the way." He paused. "Let's see—I seem to remember eating a decent meal at the Air-Conditioned Café. A lot of Europeans eat there, but you can have Indian food, too. It's hot!"

With this, Mumford was referring not to the food but to the weather. Rambir did not need to be reminded of how hot it was. The sweat was dripping down his collar and making the shirt stick to his back. It was never this hot in Hamara Nagar, he reflected.

"What do you want, veg or non-veg?" said Mumford.

"Either will do," said Rambir weakly.

Over vegetable biryani, Rambir watched Mumford shovel in his food, joke with the waiters, exchange addresses with some Americans at the next table, and generally fit into the scene with apparent relish and ease.

"So, you're living in a cowshed up there in the village," Rambir said.

"Yup," said Mumford. "Still got cow shit on the floor. Oh, sorry. We're eating."

Mumford ate daintily with his fingers, not getting any food beyond his first knuckle.

"Electricity?" asked Rambir.

"Are you kidding? I have a kerosene lantern, though. In the evening, I read or write up my notes. Sometimes people will come over to my hut to use the light, too, if they want to mend something. Or listen to the radio!"

Rambir thought of the kerosene stove in his kitchen,

which he hated to light, and of how he swore and grumbled when the electricity went out in town.

"Actually," said Mumford, "the radio was one of the first things that won people over. The first six months, no one wanted to talk to me. Now I think I know everyone in the village. Who's related to whom, what they call each other. When I get home, I'll have to write all that up as mystifyingly as possible. If it's very arcane, they will award me a PhD."

"Where are you doing your studies?" asked Rambir.

"University of Chicago."

They walked back to the Coziest Possible Hotel. With the sun having gone down, the temperature was more bearable, and a slight breeze cooled the sweat on the back of Rambir's neck. Still, going inside was not a tempting proposition, and he and Mumford looked for a place to sit and continue their conversation. Wandering down the road, they came to a small park, and by luck found an empty bench. Whole families were outside taking the air, some cooking and picnicking on the ground.

"What is your family?" Rambir asked, and then realized the question sounded odd.

"Which *jati*, you mean?" Mumford joked. "That's what the villagers always want to know."

"No, I know you Americans don't have caste as such. But . . . surely your parents are well off, university-educated, all that."

"My father makes toys," Mumford said.

Rambir pictured a workman sitting in his shop and carving dolls, like the maker of—what was that story called?— Pinocchio. But this turned out to be a romantic notion. Mumford's father actually owned several huge factories that churned out toys by the thousands, plus the trucks to ship them all over the country.

"So—*you* are striking out in a new direction," Rambir said. "Not being involved in the toy business."

"Oh, my dad wanted me to go into the business," said Mumford. "He called my choice of career weird, useless, and a number of other unflattering things. But he came around. My mother stood up for me. She can usually talk him into her point of view."

"Oh." Rambir thought of his own mother, who, to his great disappointment, had not "stood up for him" on the question of marrying Ritu.

"How long are you going to stay in India?" Rambir asked.

"I think I'll need at least another six months for my research," Mumford said.

A lot of time, thought Rambir, to be stuck in the middle of nowhere. Aloud, he said, "You'll end up knowing India better than I do."

Mumford snorted. "No one knows India! I know one village. Of course, when I write up my findings, I'll have to make it sound as if I know more than I do."

"No, really," Rambir said. "I'm sure you know things most Indians outside that village don't know." He felt, for a moment, like more of a foreigner in his native land than this foreigner.

"If you studied a little village in the U.S., you'd know things *I* don't know," Mumford Stein said generously. "It's a question of taking the time to find out."

"Perhaps," Rambir said.

"You're a journalist—you know that."

They stayed outside until driven by fatigue back to the hotel. Rambir did not sleep well that night. Mumford snored; a dog down below kept barking; the room was hot and airless. By morning, Rambir felt as if someone had sucked the blood out of his head, making it impossible for him to think.

In contrast, Mumford woke in a cheerful state, despite having to look forward to the dentist.

"I'll see you back in town sometime," he said. "Hope your wife's train gets in on schedule."

"I hope so, too," said Rambir.

He went back toward the train station. Outside the depot, he saw a strange amber-eyed fellow in a *dhoti,* naked to the waist, telling fortunes from people's shadows.

"The time to tell is now, sahib," the man said. "When your shadow is longest."

"What nonsense," said Rambir, turning to yell at two boys who had run by and jostled him. The fortune-teller lunged at the boys and gave them each a whack.

"You have had bad fortune, sahib! Big loss," the man said to Rambir. "Sahib! I've got something for you."

Rambir gave an impatient shake of his head and strode into the station.

ᴄᏰ *A Shadowy Fortune*

The train was due at seven A.M. Rambir looked at his watch every five minutes; by nine A.M., he calculated that he had looked at it twenty-four times. Pacing the platform, he gave it a twenty-fifth glance. Vaguely, he took note of some workmen putting up bunting and hanging long ropes of green, white, and saffron paper flowers from post to post. Other workmen ushered out a cow that had been nosing in a rubbish bin, and a guard ordered a grandmother, mother, father, and four children to pick up their bedrolls and take a nap somewhere else.

"What's going on?" Rambir asked.

"Prime minister is coming through . . . special train this

afternoon. All trains confused today, sir," said a bookseller wheeling his cart of books. Moments later, the bookseller had to clear out, too.

Well, I'll be out of here before *that,* Rambir thought. Although it might be interesting to stay and see the prime minister, if Ritu agrees. Probably she won't want to, though, after her long journey.

Finally, a whistle could be heard in the distance and, minutes later, at nine-twenty, the train steamed in, and people started pouring out of the brick-red cars. Rambir felt as if he were standing in the middle of a river, with the currents swirling around him. And then, suddenly, the train was empty. A dozen ladies and girls had descended from the women's compartment, but no Ritu.

Rambir searched out the stationmaster in his office. "Did you happen to get any telegram for me? Rambir Vohra. My wife is supposed to be here. She was traveling in the women's section."

The stationmaster said, "We can phone to Delhi. See if there is any message for you there."

"I'm worried she may have been taken ill," said Rambir.

A dreadful thought caught Rambir in the chest, like a ball driven from a hard cricket bat. Ritu was not there yet because she was not coming at all. She had stayed with her lover, the one who had made the dedication to her of "Love Potion Number 9" on the radio.

When the phone call to Delhi produced no new information, this conviction grew.

"Maybe your wife is coming on the evening train," the stationmaster said. "Or—though it's not very likely—on the special train. There was one normal car in addition to the celebrity cars."

"Yes." Rambir grabbed at that possibility. "That must be it. She's on one or the other."

The only problem was, now he had an unknown number of hours to wait.

The stationmaster said, "Sir, please relax. Why don't you take a nice tonga ride to the Forest Research Institute? You can roam about the grounds. It will be cooler there."

It seemed incongruous to play the part of a tourist, but better than sitting, Rambir thought, and the workmen were now sweeping the floor, shooing people out before them. Rambir went outside, found a tonga, and found himself growing somewhat more composed as the horse clopped along. But when they got to the gate of the Forest Research Institute and he reached into his back pocket for his wallet, he discovered that it was gone.

"Damn! Damn! Damn!"

"Sahib?"

"My billfold's gone. Must have been that shadow fortune-teller in front of the station. Can you take me back? I promise, my wife is coming in with money, you will get paid." He sat in the tonga, refusing to get down. Skeptically, the tonga wallah agreed, and they retraced the route, Rambir glad to have the tonga's roof up, for the sun was now beating down.

Outside the train station, the fortune-teller was still offering to analyze people's shadows.

"You have returned after all, sahib. Still don't want a fortune?"

"You scoundrel!" said Rambir.

"But, sahib . . ." The fortune-teller held up Rambir's wallet. "You don't want this after all? Those boys were stealing it; I gave them a good cuff and grabbed it back."

"Good God! I . . . oh . . . I'm sorry . . . Thank you, yes, I do want it."

And now he had to eat humble pie. He took the wallet, paid the tonga wallah, and gave the rest of the cash to the fortune-teller.

"Not necessary, sahib," the fortune-teller said, handing the notes back.

"But here, at least take a ten," Rambir said. "And please tell me your prediction."

The man thought it over, took the note and stared fixedly at Rambir's shadow. Then he said, wearily, "Faith is lacking, sahib. If you continue in this same direction . . ." The fortune-teller shook his head ominously.

Oh no, thought Rambir, he's going to give me a lecture on religion.

"Fretting is no good," the shadow fortune-teller said. "Do you have faith in your friends? Do you have faith in your family?"

"I . . . I suppose I do," said Rambir.

"Not enough," said the fortune-teller. He looked again at Rambir's shadow. "The shadow is showing—shortness of faith."

Rambir paused, puzzled. What kind of nonsense was this half-naked fellow spouting?

"My shadow would be longer if I just waited until later in the day," Rambir pointed out.

"Ah, so maybe your faith will become longer, too. See, I am telling you. More patience is required. I am thinking that your friends and family deserve it. Also, I am telling you one more thing."

"What is that?" asked Rambir.

"Always give thanks."

"To whom?" Rambir asked.

"Anyone," said the fortune-teller, with a wave of his arm. "God. Your wife. A stranger. Myself."

Rambir paused for a moment. "Thank you."

"Think nothing of it," said the fortune-teller.

To the Railway Station

◦ß A Ride for a Bird

Mr. Kilometres had kept the gray Hindustan in view almost the entire time they were hurtling down the mountain road, and now he was gaining on the car. In the back seat, Jana and Kenneth were flung back and forth and against each other. They saw Tilku's terrified face looking out the rear window of the Hindustan.

After a seemingly interminable time they got down into rolling soft hills; the road inclined more gently, and the forests were a dappled light green. All of a sudden, the Hindustan swerved onto the side of the road, stopping abruptly in a scrubby area, and the thin man jumped out of the driver's door and headed toward the forest at a run. Jana, looking ahead, saw the reason: two police jeeps, a wooden pole barring the road just behind them, and half a dozen uniformed men with clubs and revolvers.

Mr. Kilometres stopped his cab, leapt out with a cry, and chased after the thin man, with Kenneth Stuart-Smith right behind. They were closing in to lunge at their prey when the birdnapper dodged, changing direction, and ran straight into the arms of the oncoming policemen.

Meanwhile, Tilku had jumped from the back seat of the

Hindustan and ran toward Mr. Kilometres's taxi, with Aloo's cage banging against his leg and Aloo gripping the bars in silent terror. Panting as if his lungs would give out, Tilku came to an abrupt stop, set the birdcage down, and threw his arms around Jana's waist.

"I never thought you'd survive that ride!" Jana exclaimed to him. "And I wasn't at all sure about us, either."

Mr. Kilometres, returning briskly with Kenneth to the taxi, overheard her and looked hurt.

"Mrs. Laird, you know you can trust my driving! All trips are successfully completed."

"But this is the first time you have had to actually *chase* another car, isn't it, Mr. Kilometres?" Jana asked.

"Yes, yes. But you see, Mrs. Laird, I was prepared. All those thousands of trips were merely preparation for today."

"I didn't like being in that car!" Tilku said. "I thought I was going to die, for sure."

"But, Tilku, why did you get in the car with that man?" Jana asked.

"Jana mem! He told me *you* said for me to go with him. He brought out this piece of paper with your handwriting on it. He said it was instructions from you."

Jana saw, with a start, that it was the missing sheet of staff paper with old Ian's nice little air on it. So that was where it had gone! The impostor reporter must have pinched it the day he came for the phony interview.

"Tilku," she said, "that's one of my music pieces. There's nothing on there telling you to go with him."

Then she saw Tilku's mortified look and said, more gently, "Don't feel bad. You thought you were doing what I wanted."

Aloo gave a pathetic little flap in his cage.

"Are we going to get Mr. Ganguly back?" Tilku asked. "And what are we going to do with this other bird, now that he has not been kidnapped after all?"

Mr. Kilometres, who had been listening, said, "I have one idea."

The thin man had been trussed and thrown into one jeep and borne away, leaving the other jeep and two police officers behind. Kenneth greeted them each with a handshake.

"Excellent work, gentlemen."

"Thank you, sir. But I must tell you, today was a hard day to do this. We were short-staffed. When it rains, it pours."

"Oh?"

"We're very busy today, Mr. Stuart-Smith," the other policeman told him. "Today is the day that Prime Minister Nehru comes to Dehra Dun, on a special railway car."

"I see," said Stuart-Smith. "You mean, there will be an absolute mob at the railway station?"

"Quite so."

"I'd like to see the prime minister," Jana said. "I've never been up close to him. But we should get back, if we don't want to make the whole drive in the dark."

"I want to see Prime Minister Nehru, too!" Tilku said.

"And I," said Mr. Kilometres. "And in any case, I must go to Dehra Dun and get petrol. And to tell my wife not to worry."

The policemen had another muttered consultation with Kenneth.

"We'll take you there under police escort," the policeman said. "Some of the police from Hamara Nagar are here today to help us and to greet the visitors. Including your police commissioner, Mr. Bandhu Sharma."

Preceded by the military jeep, Mr. Kilometres pulled up outside the Dehra Dun railway station, where a plump, gray-haired lady was waiting, looking first one way and then the other.

"See, there she is. That's my wife," said Mr. Kilometres. "Do you mind if I . . . May I take the bird for a moment?" He got out of the car and opened the back door. Tilku handed him the carrying cage with Aloo, who was frozen with bewilderment.

His wife, who was obviously not accustomed to running, came scurrying up to him, her bosom heaving, her feet slipping around in her *chappals*. "Where *were* you?" she cried. "I was thinking you had gone off the mountain road."

"Why?" Mr. Kilometres exclaimed dismissively. "I have driven that road hundreds—thousands—of times! Never have I gone off."

"And what's this?" Mrs. Kilometres bent forward and peered into the cage, and her face softened. "Oh! He's so *sweet*!"

By now, Jana and Kenneth and Tilku had also gotten out of the car, and Mr. Kilometres drew Jana aside.

"Mrs. Laird, may I speak to you one small moment?" he asked. "As you wish to get rid of that bird, and my wife seems to have taken a liking for it, this is a fortunate situation! If you let her take the bird, I will give you a cheap taxi ride back up to Hamara Nagar."

"But the bird can't talk," said Jana. "I thought you told me, that day I was going to the dentist, that your wife wanted to teach a bird one hundred words."

"Oh, I think she will be satisfied with a quiet bird after all," said Mr. Kilometres. "Look how they are making friends."

They watched as Mrs. Kilometres opened the door to the carrying cage and, in an unthreatening manner, eyes averted, offered her arm to Aloo. After a few moments of hesitation, the bird climbed onto her wrist, and soon was nuzzling his head against her hand.

"Extraordinary! You'd think he'd never a trust a human being again," said Jana. "She's got the touch. Yes, she *must* have him."

Mr. Kilometres's face broke into a big smile, and when he transmitted this news, his wife's did, too. "Thank you," she said, "thank you, thank you!"

"You're quite welcome," Jana said. "I'm delighted that we got him a good home."

Mrs. Kilometres turned to her husband. "Did you give the lady her thermos bottle?"

"I did," said Mr. Kilometres.

"*Achcha,*" said his wife. "I've been reminding you for a long time."

ᴄ᠖ *Waiting for the Prime Minister*

At that moment, near the taxi queue, Jana saw a pair of people she was surprised to find standing and talking together: the shadow fortune-telling man she'd met last year, when she'd first arrived, and a figure who looked both familiar and strange. Familiar, because it was her friend Rambir, but strange, because instead of his usual neat and tidy appearance, his hair was disheveled, his shirt was half out of his trousers, and his shoes were covered with dust. He was carrying an overnight bag and looked exhausted.

"Rambir! What's happened? Why are you here?" said Jana.

"I . . . I had a rather long night," said Rambir. "I spent it in Dehra Dun. I had decided to meet Ritu's train this morning, but she wasn't on it."

Jana said, "Surely she'll be on the next one, then."

Rambir said, "Ritu can be, well, absentminded, you know.

Brilliant people often are. And she can't see all that well! Maybe she lost her specs. She might have gotten on the wrong train. And today is an unusual day—all the schedules are confused, with the prime minister coming through and everything."

"Yes, that's why we're here," Jana said. "We have to get back to Hamara Nagar, but first we thought we'd see the PM."

The area around the station had filled up with people, as shopkeepers, camel drivers, bullock cart drivers, and farmers coming in from the surrounding area pressed toward where the prime minister would be arriving.

The policeman who had escorted Jana and her group to Dehra Dun now gestured to them to follow him. Cutting through the crowd, they found themselves in a roped-off section of the station labeled "VVIP." They took their places under a large banner that said, "Welcome, father of our country!" next to a dozen men in white kurta pajama, with white Congress caps on their heads. At the end of the line stood Police Commissioner Bandhu Sharma, with whom Jana exchanged a perfunctory namasté.

A veritable army of schoolchildren were there, holding ropes of green, white, and saffron paper flowers, and waving little flags.

When Prime Minister Nehru disembarked from the train, the crowd went into ecstatic cheering. The children chanted, *"Jai Hind! Jai Hind!"* and *"Pandit Nehru ki-jai!"* Nehru, looking a bit old, Jana thought, came wearily toward them; then, at the last minute, he seemed to buck himself up, promptly to be smothered with garlands of marigolds. A brass band broke into the strains of the national anthem, and all stood at attention.

And then the prime minister and his aides were whisked away. All of a sudden, the train station seemed empty. Rambir said worriedly to Jana, "She doesn't seem to have come on this train." But Jana was looking way down to the end of the platform, where one last car was unloading. Red-turbaned porters were hoisting suitcases and trunks to their heads. Jana saw a young woman, verging on plumpness, with a geometric haircut. Ritu! Jana turned to Rambir and gestured down the platform.

Rambir stared, transfixed.

"It couldn't be," he said.

And then he started to run forward.

✿ *A Reunion*

Rambir's heart pounded. All the fatigue and anxiety of the day had disappeared. He was running toward Ritu, and Ritu was not only alive but obviously fine, and smiling and waving at him. But she was not alone, and Rambir's heart leapt at the sight of the couple she was with, the elderly man making his way along painfully with a walking stick, the frail woman allowing Ritu to guide her elbow.

Both white-haired now, he thought, both totally white. His father, his forehead so lined, his mother, so stooped. How slowly they walked. Even the photographs that his brother Jai had sent him had not prepared him for this.

A thought flashed through his head: Ritu has done a miracle. She's done it. He understood all. Disregarding his advice, she'd gone to their house in Delhi, despite the risk of being turned away at the door. She'd gone to her conference and given her paper, and then she'd stopped over in Delhi and had turned her attention to mending his family. The very thought was mending his heart.

Ritu and his parents had stopped walking. Ritu was gesturing in the direction of Rambir, and his parents were looking toward him. The last time he had seen his parents, he had read nothing on his father's face but anger and disapproval, and nothing on his mother's but sorrow and confusion. But now all he saw, on both faces, was joy, although the tears were streaming. Ritu got a handkerchief out of her handbag and handed it to Rambir's mother.

Rambir felt tears welling in his own eyes, and when he got to his parents, he was crying in earnest. He bent down to touch his father's feet, performing the gesture of filial respect that he had not done in so long. But his father, intercepting the gesture, held out his arms, and Rambir found himself in a three-way hug, sandwiched between his father and his mother. Then, as Ritu joined them, the hug turned into a four-way one, close and soul-satisfying, like a long drink of water after a bitter thirst.

"You picked a strange day to come to visit me," he said, and they all broke into laughter, and then started crying again, and laughing some more.

"Our daughter-in-law picked it for us," his mother said.

⸂ *The Last Passenger*

Rambir's party departed from the station, and Jana and Kenneth turned to each other.

"What now?" Jana said.

"Tea, what else?"

"I, too, want tea!" Tilku announced.

The three of them had started off in search of tea when Jana saw, way at the end of the platform, one last passenger getting off the train. There was something about the man that rang a bell in her memory.

"Hold on," she said to Kenneth. "I want to see something. I wonder . . ."

They waited as a short man, roundish but not fat, approached. He was using a walking stick, but the stick seemed more a fashion accessory than an aid to balance; his gait was jaunty, and he kept ahead of the porter who was balancing a brown leather suitcase on his head. The man, carrying a corduroy jacket over his arm, looked as if he had dressed for winter and found himself surprised to be in a summer climate. As he approached, Jana saw a boyish, even puckish face, although the fringe of hair behind his ears was snow white.

Then she knew. This was Miriam's pen pal. It was Marcus Phillips! Jana had almost laughed at his photograph, in which his head and ears had seemed gnomishly pointed. But Miriam had been right: he was far more normal-looking than the photo would suggest. His eyes were a greenish hazel and quite pleasant, with a smile to them. She caught his eye, and he stopped in front of her.

"Are you perhaps Mr. Marcus Phillips?"

Startled, the man opened and closed his mouth, then replied, "Yes, I am."

"Are you looking for someone?" Jana asked.

"No," said Marcus Phillips, "I'm actually here to surprise someone. She doesn't know I'm coming."

"You've come to see Miss Miriam Orley! Haven't you?"

"I have." A look of alarm flitted over Marcus Phillips's face. "Why? Is there something wrong with Miss Orley? She's not well?"

"She is perfectly well," Jana said.

"We spoke on the phone," Marcus said.

"I know," said Jana.

"And the connection was so bad that I'm not sure she

understood that I had bought my ticket and was about to leave for India."

"I don't think she did," said Jana. "She's probably writing you a letter as we speak."

"I'm earlier than I thought I would be, though. A relative of hers, a Mr. Niel Powell, is supposed to meet me—but not until tomorrow."

"Come with us, now," Jana said. "We'll get you to his house tonight."

Eyes on the Sky

Rambir got to the Jolly Grant House an hour before he and Jana were expected at Aunt Sylvia's. Jana showed Mr. Ganguly the carrying cage, which at first made him turn his back, but when she said, "Let's go see Aunt Sylvia," he stepped into it without fuss. The rickshaw having arrived at the front gate, Rambir and Jana got in with the birdcage and rolled off, with a wave to Tilku and Mary.

"How is the press working?" Jana said.

"It's as cranky as ever," Rambir said. "But—here's the news! I have found a new one. Well, not new but *newer*. I'm going to Dehra Dun soon, to take a look at it."

"That's good news," said Jana. "We don't want any more accidents."

"Oh, it will be a lot safer," Rambir said, wincing at the memory of Tilku burning himself. "This time, maybe no one will get hurt with it."

"That was my fault just as much as yours," Jana said. "The child should really be in school. I'd happily pay the fees, if we could only find him a place in a good one. But every time I've brought up the subject, he says he'll run away if he has to go to school. He says he's quite happy as a messenger boy."

Rambir sighed. "And Ritu spends her time trying to persuade girls that they should be physicists! And they say their
parents just want them to get married and produce grandchildren as soon as possible. How to get people to aim high,
that's the question."

Jana said, "Then, when they do aim high, what if they
fall on their faces? University graduates have a hard enough
time getting jobs. Maybe Tilku is right—especially if he's
already happy. Still, I'd rather he had an opening into something else."

They had turned off onto Maharajah's Hill, and Jana
pointed to the gleaming white villas. "Like these houses, for
example. As an owner, not as a servant."

Rambir laughed. "I, too, would like an opening to one of
those."

When they got to Aunt Sylvia's, Jacob John, his uniform
newly washed and starched, met them at the gate and showed
them back to the terrace. Aunt Sylvia, delicately pretty in a
pale-pink ruffled dress and pink shawl, was sitting under the
sun umbrella.

"You're here!" she cried, and put out her arm for Mr. Ganguly. "Hello, sweetie, give me a kiss." Then she turned to the
humans.

Jana introduced Rambir, and within minutes, it was not
"Mrs. Foster" and "Editor Vohra," but "my dear aunt Sylvia,"
and "Rambir, my pet." Jana felt that bringing them together
had been a stroke of genius.

"LPN10 for all, I presume," said Aunt Sylvia.

"Please," said Jana, and Jacob John poured it out of a
decanter, into tiny brandy snifters.

"You know," Rambir said, "I've got a bottle of that at home
I'd completely forgotten about!"

"Taste it now," said Aunt Sylvia. "It does wonders for my
arthritis."

Rambir took a sip. "I can see how it would."

"And have some of these sandwiches."

Once they had consumed the lunch (light, as requested and promised), Jana reminded Rambir and Aunt Sylvia of their mission.

"Rambir," she said, "Aunt Sylvia feels that she hasn't yet fulfilled one of her desires in life, and that is to voice her opinions to the world."

"Indeed, I would!" said Sylvia. "I understand that, in three days, two of the most powerful men in the world will be meeting in Vienna. I have a message for them."

"If you dictate," said Rambir, "I will jot it down," and he took out a notebook.

Aunt Sylvia cleared her throat. "Mr. Kennedy, you are a young man. Mr. Khrushchev, *you* are not so young. I have been alive longer than either of you. I've lost two husbands and four sons to wars, and I've never accepted the idea that they died for any noble purpose. Therefore, on behalf of the ordinary people of the world—and the infinitely varied members of the animal kingdom—I make this plea: Take your atom bombs and tanks and guns and submarines and jet planes and missiles and turn them into plowshares."

She sat back in her chair.

"Is that all you have to say?" Rambir said.

"Isn't that enough? Why dilute the message with other messages? Brevity is the soul of wit, isn't it?"

"Yes, of course it is," said Rambir.

"Really, as long as you can get that message to those two men, I will be happy."

"I will publish it," said Rambir. "And I will send a copy to the international edition of the *Herald Tribune*. And to the American embassy and the Soviet embassy as well."

"You *are* obliging, Rambir dear," said Sylvia. "Now, you tell *me* what you think about the state of the world."

Rambir was happy to do so. The two chatted into the afternoon. Mr. Ganguly got bored and nodded off, and Jana, too, found herself getting drowsy.

They parted with Aunt Sylvia grasping Rambir's hand and saying, "Thank you, thank you. You have given me a voice."

"May I visit again?" Rambir said. "You can address your thoughts to other world leaders. Charles de Gaulle, for example."

"And Mao Tse-tung," said Sylvia. "Yes. We have more work to do. It would be my pleasure to see you again. Soon."

On the way home in the rickshaw, Jana said to Rambir, "You gave her a great gift. She seemed to get younger as you talked. Now, the other thing she wants is a husband. Got any candidates?"

"Now you want me to matchmake?" Rambir said.

"I know, it can be a dangerous endeavor," said Jana. "But keep your eyes peeled."

✿ *Captain Tilku*

"Jana mem."

Tilku's voice is changing, Jana realized with a start. Just in the last couple of days. She looked up from her work on her music transcriptions and saw the boy with an uncharacteristically intent expression on his usually happy-go-lucky face.

"Yes, Tilku?" she said, hoping there was nothing wrong.

"Jana mem, I have something to tell you."

"Yes, of course."

She waited while he gathered his thoughts. Perhaps, she thought, he would feel more comfortable talking outside.

"Shall we go down to the terrace?"

He nodded, and they went down behind the house, where she settled on the stone parapet. Tilku, not used to sitting in her presence, looked hesitant.

"Sit, sit," she said, patting the parapet.

Hesitantly, he sat down, leaving a large amount of space between them. Finally, he spoke. "Jana mem, you said I should go to school."

"Yes, I did, Tilku." Jana paused. "And I still think that you should."

"Jana mem . . . I am willing." With that, Tilku folded his arms and looked her in the face.

"Willing to go . . ."

"Yes, to school," he said firmly.

"You are? Tilku, bravo! *Shabash!* But what made you change your mind?"

Tilku said, "Before he left, I went to talk to pilot sahib at the hotel. I sat on the verandah outside pilot sahib's door, waiting for him. Finally, he came out. I jumped up and saluted. Like this."

Tilku demonstrated, and then remained standing.

"And?"

"At first, I didn't think he recognized me. I said, Pilot sahib! I am Tilku!"

"Very brave of you," said Jana.

"I am Tilku, I said. Your copilot! In the helicopter. Hiller UH-12B. With Jana Bibi memsahib. Then he gave a smile and said, Hello, copilot!

"So, then I felt better. I said, Sahib, I want to be a pilot. And he said, Many boys want to be pilots. So, I said—just like that—Sahib, I *must* be a pilot."

Jana pictured Tilku fixing Maximilian King in the eye and giving him this pronouncement.

Tilku went on: "I asked, How can I become a pilot?"

Jana said, "And what did he advise?"

Tilku let out a huge breath. "Oof! He said, training this, flight certification that, all sorts of things. I couldn't even follow very well. But then he said something *I did* understand. Tilku, he said, you need good reading and writing. And you must understand numbers. Be able to calculate how much time it will take to get from here to there. How much fuel you will need. That sort of thing. Do you get high marks in school?"

Tilku made a wry face. "I didn't dare say to him, Pilot sahib, I don't even go to school. I just said, Not very high at the moment—but from now on, I'm going to get *highest* marks."

"Bravo, Tilku! You said just the right thing."

Tilku smiled. "After we had this talk, he took me back behind the hotel. They were getting the helicopter ready for flight. He said, Do you want to sit in the pilot's seat? I said, Yes, please, sahib. Jana mem, I sat in the seat! In the center. Looking straight at all the dials. My feet didn't reach the pedals. Pilot sahib said, Don't smoke *biris,* they stunt your growth. So! I am not smoking *biris* anymore, either."

My lecturing and Mary's have been for naught on this problem, thought Jana, but Maximilian King had turned Tilku around with a word.

"Tilku," said Jana, "we'll start right away to get you a place in a school."

Tilku faced Jana squarely. "Jana mem, if you pay the school fees, I will pay you back as soon as I am big!"

Jana started to say, "You don't have to pay me back," but something in Tilku's determined small face stopped her. Perhaps such a remark would insult him.

"When I am a pilot," Tilku said, "I will pay you back a hundred times. I will give you free rides. Take you to the dentist in Dehra Dun. Take you *anywhere* you want to go. You will be proud of me, Jana mem!"

"I am proud of you," said Jana, feeling the tears spring to her eyes.

Tilku saw that and said, worriedly, "You're sad, Jana mem? I'm making you sad? You don't want me to be a pilot?"

"No, not sad." Jana gave a half laugh, shook her head vehemently, and sat up straighter. "On the contrary. I'm *very* happy and *very* proud."

Still feeling a lump in her throat, she smiled, and then looked away for a moment, toward the sky. This same sky had so many different aspects and colors: the blue-black of night, when it was barely distinguishable from the hills below; the pewter and white of the monsoon season, when a pitch-fork of lightning could split the clouds and bring down relent-less sheets of rain. Today, it had a generous, lazy face. Against the calm, hazy expanse of blue, the huge bearded vultures wheeled and circled high above, while closer to earth, the crows flapped and cawed and flew across the ravine. She turned and faced Tilku again, gesturing to the wide expanse that he would one day move into and navigate without fear.

"Captain," she said, bringing her hand to her forehead in a salute, "Captain Tilku, the skies are yours!"

Matrimonial Advice from Mary

"Jana mem, what do you want for dinner tomorrow night?" Mary asked. "Chicken wallah comes tomorrow morning. I can buy a chicken already plucked. Or live, if you want it one hundred percent fresh."

"Oh, Mary, good thing you asked!" Jana said. "I'll be out

tomorrow night. At the Victoria—I mean the Victory. With Mr. Stuart-Smith."

"*Achcha* . . ." Mary's eyes widened, and she drew out the word. "Hmm, very good."

Jana was amused. "Yes, he'll be leaving for Delhi the next day."

"Stuart-Smith sahib is a very nice man," Mary said. "Don't worry about divorce."

"Divorce?" Jana said, puzzled. "We're just having dinner."

"No, I meant don't worry that Stuart-Smith sahib got divorced. Not his fault. Stuart-Smith sahib is a very good man. Very calm. Very good to everyone. Knows everyone's name, what they like, what their family is."

"He's good at gathering information, that's true," said Jana.

"And he tips the bearers at the hotel very good tips. They told me. And they say he's an easy man to take care of."

Kenneth was not the only one good at gathering information; that much was clear.

"My idea is . . ." Mary paused. "My idea is that he should get married again."

"Well, he probably will," Jana said. "He's an attractive man, has a good career, healthy, personable . . ."

"Women will be trying to get him for a husband," Mary said.

"Yes," Jana said.

"Don't say I didn't tell you," Mary added darkly.

"Thank you, Mary." First Lily, then Aunt Sylvia, now Mary! thought Jana. Everyone else knows what's best for me—and they think it's marriage. She winced at the memory of Lily's picnic, and at the image of Max King's triumphant expression as he received congratulations on his engagement. Firmly, she changed the subject.

"Mary, Tilku is going to go to school next term. Perhaps

you and I can coach him a bit on reading and writing before he starts."

"I am very busy, madam," Mary said.

"Well, maybe you can find a stray moment here and there."

"Only if he is properly respectful," Mary said.

"He will be," said Jana.

The conversation was interrupted by the front doorbell, and the Ramachandran girls came in. Each was wearing a flower in her hair, but Jana couldn't remember which one was supposed to wear it behind the right ear and which behind the left.

"All right, girls, tell me who's who," Jana said and, for the moment anyway, was able to distinguish between them. They were both bubbling over with identical news.

"Auntie Jana! We have to tell you! We got our results back from the final exams."

"I take it the results were good," Jana said.

"Yes!" said Bimla. "We tied for first place in physics!"

"My word!" said Jana. "I *am* impressed. I'll bet Mrs. Vohra is proud of you, too."

Asha said proudly, "Yes, we're going to send a message to her. A dedication on Radio Ceylon. We're going to say, Thank you to the best teacher in the world."

Then the twins looked at each other and started giggling.

"What are you girls laughing about?"

Bimla said, "It was Asha's fault."

Asha said, "It was Bimla's."

"Now, come clean," Jana said severely.

Asha finally explained: "Last month we sent in a dedication from Quantum to Ritu. A lovey-dovey one."

"*Who* is Quantum, may I ask?"

"Mr. *Physics*," said Bimla. "We *told* you about him. The

stick man Mrs. Vohra draws on the board. In the dedication, he said he was sliding down the inclined plane of love."

"That wasn't very respectful," said Jana sternly. "And she probably figured it out that it was you two daft girls. If she heard it, that is."

The two went into another fit of laughter. "But it doesn't matter now! The exams are over, and we came first!"

᪲ *All Roads Lead to Hamara Nagar*

Kenneth came by to have an LPN10 and soda before escorting Jana to dinner. They went up to the tower room, Jana with Mr. Ganguly on her shoulder. She settled the bird on his perch, then poured the drinks. They sank into easy chairs. The sun was low in the sky; soon it would disappear suddenly, as if dropping into a deep sea to be extinguished for the day.

Jana said, "Tell me! I don't know yet what happened to that sinister man who snatched Tilku and Aloo. D.P."

"Oh, D.P. turned out to be all too willing to talk . . . The Dehra Dun police held him until the C.I.D. picked him up. And they ended up catching a couple of the higher-up members of his gang, too. So you can relax about Mr. Ganguly."

The bird, hearing his name mentioned, straightened up and said, *"Merci!"*

"He seems happy to be home," Kenneth said.

"Well, *I'm* happy to have him back," Jana said. "He actually got along famously with Aunt Sylvia, though. I've got competition."

Kenneth chuckled.

Jana went on: "Aunt Sylvia has demanded a weekly visit—at least from Mr. Ganguly, and also from me, if I want to come. She's decided *not* to go to Australia with Marcus and Miriam, although they invited her. She says she'd rather deliver her messages to the world from here, with Rambir's help."

"So," Kenneth said, "Miriam *is* retiring from her Latin proverbs."

"Only from teaching them," Jana said. "She and Marcus Phillips are exchanging them right and left."

"Proclaiming *amor vincit omnia* and singing bits of 'Gaudeamus Igitur'?"

"I think so. Well! I'm impressed by *your* Latin."

"That's about all I know," said Kenneth.

Jana returned to the topic of Miriam and Marcus. "I'm so happy for them. Miriam's going around with an enormous pearl-and-opal ring on her finger. Feroze is making her a wedding dress. In palest violet!"

They finished their drinks, and Kenneth said, "Shall we proceed to the hotel? We don't want to make Dizzy nervous. He'll be looking at his watch and wondering where we are."

"I'm looking forward to a good meal," Jana said. "The cook there learned quite a lot from the Kings' culinary team, and now that they're gone, he can claim he made up the new recipes himself. You'll have something new to put in the updated *Globe-Trotter's Companion*."

"Parisian and Parsi—an inspired combination! The gastric juices trickle at the very thought."

They took Mr. Ganguly down to the salon and found Mary and Tilku at the table, both bent over the same newspaper. They jumped when Jana and Kenneth approached.

"Don't worry, stay there," Jana said. "We're off to the hotel."

On their way out, Jana stopped in the hall and glanced back into the salon. She thought that Mary had relented and was coaching Tilku on his alphabet, but as she watched them for a moment, she realized she was wrong.

"You see this blade turning?" Tilku was pointing to a picture and explaining to Mary how a helicopter worked. Jana exchanged a glance with Kenneth, and they both smiled. They crossed the courtyard, the evening sounds of the bazaar now close.

Lal Bahadur Pun held open the gate, and gave Jana and Kenneth an approving look.

"Have a good evening, sir, madam," he said.

"Thank you, Subedar-Major," they said in unison.

The sunset call to prayer sounded from the mosque; some shops were closing down, and others were turning on their lights. Cooking smells wafted from the side streets as Jana and Kenneth made their way through the bazaar, passing street vendors wheeling their carts home. They made a detour around a cow that had settled down in the middle of the street.

"Have you ever noticed," Kenneth said, "how one thing just seems to flow into the next in this country? You can't keep anything separated from anything else."

"You wouldn't want it orderly and bland and boring, would you?"

"No, of course not. Look!"

At Abinath's Apothecary, a new sign read, "LPN10, the medicine of choice of French aviators." The usual evening customers, with their foreheads wrinkled from a variety of complaints, were going in, and others were coming out, most carrying brown bottles and wearing already happier looks.

"All roads," Jana Bibi said to Kenneth Stuart-Smith, "lead to Hamara Nagar."

GLOSSARY OF TERMS

Many of these words have alternate spellings.

Aaj Kal   "nowadays"; here, the name of a fictional printing press

almirah   a freestanding closet or wardrobe

aloo   a potato

anna   a coin worth 1/16 of a rupee

aré   an expression of surprise, dismay, alarm

ayah   a nursemaid or lady's maid

badmash   a villain, scoundrel

bearer   a waiter

bhai sahib   a friendly form of address to a stranger

Bharat Mata   the personification of Mother India; here, a fictional movie theater

Bharatanatyam   a classical Indian dance style

biri   a small cigarette consisting of a twist of tobacco in a tobacco leaf

C.I.D.   Crime Investigation Department

chapatti   a thin, round, unleavened whole wheat bread cooked on a skillet

charpoy   a wooden-framed bed or stringed cot

chokidar   a watchman

darzi   a tailor

dhansak   a savory stew containing lentils, vegetables, and meat; popular with the Parsi community

dhobi   a laundry man

dhoti   a traditional men's garment consisting of a length of cloth wrapped around the waist and legs in various ways

driver   a chauffeur

ekdum   right now, immediately, completely

goonda   a thug, hooligan

Gurkha   a soldier of Nepalese origin in British or Indian armies

harmonium   a keyboard instrument whose sound is produced by hand- or foot-operated bellows; depending on its size, it can be positioned on a table or on the floor

hill station   a resort established in the mountains, at first for colonial rulers; later used for general tourism

Hindustan   India

Inshallah   "If Allah wills it"

Jai Hind!   "Long live India!" or "Victory to India!"

jati   a sub-caste

ji   a suffix indicating respect; also, an expression of assent or inquiry

kameez   a tunic, shirt, or dress-like garment

kukri   a curved knife carried by Gurkha soldiers

Mangalore Ganesh   a brand of *biri*

Manipuri   a classical Indian dance style

memsahib   ma'am, Mrs.; may be shortened to *mem,* informally

namasté   "Hello," "Good day," or "Good-bye"

nawab   a Muslim ruler, prince, governor, nobleman

Nehru, Jawaharlal   the first prime minister of India

ophrysia   the Himalayan quail, thought to be extinct; here, the brand of a fictional beer

paan   a chew made of betel leaf wrapped around areca nuts and various spices and flavorings

pakora   a deep-fried fritter, usually made of a vegetable

paratha   an unleavened flatbread made of layers of dough, sometimes stuffed with potato, vegetable, or an Indian cheese

puja   worship

pukka   good, genuine, solid, completed (literally, "cooked")

puja   worship

Radio Ceylon   a popular radio station established in 1923; now, the Sri Lanka Broadcasting Corporation

sahib   sir, mister, man of importance

salaam   an Urdu greeting; "Hello" or "Good-bye" (literally, "peace")

samosa   a small triangular-shaped pastry with a savory filling, usually fried

shukriya   "thank you"

subedar-major   a senior rank for a viceroy's commissioned officer in the Indian army during British rule (similar to a noncommissioned officer elsewhere)

syce   a groom

tamasha   a big commotion or to-do

tonga   a horse-drawn cart

wallah   a person associated with a particular trade, place, activity, situation

zindabad   "long live!"

ACKNOWLEDGMENTS

How can I adequately thank my agent, Suzanne Gluck, my editor and guide, Marjorie Braman, my champion, Elizabeth Berg, and my first reader, Lee Woodman?

Or keep from smiling when I think of Joanna Levine's drawings of Mr. Ganguly? Or from chuckling at Captain Rustom Captain's fascinating anecdotes?

Or express my awe over Bonnie Thompson's superb copyediting job?

I'm blessed not only for what they've done for me, but for what they've taught me.

Speaking of teachers, I must add a grateful note in memory of my teachers at Woodstock School. Now I realize that they were evolving, too.

Finally, thanks to Dr. Lawrence Ballon for his observations on post-Freudian dream interpretation and love to my sister Deborah.

ABOUT THE AUTHOR

BETSY WOODMAN is the author of *Jana Bibi's Excellent Fortunes*, the first book in this series. She spent ten childhood years in India, studied in France, Zambia, and the United States, and now lives in her native New Hampshire. She has contributed nonfiction pieces and several hundred book reviews to various publications, and was a writer and editor for the award-winning documentary series *Experiencing War*, produced for the Library of Congress and aired on Public Radio International.

To contact the author, please visit her website: www.betsywoodman.com